Flora

FINA
ROMANTIC NOVEL
DEBUT ROMANTI
20

Praise for Flora Dunn

"Had me on tenterhooks right up to the end."
Lynne Shelby, author of *Rome for the Summer*

"Wow! I will be reading more from this author. What a fabulous, funny and romantic story. I loved every bit of it and now I am a bit sad the book's finished. Well worth a read!"
Lucy Mitchell, author of *The Car Share*

"Enjoyable, engaging and entertaining."
Reader, Wimbledon

To Rebecca
congratulations
from Flora

ALSO BY

Flora Dunn

Summer at Tillingford Hall

Finalist, Romantic Novelists' Association Debut Novel 2025

A Little Treat on Honey Street

both available as
e-book and paperback on
Amazon and www.floradunn.com
and audio books from
Audible

PRAISE FOR
Christmas at Tillingford Hall

"I loved the real, believable and loveable characters with their quirks and flaws. The setting is great, the variety of personalities and situations feels real and alive and the happy ending well deserved for our couple."
Ruth Kramer, author of *Things we do for Love and Science*

"One of the loveliest Christmas romances I've ever read!"
Chris, reader, Florida

"A fantastic Christmas romance
with a superb cast of characters and all the feels!"
Angela Pearse, author of *Flossed in Love*

Christmas
AT
TILLINGFORD HALL

Flora Dunn

an uplifting romantic comedy
about forgiveness

LUMINA

First published in Great Britain by Lumina Publications 2025

Paperback ISBN 978-1-0687494-4-5

eBook ISBN 978-1-0687494-5-2

First edition.

Cover design: Berni Stevens,
www.bernistevenscoverdesign.com

Cover illustrations:
Sajeela Kiran (Instagram: @sajee_artandpatterns)
Dijana Peter (Fiverr: @burntredhen)

To my parents.
It's not *The Bunny Christmas Special*,
but I hope you like it.

Dear Reader

Thank you for picking up *Christmas at Tillingford Hall.* It's Charlie's story, which follows on from my previous book, *Summer at Tillingford Hall.* You don't have to have read that book to enjoy this one; but I'm just letting you know that *Christmas at Tillingford Hall* contains lots of spoilers for *Summer at Tillingford Hall.*

Christmas is a time for love, forgiveness and living in heavenly peace. This book tells the story of some people who really need a bit of that in their lives. It's a funny, feel-good romance with a bit of grit but a happy ending, because that's the kind of book I like best. I hope you'll enjoy reading it as much as I've enjoyed writing it.

I love to hear from my readers, so please contact me on Instagram @floradunnbooks or by email, flora@floradunn.com, to tell me what you think of my books. And why not sign up for my newsletter at www.floradunn.com, so you can win prizes, discover more about the world of Tillingford Hall and find out what's next?

Enjoy!

Flora

Prologue

At the Christmas concert

I'm hiding in the oak-panelled cloakroom under the grand staircase at Tillingford Hall. My breath is quick and shallow. Even though I'm dressed in a slinky black satin ball gown, I feel like some terrified Christmas elf Santa accidentally left behind.

I came in here to try to calm down, to wipe the shock and anger off my face, before I go back out to the crowd of concertgoers seated in the ballroom of Tillingford Hall.

But I took too long. Now I'm trapped in the loo by the shuffling crowd of choristers assembling in the imposing entrance hall, just outside my hiding place.

Over the sound of the choristers' suppressed giggles and swishing robes, I can hear the audience in the ballroom quietening to a hush. The Honourable Guy Tillingford gives a short welcome address. There's a bit of laughter, and some clapping.

Then the shoving and shushing just outside my little prison suddenly stops.

There's a spine-tingling silence for several seconds before the purest sound, like a crystal blade cutting the ether, breaks out right in front of me.

A single treble is singing:

Once in royal David's city stood a lowly cattle shed.

The shuffling starts up again as the choir processes into the ballroom. I actually can't breathe as the treble's voice fades into the distance, until I can barely hear him ending the verse:

Mary was that mother mild,
Jesus Christ her little Child.

Then, after a beat, the whole choir – bass, tenor, alto and descant – bursts into full harmony for the second verse of the carol.

As I lean back against the dark wood panelling, I take a deep, shuddering breath. I finally begin to notice the smell of cinnamon, orange and clove wafting from the Christmassy reed diffuser propped on the cistern.

How did I, Charlie Patcham, garden historian, end up hiding in the downstairs loo of an English country house, hoping I'd never have to come out and face the music?

I guess it all started with the walled garden.

Damn Sebastian.

Chapter One

Mid-October

"It's like in *The Secret Garden!*" squeaks my eight-year-old god-daughter Hatty, as Guy, Alice and I pause expectantly outside an old wooden door, set in a ten-foot-high, red-brick wall in the grounds of Tillingford Hall.

The door is firmly locked; but I'm pretty sure it leads to what would have been the old walled garden.

"There was a brilliant TV programme my mum showed me on DVD, when I was a child, called *The Victorian Kitchen Garden.* I guess it was a kind of early reality TV show. This garden historian decided to restore an old walled garden to show how it would've been in Victorian times. He found an ancient head gardener who remembered the old ways and presented the programme with him. They grew the kind of stuff the Victorians would have, like cardoons and salsify and couve tronchuda."

"What the hell's that?" asks Guy, laughing.

"I'm not sure – some kind of Portuguese cabbage, I think. And they used arsenic and pure nicotine to kill the bugs. It probably killed off the gardeners too! It really stayed with me. I think that programme might have been one of the reasons I became a garden historian."

Hatty starts running about, laughing as she tries to catch the fluttering autumn leaves shaken from a massive oak tree by a playful gust of wind. Bailey and Bertie, the Tillingford beagles, career around her, picking up on her excitement.

Hatty's mother Alice, my best friend from uni, who I've been reconnecting with recently, has invited me to stay the weekend at Tillingford Hall, the massive old country pile that is the ancestral home of her new partner Guy. He's a bona fide aristocrat – his father is actually a baron – but I'm trying not to let that intimidate me. She wanted me to meet him and have a look at the grounds. They are in desperate need of restoration: a bit like my worn-down Doc Martens, which are starting to let the damp in.

Guy effectively owns and runs Tillingford Hall, now that Lord Tillingford, his father, has retired to London. Guy looks at my playful little god-daughter with undisguised warmth. He seems to adore Alice's daughter almost as much as he adores Alice.

Alice came to Tillingford Hall last summer to catalogue the family's unrivalled collection of miniature portraits. She was divorced and skint; so when she and Guy had a whirlwind romance, it was like something out of a fairy tale.

Sustaining a new relationship between London and Hampshire, and working full time while bringing up a young child more or less alone (because her ex-husband, Phil, is a bit hands-off with Hatty) must be challenging. She seems really tired. She was certainly looking pretty shit at breakfast. But the colour has come back into her cheeks, so I guess she's got over whatever it was.

She's clutching an old mahogany casket inlaid with brass. "We call this the Box of Shame. It's full of orphan keys. We're not sure what they're all for, but we dare not throw any away. There must be a thousand locks at Tillingford Hall, so we keep any key we find, just in case. Come over here, Hatty, and hold the bag open."

Alice gets Guy to hold the casket so she can rummage through it more easily.

She drops a handful of tiny keys into Hatty's little plastic bag. "These ones are all too small."

"I can't imagine *this* one would unlock a garden." Guy holds up an ivory one inlaid with gold and wrapped in tissue paper. "And those Yale ones can go."

"That orange one is for a Kubota mower," I add, pointing to it.

But then we find some big, rusty-looking keys that are probably just what we're looking for. Alice hands them to me and I try each one in the lock, giving them to Hatty to put in the bag once I've tested them. It's trickier than it sounds, as she won't stop hopping and pirouetting.

I'm not sure it needs four people to do this job, but it's kind of fun – a sort of ritual – and there's a crackle of anticipation between us. We're all really keen to find out what state the old walled kitchen garden is in. Guy says it hasn't been opened since the end of the Second World War, when there weren't enough people to staff the gardens any more. I point out that the undergrowth round the door has recently been cleared away. And the door isn't covered in ivy and cobwebs, as you'd expect if it really hadn't been opened for eighty years.

Gradually Hatty's bag becomes heavy, the Box of Shame starts to empty, and none of the keys fits.

"I'll have to pick it," Alice says.

She takes the plastic bag from Hatty and hands it to Guy to put back in the Box of Shame. I'm gobsmacked when Alice takes a cordless Makita screwdriver out of a pretty William Morris tote bag on her shoulder and starts dismantling the lock. Guy doesn't react, as though this kind of thing goes on all the time round here.

He notices my look of surprise. "Alice was so desperate to get into some cabinets in the billiards room, when she was cataloguing the miniatures this summer, that she used YouTube to teach herself some basic lock-picking skills.

It looks so funny seeing my quiet, academic friend wielding a power tool, especially as she's wearing a baby pink, full-skirted wool overcoat, the hood lined with faux rabbit fur, and tiny little Victorian-style patent leather lace-up boots.

I take a photo.

"Stop that, you minx! You'll be laughing on the other side of your face when I get us in!"

And a few seconds later, the door soundlessly swings open on its surprisingly well-oiled hinges.

The others march into the garden; but I stop on the threshold, absolutely transfixed.

Someone has restored the old kitchen garden.

Passing under a rose arch, alight with hips, I take in raised beds filled with produce. Or the remains of it: slimy, rotten lettuces gone to seed, harbouring hundreds of slugs and snails; overblown carrots, parsnips and onions with seed heads like rockets frozen mid-explosion; leeks that are just ready; and some healthy-looking kale, cabbage and cauliflower – all under nets to protect them from marauding pigeons.

Looking up at the high, red-brick walls, I can see dozens of ancient but carefully pruned pear and apple trees trained in cordons and espaliers, many of the fruits now rotten or mummified. But a few are still perfect for picking.

And, everywhere, the dying embers of flowers: roses, alliums, lavender, hollyhocks, knee-high tangles of once-rampant nasturtiums, now peppered with knobbly seed heads. And here and there are small playful details: a little carved wooden gonk peering out from behind a water butt; a windmill made from flattened Coke cans; a nest box painted like a beach hut, with a miniature surfboard glued to one side; a hedgehog home made out of an old wooden champagne box.

Every single corner of the garden has been tended lovingly and with care, except the glass houses, which are still in a dilapidated state: overgrown with brambles; the panes all broken. There are even a few small trees poking through. Whoever started this project clearly didn't have the time or the means to finish it.

Alice and Guy are walking round, talking in low voices. Hatty and the dogs are into everything, Hatty exclaiming and pointing at every surprise detail she spots.

I sit, overcome, on a lovely bench carved from a whole tree trunk, and just stare.

I take the purple velvet tobacco pouch out of my pocket, brush off the crushed leaves and other debris it's picked up in there, and absent-mindedly pull out a cigarette paper.

"What do you think, Charlie?" asks Guy as he approaches.

For a moment, I can't speak. I silently run a thin line of

tobacco along the paper. Then I lick the paper, take a deep breath and say, "Someone's restored the entire garden … apart from the glasshouses."

I start to roll the paper up. "When you said no one had been here since the war, I expected there'd be full-grown trees in here – brambles as high as your head. It should have been impossible to get in here. Who could do such a thing? How? Why?" I tap the roll-up on the bench. "Do you mind if I smoke?"

"So long as it's only tobacco," says Guy. Alice wrinkles her nose steps upwind of me, arms crossed. "It's fine," Guy reassures me as he comes to sit next to me. "We're outside."

I hesitate for a moment but, noticing that Hatty has run to the far end of the garden with the dogs and is examining the hedgehog house, I put the roll-up in my mouth and pull my lighter out of my pocket.

"There's only one person who could have done this," says Guy softly, rubbing his beard.

"Who?" I ask in bewilderment, my lighter halfway to my mouth.

"Sebastian."

I feel like I've been flattened by a nuclear blast. For a moment, I can't say anything, my lighter still poised.

I can't believe someone like *him* could do something so wonderful.

I take the roll-up out of my mouth.

"Sebastian?" I check I've heard right. "Like, *that* Sebastian – who stole your art and slept with your mother?"

Guy winces. I don't think he appreciated me mentioning that. "It had to be him. Our old gardener Herbert only did what was needed, nothing more. I don't know when Seb started doing this and I don't know if he was doing it for himself, or … or for my mother … But it's got his hand all over it: secretly working hard to make something beautiful; letting people think he was bunking off when, really, he was coming here, working his arse off."

"It must have been a herculean task to do it alone. How do you think he managed it without anyone hearing or noticing?" asks Alice.

"The walls," I explain looking up at the thick, twelve-foot-high red-brick structures encircling the whole garden. "They didn't just keep the fruit trees safe from frost and protect the crops from the wind. They also had them so the lords and ladies in the big house wouldn't be disturbed by the sight and sound of the gardeners working."

"I wonder where he got the materials from," Guy muses, taking off his glasses and rubbing the bridge of his nose.

"It's all natural or recycled stuff he could have got from around the estate," I point out. "He's used wood chips for the paths, willow and hazel for the fencing, old plastic bottles for cloches – everything's reused or recycled from somewhere. This bench is straight from a tree. He must have brought it down with a chainsaw, which would have been tricky on his own: this trunk is massive." I pat the bench. "It looks like he carved it with a chainsaw too, which is very skilful … and dangerous."

My mind's eye is filled with the image of Seb, a massive, ridiculously good-looking guy – six foot four and broad in proportion, with a full beard and long golden hair, tied back with whatever he could find – bringing a whole tree down with a chainsaw; and I'm suddenly flooded with heat. I take a deep drag on my cigarette and wish I had something stronger to calm my nerves.

Guy stands up and looks more carefully at the bench. "Look – he's carved a dove at either end."

"They're beautiful," says Alice.

Guy sits back down thoughtfully. "It's his spirit animal."

"Is he a New Ager or something?" Alice asks.

"A bit." Guy smiles indulgently. "He's certainly a free spirit – a bit of a child of nature."

My guts twist as I recognise myself in that description. I remember the weekend I spent with Seb and some of our mutual friends at the Melksham Aquarius Festival last summer, and how we both knew all the lyrics to all the songs by Pentangle, the seventies hippy band who were headlining.

"A dove, though?" I ask.

"Why not?"

"They're symbols of peace, hope and compassion." I explain, frowning and clenching my teeth. The chainsaw image has dissolved in a puff of black smoke. In *my* mind, Sebastian's a rat, a snake, a dung beetle or some kind of dysenteric amoeba. So whoever thinks his spirit animal is a dove is utterly deluded.

I thought I loved him once. He was huge and strong and gorgeous. But then it turned out he was cheating on me – *with Guy's mother* – and helping her steal art from Tillingford Hall and sell it on the black market.

They betrayed us all.

And then I set fire to his camper van.

Wrote it off.

But I don't see why I should apologise to *him* – not after what he did. And if I ever meet Lady Tillingford, I'll probably kill her with my own bare hands, if I don't have my mattock to hand.

I turn away in disgust and suddenly this garden looks like a big old mess, most of it ready for the compost bin. I stub out my cigarette on the bench, leaving a tiny brown burn mark.

Guy kneels down to look at the carvings again.

"Sahara's is a dove too. That's why he's made one on each side."

Alice looks away, pursing her lips.

Sahara Seaton-Smyth, the ex-supermodel, used to be engaged to Guy. Alice finds that particular bit of Guy's past a bit challenging. I don't blame her: I know I would.

If Sebastian's memorialising her on a bench, then I guess she's been *another* woman in his busy life. How Guy can be so calm thinking about his best friend – who not only slept with his mother but presumably his ex-fiancée too – I have no idea. But I'm hardly going to ask more about it, with Hatty jumping around; and I'm not sure I really want to know anyway.

Guy sits down on the bench again, clearly weighed down by thought.

"Why would he do this without telling me or asking me?"

"If he'd asked, would you have let him?" queries Alice.

Guy thinks for a moment. "I'd have told him it was too big a project – not a priority, too expensive – and that he should focus on the lake and the shrubbery."

I'm nodding. "I'd have said the same. But," I admit grudgingly, "I couldn't have done a better job myself with a whole team of gardeners helping me."

"He must have done it all in his own time. I mean, we knew he was bunking off a bit, just like Herbert did, but he still put in more or less a day's work."

"But why?" asks Alice. "Why do this?"

We're all silent for a moment.

"Seb's a bit of a mystery," says Guy. "I don't think even he knows why he does stuff sometimes. But I'll bet he did it for *someone*. It's how he is. He was – is – the most generous person I know. He'd always do things for other people without even questioning whether he had the time, the energy, the desire – or whether it might get him into trouble. He'd even burn himself out sometimes. I think it's because he needs validation. He's always looking for someone to be pleased with him, to praise him, to thank him for what he does. Maybe because he had nothing from his parents. Maybe he did it for my mother, which is sad because she honestly wouldn't have been interested." He runs his hands through his hair. "Seb's a good guy. He's had a shit life. But he's the kind of friend who would secretly restore your walled garden, just to do a nice thing."

Alice snorts.

Guy looks at her and then at me as both of us burst into fits of giggles.

"What?" he asks, bewildered.

"That sounds *so absurd*, Guy. Like people in general have walled gardens!" Alice exclaims, giggling. She sets me off again.

Alice has explained to me that Guy takes his role as the last scion of an aristocratic English family very seriously; but she says he's the most unsnobbish, level-headed man you could hope to meet. I hope she's right because I can't bear airs and graces. I had enough of that growing up in a clergy family.

"Come on, Peasants," says Guy giving her a look of mock disdain. "Let's go in!"

"Yes, let's. I'm getting cold!" Alice pulls her furry hood up, giving herself the look of a squirrel that's accidentally put its pelt on inside out.

But I can't drag my eyes away from the decaying remains of the garden. I can hardly breathe as a maelstrom of confused emotions tumble over one another, threatening to overwhelm me. Sebastian – the liar, the cheat, the criminal, who didn't just lie to *me*, but to his best friend; Sebastian, who I swore I'd never see again – made *this*: the garden of my dreams.

Chapter Two

Alice and I are lolling on one of the huge, plush sofas in Tillingford Hall's beautiful Victorian-style salon. The autumn sun is lowering in the sky, casting long shadows across the estate. Dust motes dance in the weak shaft of amber light that makes its way through the tall sash windows.

Alice gets up to pull down some translucent blinds.

"Sorry to block out what little sun we have at this time of year; but we have to protect the pictures."

We've just had a lovely Sunday lunch made by Mrs Powell, the Tillingfords' housekeeper. She was a bit dismayed at having to cater for a vegan, apparently, but rose to a really tasty bean hotpot. It came in a cute, individual Le Creuset casserole dish that gave me cookware envy.

Guy's helping her clear up and Hatty is watching *Horrid Histories* in the snug downstairs while Alice and I enjoy a private chat up here. Alice pours some coffee out of the cafetière into a proper china cup.

"I've had a great time, Alice. Thank you for inviting me. This place is absolutely stunning – and so is Guy! You've really landed on your feet."

"I know," says Alice, blushing and offering me the sugar bowl. "Guy is the loveliest man on the planet."

I can totally see why she was bowled over by him: he's a tall, athletic, blond aristocrat, with a huge estate in Hampshire. And he's really nice too. But he's not my type: he's too preppy and business-like, with his steel-rimmed specs and Oxford shirts. I like a guy who's a bit more laid-back; but for Alice, Guy is just right.

"It's hard juggling everything, though," she admits as she pours coffee into her own cup. "I've got to get Hatty to and from school, go into town every day to work and then come here every weekend, as well as run a household and all the usual stuff. And I've got to finish my PhD by the end of the academic year, or they'll chuck me off the programme. I'm exhausted."

"You *do* look tired," I admit, putting my cup down and scrutinising her.

"Hmm. To be honest, Charlie, you don't look amazing yourself."

"Huh. Thanks. Maybe we're just getting old, Alice."

"Thirty-seven's hardly old, is it? Seriously, Charlie. I'm saying, as a friend, couldn't you consider dropping the vegan diet? Or give up smoking? You just don't look healthy."

I can see she's actually worried about me, not judging me or bossing me around; so I take her comment as it's meant. "I don't think it's my habits, Alice," I sigh. "I told you before, I actually have more energy now I'm vegan. I know smoking's obviously not good for me, but I only have a couple a day. But d'you know what I reckon it is? I'm just so pissed off, Alice. Work's shit."

"But I thought the Bath Physick Garden was your dream job!"

"It *was*, but it's turned into a nightmare: the funding's dried up; I've got no staff; and the place is just going to pot. I've applied for a bunch of other jobs. But the longer I'm presiding over a pile of crap, the harder it is to persuade anyone else to take me on. And to be honest, Alice, this business with Seb has knocked me for six."

"You really loved him, didn't you?" she asks, reaching for my hand.

"Oh no, it was just a casual thing," I say in a small, clipped voice, trying not to well up. It *was* a casual thing, obviously, from the fact he hadn't bothered to tell me he was sleeping with someone else at the same time as me. But think I might have been in love with him. I know it sounds a cliché, but I really *had* never felt that way about anyone before. Not only was he incredibly good in bed, but I loved the way he made me feel when we talked nonsense into the night: free and light … and safe.

But it turns out he was a snake in the grass. And now I feel betrayed and violated.

"I still want to kill him," I mutter. "And bloody Lady Tillingford."

My teaspoon clatters in the china saucer as I lift my cup angrily.

"I think we all want to kill Maxine," admits Alice. "Honestly, if you hadn't helped me catch Seb trying to sell that Thomas Lawrence portrait to that drug dealer, I don't know if Guy and Giles would ever have realised that Maxine was taking pictures from the collection and selling them on the black market. And that Seb was helping her."

Alice gets off the sofa and picks up a silver-framed photo from the piano. "I'm not sure if it helps, but she would have been about our age when it started … and stunning." She thrusts the picture at me. I can hardly bear to look at it; but, yes, the blonde woman in the picture isn't a minger.

"That really doesn't help, Alice."

I'm sick to my stomach at the thought of that gorgeous boy being seduced by his best friend's *mother,* for goodness' sake, no matter how pretty she was. I know he had thought, since he was fourteen (along with all the boys in Guy's class), that she was "a MILF"; and that he'd "become a god" when he'd started sleeping with her five years later, because he told me so himself.

I want to vomit at the recollection of my last-ever conversation with Seb.

"Whose side are you on?" I growl.

"I'm not taking sides. I'm just trying to help you understand how it could have happened."

"Don't go on about President Macron's wife again. It doesn't help! He was *nineteen*, Alice! Would you hit on a nineteen-year-old?"

"No. But then I'm not the 'hitting on' type." She flops back down on the sofa with a sigh. "I'm not condoning it, Charlie. But he was well above the age of consent by the time they became lovers. And she was still youngish – our age. And Lord Tillingford, Giles, her husband, knew he was gay. And so did she."

"Shit the bed!" I sit bolt upright. "I didn't know *that*!"

"He and Maxine had an understanding. So long as she was discreet, he encouraged her to … to find her pleasures elsewhere," Alice says prudishly. "They kept up the pretence until, well … until my research blew everything out of the water and Guy realised that Giles isn't his biological father."

"*What?*"

"You haven't met Giles yet, but you'll see Guy looks nothing like him." She hands me another photo of a tall, gangly man, with receding dark hair and a slight overbite; his arm around his athletic, blond son. "Please don't tell anyone. I'm only telling you so you can understand!" Alice draws her legs up on to the sofa and wraps her arms around them. "Although people are probably going to work it out soon, now Giles is living with Desmond. He's such a socialite; and *Antiques Roadshow* has made him a kind of D-list celebrity, so it won't be long before people start asking questions and the media come sniffing round.

"Apparently, Giles met Maxine in Zermatt when she was working as a chalet girl. She was only twenty and she'd run away from her family in America because she was pregnant – with Guy – by a family friend: an older married man, called Brad, who was never going to leave his wife. Giles had realised he was gay. But it was the mid-eighties, the height of the AIDS pandemic. As an aristocrat, he felt he needed to father a son to carry on the family line. It suited them both to marry fast and pretend the child was Giles's. But they never told anyone, not even Guy or his half-sister Chelsea."

"They left that to you."

"Effectively. As you can imagine, Guy was pretty upset. Finding out in his thirties that Giles isn't his biological father, and the girl he thought was a family friend is actually his sister, has turned his world upside down. The strain of it all almost broke us up. But he got his head around it and realised he shouldn't shoot the messenger."

"Good. It was hardly your fault."

"Of course not. But it was a horrible shock for him, so I understand he was a bit confused. People can do stupid things when they're upset – like set fire to camper vans – but it doesn't make them bad people."

I look at her ruefully and we lean across to give each other a hug. It's funny how you can have some friends who will always be close even if you're not brilliant at keeping in touch.

At that moment, Guy walks in.

"What time's your train, Charlie?" he asks.

"17.23 from Winchester."

"I'll need to get going before then," sighs Alice. "Hatty's got some homework to do and I've got a Sainsbury's delivery coming in time for supper."

"Don't worry, Darling. I'll take Charlie to the station. But we've got time for a chat with Charlie *now*, haven't we?" He sits down on the other huge sofa opposite us and leans forward, with his elbows on his knees, his hands lightly clasped together. "So, Charlie, what do you think?"

"Of what?"

"Of the grounds."

"Well, they're stunning – amazing – but they do need a lot of work just to make them safe. And actually restoring them to their former glory would be a massive project."

"I'm opening the house and gardens to the public in eight months' time; and I want to hold a gala Christmas concert in ten weeks. Herbert's retired and I've only got Milan now. He's a steady pair of hands; but he's got no training and he's only planning to stay a few more months. I need a head gardener, Charlie. Right now."

"Well, they'd definitely have their work cut out for them. You'd need a massive team and a hefty budget if you want the grounds to be safe and accessible by Christmas."

I pick up my coffee and take a sip wondering where this conversation is going.

"We'd only need the car park, toilets, drive and the front of the house done by Christmas. Then there'd be another six months to get the rest done."

"It's still more of a job for a project manager or a construction company," I say, putting my mug down.

"But I need someone who knows how to do those things in a historically sympathetic way; who can liaise with English Heritage; who can explain to the contractors what needs doing and how. Someone with energy and vision who fits in here and gets what we're about. So I'd like to offer you the job."

For the second time this weekend, I'm floored.

I stare at Guy, blinking; then look from him to Alice. They're completely serious – and look like they weren't expecting this reaction.

I take a deep breath.

I have to say something.

"Y-you need a proper, experienced head gardener," I gabble. "I'm r-really just a garden historian, not a gardener." Although, I'd admit to myself, that's a bit of a joke given that, in my current job, I'm not using my historian's skills at all and spend more time answering the phone and cleaning loos than actually gardening. "Look, I can think of a couple of people just off the top of my head who'd be good for you: Andrew Potter, who's done a lovely job restoring the knot garden at Batheaston Court;

and Taylor Waites at Chennings in Oxfordshire. I trained with her. She'd be brilliant. And you could advertise in *Horticulture Jobs* or with the Professional Gardeners' Guild."

"I don't have time for all that! I need someone now," says Guy.

"Charlie," says Alice. "We really want *you* to do it. I know you've got the brains for this – you've been so underemployed in Bath for the past ten years. This would be a good opportunity for you. And you'd really fit in here too."

I look down at my ancient Doc Martens and ripped jeans. Then I glance at Guy, in his cashmere sweater, and Alice, looking like some Pre-Raphaelite muse, lounging on the sofa in her paisley needle-cord frock. I wonder where she could have got that idea from.

"I'll pay you double what you're earning in Bath. And there's a tied cottage, so you wouldn't have any accommodation costs," explains Guy. "And you'd obviously manage a team. We've got Milan already; but you could hire whoever else you needed."

I know that's more than fair. But I'm not sure I want to be part of all this fancy schmancy English Country House business or be a gooseberry to Alice and Guy. And I don't want to be reminded of Sebastian or think about what he and Maxine might have been getting up to in every secluded nook I come across.

Nope. It's not for me.

"At least consider taking on an assistant role if you don't want to be the head gardener," Alice pleads. "You just told me you're not enjoying your job in Bath."

I'm *really* not enjoying my job. And it would be a fresh start: a chance to finally progress in my career; and the opportunity to do something properly exciting. There's so much that needs doing here right now and enormous potential for grand projects for years to come.

But I don't want them to assume I'm the best person for the job just because I'm Alice's friend. It would be a huge undertaking and I'm not sure I'm up to it: I've never had experience of something as big as this. I was supposed to manage people and motivate volunteers in Bath, but I haven't been very good it. And I'd have to move away from my friends and my flat; although, to be fair, it is only a stinky little garret I share with my gross flatmate, Scuzzy Susie.

"Let me sleep on it."

"Okay," says Guy, standing up and rubbing his hands together. "But I'll need an answer this week."

Chapter Three

I feel I should put a towel down on the seat before parking my muddy jeans on the cream leather upholstery of Guy's James Bond-style Aston Martin. But, as that's not an option, I just lower myself into the car and strap myself in. As Guy starts the engine, the sound system blares out the raucous tones of Nirvana, the nineties grunge band. He snaps it off.

Seb liked Nirvana too, I remember. The memory of nights in his camper van, with him picking out a few chords on his guitar, doing his best Kurt Cobain impression, come back to me, twisting my heart with painful, unwanted longing.

At least Nirvana gives us something to talk about as we drive down Tillingford Hall's half-mile-long drive, spooky in the twilight. We glide through the village of Tillingham, where the lights are coming on in cosy little cottages, and out towards Winchester, along the A31.

"Please don't drive past the cathedral," I plead in my mind as we come into the outskirts of Winchester. But the ancient building inevitably comes into view, glowing eerily in the floodlights. I feel my breath start to shorten and I grip the seat.

"Are you okay?" Guy asks, his concerned eyes flicking over to me, then back to the road. He opens my window from his side. "Shall I pull over?"

"No!" I manage, but memories are flooding in.

We pull smoothly into the station car park, with fifteen

minutes to spare. He brings the car to a stop in a space near the station entrance. "Something really spooked you back there."

"Sorry about that," I reply. I'm about to say *it's nothing*, but there's something about Guy: his kindness just shines out of him. I decide to tell him the truth.

"My mother was headmistress of Tatchester Cathedral Choir School. So I went there with my four brothers because she got money off the fees. And she was really busy, so it was just easier to have us all at the same place. I was the only girl in the school. But I had to do all the things the boys did, except that I had to use the ladies' staff toilet as my changing room. Can you imagine having to get into your gym kit while your chemistry teacher is peeing in the next cubical? It was really weird and stressful. And there was *so much* music. I had to learn the French horn and the piano, whether I liked it or not; and do an hour a day of choir practice, even though I couldn't be in the choir because I wasn't a boy. Later on, they let me swap French horn for guitar – classical guitar, of course – but I still had to do two instruments until I'd finished my A levels when I was eighteen. So, whenever I see an Anglican cathedral or hear choristers, it stresses me out."

"That sounds tough. Seb's like that too. He can't come into Winchester – it triggers too many awful childhood memories. Sorry … Alice made me promise not to mention him again. But he's like a brother to me, Charlie – I can't just forget about him. I feel bad about what happened between you two."

He rakes his hand through his floppy blond hair.

"Don't worry, Guy. He's not a problem any more. And it's not your fault he was a tosser."

Guy gives me a sharp sideways glance, and his jaw tightens. He takes a deep breath. "I feel like I should have kept more of an eye on him; kept him under control."

"What do you mean?"

"After his mother died, he had such a shit home life, us Tillingfords effectively adopted him and his sister. He became like a kind of brother to me. I've always felt kind of responsible for them, like *someone* had to look after them."

"That's quite a burden to take on yourself, Guy."

"I know, but I'm like that." He stares ahead into the floodlit car park, drumming his fingers on the steering wheel. "I'm sorry about how he treated you, Charlie."

"Seriously, don't worry about it. It was only a casual relationship," I say, trotting out the same old chestnut I tried to use on Alice.

"Really? That's not how it sounded. Seb told me he'd met this *amazing woman* in Bath. He …" Guy hesitates. "I don't know if I should say this, but he told me he thought she might be 'The One'. The way he described her … Now I've met you, I'm sure it's you he was talking about."

I feel like the car's just tipped on its side. I just can't believe that! He must have been talking about someone else or, surely, he wouldn't have treated me the way he did.

"He was sleeping with your mother, Guy!" I burst out, turning angrily to him. "How could he have meant that?"

Guy's face is etched with pain. "He was. But she didn't love him, obviously – she was just using him. And I'm sure he didn't have feelings for her. I honestly didn't even know it was going on," admits Guy, "until Alice worked it out and stopped their little game – with your help. I'm sorry he hurt you, Charlie. He's not a bad person; he's done some bad things, but it's not what he was made for. He needs someone to keep believing in him."

A silence falls between us for a moment as I try to process what Guy's just said, but it's just way too complicated. I feel sure I'm better off putting that unfortunate episode behind me and forgetting all about it.

"It's such a pity that Seb comes across like a total waster, because he's so talented and skilful. He does everything with painstaking care and with such an eye for detail. It's just the bigger picture stuff – life, relationships – that he sometimes struggles with. But I'm going to find him and bring him back here so I can help him get his life back on track."

"What?"

"Yeah. The last thing he needed, when the shit hit the fan, was me pushing him away. But I just had too much of my own stuff going on to be anything other than angry with him back then. Now Mum's settled in Boston, with Brad, and I'm coming to terms with everything that's gone on, I've realised I can't leave Seb to rot in Cornwall – if that's even where he's gone. Seeing what he did with the walled garden – single-handedly – made me I realise how wrong I was to send him away. I can't believe I don't actually know where he is right now. He's not answering his phone. I don't even know if he's okay – *alive* even. Sahara's really worried about him, so I've promised her I'm going to take this week off and we're going to go find him."

Does *Alice* know he's taking off to Cornwall with his ex for a week?

"What's Sahara got to do with this?" I ask, angry

on Alice's behalf.

Guy turns to look at me, surprised.

"She's his sister."

"You're telling me the supermodel Sahara Seaton-Smyth, *the Face of the Noughties*, is Seb's *sister*?"

"Sorry, I just assumed Alice had told you everything."

"No. Funnily enough, it's all been a bit of a non-subject between us."

He leans his elbows on the steering wheel, his head in his hands. "Yeah. I can understand that."

"Huh." I turn to look out of the window. This I had not expected. "Seb totally lied to me about who he was. It was just a crazy coincidence that he used to hang out in the same pub as me in Bath, and Alice happened to be visiting me when he walked in that time."

"Ah, yes, that makes sense. He goes to the George and Dragon when he's in Bath, because of Tristain. We were all at school together."

"No way! Tris says he grew up in a commune near Glastonbury."

"Bollocks! He certainly grew up near Glastonbury – his parents own the largest dairy farm in Somerset – but he was at Winchester with us. He got chucked out for snorting coke in a Latin lesson."

"What?"

We both burst into laughter.

"Seriously – it's true!" Guy's eyes crinkle. "Look, Charlie, I hope Seb coming back isn't going to be awkward for you. Obviously, I'm still super keen for you to come and work for me."

"I'll give it some thought." I try not to sound too brittle.

I'm shaken up like a snow globe: realising I really didn't know who Seb was; raging at how he treated me, at Maxine, and all these people and their stupid, complicated lives sending seismic waves through the whole universe; battling with the ghosts of Seb's touch on my skin and the fluttering of my heart every time I hear his name.

If *he*'s going to be working at Tillingford Hall, then this job they're so keen for me to do is an absolute no-go. I can't go round feeling like *this* every day.

I can see my train pulling into the station.

"I've got to go now, Guy."

I grab my shabby rucksack and run like the wind.

Chapter Four

The train is full of the usual tired, hungover Sunday afternoon crowds and their whingy, overwrought kids. The two opposite me are fighting over a thin selection of cheap colouring pens, severely hampering their attempts to complete their pictures of Cinderella and Simba the lion cub. Their exhausted mother, sitting next to me, studiously ignores them, riveted to a copy of *OK!* magazine.

Over her shoulder, I catch sight of a headline: *SAHARA'S HEARTBREAK*, it reads. I'm just taking in the standfirst – *James Irving-McAuley breaks up with "Face of the Noughties", Sahara Seaton-Smyth ... again* – when the woman rattles the magazine in an irritated way, showing she's aware of me staring over her shoulder. She slams the magazine shut and tells the kids off, even though they've actually calmed down a bit now.

I stick my tinny Poundland earphones in and put on some Nirvana, but it reminds me of Seb. I turn it off. But I can't stop thinking about him anyway, now I've just seen that article. Of course, I didn't know he was Sahara Seaton-Smyth's brother: I didn't really know him at all. He told me he was a chippy from Twerton who worked away during the week. I certainly didn't know he was Lady Tillingford's lover, a drug dealer and a thief.

I can't believe Alice didn't tell me; but then we don't talk all that often – what with her being so busy, and me being a bit disorganised about that kind of thing. And anyway, I guess we both thought me setting fire to Neville, Seb's camper van, and him disappearing would be the end of the story.

I grit my teeth and turn to look out of the window but can only see myself – alone – rushing through the darkness.

I turn back to my phone and choose the *Divertimento* from Mozart's *Gran Partita.*

Sometimes, I need to come back home.

I settle my head into the greasy headrest and close my eyes, letting the beautiful classical music wash over me. Mozart soothes and cleanses my thoughts, helping me feel grounded and uplifted at the same time as I ponder the dilemma I'm now faced with.

Guy and Alice have offered me my perfect job: a great opportunity and exactly what I trained for. But I'm not sure I want to be a gooseberry to Jammy Alice and Gorgeous Guy, watching them play happy families with Hatty in the world's most expensive Wendy house.

And if Guy really is going to bring Seb back to Tillingford Hall, I'd have to negotiate the Tricky Ex Situation. I'm astonished that Guy's even considering bringing him back into the fold, after everything he's done. I don't think *I* could ever trust him again, no matter how much he cares for *me*; no matter how much Guy pleads for him.

No matter how much my body aches for him, his insane kisses, his strong but gentle lovemaking, the weight of him, his … I mentally slap myself and remind myself for the billionth time today that Seb is Bad News.

But if we're working at the same place, I won't be able to avoid him.

My heart contracts with pain and tears prick my eyes. I was head over heels with that man. If he'd just been a passing interest, a casual fling, I could maybe have got over it.

But I *really* liked him.

The mum next to me has given each of her kids packets of Hula Hoops and they're quietly chomping away. They giggle as they slide them on to their fingers like rings and then nibble them off, licking the salt from their pen-stained hands. It's pretty gross and yet kind of endearing, watching their little faces scrunched up with enjoyment on just the right side of naughtiness.

They're actually quite cute kids. The girl has a really sweet face. The boy looks a bit feral, but there's something disarming about his cheeky grin.

And then suddenly the mum's yelling at the kids while trying to pack up their stuff. She's just realised they've reached their stop. I jump up to let the mother out of her seat and help her shove their things into their bags. She thanks me as she hurries the children off the train, just before the doors beep shut.

I'm grateful for the peace and quiet, but the seats opposite seem to ring with their emptiness. My abdomen gives a sudden dull kick. I've always wanted a family; I've just never been in the right place with the right person to start one.

I guess if I really want kids that badly, I could just get myself pregnant using a turkey baster and a willing volunteer. But I'd at least need to have a home and a job first.

I look down and realise that the woman has left her two-month-old, tattered copy of *OK!* on the seat next to me. I read the article, a double-page spread; I look at the pictures first. There's one of Sahara and James Irving-McAuley, a well-known playboy, at a society do, artfully "torn" down the middle; another of a teenage Sahara in her modelling heyday, pouting at the camera; and another that stops me in my tracks.

It's a famous poster, which I remember seeing on billboards when it came out, maybe fifteen, twenty years ago: Sahara, in Calvin Klein bra and knickers, has looped her arms around an oiled-up boy with a buzzcut, wearing nothing but similarly branded bulging briefs. They're both pouting at the camera. The poster's reproduced very small in the magazine, so I have to squint to see it properly. But I can see the boy is definitely Sebastian. And I say "boy" because they really are just teenagers in this picture. What were their parents thinking? And who thought it was okay for a brother and sister to pose together like that?

I feel weirdly voyeuristic staring at the picture of this kid, knowing that, at some point that summer, a million other women across the UK probably looked at this picture and wondered what it would be like to sleep with him. And knowing that I have done so makes me feel … what? Special? Dirty? When you're my age, is it okay to drool over a photo of your former lover as a nineteen-year-old?

But it's like this kid is a totally different person; not the mature man in his prime, with a beard and long, curly golden hair, who used to light up my weekends – and who I never want to see again.

And so I make a decision.

I'm going to go back to the Physick Garden, focus on recruiting more volunteers and fundraising so I can appoint an assistant. And while I'm doing that, I'm going to look very hard for another job – preferably somewhere far away like Scotland … or Australia – and maybe set up a side hustle as a garden designer so I can start paying off my debts and maybe even start saving. It's not like my day job is actually stretching me, so it should be easy to put in a few hours' moonlighting.

But I'm definitely staying in Bath for now. I've got friends, a job (of sorts) and a life there. As soon as I get home, I'm going to clean my flat and tell Scuzzy Susie, my hot mess of a flatmate, to get her shit together or get out. I'll give notice to the landlord and look for a cheaper place where I can afford to live on my own.

I'm going to be a strong, independent woman.

Yes, I'm raising my standards – but on my own terms – and I'm taking my life back.

Chapter Five

When I arrive at the Bath Physick Garden on Monday morning, it's looking drearier than ever. The brown skeletons of dying plants, left for their "architectural interest", are slowly rotting under damp spiderwebs.

In the middle of one of the herb beds, I find a large piece of foam from an old car seat, which someone has chucked over the wall from the supermarket car park next door. I realise, just a tad too late, that an excited fox cub has done what excited fox cubs do on interesting bits of discarded junk.

Trying not to breathe in, I rush into the staff toilet and wash my hands three times with Happy Santa Handwash, which was on special offer in the Londis across the road.

But I know that stink is going to linger for the rest of the day no matter how often I wash.

I know I should love the "season of mists and mellow fruitfulness"; but right now, the only mist I can see is the red one that starts to swim before my eyes. So, when I realise that tin cans and other rubbish are starting to rain over the garden wall, I shoot out of my tiny office-cum-kitchenette, like an angry dragon bursting out of a cave.

"Oi! What are you doing?" I yell at the unknown assailants on the other side of the wall.

I hear a cry of "Piss off, you old cow!" and loud, cruel laughter.

"Who are you calling *old*, you little shits?" I scream as I run towards the gates, determined to find the brats.

And then they invade.

They're not the couple of relatively harmless, little ten-year-old truants I've seen round here before. It's four spotty teenage girls, wearing oversized hoop earrings and coordinated velour tracksuits with diamante detailing.

"Who are you callin' *little*, Bitch?" barks the one in pink.

The brunette in green flexes her crudely home-tattooed arms, lifts a Victorian glass cloche and smashes it on the ground while Pink crushes a whole swathe of autumn crocuses with her inflatable trainers. The other two start to climb the three-hundred-year-old mulberry tree, around which the Bath Physick Garden has been built, deliberately snapping the branches as they go.

For a second, I'm rooted to the spot.

I know I'm outnumbered and there's only one thing for it.

I run into the office, bolt the doors and call 999, looking on in horror as my precious herbs and medicinal plants are crushed, ripped and shredded. By the time two police officers stroll into the garden an hour later, the girls have left and the garden is totally trashed.

PC Chris Knighton looks bored as he takes my statement. "And you say these … *herbs* … are *valuable*?" he asks, dubiously. I give up trying to explain what the point of a physic garden is. He's clearly never been here before and probably didn't even know it existed. He doesn't get that we're all about providing *a calming space*, where local people can connect with nature and learn about the special properties of medicinal plants.

"This is a public place, Officer," I explain. "And I work

here. I was harassed and intimidated by four pretty scary young women. This garden is run by a charity for the benefit of the people of Bath. Those kids have ruined it for everyone! And it's going to cost thousands of pounds – which we don't have – to put right. But more importantly, I feel scared. What if they come back?"

"Did they physically threaten you, Charlotte?" asks his bobbed sidekick, PC Annette Porter, more gently.

"Erm … they called me a bitch."

The plods look at each other sceptically. "If you don't mind me saying, *Madam*," says PC Knighton, "I wouldn't really call that harassment these days."

"But this is *Bath*!" I realise I sound just like Alice, who thinks everyone should behave like someone out of a Jane Austen book.

PC Knighton snorts and puts his notebook away.

"Well, aren't you going to *do* anything?" I ask.

"I suggest you make a nice strong cup of tea and have a biscuit. We'll send you a link to upload your CCTV footage. And when we've had a look, we'll be in touch with you if it shows anything *useful*."

I don't need a cup of tea, I think, as I show the police officers out. I need something a lot stronger. In the absence of anything else that will do the job, I mechanically put the kettle on and then grab the box of Spooky Pumpkin Cakes, which were supposed to be a reward if I made it through to Friday. I look dejectedly at the autumnal garden and watch the cascades of leaves falling, dull brown and dirty yellow in the dim light.

The thought creeps up on me that Seb wasn't scared of

anyone – even Scorpio, the leader of our local drug gang – would have seen those kids off. Seb would also know how to weave a spell to make this sad little place beautiful again, just like he did with the walled garden at Tillingford Hall.

I feel like my heart's going to break in two.

I hear footsteps on the gravel outside. I freeze – afraid the Terror Teens have returned.

"Charlie?" drawls a familiar voice as the door handle rattles. I immediately relax and get up to unlock the door to my friend Tristain. Something like a smile returns to my face.

"All right there, Charlie, M'lover?" he asks in his thick Somerset accent, flicking his mousy dreadlocks back over his shoulder and languidly enveloping me in his smelly hippy jacket. I like Tris. We've slept together a few times over the years but we're not together. He doesn't believe in exclusivity, although he and Ama are effectively a couple.

Surely Guy had to be confusing him for someone else when he said they were both pupils together at Winchester College, one of the country's most exclusive fee-paying schools?

Tris flops down on the ancient charity shop sofa behind my desk, which serves as our "staff room", and pats it, beckoning me to join him. "Ama had a notion you was in trouble."

Ama's mother is a shaman (even though she's called Trisha and hails from Budleigh Salterton). Oddly, Ama seems to have a sixth sense, so we tend to trust her intuition.

Tris rolls a spliff, lights it and takes a deep puff to get it started before handing it to me. This'll hit the spot those Spooky Pumpkin Cakes never will. I snuggle up to him and tell him, as we pass the spliff back and forth between us, about how I hate working in this grotty place; about the invasion of the Terror Teens; and how it's going to take for ever to get it all tidied up.

He kisses my forehead.

"I'll help you."

"You'd do that?" I ask, gazing out of the window at the strange colours on a jay that's hopping about in the wreckage of the mulberry tree. I think it would be nice to absorb its hues into myself and feel more soft pink, with just a hint of iridescent blue.

"Of course, Charlie. Anything for you." He grins, showing a row of uneven, yellowing teeth.

And then he kisses me properly. It feels kind of nice; but I've never been quite comfortable sharing him with Ama, even if she really doesn't seem to mind. Tristain says it's just that "conventional bourgeois upbringing" coming back to haunt me. I try to believe him, but I think it's more than that. Call me a hopeless romantic, but I do believe that – *one day* – I'll find *The One*. And, although I'm trying not to, I can't help thinking I'm going to compare anyone I meet from now on with Sebastian. Even if he was a two-timing crim, he did at least wash his clothes occasionally and have a decent set of teeth on him.

"Remember, it's Samhain next week, M'lover." Tris, pronounces Samhain "sarr-wayn", adding in a Somerset *aarr*. "We're going to Glasto again. You'll come, won't you?"

"I think it's pronounced 'sow-inn', like a pig and a pub, Tris," I point out, like I do every year.

Samhain is the pagan festival of harvest and autumn that marks the beginning of the darker half of the year. Christians turned it into Hallowe'en. But Tris and Ama aren't Christians.

I'm not really sure what I am. I'm not a pagan exactly. But I kind of go along with it when I'm hanging out with people who are into all that. It's just a way of being part of a group, really, isn't it?

My parents, on the other hand, are very Anglican. My father became the Bishop of Bath and Wells five years ago, after a long stint as Dean of Tatchester, where my mother was headmistress of the cathedral choir school. They'd be horrified to know I regularly take part in shamanic rituals and pagan festivals. I speak to my mother quite often, but I'm very selective about what I tell her.

The particular Samhain celebration that Tris is talking about is basically a massive stoners' orgy in a forest near Glastonbury. I don't think there's actually anything religious about it or, at least, not for most of the people who go. People just get out of their minds on mushrooms and then all have a lot of sex with each other. I still can't forget that when I went last year, I was pretty sore for days afterwards. It's a miracle I didn't bring home a party bag I didn't want.

"I don't think so, Tris. Not this time."

To be honest, I'd rather run a hot bath and read a good book.

"That's okay, M'lover. I respect your choice," he says, cuddling me. Then he turns to look at me. "I needs to tell you something, though. Ama and me are moving, Charlie. Some mates have got hold of this lush house over Batheaston way. You should join us – the more the merrier, y'know."

"Join what, exactly, Tris?"

He looks into my eyes. "A group of likeminded people who want to share their lives."

"So, it's a pagan polyamorous squat?"

A tiny bit of hurt flickers across his smudgy face. "You're so bourgeois, Charlie."

I extricate myself from his embrace and stand up, slightly wobbly but still very much in control of myself. "Okay, Tris. If being *normal* is *bourgeois,* then that's what I want to be. I like you guys a lot – we've had lots of fun together. But, you know what? I'm thirty-seven years old and I'm still living in a shitty flat share. I don't even earn enough to own a car! Not that I want to because I do actually really care about the planet. But it would be nice to feel I had a choice – maybe a big gas-guzzling SUV, with a couple of car seats in the back containing some carbon-producing new baby humans. I'm sick of cycling ten miles through the rain to go to my bloody basket-weaving class. I'm tired of having to buy my clothes from Oxfam. I'm sick of going to festivals in the middle of fields because I can't afford to go anywhere nice or do anything fun!"

"All right! I get it. You're bowing out." He looks sad.

"I'm not *bowing out*, Tris. *You lot* have all bowed out of normal society. But – and I'm sorry – I don't want to keep living like this."

I'm about to say more but I don't want to hurt his feelings. No one forced me into any of this. None of this is *his* fault; he's been nothing but lovely to me. I'm just sick of being a useless waster, with no life and a dead-end job.

He gets up. "I guess I'll be going, then."

So now it looks like I've got no friends either.

My heart clenches. I really do like Tristain; but maybe the Terror Teens have just struck some sense into me, like a visiting angel who's burst into the room and asked me what I'm doing with my life.

I'd never be Lady of the Manor, like Alice, but I could at least be Homebase Mum, with a couple of kids, a dog, a Volvo and some kind of vaguely respectable man in my life. And, maybe, a set of those nice Le Creuset pans ...

"Hey, Charlie." Tristain breaks into my reverie by enfolding me in a huge hug and kissing me full on the lips again in a way that almost makes me change my mind. "Don't go feeling bad now. You have to do what's right for you. Just see it makes you happy."

Right now, I'm not sure anything will make me happy ever again.

"Shall we crack on and tidy up outside?" he says.

"Don't worry about it."

"You reckon you don't want any help, then?"

Of course I do! I can't bear the thought I'm going to have to clear this all up by myself because all three of my volunteers have called in sick this week. But I don't want *Tristain* to help me after the speech I just made.

"Don't worry, Tris. I need to take photos of the damage for the insurance company and for my report to the trustees before I start doing anything."

"*Report to the trustees*!" he sniggers. He's always thought I'm funny for having an actual job. "Bye, Charlie. I'll send you our *address*. Listen to me – all posh!"

And given that he and Ama have been living in a camper van as long as I've known them, I guess a squat in Batheaston is a move up for them.

“Thanks, Tris. See you around.”

“Yeah, Charlie. See you around.”

Chapter Six

I'm about to drag myself away from my fuggy office and actually do some work in the cold outside, when my phone rings. It's my mother. Normally, I wouldn't pick up during work hours but, as I'm doing literally nothing and really don't want to go outside, I can't think of a good enough excuse not to.

"Hi, Mum!" I say as cheerfully as I can.

"What's wrong, Tottie?"

My parents always called me Tottie when I was little. But when my mother became head of the choir school and enrolled me as a pupil, you can imagine the field day the boys had with my name on the first day of year seven. On day two, I changed my name to Charlie and, taking my brothers' advice literally, I made it widely known that anyone who called me anything else would get their nose broken.

I suspect George Willoughby-Parton still tells everyone it was a rugby injury, especially as he was in year eight and a good six inches taller than I was.

Nicknames aside, my mother has an annoying instinct for knowing when I'm down, which is a lot of the time these days. But I don't like to share my problems with her as I'll only get advice and judgement instead of sympathy. So, I decide to stick to the facts of the Raid of the Terror Teens. She's shocked – and disgusted, of course – at the lack of support from the police and shares her thoughts on what I ought to Do About It All for some minutes.

Eventually, after advising me to make sure I take my vitamin B12 because my vegan diet won't give me all the nutrients I need, she pops the killer question.

"What are you doing for Christmas, Darling?"

"Erm … I hadn't really thought about it," I admit. "It's only October."

I look out of the window at the plane trees: their leaves have barely started to turn brown, though piles of them are gathering in corners. The gift shop and the bookshop in St Alphege's Square were both sporting pumpkins and spiders when I walked past this morning; but I know that it won't be long before they're cleared away and replaced with Christmas trees and fairy lights.

"It comes around quickly, Dear, and I need to know how many spaces we've got for other guests. There are lots of people who are keen to have Christmas lunch with the bishop. I need to make sure my numbers are balanced and order the turkey soon."

"Well, obviously, I won't be eating any; so that shouldn't be a problem."

"Oh, Darling, surely you can make an exception for Christmas? They're free range, you know. You can see them, on the 'Turkey Cam' on the farm's website, having a whale of a time, running around the fields."

"Do they show them in the abattoir as well?" I ask, reading the ingredients on the Spooky Pumpkin Cake box and realising they include dairy butter.

"Don't be facetious, Tottie. If it were wrong to eat animals, our Lord wouldn't have eaten fish and lamb, would he?"

Not this again! It usually leads to me bringing up the wedding feast at Cana and that never goes well.

"It's lovely of you to invite me, Mum, and I'll give it some thought. I'll let you know very soon."

I guiltily open the Spooky Pumpkin Cake box, knowing I'm going to eat one, despite the baby calves who got turned into dog biscuits.

"I need to know soon, Tottie. And I assume there's no one else we should be inviting? A new man, perhaps?"

"No, Mum. There's no 'new man' I can bring, I'm afraid."

"I suppose I'll have to invite the canon theologian to balance you out," She sighs dramatically. "He's single too you know, but you wouldn't be his type; he's a bit young for you – only thirty – and I'm sure your nose ring would frighten him off. Is your hair back to its natural colour now?"

I don't even answer this. I have a single, greyish blonde streak that used to be purple in my otherwise dark brown hair. I haven't bothered to touch it up recently and I really don't want to get into a discussion about my hair right now.

"The important thing is that you should keep safe, Darling. Please look after yourself. And do come and see us soon, so I can feed you up a bit."

And you and the Bishop of Bath and Wells can lecture me about how I'm wasting my life and education and really should get my act together. No thanks.

"I'm eating fine, Mum." I say, unwrapping a Spooky Pumpkin Cake. "Everything's *fine*!" My voice is just a bit too bright. "I've got to go now and photograph this mess in the garden."

"Of course. Back to work, Darling!"

I drag myself out into the dank, chilly garden and start to

look around. I'm going to have to get a tree surgeon in to see to the mulberry. It's a crying shame. If those girls knew the significance of that beautiful tree … well, they wouldn't be the kind of girls they are. I guess it's not their fault. To them an old tree is just any old tree.

By the end of the day, my head's aching, my back's aching and my heart's aching.

Normally, on a day like today, I'd meet up with Tris and Ama at the George and Dragon pub but, after this morning's conversation, I'd better give it a miss. And anyway, "The Chase" (as we regulars jokily call it, referencing 'chasing the dragon' because it's a bit druggy) reminds me too much of Seb.

To cheer myself up and because I feel a bit lonely, I decide to get supper from the Van of Life, even though I can't really afford it, because I'm hoping Cobain's on shift tonight. I've always thought he's really cute. Maybe I should be brave and ask him out. It would be nice to have a date for a conventional Hallowe'en party in one of the smart pubs in town, rather than go to the Samhain orgy in the forest. What if Mum didn't need to invite the canon theologian for Christmas because I actually had someone to bring?

And so, I dig around in the bottom of my rucksack for the ancient stub of lipstick that sculls around in there somewhere, slick a bit on my mouth and rub a little bit on my cheeks to give them some colour. Then I lock up and head out into the autumn night for an early supper.

The leaves flurry across St Alphege's Square like snowflakes in a snow globe. A middle-aged lady in Regency costume walks by, pulling her cloak a little tighter round her ample body.

She's probably just left the new Bridgerton Experience that has opened in an old warehouse near here. I wonder what leads someone to end up in a job like that, if you can call it a job. And I start to think of all the people I went to uni with and how successful they've become. One's a KC already, another a Royal Academician and one's made a breakthrough in finding a cure for pancreatic cancer. And, more often than not, they now have kids.

The Van of Life, parked up next to a Thai street food van in St Alphege's Square, is spray-painted with tropical-looking greenery. The cheery words "The Van of Life" are painted in orange in a fat-footed, seventies-style font. A string of cheerful chilli-shaped fairy lights hangs all around the hatch, giving it a jaunty vibe.

"What can I get you, M'lover?" says Cobain. He has surfer-dude good looks: broad shoulders, chin-length, curly fair hair, which is still slightly sun-kissed, and a smile that would light up a beach.

"A falafel wrap, with extra vegan dressing, please, Cobain."

"Comin' up!" he says in his trademark upbeat manner as he tosses and flips and chops and wraps at lightning speed.

I draw my scarf tighter round my neck as another gust of wind tries to creep inside my top.

"Cobain?" I ask as he works. But he's concentrating on making my wrap and I don't think he's heard me, so I wait until he hands it to me before I try again. "How long are you on shift for?"

"Until six, then Magda's taking over. Why?" He picks up the card reader.

"Would you like to have a drink with me?"

He stares at me, card reader suspended in mid-air. "Like, as in a *date* drink?"

"Yeah, if you like, as in a *date drink*," I reply, getting my bank card out so it's easier to hide my face.

He puffs out his cheeks and looks around awkwardly. "Erm … Charlie, it is Charlie, isn't it? I mean, I'm flattered, obviously, but aren't you like *forty* or something?"

It's like a tsunami's just hit me. Do I really look *forty*? I'm thirty-seven, which is as near as dammit, but still.

"I mean," he goes on, "you're really nice and everything – but I'm looking to date someone more my own kind of age, if you know what I mean?"

"How old *are* you, then?" I ask.

"Twenty."

My blood runs cold.

He looks so apologetic that I can't be cross with him. Inside, though, I'm feeling like that Nazi *Kommandant*, in *Indiana Jones and the Last Crusade*, who goes through the ageing process and becomes a crumbling skeleton within five seconds.

"Yep, of course," I blip my card on the reader, attempting to smile while I keep my eyes down. "Makes sense."

"Here, have this … on the house." He hands me a can of Coke.

I stare at the can. I can't remember when I last had a Coke. Probably when I was about his age.

Which was nearly twenty years ago.

Oh shit.

I start to walk away.

"Hey, Charlie."

I whip round.

"Don't forget your wrap."

Twenty years.

"You take care now."

I pick up the wrap and want to creep away into a hole to die.

I can't even be bothered to walk home with my supper. I just sit on the first bench I can find, out of sight of the van, and eat my bullet-hard falafels while the leaves drop off the plane trees on to my food. Alice was right. The food from The Van of Life is shit. I now realise I only went there because Cobain was so cute; I guess his broad shoulders and surfer-dude good looks remind me a bit of Seb.

And then I remember that conversation with Alice in the salon at Tillingford Hall.

Would you hit on a nineteen-year-old?

I pull my hood up over my head, throw the rest of my horrible wrap in the bin and hurry away.

Chapter Seven

Hugo, our chair of trustees, harrumphs. "You should have called the police the moment those oiks started throwing rubbish over the wall," he says, rubbing his hands on the thighs of his red trousers. I notice they're thick needlecord today: a sure sign we're in autumn.

Despite my hideous experience with the Terror Teens and Cobain, I've tried to keep upbeat and carry on with my plan to level myself up. At the garden, I've been updating the website and working on a volunteer recruitment pack. And at home, I broached the subject of parting company with Scuzzy Susie.

Luckily, she said she was happy to take over the lease of the flat, as her girlfriend and another friend of theirs want to move in: the rent will be more manageable between three of them. So I've now got to clear out by the weekend, which is brilliant news for my bank balance but a little scary as I haven't found anywhere else to move yet. At least it means I won't have to waste time deep-cleaning the flat; instead, I can focus on reorganising and packing what little stuff I have.

Hugo has called an emergency trustees' meeting because of what happened on Monday. Only the retired trustees can make it at such short notice, though, which means that Emma, a teacher and Chris, an accountant, who I've always got on with pretty well, can't make it.

"Charlotte!" calls Posh Timothy, waking me from my

reverie. His mustard cords are probably the only way you would distinguish him from Hugo. He steeples his fingers and looks over his reading glasses at me. “We seem to have lost you. I asked, weren’t you checking the CCTV?”

“I can’t be in the office watching the CCTV if I’m in the garden or cleaning the toilets, can I?”

“That’s true,” says Patricia, who is, at least, always fair, even if she is a cold witch. “But it’s incredible that you didn’t think to check the cameras were in position, and the machine was actually recording every day.”

“I acknowledge that, on this particular day, I let that slip,” I admit. It’s a fair cop: the footage was useless. I had deliberately disconnected the camera in the office, so they wouldn’t see me smoking in there; and the other one – pointing into the main part of the garden, which might have caught the girls – had been angled downwards at some point, presumably by some other vandals. The only camera that was working showed the main entrance, where literally nothing happened until Tris walked in.

“We’re quite concerned, Charlotte,” says Patricia.

Teresa, who never says anything in the trustees’ meetings, except to agree with Patricia, nods and takes one of the mince pies from the cracked earthenware plate that normally acts as a saucer for my Swiss cheese plant.

“I’m not sure you’ve really met your targets for this year.” Patricia shuffles some paper. “I have your appraisal here and we agreed that …” She starts droning on about all the things I’m meant to have done while I eye up the mince pies, but I don’t reach for one. I have some sense of propriety: it’s October, I’m a vegan, and I’m apparently getting a dressing down from my employers, although I've kind of switched off by this point.

"What do you have to say?" asks Patricia as Teresa swishes the crumbs off her skirt on to the floor, oblivious of the fact it will be me who has to sweep them up.

"To be fair, you do expect a lot."

Hugo starts harrumphing and Timothy opens his mouth to say something.

"Hear me out," I plead. I give an account of all the multifarious, shitty things they expect me to do; how we now don't have funding to get any staff at all, even a cleaner; and that although they seem to expect *me* to do it, fundraising isn't on my job description: it's meant to be *them* doing it.

"You're right," huffs Hugo. "We'll need to change the way we do things."

I breathe a sigh of relief. Finally, someone's listening to me!

"We all agree that we can't carry on with the current arrangements, so we've decided to restructure," he goes on.

"What?"

"We're putting you on consultation, as of now, while we make the final arrangements. We think it would work better to have a part-time curator, with a high level of expertise, and a full-time garden assistant. That way, we'll be able to cover holidays, sickness and so on with paid staff. The curator can then spend more time on the admin, fundraising and volunteer management. The garden assistant can do most of the dirty work, including cleaning the lavatories."

"But …"

"Obviously, if we make you redundant, you'll get an appropriate severance payment and then you can reapply for one of the roles," Hugo explains.

Either job is going to pay me less than I'm on now, and I can't afford that! I need to work full time. And I couldn't be an assistant to someone who's stolen my job from me.

Either way, I'm stuffed.

I'm not just stuffed, though. I'm outraged!

After all this time, after all my striving and pleading and …

The red mist that descended when those shitty teenagers came to trash the garden floods my brain again and I jump to my feet.

"You know what, Hugo? You can stuff your severance payment because I resign!"

I grab my bag, ram a few bits from my desk into it and stomp out of the room.

I run all the way back to the flat and cry a lot, surrounded by my half-packed grocery boxes and those woven plastic bags my friends and I used to call Chinese laundry bags when we were students.

Not only do I no longer have a job, in a few days I will be homeless.

It seems the universe needs me to be at Tillingford Hall.

After a couple of hours, the bell rings. It's Tristain and Ama. Somehow, they always know.

Together, we pack all my stuff up; it takes only a couple of hours between the three of us. Everything I've accumulated in nearly four decades on this planet fits into ten half wine cases, a rucksack and five giant woven plastic bags. And that easily fits into a camper van. By now, it's early evening; so we agree to set off the next day and all sleep together in the van.

Thankfully, sleeping is all we do.

***

By ten o'clock the next morning, we come to the private drive leading up to the Hall. We rattle over the cattle grid, and I jump out to swing open the five-bar gate.

I can't wipe the grin off my face. I can't believe this place is going to be my home! I'm excited about the job. But I'm also nervous; I feel the same as ever about working for Guy and Alice. And the thought that Seb might be here too makes me want to throw up.

I guess I'll just have to do my utmost to avoid him.

I take a great big gulp of the damp autumn air. A late acorn hits the ground, just missing me. I pick it up, and it makes me smile. I remember making acorn men with my brothers when I was small; we'd use dressmaking pins for arms and legs and draw faces on them with a stub of pencil.

I shut the gate and jump back into the van.

"How can you do this, Charlie?" asks Tristain as the magnificent red-brick, Queen Ann façade of Tillingford Hall comes into view around a bend in the road. "Reckon these fellas made their cash from slavery," he mutters as the van stutters into second gear.

"The Tillingfords were abolitionists and liberals, so that's not very likely."

"They got their filthy lucre someways – from exploiting people or the land."

"They got given the estate of Tillingford Abbey by Henry VIII, during the Reformation."

"It's like I told you, then: privatising charity land," says Tris, as though this conclusively proves they're bad people.

Ama's green eyes narrow. "But there's an energy here." Her face starts to take on that weird look she has when she's going all mystical. "There!" she says as we pass a truly magnificent oak tree. "Stop, Tris!"

He's used to this kind of thing, so he obliges and she jumps out, getting her flowing tie-dyed skirts soaked as she walks barefoot through the long grass. She leans on the fence and stares at the tree. After a couple of minutes, I sigh impatiently and Tris toots. She turns back to us and hops back up into the van. "It is one of the ancient giants. A ley-line marker. This place has a very powerful energy."

"Great!" I'm unsure how else to respond.

A minute later, we pull into the stable yard of Tillingford Hall. Even though I don't want to be a gooseberry and I'm tied in knots knowing Seb could be here, I can't deny I'm really excited about this new challenge, about having a proper job: twice the money, a tied cottage and a team to manage! And a cloud is lifting from me as I really start to feel I'm leaving my old problems behind me in Bath.

I've got butterflies in my tummy as I ring the tradesmen's bell. There's no answer, although I thought I saw a movement in the kitchen, a light flickering off, but I can't be sure.

I should have rung ahead – obvs.

I sometimes forget that Normal People do stuff like that.

I try the boot room door. Bailey and Bertie are barking furiously, scrabbling against the door, but no one answers. I walk round the house and try the library door. Obviously, the

French windows of the salon and the ballroom aren't going to provide a way in. And then I make my way round to the front of the house and try the main bell. No one replies. Are they all out?

I slink back to the van.

"I guess we'd better wait, then." I say, disconsolately.

Tris lights up and we three share a smoke peacefully. I wonder if Milan the assistant gardener might be working somewhere out in the grounds. I'm just about to suggest we go looking for him when we hear a car approaching on the gravel.

But when we see the blue light flashing, we go into panic mode, trying to stub out the spliff.

Why are the police here?

But I think I already know.

A police car stops right in front of us, light still flashing and the plod gets out. "I'm going to have to ask you to leave."

"Why?" Tris asks through the open window.

"You're trespassing."

"No, you don't understand! I'm going to be the new head gardener here."

"A likely story, Miss." He looks suspiciously at Tristain and Ama. They've stubbed out and hidden the remains of their enormous reefer, but a tell-tale acrid smell is still hanging heavy in the air. "I've just had a call from the housekeeper. She said some suspicious people have been hanging around, acting oddly. I'm going have to ask you to leave."

"But …"

"Don't make this harder than it needs to be. I think Mrs Powell would know if the new head gardener was starting today, wouldn't she?"

"I only decided to take the job last night and I haven't told them yet I've accepted." I twist my fingers in my hair.

The policeman chews his lip and just looks at me.

"Okay," I sigh, realising no one's going to believe a story like that. I roll up the window and Tristain starts the engine.

The police officer returns to his car and manoeuvres to let us out; he keeps close behind us all the way down the drive until we're safely off the premises.

I stare out of the window and bite my lip while Tristain drives back towards Bath. After a couple of miles, he stops in a lay-by.

"See what these people are like? Come to Batheaston with us."

"It's your destiny, Charlie," says Ama. "You are manifesting your true desires to find your bliss in our circle."

"Right."

She strokes my cheek and kisses me behind my ear, the smell of dope still lingering in her hair.

I'm not sure living with Tristain and Ama in a polyamorous squat in Batheaston is manifesting my desires, but I don't see that I have a choice. Is the universe really telling me to go back to Bath, or do I just need to get more organised and actually tell people my plans before I make them?

I've really messed up, haven't I?

Chapter Eight

Two hours later, Tris parks the camper van half up on the pavement opposite a double-fronted Victorian villa in Batheaston. He cuts the engine, slides casually out of the driver's seat, plods nonchalantly across the road and up the stairs to ring the bell.

I get out to stretch my legs and notice a "For Sale" sign has been dumped in the front garden among the brambles twining around a shopping trolley full of road cones. The windows are all boarded up, apart from two on the first floor, which have tie-dye throws hanging in them in place of curtains. One of the glass panes in the front door is held together with duct tape.

Having received no answer to the bell, Tris knocks loudly on one of the unbroken glass panels. "Looks like no one's home today," he laughs.

As we stand on the doorstep, I look up and see that the guttering has gone and a buddleia is growing out of one corner of the parapet. Several chunks from the other side have completely fallen off into the garden and there is a large, mossy green patch on that whole side of the house. Whoever does buy this place is not only going to have to get the squatters out but also do *a lot* of building work.

Eventually, we hear footsteps.

A small, mousy girl, wrapped in what looks like a curtain, answers the door. She doesn't look much older than eighteen, but her eyes are tired and old.

"Oh sorry. Were you in the bath?"

"No."

"Is Selena here?" asks Tris brightly.

"Might be."

"Can we come in?" asks Ama kindly.

"Guess so."

The girl leaves the door open and walks back into the building, the curtain or throw, or whatever it is, trailing behind her. Her light brown hair is matted – she doesn't have dreadlocks like Tris – her hair is just long, unwashed, and she has sores on her back that look like deep scratches.

"They're doing a ritual," she explains dully. She points to a mossy brown velour sofa that is blocking up the hall and looks like it's just come from a dump. "You can sit there and wait if you like."

Then she slopes off upstairs and leaves us there, the door still wide open.

"This is our new home!" Tristain kisses me and then Ama. Ama strokes my cheek and looks lovingly at me; but I turn away and purse my lips, willing myself not to cry. I'd sleep with Tris if I was feeling lonely. But I definitely don't want to *live* with him. And Ama's my friend but I don't want to make love to her. I can't help thinking about the girl with the matted hair and wonder what the hell goes on in this building.

I'm going to have to find somewhere else to be.

My phone rings. It's a number I don't recognise. I move a few paces away to answer it.

"Charlie, where are you?" a deep voice asks urgently and breathlessly.

It takes me a second to realise it's Sebastian.

I feel such a punch in the guts I think I'm going to be sick. I lean against an ornate column in the hallway. I'm about to tell him to get lost and mind his own business, but I have to get out of this place. I step outside the front door to get a better signal.

"Thank God I managed to get hold of you," he says, when I finally reply. "I'm back at Tillingford Hall again – Guy's giving me another chance."

"That's nice for you, Seb. But what's that got to do with me?" I reply tartly.

"When the police told Mrs P what you said, she put two and two together and realised you must have come for the job. She couldn't understand why you hadn't rung ahead, arranged things with Guy."

"I know. It was pretty stupid."

"Huh. It's just the kind of thing *I* would do."

He laughs and I can't help but join in, even though my nose is tingling and my eyes are pricking.

"Where are you now?" he asks. I clench my jaw to stop the tears that are threatening to fall and tell him what's happened.

"Tell me *exactly* where you are, Charlie. I'm coming to get you," he says.

I've never felt so relieved – and so confused – in my life. What I do know is that I can't stay in Batheaston. I'll worry about *what next* when I'm safe at Tillingford Hall.

"I'll send you a pin." I put him on speakerphone and get Google maps up.

"I'll be with you by three," he reassures me. "Do you think your stuff will fit in the Range Rover or shall I bring the trailer too?"

"I think probably just the Rangie," I say, sheepishly. I want to cause the least amount of fuss; and I want him to get here as quickly as possible. I can always leave a couple of boxes of unimportant stuff here.

"Don't worry about a thing, Charlie. I've got this."

"Thank you, Seb," I croak.

I hang up, my heart pounding, whether with stress or just *that thing* that his voice does to me, I can't tell.

I lean my head back against the door frame and take a deep, shuddering breath. And then I stare at my stuff piled inside Tristain's van. I don't know how I'm going to explain this to Tris and Ama. And I don't know what happened to being a strong, independent woman. But right now, I don't care: I just want to get out of here, even if I have to swallow what little pride I have left.

Ama emerges from the house, her arm round the waist of an incredibly tall woman with white eyelashes, huge blonde dreadlocks and more piercings than a knife-thrower's assistant. She looks like Tilda Swinton as the White Witch of Narnia, with baubles.

"Hey, Sweetie. This is Selena."

"Hi Selena." My voice quavers: I don't feel entirely unafraid in the presence of this frosty amazon.

"Welcome, Charlotte." She tastes my name like a Bond girl licking an olive.

Thank God I don't have to live here and change my name to Rain or Sequoia.

"Ama, I need to speak to you. Alone."

"No secrets in this house, Charlotte," says Selena.

"Whatever!" I don't need to keep the White Witch on side *now*, do I?

Selena recoils, her eyes narrowing. She gives Ama a very intense look before stalking off.

Ama's wearing her sad face. She only pulls this face when she has a message from The Universe for someone that involves some kind of personal development goal. Otherwise, she's always got a look of blissed-out contentment, which might be as much to do with her dope habit as her connection with the love-energy of The Universe.

"Charlie, Sweetheart, Selena's our priestess and due your respect." Ama gently rubs my arm.

"I'm sorry, I have no respect for someone who dresses like Jadis of Narnia on a weekday. Look, Ama, you've been a lovely friend …"

She's now stroking my face and looking deep into my eyes. "Aren't we more than just friends?"

"I'm sure we'll keep in touch, Ama, but I just need to break out on my own right now. I really appreciate you and Tris helping me out, but I'm going back to Tillingford Hall tonight."

"How?" A strange light comes into her eyes, like she's searching her sixth sense for an intuitive answer and is puzzled that she can't find it there.

"They're coming to pick me up."

Her face lights up. "It's Sebastian! And you're still in love!" She says it in such a gloopy voice I'm almost expecting her to say "Aww!" afterwards.

"*No!* He was never in love with *me*."

Ama looks at me pityingly. "Oh Charlie, you really don't

get it, do you? Your aura is soooo confused, Sweetie. You are all over the place! Let's just get you into the house and you can have a nice smoke, and Selena and I can give you a massage to settle you in. Luna makes these amazing oils that will totally relax you and resettle your aura."

"No, Ama. I don't want a smoke or a massage. Or reiki. Or a shamanic ritual or aura-bonding crystals or anything like that! I just want a cup of PG, a bath and *Strictly* on catch-up."

"Oh!" She pulls exactly the kind of face you'd expect a middle-class English woman in her thirties to pull when her best friend tells her to piss off. Then she takes a deep breath and half-closes her eyes, gazing into her inner realms. After a few breaths, she opens her eyes wide. "This is it, isn't it, Charlie?"

"We'll stay friends, obviously."

"The Universe will decide."

Stuff The Universe, I think to myself. I can't wait for Seb to arrive and take me away from this.

And no, I'm not *in love* with him *anymore*, obvs. Why did she say that?

I start to get my things out of the van. Seb might be a while, and I don't want Tris and Ama to use the opportunity to hijack my stuff to force me to stay with them. "Will *you* tell Tris?" I ask her.

"No, you must speak to him yourself."

"Where is he?"

"Preparing for his initiation ceremony, which we'd hoped you'd be part of. He'll be hurt, you know, and it will disturb the serenity of the ritual. You should tell him afterwards."

“How long will it be?” I ask, putting the wine boxes on the pavement.

Ama looks at me pityingly. “When?” and “How long?” are not questions you ask Ama.

“Lovely, sad Charlotte. Sometimes you just need to learn to let go a bit.”

Let go? Bloody hell. I’ve done nothing but let go for the past decade and look where it’s got me! Homeless, friendless and desperate; relying on my ex-lover to rescue me and my tatty Chinese laundry bags from outside a squat before I’m ravished by the White Witch.

Chapter Nine

A misty drizzle starts to fall and I'm regretting having got my stuff out of Tris's camper van so soon, when a shiny, forest-green Range Rover careens round the corner. It screeches to a halt just outside the squat.

Sebastian flings open the door and it's like the sun's come out. His long, curly golden locks always remind me of the sun's rays when they flow loose over his shoulders, like they do right now. He wordlessly wraps his arms around me and relief floods over me.

For a moment, I rest my head on his chest, absorbing the warmth from his solid body, and I feel like I could stay there for ever. His hair brushes my face and his neat bronze beard touches my forehead. Tendrils of his cypress and driftwood cologne arouse memories of joyful nights together and then I begin to feel something that isn't just relief. My lips start to tingle, a fuzzy feeling takes over my brain, my breath quickens. I can feel his heart beating faster too, his grip tightening as he starts to respond to me.

He bends as if to kiss me, but I stiffen; I turn my head quickly so his lips just meet my cheek. Then I pull away; but I can still feel the heat of him, even though we're not touching. Tears prick my eyes; and I blink fiercely, biting my lip. When I look up, I see his eyes are fixed greedily on my mouth.

No one has a right to look that good in a holey, faded

sweatshirt, I think crossly.

I don't want to feel this way about him.

"I'm sorry for being such an idiot," I say, through gritted teeth, the apology costing me.

He searches me with those amber eyes, flecked with green. "We all do stupid things sometimes, Charlotte, but that doesn't make us idiots."

It's the first time he's ever called me by my full name. Something in the way he says it doesn't sound cold or distant: it's more like a mark of respect. Given how awkward this all is, I really appreciate that; and it softens me a little towards him.

His hair is even longer than it was last summer. His beard is full but tidy. He looks leaner and somehow older than he did. It suits him, although the shadows under his eyes and the deepened frown lines on his forehead suggest it's not been the easiest three months of his life.

"Come on, let's get you outta here!" He pulls a piece of string out of his pocket and ties his hair back while I start to grab my things, desperate to stash them in the Range Rover as quickly as possible. But Seb gently tells me to put them all down. He takes a minute to look at the size of the pile on the pavement and the size of the car. And then he's somehow fitted everything in, like a giant three-dimensional Tetris puzzle, with not an inch of space to spare.

I'm just about to get in the car when the front door of the squat swings open. Tris is standing there in a skimpy whitish tunic. "Charlie!" he calls. He hesitates for a moment when he sees Seb but jumps down the stairs, two at a time; Ama appears in the doorway behind him.

"I missed you at the ceremony, Charlie," Tris slurs as he approaches us, barefoot on the wet pavement. "All right, Seb? You come to join us too?"

"No, Dude; I'm taking her to Tillingford Hall."

"Oh." His pupils are weirdly dilated, his dreadlocks loose around his shoulders. He envelopes me in his arms, pressing up against me so I can feel every contour of his body. "But I understand; you have to go where your spirit leads you." He intertwines his fingers with mine so I can't quite extricate myself. "I'm going to miss the taste of Charlie. You take good care of her now, Seb."

"I will," mutters Sebastian, rubbing the back of his neck. I swear he adds, "If she'll let me," under his breath.

"We'll come over to Hampshire to check up on how she's doing."

"Cool," says Seb, crossing his arms.

The White Witch appears behind Seb and Ama.

"We've been studying the ley lines," Selena announces. "The Spine of Albion ley line goes right through the grounds of Tillingford Hall. We want to hold our winter solstice festival there."

"Yeah? No worries! We'll see you then!" says Seb, getting into the Range Rover, with a wave.

As we clunk our car doors shut, I turn to him. "Oh my God, Seb! What have you done?"

"What?" He turns to me with an angry frown.

"You've just invited twenty pagan squatters to Tillingford Hall for the twenty-first of December. What's Guy going to think? What about the Christmas concert?"

"It was only a polite invitation!"

"You know these guys, Seb! They're not into upper-crust social niceties: the difference between a 'polite' invitation, a 'social' invitation and a 'firm' invitation is a bit lost on them. It was an *invitation*, and they are going to come! They're going to hold a bloody pagan winter solstice festival at Tillingford Hall – at the same time as Guy's Christmas concert! You're going to have a lot of explaining to do!"

"You think so, Charlie?" Seb raises one eyebrow. "I think you're the one who's going to have to explain to Guy why I didn't finish getting the old stables cleared this afternoon. *Thank you for rescuing me, Seb. I would just be starting my initiation ceremony into some kind of weird pagan cult if you hadn't rescued me!*" He uses a silly high-pitched voice that doesn't sound anything like me. "Don't mention it, Miss. Any time, Miss," he tugs a lock of hair on his forehead, like a serf grovelling to the lord of the manor.

I harrumph and hunch my shoulders as he turns on the sound system and guns the Range Rover down the road, Kurt Cobain's raucous tones filling the car.

We soon hit the open countryside, the windscreen wipers at full tilt to try to clear the glass of wet leaves. I stare out of the windows in sullen silence as Somerset and Wiltshire rush past us. Disconsolate sheep huddle under dysfunctional trees that offer no shelter. I try to lean as close to the window as I can, away from the heat emanating from Seb's body and the gentle scent of the ocean he carries with him. But nothing can stop the tingling of my entire body.

If Ama was here, she'd tell me my aura's wrapped right

round his.

But I don't think *his* aura's going anywhere.

And I don't want to feel this way about him. Even if he did single-handedly restore the walled garden, even if he did just rescue me, even if he is the best lover I've ever had, Sebastian Seaton-Smyth is bad news and a grumpy sod at that.

The traffic slows as the A303 narrows. Stonehenge appears across the plain, stark on the rise of the slight hill, the stones the colour of the rain; a few dejected ravens are being buffeted across the lowering sky.

"Perhaps we could persuade Selena's lot to come down *here* for the solstice instead," says Seb, the first words we've exchanged in over an hour.

"What, when they've got an ancient oak sitting on the Spine of Albion, in a nice big field all to themselves?" I reply. "Not likely."

Then he takes a deep breath. "I know you hate me, Charlie, and I guess deserve it. But please give me a chance to explain."

I take a deep breath in.

"I don't *hate* you, Seb," I say, but it's not entirely true. "And I certainly don't need you to *explain*. Everyone's told me about your difficult childhood; how you were in thrall to Maxine and now she's dumped you. They all feel sorry for you and expect me to do the same."

He bites his lip. "I don't need you to *feel sorry* for me, Charlie. My mistakes are all my own and I take total responsibility for them, including hurting you, for which I'm truly, deeply sorry." He looks across at me for a second. "But we do at least need to get along if we're going to be colleagues."

I turn away. He's absolutely right, of course.

"That's fine, Seb. I can do that."

"And don't think I'm going to rescue you again."

"Nope. Understood. You can just leave me to burn next time. Let's just end it there, shall we?"

I return to staring out of the window; but, when I glance across at him, his jaw is rigid and his eyes are tired. I try to close my heart and forget how I felt about him once, but I can't. It's like that doorframe has warped and I'll never be able to close the door properly again.

But even if I could forgive him, he's made it clear he never wants to go back to how things were.

Despite the way he held me, the kiss he almost gave me back there in the rain in Bath, I have to stop thinking about Sebastian as anything other than a colleague – and a somewhat annoying one at that.

When we finally arrive at the entrance to the Tillingford estate, it's a relief to jump out of the Range Rover to open the gate. For a moment, I glance around at the skeletal trees, silhouetted against the early evening sky – gunmetal grey with streaks of burning pink – and I breathe the fresh air deeply as the Range Rover judders across the cattle grid and I shut the gate behind it.

This is my new home and my new place of work: a fresh start.

As I gaze out at the rain-washed fields and trees, I realise I need to think of Seb as a new workmate I just met today.

He toots and I hop back in the car, smiling.

He smiles back. "Unreal, isn't it?" he says as we ramble

up the drive. The beautiful landscape rolls away in front of us, revealing the lines of Tillingford Hall as we come round the bend in the road.

"That's *something* we can agree on," I admit. The corner of his full lips turns up in a little smile as he glances over at me. For a second, I wish we were back where we were three months ago, before I knew who he really was.

Back before I was angry with him.

Back before anyone knew what he and Maxine were up to.

But now we do.

And that's that.

Chapter Ten

"Did you sleep well?" asks Alice as I come down to the kitchen for breakfast the next morning. It's a Saturday: one of Hatty's "on" weeks.

"Like a log! The bed in the Rose Room is so comfortable."

"You can stay there another night, if you like," says Guy as Alice pours me a cup of tea from the big Brown Betty teapot.

"Oooh. I'm tempted," I say, thinking of the four-poster bed and the lovely view of the grounds. "But I can't wait to get into the gardener's cottage. It's such a long time since I've had my own space."

"I totally get that – we'll get you settled in there today." Guy passes me the toast. "I can't tell you how glad I am that you're here at last."

"Me too!" says Hatty. "I've never had a fairy godmother before!"

"I'm sorry, Hatty, there's nothing remotely magical about me! I'm just your boring old *normal* godmother. I'm supposed to tell you how to be a good girl."

"Well, that *is* rather boring. But it's not your fault," she adds brightly, looking up at me. "You can't help being a grown-up."

Alice looks at me and we burst out laughing while Guy gazes at Hatty adoringly, like that's the cutest thing anyone's ever said.

I can't help thinking how lucky Alice is to have found a

partner who not only loves her but is clearly besotted with her eight-year-old daughter too; not to mention the fact that he's one of the most eligible men in the country.

Alice keeps trying to tell me that Guy's actually skint because Tillingford Hall is a money pit and the estate hasn't made a profit for five years. But when I think about the clothes he wears, his Aston Martin, the swimming pool, I don't think Guy's quite on the breadline yet.

As we share out a second round of toast, Hatty, who's moved on from Disney films and is now obsessed with the Tudors, tells us about *Amber Lynn* and the castles she lived in. Then we start talking about what Tillingford Hall should be offering when it's opened to the public.

"I think you should have more ladies' loos than men's because there's always a *huge* queue for the ladies," says Hatty. "But there should be baby changing thingies in both, because lots of daddies change stinky nappies too. And it's helpful to have a family one like at Legoland, so there's room for mummies and daddies to push buggies inside and help the little children. I don't need help because I'm big now. But I remember when I was really little, we used the family loo at Legoland, and it was much better than trying to squeeze *into a tiny little …*" and she scrunches up her shoulders and sucks in her cheeks as if to illustrate the point.

"Well said, Hatty," says Guy, and she beams at him.

"And we must also have swings and slides and a pirate ship."

"A *pirate ship*?" asks her mother, cradling her Jane Austen mug.

"Not a *real* one, Silly Mummy, but a big wooden climbing

frame that *looks* like one. We've got one at school and everyone loves it."

"I'm not sure a pirate ship is really relevant here at Tillingford Hall. Maybe we could have a castle instead?" Guy suggests kindly.

"A castle like the Tower of London?"

"Maybe not quite *that* big!"

"Where would you put it?" asks Alice, starting to peel an orange for Hatty.

"There's the rub." Guy runs his hands through his floppy blond hair. "If we build a playground, it has to be near enough to the house and tearoom so small people can easily walk to it. But we need to make sure there's room for it to expand as our visitor numbers go up. It could become a feature."

"But it has to be far away enough so we don't ruin the view of the house," argues Alice. "People aren't going to come just for a play area. And if it dominates too much, it might even put off people without children. You have to appeal to retired people as much as families. I think getting the miniatures housed in their own gallery, separate from the house, is at least as urgent."

"But that would be a massive project!" Guy pours himself another cup of coffee from the oversized cafetière. "Anyway, I prefer the idea of having a trail through the house so people can hunt for them."

"Oh no! That would be a security nightmare – we'd need custodians in every room," insists Alice.

"I think a trail sounds fun!" Hatty butts in. "Maybe we can glue the pictures to the walls so no one can steal them!"

"But that's all in the future," says Guy. "The most important thing is to get the car park and toilet block ready; and the front of the house spruced up in time for the Christmas concert, *which is only nine weeks away!*"

It's exciting hearing this new little family talking about their plans. I'm feeling incredibly daunted by what lies ahead, and still in a bit of a state of shock and exhaustion after the events of this week; but I can't help being infected by their enthusiasm.

"Has everyone finished?" Guy jumps up from his seat, and we all nod. "Then let's clear up and give Charlie the tour."

I realised from my last visit that, despite its grandeur, the Hall has hardly any staff these days; and, generally, everyone mucks in with the chores like a normal household. I don't mind at all: I'm just happy that I've got a table to sit at for once.

"I'll join you in a bit. I need to help Hatty with her homework. And I'm feeling a bit under the weather." Alice certainly does look a bit pasty.

"Are you sure, Darling?" Guy looks concerned. "Do you want to go back to bed?"

"Don't worry. It'll pass."

"Give me a ring when you're ready to come out and we'll tell you where we are," he says, stroking her arm.

"Okay. You two get off. Hatty and I will clear up."

"I won't hear of it!" Guy takes plates, cups and glasses off the table so Hatty can pop them in the dishwasher. "You should definitely go back to bed for a bit if you're not feeling well," Guy insists, rubbing Alice's shoulders. "We can take Hatty with us and give you a break."

"Honestly, Guy, stop fussing!"

He looks a bit taken aback, and I'm not surprised. I wish I had someone to clear up and look after me when I'm feeling ill. I stifle a sigh, then I grab a J-Cloth from the side of the sink and wipe down the surfaces while Guy and Hatty put the jam and butter away in the giant American-style fridge.

As Guy and I enter the boot room, Bailey and Bertie, the Tillingford beagles – one old and arthritic, the other livelier – jump up expectantly. Guy grabs a smart new Barbour from the old-fashioned coat stand and shrugs it on over his cashmere sweater. I slip into my battered Doc Marten boots and pull on my very old Mountain Warehouse jacket, which was once waterproof but now leaks a bit at the seams.

Bertie, the younger beagle, with a white patch over his eye, looks at me imploringly, beating his little tail on the floor. He seems delighted when I kneel down and scratch him behind the ears and begins to lick my face.

"Get off her, Bertie," commands Guy.

"No, it's fine. He *soooo cute*," I say in a doggy voice, rubbing his ears and get another lick in return.

"Seems like he's taken a shine to you."

I make a fuss of the little fellow. "I love dogs!"

"That's good! There's never been a shortage of them here. Dad took his Great Dane to London with him, but I expect you'll meet him soon. How Algie fits in Desmond's flat in Belgravia, I have no idea – I'm surprised they're even allowed pets."

"I've always wanted a dog," I admit. "But I've never lived in a suitable place or been able to afford it."

Bertie comes up to investigate and I give him a scratch behind the ears too.

"Bertie, Bailey!" Guy calls to the dogs as he straightens up and strides towards the door, zipping his Barbour right up to his chin and hunching his shoulders against the cold wind.

"So when did Herbert retire?" I ask as we crunch across the gravel.

"A month ago – around the time my father went up to London. Herbert had been here for forty years. He was over seventy, so I guess it felt like the end of an era. I don't think Dad had put his wages up since the millennium and I'm not sure he ever actually had any horticultural training. He just kind of kept the place from turning into a wilderness. He wasn't pro-active and didn't know anything about the historical context."

"What about Milan?"

"He doesn't have any real gardening experience, but he's keen and strong. We'll probably see him around," Guy replies.

"Milan works on a *Saturday*?"

"Yes, he's just here for the year to earn cash to send home to his fiancée in the Czech Republic, so he's happy to do a six-day week and I'm glad he can do those extra hours – we're all pulling all the stops out at the moment. And Seb's a hard worker too – I can't get him to take a day off. He'll be joining us in a few minutes."

"Ah ..."

"Listen, Charlie." Guy stops in his tracks and turns to look at me. "You and Seb are just colleagues now, okay? You have to put your history behind you. And I've said the same to him. You've taken up this job freely, knowing Seb's part of the team here. If you don't think you can handle that, then you're welcome to stay for the rest of the weekend as our guest but we won't be signing that contract on Monday. Is that clear?"

"Yes," I say meekly, shuffling my foot in a pile of leaves.

Chapter Eleven

We walk round to the formal rose garden on the west side of the house. Some of the shrubs are still blooming but, on most of them, the bright red hips are hanging like jewels amid the spiderwebs. I can hear the snip-snip of secateurs and, when I look more closely, I see a young man at work among the bushes.

This must be Milan. With his angelic golden-brown hair, full lips and pale brown eyes, he reminds me of Botticelli's self-portrait in his *Adoration of the Magi*.

Guy introduces me to Milan as his new boss.

"I understand you don't have any gardening experience," I say.

"When I was student in Olomouc, I mow lawns for old ladies. But I am philosophy graduate, not gardener," he replies, with a shrug.

"Do you mind?" I ask, holding out my hand for the secateurs.

He hands them over, bemused and I cut one stem right back.

"There!" I hand back the clippers. "This isn't a shave – it's a haircut! Right back to the old wood, remember!"

"Sure, okay, Boss!" He grins and turns back to his work with gusto, hacking into the bushes with an abandon they'll thank him for.

Guy sees a dark red bloom that's still clinging to the bush, despite the lateness of the season; he pulls it towards him and inhales deeply. "I love this one. It reminds me of Granny Bea. She adored the garden and, on a summer's evening, her favourite thing was to come down here and deadhead the roses. She used to collect the petals and dry them with lavender to make potpourri. My mother never had time for the gardens – that's one of the reasons they've got a bit neglected, I suppose."

'A bit neglected' is an understatement. It's an impossible task for a single gardener to look after such a large estate properly. Mowing the lawns alone would take a full day every week in the summer, but that doesn't account for the other nine man-days Seb and Herbert should've managed between them.

Suddenly the beagles shoot off at top speed towards a nearby oak, startling a squirrel who was busy stuffing an acorn into his mouth. The squirrel careers up the tree, loosening dead leaves, which flurry down on to the dogs below. He sits, scolding and chattering, on the lowest branch, twitching his tail in outrage while the dogs bark up at him. Guy laughs and calls the dogs back. Bertie bounds up and stays close to me as we walk on; Bailey stiffly trots a few paces behind.

"So, this is the shrubbery." Guy glances at his phone. "I've asked Seb to join us here so we can talk about the plans for the grounds and the exterior of the house holistically."

I'm getting twitchy for my first nicotine fix of the day, so I take a drag on a vape: this doesn't seem the moment to be making roll-ups. I hardly ever use vapes because of the plastic and the lithium, which are so bad for the environment, but oddly vapes seem to offend people less than roll-ups.

"So where does Sebastian live, then?" I puff out a sickly-sweet cloud of grape-scented vapour.

"Down at the farm with Sahara. She's still living in James's cottage."

"James Irving-McAuley?"

"Yes, the Irving-McAuleys are our tenants. Tillingford Manor Farm's part of our estate; they have it on a long lease from us. James and his sister Allegra were running the farm together; but James has ... got involved in another project abroad. Sahara was living with him but, when he took off, she just stayed in his cottage. She's got this complicated legal dispute going on, which is bleeding her dry, so she's had to rent out her London flat and doesn't really have anywhere else to go. Allegra's her best friend so I guess it works out for them. Sahara's over the moon about having Seb around: I've never known a brother and sister as close as those two."

"You've got some nice specimens here," I say to change the subject. "But everything's so overgrown. These rhododendrons must look stunning in May, but they're taking over – look, they're coming out over the lawn – and some of them are dead; they need taking out to make space for new growth. Children love playing in rhodies: you can get right inside them. Look at this one, it's made a real little cave. You could open this all up with some paths and encourage people to explore – like a kind of maze. That's definitely something Milan could start on right away. I assume you've at least got a hedge-trimmer and chainsaw?"

Guy grins. "A couple – I'm a sucker for power tools!"

"Me too!"

"But I leave all the dangerous stuff to Seb."

Right now, I feel like I could do with taking things out on a few hapless shrubs. But it's all I can do not to think about Seb in a tight, sweaty T-shirt, bracing himself against the kick of a chainsaw.

"Talk of the devil," says Guy as Seb comes striding towards us. Despite the chill in the air, he's only wearing an old jersey grandad shirt; and it's as tight as the one I just imagined, showing up the line of every muscle in his chest and arms. Any other man would look stupid in a holey grandad shirt, his mass of golden curls tied back with a torn-off strand of Virginia creeper. But Seb somehow manages to look even more gorgeous when he's scruffy like this.

I look away and take a deep drag on my grape vape.

"I see you've given up the roll-ups, Charlie," Seb comments.

"Nope. Just don't want my fumes to kill anyone." I bite back the sarky comment I want to spit out, determined not to be a bitch. I glance over at Guy, looking for his reaction, hoping my response doesn't come across as too snippy.

Bailey and Bertie lead us up some steps, under a canopy of plane trees. Beneath their overhanging branches lies an ornamental pond ringed round with ancient, lichen-encrusted statues of Roman gods.

"Oh wow! Is this the famous pool?" I ask.

Guy nods and laughs.

I try to imagine how Alice ever thought it was a good idea to swim in *this*: it's green with algae.

"Do you remember, Seb, that first day Alice came here, and she thought this was the swimming pool?" Guy asks his friend. "It was so funny – and so Alice to assume we swam in a marble pool full of shit!"

I can't help but laugh with them at the thought of prim little Alice, in her bathing suit (probably one of those long Edwardian ones, with a skirt and legs), emerging from the pool, covered in pond weed, to find Guy – who she'd never met before – standing there, wondering what the hell she was doing.

Seb doesn't laugh. "When you brought her round to the real pool, she was covered in green slime. And yet, somehow, you fell in love with her! It's funny how falling in love can blind a guy to slime."

Guy gives him a sharp look as I momentarily wonder if that was a dig at me; but I'm not going to rise to anything. I snap back into work mode. "These plane trees won't shed until late November; but when they do, we're going to have several tons of leaves in the pond."

"It's on the schedule to net it this week," says Seb. "We were going to catch them all and put them on the compost. But that's up to you now."

"That's all good – exactly what I would have done. I'll do it with Milan on Monday. Are there fish in the pond?"

Guy peers dubiously into the slimy depths. "I don't think they'd like it much in there."

"But wouldn't it be fabulous, stocked with hundreds of goldfish?" Seb says. "They'd probably survive how it is now; but you want it to be clear enough to see them, so you'd just need a hidden filter and pump system."

"But that would take a ton of energy – and be a massive faff to maintain – and I'm assuming you want to aim for carbon neutral." I look at Guy, questioningly.

"Of course!" Guy looks like a rabbit in the headlights. I wonder if he's even begun to think about things like a sustainability policy.

I follow an overgrown path towards a wall. Pushing aside

the matted briars and rhododendrons, I find a small domed structure. "What's this? Looks like you've got an ice house."

"Huh. I had no idea," says Guy with delight.

"Every great house would have had one – it was an early form of refrigeration, filled with chunks of ice gathered off the lake in the winter, and meant they could show off by serving cool drinks and ice cream in the summer. You should reopen it – kids would love coming down this little path and peering inside."

"We'll have to get a surveyor to check it's safe," says Seb. "And we don't really have time or budget for that kind of thing this year."

"But it's so cool!" says Guy. "There's so much about this place I don't even know. I guess you've seen a lot more country houses than I have, Charlie."

"I think I've visited every National Trust property south of Derbyshire and half of the ones up north," I admit, picking up a stick for Bertie.

"How did you find time to do any work?" asks Seb.

"I went with my parents as a child. And I visit some for my degree and my post-grad course. This is my *profession*." I sound slightly snippier than I mean to. I chuck a stick for the enthusiastic beagle and Bertie goes careering off into the undergrowth.

Despite Seb's continual sniping, I'm starting to feel quite excited: the restoration of the grounds will be the most amazing project. They were designed by Capability Brown, one of the most famous Georgian landscape designers; they have wonderful bones and so much potential. I'm staring at the steps of the ornamental pond and asking myself why they're there. Was it a bathing pond as Alice thought or …? I find a sturdy stick and start poking. "Look, there were *other* steps! Here's a plinth. Some rubble."

We go deeper and deeper into the undergrowth until we come across some bricks, a foundation and a couple of large rocks. "They weren't steps for people to get into the pool – it would have been an elaborate waterfall. Is there a spring that feeds it?"

"I have no idea."

"If this was part of the original Capability Brown landscape, I doubt he'd have used a steam pump, so it has to be some kind of natural water flow. Probably, this cascaded all the way down to the lake. Look!" I point down between the trees and shrubs to the grassy area by the lake, where the imprint of a former channel is still clearly visible. "I wonder where the spring flows now? Tell me you've got archives somewhere, Guy?"

"There are boxes of papers up in the attics – probably a job for Alice."

"It's so exciting!" I squeak.

"I never expected something like this!" says Guy, nodding in agreement. He puts his arm round my shoulder and gives me a squeeze.

"It's quite a project!"

"That's major money territory, Dude," Seb points out.

"Our major donor is supporting us to get the Hall open to the public; but that money won't be enough for something like this as well," Guy admits as we start to walk down the slope towards the lake and Bertie comes running back towards us.

"We can't be getting stoked about stuff like this when we need to focus on restoring the house. I don't reckon the chapel roof's going to see out another winter," says Seb.

"I bet you could get Heritage Lottery Funding," I suggest as I take the stick back from Bertie.

Guy pulls out his phone and makes a few notes. "I don't know the first thing about fundraising."

"There are professional fundraisers for hire out there," I point out. "It's something you should think about. And remember, with your connections, you could get more major donors and some corporate partners, as well as Lottery funding – and money from trusts and foundations."

While I continue on down the slope in a daze, I notice one of my laces is undone and kneel down in the long grass. Bertie comes running back towards me with a stick and then drops it to give me another big lick, almost tipping me down the hill.

"He's right mental," Seb mutters.

"Well, I think he's adorable!" I stand up and wipe the drool off my face.

Seb picks up a stick and throws it so Bertie charges after it, running away from me down the slope. Why does Seb have to kick back at every single thing I've said this morning, when I'm trying so hard to be nice? Is this some kind of test?

"So, what do you think is the absolute priority, then, Charlie?" asks Guy.

"The trees. The avenue has some dangerous branches that need trimming back. We can't allow the public on to the site without doing that as a priority, before the autumn storms pull them down for you. A falling tree could block the drive or cause serious damage to a wall or fence."

"We'd best get Steve Silver in to give us a quote," says Seb.

"Who's Steve Silver?"

"Local tree surgeon."

"He sounds more like a pirate!" I say with a grin.

"He'll certainly make a few pieces of eight out of me," Guy says.

"We have to prioritise," Seb insists, rubbing his neck. "I know there's a lot of work to do on the trees, but it's kinda spendy. And we can't be distracted from getting the car park and toilets done and getting the house ready."

"Yeah, but *I'm* here to restore the gardens, right?"

"We have to work as a team." Guy frowns at us both. "And that means, between now and Christmas, we can't be too siloed – you two are going to have to pull together."

Chapter Twelve

The gardener's cottage at Tillingford Hall is a Victorian two-up, two-down behind the old stables. I get it completely rent-free as part of my job. It's the first time I've had a place *all to myself*, so I've been personalising it and making it as homely as I can. Mrs P and Milan helped me do a deep clean, taking down the Bob Marley posters (I liked them, but they were pretty tatty) and generally getting the place spic and span after forty years of occupation by my predecessor, Herbert. I've kept the old Jamaican flag that he used as a throw to cover up the tatty old sofa. It gives the place a jaunty air and it's a kind of tribute to what went before.

Guy suggested I ask Seb to help me redecorate and paint over the orange-and-brown seventies floral tiles in the kitchen and the varnished pine cladding in the living room. But I quite like the cosy retro look, and I don't want to ask Seb any more favours.

The Friday after I arrive, I find Alice is standing on my doorstep. I guess she's just got here from London. I hesitate before letting her in.

"What's wrong, Charlie?"

"I'm not sure I'm meant to hug you now that you're the Lady of the Manor."

"Don't be silly! Nothing's changed: you're still my best friend and always will be. Guy and I want no formality and no deference from you. And anyway, we're not even engaged yet and his father is definitely a long way from dying, so the *Lady Tillingford* thing is definitely not a done deal."

Nevertheless, I make a sweeping bow. "Drink, ma'am?"

She teasingly cuffs me round the ear with her mittened hand. I take her flayed-squirrel coat and hang it on one of the wooden pegs by the frosted glass door.

She glances up at the kitchen clock. It's half six in the evening – definitely gin-and-tonic time – but she asks for a cup of tea. I get the kettle on and pull out my new-to-me, apple-and-pear-patterned Royal Worcester teapot, which I got from the Winchester Dog Rescue charity shop in Alton. I'm pleased to have an excuse to show it off.

I put on the kettle as Bertie shuffles disconsolately towards Alice and half-heartedly checks her out.

"How's Bertie settling in?"

"He seems content," I reply, popping a couple of tea bags into the pot. "But he's definitely pining."

Two nights ago, I got a late-night call from Seb asking if I could look after Bertie. Seb and Sahara have been keeping the beagles on the farm while there's no one living full time at the Hall. Seb needed to take Bailey to an emergency vet appointment and Sahara was up in London. Sadly, Bailey didn't make it through the night. He was fifteen, so it was probably time. Nevertheless, Lord Tillingford was gutted. He came down with Desmond yesterday so we could have a funeral. Bailey's little casket was added to the many in the pet cemetery behind the walled garden.

Everyone agreed that since Bertie seemed to have taken

such a shine to me, and I have more room for a lively dog than Seb and Sahara, I should adopt him, which I have been more than happy to do.

"I'm sure he's better off with you than flitting between the Hall and Holly Cottage. Anyone can see he adores you." Alice ruffles his ears as he grins up at us.

I'm about to grab a faded old Usain Bolt mug but decide the new Royal Worcester ones might be more suitable for Alice. So I reach to the back of the cupboard and pull out two gold-rimmed, bone china mugs decorated with plums.

"And how's work going?" she asks.

"It's been manic. Guy wanted a fully prioritised and costed work plan by the end of the week. So I've been rushing round the grounds on a quad bike – I *love* the quad bikes, by the way – meeting contractors and working out what's essential to get done before this bloomin' Christmas concert and what can wait until the new year."

"The concert's a bit of a shocker," says Alice. "I honestly don't know how we're going to manage it. It's going to be a security nightmare to put something like this on before we're properly set up for opening, but Guy's adamant."

As I pour the tea, Alice admits she's a bit downhearted about her day job at the London Portrait Gallery. "You know Desmond's retiring?"

I nod. Desmond was Alice's boss. He got together with Guy's father, Giles, when he came down here in the summer to help Alice sort out the Tillingfords' art collection.

"I meant to apply for his role but, somehow, I missed the deadline. I think it was because, subconsciously, I didn't really want it. I need time to finish my PhD. And Guy's keen for me to give up work and come and help at the Hall."

"So, why don't you do that? It seems like the ideal solution. You could work here part time and finish your PhD."

"I'm worried it's too soon: we've only been together for a few months. And Hatty would have to move schools; and I'm not sure I could face packing up and moving out of the flat."

"You wouldn't be under pressure to do that, though, would you?"

"But if I'm not working, how am I going to pay the rent? I can't expect Guy to pay it if I'm living here, can I?"

She seems tired; not just in a Friday-evening kind of way but really *weary*.

"I'm not sure I can do it again, Charlie." She stares into her mug.

"What?"

"Have another child. But it's what he wants most in the world. He deserves the chance to be a dad; and he needs someone to pass the title on to. It's really important to him. You're so lucky not having to worry about that!"

"*Alice!* Don't *ever* tell someone who doesn't have kids that they're *lucky*! I want to be a mum too. I want to have my own little Hatty to love and to cuddle and to worry about. Don't you see? The worry is part of it. Having someone who needs you to get up for them in the morning; having someone who makes your home a home; who helps you see a future. I'd do anything to have that."

I realise with blinding clarity that's exactly what I've really wanted all this time; but I've spent far too long mucking about and now I'm running out of time. I need to find a decent bloke and settle down if I'm ever going to be a mother.

There's a knock on the door and I jump up to see who it is.

Milan is standing on the doorstep.

"Mrs P offer lift to pub when she go home," says Milan in his broken English. "You like come?"

I've got to finish the work plan and do the job descriptions for the new staff this evening, I think. Then I look back at Alice, slumped over a cup of tea. Sod it, I don't have to be all responsible just yet! I'm tired and overwrought and could do with a bit of down time. "Just a sec, Milan. I've got Alice here and I just need to check that's okay with her."

"Its fine. I need to get over to the Hall for supper with Guy anyway."

"It's a date then, Milan. Let me just put my boots on. Will Mrs P be okay having Bertie in her car, do you think?"

"Mrs P, she like dogs," he assures me.

"I'll be on the drive in ten, then."

***

The warm yellow light shining through the mullioned windows of the Tillingford Arms invites us in. A wave of chatter sweeps over us as Milan holds opens the door and ushers me and Bertie inside.

Seb's at the bar, a couple of inches taller than anyone else; the overhead lights burnish his curls. He's leaning forward, arms resting on the counter, emphasising the muscular set of his shoulders, the taut contour of his backside. I feel a sudden jolt, like a kick in the guts.

"Yo, Dudes," he says in a neutral but not unfriendly way. "I'm next. What can I get you both? The local ale's Old Cressy or there's a good scrumpy: Susan's Cloudy," he suggests, knowing I'd be unfamiliar with the local brews.

I ask for a pint of Old Cressy, while he gets Milan a pint of Staropramen Czech lager. I'm quite surprised to see it available in a country inn but soon realise, glancing at the food menu, that this is an upmarket gastro pub, not your average spit-and-sawdust place.

While Milan goes to bag us a table, Seb orders a lime cordial. I wonder why I've never seen him drinking, when he doesn't seem to have any objection to drugs.

As we're waiting for our drinks to be poured, a wiry man, with short silver hair and a confident, patrician air, props up the bar next to a noisy gaggle of other middle-aged blokes.

He turns to Seb, appraising me. "I'm guessing this is your new head gardener."

"That's me!" I answer for myself, leaning back on the bar. "News does travel fast round here!"

"Faster than his lordship's Lambo!" He winks at me as he takes a swig of his pint.

"He has a Rangie," I point out, noticing the twinkle in his warm brown eyes.

"We've got a quick one here!" he turns towards his mates, jabbing his thumb towards me over his shoulder. He turns back towards me and holds out his hand. "I'm Steve!" I take it tentatively, not sure who he is. "Tree surgeon," he explains, seeing my confusion. His hand is warm and calloused, his grip firm. And he doesn't let go of my hand. "You've only been stalking me all week!" he says with a rich, infectious laugh.

"Oh, *that* Steve! This is brilliant! I really need you to come as soon as possible."

"Here that, lads? She's gagging for it already," says one of Steve's mates.

"Let's have some respect for the lady, please," growls Steve, finally letting go of my hand.

"Don't mind Ron," says another of Steve's mates, rolling his eyes and pointing to the offender. "He's a dickhead. Probably hasn't seen a woman in, like, ten years or something."

It's all typical, good-natured pub banter.

I instantly like Steve. He's good-looking, with a cheeky smile and a glint in his eye; and I've got a bit of a thing about tree surgeons. I think it's that sweet-and-sour combination of manly ruggedness and caring about nature: like us gardeners, only with bigger muscles and more straps and power tools.

"Why don't I buy you a drink and we can talk about it?" suggests Steve.

"Thanks, Seb's just got me one. Cheers!" I say to Seb as he hands me my drink and nods to Steve.

"Wahay! She drinks pints!" quips the one called Ron.

"Right up your street, Mate," says the other guy.

And his friends mutter more laddish comments while I lead Steve over to our table to talk trees.

"Good evening, Steve," says Milan, standing up.

"Wotcher, Milan," says Steve, clapping him on the back. "All good?"

"Thank you, yes. I hope you are well also?"

"Yeah. Even better now you've got yourself a foxy new

boss!" he says raising his glass to me. "Better looking than that Jamaican bloke, anyhow!"

"Oh thanks, Mate," I say, digging him in the ribs while he chuckles infectiously.

"And Seb. You alright? How's that lovely sister of yours?"

Seb just nods and takes a swig of his cordial.

"So, what do you need?" asks Steve, his eyes twinkling. "A bit of muscle? My mighty chainsaw? Or is it my brains you're after?"

"All three!"

Do I see Seb roll his eyes? He turns aside and asks Milan about the football scores, so he's obviously ruling himself out of this conversation; slightly rudely, I think.

I start to explain how much there is to do to get the estate safe and ready for the public. Steve listens intently.

Seb and Milan spot a friend in another corner of the pub and excuse themselves. The atmosphere immediately lightens.

"I'll tell you what," Steve says with a grin, "it's going to be a real money-spinner when they get the place open."

"I don't think so. I think it's going to be a challenge to turn a profit – you won't believe the state of the place – but if it can at least help cover the costs, that would be something."

"Don't listen to these bleeding-heart aristos. Have you seen what car *The Honourable* drives? He's not short of a bob or two. Although," he leans towards me conspiratorially and says in a low voice, looking significantly over at Seb, "when Lady T ran off with the family silver, I bet that was a bit of a shocker."

How does he know about that? I guess these things get out in a tight-knit community like this one.

"I'm surprised Seaton-Smyth's back, to be honest. None of us understood how they didn't get the police involved. He's a rotten apple that one. Still, it's all work for you and me, eh, Princess. Another pint?" he asks.

I drain my first one. "I don't mind if I do."

I go up to the bar with him. "Do you smoke?" I ask Steve as we take our drinks.

He puts his hand on the small of my back and leads me to the darkness of the beer garden.

"What's your smoke?" He takes a pouch out of his pocket. Inside, nestled next to a couple of normal-looking roll-ups is a massive reefer, and I smile.

Half an hour later we return to the bar, his arm around my waist. I've got myself a promise that he'll come to the estate first thing on Monday to look at the trees.

And also, a date. A real date. Tomorrow. At a very posh-sounding restaurant.

Chapter Thirteen

I don't think I've actually been on a date – I mean, a proper *Let me treat you, Princess* kind of date – since, well, probably for ever, really.

Steve said I need to "dress up nice", but I honestly don't have anything *nice*: leggings, jeans, cargoes and a pair of baggy corduroy dungarees that have seen better days; definitely nothing suitable for a fancy restaurant. Guy hasn't paid me yet and, even if I did have money, I've been too busy to go shopping; so, I've had to borrow a dress from Alice.

After dropping Bertie off with Milan, I hurry back to my cottage. I have a quick bath and shave my legs for the first time since the summer. As well as the dress, I have to steal a pair of Alice's tights, a cashmere wrap, a necklace (not the Tillingford Diamonds, which I expect are in a safe somewhere) and – since I can't wear my Doc Martens or sneakers with this ensemble – a pair of ballet pumps a size too big for me.

I attempt to curl my long, dark hair; but it's gone a bit weird and frizzy, so I pull it up into a sort of bun-chignon thing, pull a couple of curls down and wind them round my fingers, hoping it doesn't look too scruffy.

Just as I sit down, the bell goes. I open the door and Steve is standing there, looking very foxy in a snug-fitting, royal blue suit with an ice-blue shirt and tie that set off his silver hair perfectly.

"You look great!" He puts his hand on my arm. "And you're

ready!" He seems surprised, as though he's used to taking out the kind of woman who would keep him waiting.

Then he leans in to kiss me on the cheek. He's wearing a strong musky aftershave that smells of cloves. It puts me in mind of those fancy wreaths made of ivy and mistletoe, with dried oranges and cinnamon wired into them, that you see on the doors of big country houses in property-porn magazines.

Or maybe it's Old Spice? It also reminds me slightly of my grandfather.

It's a clear night and I'm sure a frost is going to settle. I'm about to grab my coat but realise that a beaten-up Mountain Warehouse cagoule over this ensemble is going to look cringy and decide I'll just have to brave the cold. I lock up and trot across to the stable yard, where Steve holds open the door of a Lexus sports car the colour of molten silver.

"Nice wheels."

"I wasn't going to take you to the Abbey in the crew cab, was I?"

He's obviously done well for himself. In my industry, people say that tree surgeons are always loaded. I was sceptical, but now I think they might be right.

As I clamber awkwardly into the car, I joke that I was off sick the day they did "getting into a sports car" at finishing school.

He laughs and I get a thrill of pleasure that my quip's gone down well. I wriggle into the tan leather seats, noticing they are strangely warm.

When he's satisfied that I'm safely ensconced, he closes the door and gets into the driver's seat. Before he starts the engine, he takes another look at me.

"You scrub up nice, Charlie," he says with a satisfied smile.

"Thanks. You're looking pretty dapper yourself."

"Thank you, Princess. I like to make an effort for a lady. Hope you're warm enough?" he asks as he fastens his seat belt. "The heated seats are on."

"Very cosy!" I snuggle into the warm seats, guiltily wondering what the carbon footprint of this car is.

On the short drive between Tillingford Hall and the Tillingford Abbey Hotel, we talk shop: how we're making good progress taking out the dangerous dead trees; and how, provided we don't get a storm in the next week that would take the lads off site to deal with emergencies, Steve's second team can join the first one and we can pick up the pace.

In a few minutes, we're rolling up a gravel drive to a pretty country house. It's much more modest than Tillingford Hall but far older: Tudor, I'd say. I'm guessing this was the house the Tillingfords built with the materials from the abbey their chum Henry VIII had dissolved and given them.

I can't help but remember Tris's comment about privatising charity land; but it was four hundred years ago and the thought fizzles out.

A lad in Hunter wellies and a Barbour jacket comes to help me out of the car. Steve throws his keys to a similarly clad boy, who drives the car away and presumably parks it somewhere so we don't have to bother. The cold air slices through Alice's party dress and I shiver.

"Let's get you inside!" Steve whips off his jacket and puts it around me. It's warm and smells of his Christmassy cologne, with a faint musky man undertone. Now his jacket is off, I can see the muscles in his arms and back rippling under the thin cotton of his tailored-fit shirt.

As we approach the front door, another flunky in a Barbour whips open the door and wordlessly welcomes us into a double-height hallway, dominated by a huge fireplace. Antlers and swords are displayed above the massive stone mantelpiece, which is decorated with a garland of dried strawflowers, mini pumpkins and hop-bines. In front of us is a polished mahogany reception desk, sporting colourful winter squash of all kinds and a huge display of autumnal flowers in mustard yellow, ochre and orange: dahlias, chrysanthemums and Chinese lanterns.

A leggy blonde in shiny brown riding boots, spray-on jeans and a massive white mohair rollneck shakes her curls at Steve as she asks, in nasal tones, if we have a reservation.

"Silver. Seven-thirty." She taps a screen with her impossibly long fingernails.

"Amazing! Come through. Shall I take your wrap, Madam?"

"No thanks, I think I'll keep it!" I pull it tighter round me.

"Of course," she simpers. "There's a fire in the Great Chamber so you should be lovely and toasty but just let me know if you'd like a blanket."

Once we've been delivered to the "Great Chamber", we're ushered to our seats, with a bow and a scrape, by a man who sports closely cropped hair, Elton John specs and a tight dark suit, zhuzhed up with a loud tie. He draws out a plush velvet chair for me. When he's helped us scooch our chairs under the linen-draped table, he asks (in a very camp East European accent, which sounds not entirely unlike one of those meerkats on the telly) whether we'd like something to drink.

Steve orders champagne cocktails for us both, which arrive swiftly, brought by yet another smart young man in a suit; the sixth staff member we've seen so far. A different person altogether brings us menus to look at, while we sip our drinks, and discreetly passes me an additional piece of paper with some vegan options.

"What've you got there?" asks Steve, craning his neck to see.

"The vegan menu."

"What the heck's that?" he asks, taking a deep swig of his cocktail.

I explain.

"What … so not even fish?"

"That's an animal," I explain patiently, looking down the menu.

"Eggs?"

"They're from animals, too. I don't eat any animal products at all. Really strict vegans don't even wear leather or eat honey."

"Bloody hell!" He plonks his glass down on the table and takes a deep breath. Then he frowns. "How did they know you was a … a *vaygan*, anyway?"

"I called ahead."

A look flashes momentarily across Steve's face, but it's gone before I can decipher it.

We take our time to ponder the options. Nothing is just "beef" or "chicken" but "thirty-day-aged Belted Galloway *onglet de bœuf*" and "organic free-range New Forest chicken".

When flunky number seven comes back to take our order, Steve chooses something which is essentially langoustine soup and a steak (with the £10 supplement) while I have the

"Heritage Beetroot Mosaic with Fermented Cashew Cream and Herbaceous Foam" followed by the relatively normal-sounding "Freekeh and Butternut Squash Roulade".

"Sounds freaky to me," says Steve.

I muster a girlish giggle.

Then he chooses a bottle of burgundy. I'm glad he didn't invite me to look at the wine list because I can't bear to think how much that bottle's costing. I'm very much enjoying my champagne cocktail, though, as I'm quite sure he's paying. I've already realised Steve's the kind of man who would be offended if I offered to go Dutch, which is just as well because we'd have to go to a kebab shop if we were going to split the bill.

I'm also wondering about Steve driving back, but obviously I don't say a word.

I'm really enjoying looking around at the other diners, who all seem very well-heeled, and the lovely flower arrangements and antique silver perched on every windowsill; but I'm still sitting on the edge of my seat. I'm doing my best to look relaxed and happy, but I just don't know where to put anything. And my legs and crotch are feeling itchy in tights.

Steve looks directly at me.

"More of a pub girl, aren't you?" He grins.

I laugh and look down into my drink. He's sussed me out. I bite my lip before I answer and look up at him through my lashes, hoping I look alluring. "This is lovely. I've never been anywhere like this in my life."

"Then I'm glad I could treat you. Everyone should enjoy a little luxury sometimes. I grew up on a council estate in Wandsworth. My mum had two jobs just to keep food on the table and pay for our school uniform. I started mowing lawns for pocket money as soon as I got to secondary school. I've always worked hard and now I'm comfortable, I like to enjoy it."

Pondering his admirable work ethic, I take a sip of my drink.

"That's kind of the opposite of me: I went to a private school and my father's a bishop."

Steve laughs and says he'd better be on his best behaviour then.

"That doesn't mean he's rich, though," I point out. "Obviously, clergy don't get paid much. But my parents do get to live in beautiful places and mix with the great and the good, so it always felt like we were very privileged. But me personally, I really don't have two pennies to rub together."

"Then you can be my Cinderella." Steve has a look in his eyes that makes me think this evening might not end at midnight.

I take another swig of champagne cocktail and find the glass is already empty. "I think I'd like that."

Steve Silver is very good-looking in a rough-and-tumble kind of way; and I'm really enjoying the attention he's lavishing on me.

Our starters arrive.

Our burgundy arrives.

Solicitous staff bring home-made bread (the wholegrain is vegan, I'm assured).

We talk.

Our glasses are topped up, every few minutes, with tiny dribbles of wine by a hobbit whose only job seems to be doing just that.

Steve regales me with funny stories about his work, like the one about the guy who sawed through the branch he was kneeling on, plummeting to the ground like Wile E. Coyote, the hapless cartoon beast who was always trying to catch the Road Runner. The guy must've been severely injured – off work for weeks – but the way Steve tells the story, his crow's feet deepening, makes me crease up.

And our main course arrives and, somehow, my glass is always being topped up, even though I'm sure we ordered just one bottle. And we talk more and laugh. And the roulade is amazing.

Then he tells me, with twinkling eyes, about the time he felled the wrong tree. The lady of the house, who sounded like a bit of a bombshell, ended up sleeping with him because her husband blamed her and threw her out, and she had nowhere else to go. He told it in such a funny way I ended up having to cover my face with a napkin to stop myself snorting wine out of my nose.

The candle burns down.

The dessert menu arrives but I'm not sure I could manage any. Steve strokes my cheek and says I'm sweet enough but insists he's not sharing.

Glasses of pudding wine appear alongside the Vegan Pumpkin and Dark Chocolate Tart, and the Bramley and Worcester Pearmain Compote, with a Three-Cheese Crust, and Malaga *Crème Pâtissier* (apple pie and custard to you). But we spoon feed each other little tastes of our pudding: another one of my small dairy lapses.

And then, when the restaurant is almost empty and I've had

more peppermint tea and handmade truffles than I'm sure is humanly possible, I'm being shoe-horned into the Lexus, the seats pre-warmed via an app. I decide that, sometimes, a little luxury is very nice indeed.

Chapter Fourteen

"Morning, Princess," Steve whispers, stroking my back and then kissing it, sending goose bumps all down my spine as I slowly start to wake up.

As I become conscious, I realise my head's like thunder and my body aches; but a grin spreads across my face as I start to remember some of the things we did last night. "Morning, Handsome."

I smile languidly, enjoying the silky feeling of his bedsheets.

"I ran you a bath." He twines his calloused fingers through my hair.

"That's sweet of you."

"Like I said. I want to treat you right."

I roll over on to my back and smile up at him. How did I net this total fox? He presses his lips to mine and his kiss deepens before he pulls away. He straightens up and gets off the bed. "Now get in that bath before I have my wicked way with you again."

I try to get up but when I move my head, it throbs and I wince.

"I'll make you a coffee!"

"Tea, please," I croak. "Just normal tea, no milk!"

"So demanding!"

He heads downstairs, throwing me a small white towelling dressing gown. I wrap it gratefully round me and pad towards his en-suite bathroom. The glorious free-standing copper bath is frothing but I quickly realise that this isn't bath foam: it's actually a whirlpool bath.

I sink back into the bubbly water, like a happy raisin bobbing up and down in a glass of champagne.

Steve brings me tea and tells me to sit tight while he nips down to A Little Treat, the village shop, to grab some pastries for breakfast. As I put my head back into the water, some tinkly music starts up. I have no idea where the sound is coming from; there must be a speaker hidden in the bathroom somewhere. It sounds like the kind of naff music I guess they play in spas. It's sweet of Steve to put it on, though, and I sink into the bubbles, feeling like the cat that got the cream.

About twenty minutes later, just as I'm starting to feel like a prune and would be happy to get out, Steve appears with a tray, bearing a cafetière and croissants on a plate.

"I got you a vaygan one." He hands me a rather dismal one that definitely looks less appetising than its calf-killing brothers.

"Vegan croissants in Tillingham?" I ask.

"Tillingham's the height of sophistication these days! You know Sahara Seaton-Smyth, the supermodel, lives in the village?"

"Of course." I sit up: her name somehow fills me with dread.

"Well, apparently she's got this range of vaygan snacks she's been developing, and they sell all her stuff in the shop."

"Oh, that makes sense." I feel my appetite ebbing away at the mention of Seb's sister.

Steve brings a chrome occasional table up to the edge of the bath, puts the breakfast things on it, then strips off and gets in himself.

After that, I don't think there's a moment before midday when our skin isn't touching.

When my hangover finally passes, I admit I'm ravenous. Steve offers to make lunch, and I point out I don't have anything to wear other than yesterday's party dress.

"Look in Rogue's room. She always leaves stuff here and there might be something you could borrow."

I'm momentarily confused until I remember Steve told me, last night, that Tyler and Rogue are his son and daughter; they live in Winchester with his ex-wife but stay with him every other weekend.

I put on the robe and pad across the landing to what I guess must be Rogue's room. It's done in dusky rose pink, with the skirting boards and the back of the door picked out in charcoal grey gloss; there are thick carpets and plantation shutters, like in the rest of the house. Several posters of Billie Eilish, plus a tiny Taylor Swift one, cover most of the walls. There's an assortment of dusty dolls and teddies shoved in a basket in the corner. On a Barbie-pink chest of drawers, plastered with grubby My Little Pony stickers that obviously date back to an earlier phase in Rogue's life, a few bits of glittery make-up and nail varnish sit on a plastic tray.

Photos of Rogue and her friends, some from a few years back but some more obviously recent, fill the gaps between the posters. She's a big girl; not exactly pretty, but she's got strong features and a confident look.

I'm a bit nervous trespassing in this hallowed ground. Rogue looks like the kind of girl who would deck me if she knew I was borrowing her clothes, but I'm a bit desperate. In the chest of drawers, I find a pink T-shirt with "Mean Girl" picked out in diamante, a Billie Eilish hoody and some grey Nike joggers. I hold each of them up to my body; they're definitely too small. And then I pick them up again and hold them close to me as an unexpected little kick in my abdomen reminds me, as if I need reminding, how empty I feel inside; and a tear rolls down my cheek.

I put the clothes back in the drawer and, consumed with curiosity, poke my head around the door of the next room. There are unbelievable quantities of completed Lego models sitting on the shelves and hanging from the ceiling. The walls are lined with Arsenal posters, and a huge red Arsenal teddy sits on the bed. The duvet cover, pillowcases and curtains are all in Arsenal colours; and even the skirting boards are painted red.

There are two more doors on this floor: one leads into a tasteful spare bedroom, done in classy grey, and the other into a family bathroom. The whole house is clean and tidy. I notice the toilet paper in the family bathroom is folded into a little point: a sure sign of a professional cleaner having been here recently.

My mission for clothes has been unsuccessful so, five minutes later, I walk downstairs wearing one of Steve's T-shirts, a massive orange Stihl hoody, huge socks that are twice as long as my feet, and some joggers that barely stay up and which I've had to roll up at the ankle.

Steve looks away from his pans to give me the once-over as I come in and laughs. "Nice look! I preferred the sexy princess or – better still – nothing at all!" He gives a dirty laugh; I stick my tongue out.

I perch on a bar stool, from where I have a perfect view

of the modern, sleek kitchen: charcoal units with gold trims; black granite worktops; two ovens and a warming drawer; a family-sized air fryer; a massive American-style fridge, with a chilled-water-and-ice dispenser; and even a wine fridge. And a complete set of Le Creuset pans nestling, in size order, on a bespoke shelving unit.

The hob is in the middle of the island. The cooking fumes seem to be sucked miraculously into some vents at the side of the cooker; I've never seen anything like it. Steve taps something on his phone and the lighting scheme changes; another tap and some music comes on.

Steve puts a plate brimming with fried mushrooms, beans and tomatoes in front of me.

"Sure you won't have an egg?" he asks as he piles up his plate with a meat feast of bacon, eggs, sausage and black pudding.

"Thanks, no. This is really sweet of you."

"No, you're the sweet one." He chucks me under the chin, and I turn to mush.

With loads of sourdough toast from A Little Treat, this is a proper meal. I don't know what he's done with the tomatoes and mushrooms but they're really tasty; and he's added something to the baked beans, so they don't just taste like normal Heinz.

When I'm totally stuffed, I push my plate away. "You're a really talented cook," I say.

"Thanks! Let's see what your washing-up skills are like!" He holds out some rubber gloves, then snatches them back. "Just kidding!"

I carry the plates over to the sink. "Let me do *something*!"

"You can dry up!" he says cheerfully, throwing me an Arsenal tea towel.

He taps his phone and changes the music to AC/DC. For a few minutes, we work happily together, clearing up the kitchen.

"This has been lovely, Steve. Thank you. I guess I'll head off now."

"What for?" It's a reasonable question: it's only Sunday lunchtime. "I thought we could go into Winchester, do some shopping, catch a movie, have a bite in a pub maybe?"

I had been thinking of spending this afternoon doing some more research and planning for the week ahead. But it is the weekend, and I'm feeling so full and happy and relaxed: why spoil it?

"Sure. That'd be great. I need to check Milan's okay with keeping Bertie a bit longer. And I'll need to go back to my cottage to get some clothes, though."

"Give him a ring, then let me take you shopping!"

"What, like Sainsbury's?" I can't even afford a pair of leggings from Tu until I get paid.

"There's everything in Winchester: a couple of boutiques, White Stuff, JD Sports, M and S. Whatever you like, really."

"Primark?"

He tuts. "I'm paying."

"No! Why?"

"Cos you're going to be my Cinderella, and I want to buy you something nice. I bet they haven't paid you yet, have they?" I hesitate. "No arguments!" He puts a tablet in the dishwasher and slams it shut.

A foxy man is offering me gifts, and I could seriously do

with some new clothes so – what the hell? "I'd love that."

He beams at me.

We get into the silver Lexus and drive out of his road, which I see is called Spitfire Close. Now it's light, I can see the street is full of identical, nondescript eighties family homes but his – with its stylish charcoal door and window frames, uplighters and resin-bond driveway – is a cut above the others.

A few hours later, we're having tea in a sweet little tearoom near the cathedral: coffee and a hot buttered teacake for him; camomile tea and a vegan brownie for me. I'm nervous at first, being so close to the cathedral, but Steve laughs when I explain why and I'm completely calm now. Somehow, making a joke of my choirphobia makes me realise how ridiculous I'm being. He loves the story about George Willoughby-Parton's nose. Unbelievably, Steve knows George, who does some fancy job in the City these days and has a huge second home in Alton, where Steve's done work. George's nose is still out of joint, apparently.

I'm dressed in a whole new get-up, including sexy undies Steve was adamant about getting from a bougie lingerie shop. The knickers felt good going on, but they're riding up my bum now and giving me a wedgie. I also got some jeans, a T-shirt and a jumper from White Stuff (I'd have been happy with Primark, but he said they'd fall apart in two weeks and where was the investment in that?), and then a sweet little dress he insisted on. They also had some unbelievably cute penguin Christmas decorations; but we both agreed it was mad early to be thinking about Christmas and only reminded me how much I've got to get done by the twenty-second of December, the date of the Christmas concert.

Because I was still wearing Alice's over-sized ballet pumps, I picked up a pair of sturdy walking shoes as well. I looked wistfully at the coats in Blacks: I really need one for work that doesn't leak; but Steve said he wasn't here to buy me work clothes. He thought he had a spare Silver Tree Surgeons one I could borrow if that's what I was after.

I look at the bags piled on the floor around us and realise he's spent over £300. I try to talk about paying him back but he says, "Don't insult me, Princess. Let me treat you."

And next thing I know, we're having cocktails in a wine bar and then dinner in a cosy little bistro.

I decide I could definitely get used to this.

Then it turns out we have a room booked in the hotel across the high street and I come into work with Steve on Monday morning.

Chapter Fifteen

"If we use resin-bound gravel, it's going to look like the B&Q car park," I point out.

"That's not the kind of look I'm going for." Guy runs his hands through his hair.

The leaves are flurrying off the trees, gathering in drifts. I zip my warm, waterproof Silver Tree Surgeons work jacket up to my chin. Guy looks at the jacket, frowning slightly; then from me to Steve, who has just joined us. Steve's on site today to check both his teams are up to speed; the light's failing now, so they've stopped work and have started packing up.

"Why not use self-bonding aggregate? It's cheap and it looks good," he suggests.

"It's cheap to start with, but the ongoing maintenance soon builds up," argues Seb, whose obviously been doing his research. "It's fine when it's dry and compacted, but it's not that easy to push a wheelchair or a buggy over at the best of times. As soon as it starts to rain, it gets muddy and rutted."

"I agree with Steve," I interrupt.

"Well, you would, wouldn't you?" says Seb huffily, looking just like Guy as he takes in my jacket.

Is that a teensy little bit of jealousy I spy? It feels good to parade my new relationship in front of him, twisting the knife in just a little. I feel Steve's hand on the small of my back, giving me courage as I retort, "Aggregate looks better and it's cheaper.

And don't forget polyurethane is made from oil and releases microplastics into the environment when it weathers."

"A good bond will last years, Charlie. It's not going to start breaking down before you have to stress about it. A few molecules of microplastics are a pretty small problem compared to the amount of shit water companies are releasing into the ocean on a daily basis."

I frown at him. "That's not really the point, Seb. The worse some people are at protecting the environment, the more of an effort the rest of us have to make. Haven't you heard of the Tragedy of the Commons?"

"Er … no. I didn't have the chance to sit in university libraries reading clever stuff."

"I did art history, Seb. I didn't learn about environment issues at university. I continue to educate myself."

"And you're no doubt a great example to us all," says Guy tetchily. "So, remind me what the difference between *resin-bound* and *resin-bonded* is."

"Resin-bonded's when you put the resin down and scatter the gravel on the top," Seb butts in. "Like sprinkles on a fairy cake."

"What's effin' fairies got to do with it?" Steve spits contemptuously.

"Fairy *cakes*, Dude," says Seb. "The gravel sinks in a bit, but the stones basically stay on the surface. Resin-bound is when you mix the gravel and the resin together before you spread it out."

"Like rocky road?" I add sarcastically.

"Yeah, kind of like that," Seb retorts.

Guy runs his hands through his hair again. "Despite your enlightening illustrations, I still don't know what the best thing to do is."

"You need to sort out your top stuff first, Bro," explains Seb, bluntly. "The environment, cost, accessibility or aesthetics."

"Accessibility. Though Alice will probably kill me."

"You don't want to upset your missus, Mate," quips Steve.

Guy bridles momentarily. He's got no airs or graces, but I'm still not sure Steve's struck the right note calling him "Mate".

"I agree. Wheelchair users, people using walking frames and sticks, and people with buggies won't thank you if they can't get around," Seb adds.

"So, it would have to be resin-bound then," I say dejectedly, scuffing at the rough grass with my boot. "With resin-bonded, the stones can come loose, so it's not that accessible, and it's not permeable either.

"So, let's do it," says Guy.

"It's gonna cost an arm and a leg," points out Steve.

"Yeah … right. How much are we talking?"

"Could be as much as a hundred quid a square metre, depending on the quality of the stone," says Seb, "and how you lay the sub-base and what you want it to look like. Laying it's a skilled job; we'd have to get people in. But it will last really well and won't need maintenance for a long time. It will be totally accessible, *even if it does look like the B&Q car park*," he says, in that stupid squeaky voice he does when he's mocking me.

Guy winces. I'm not sure if it's because, like me, he's fed up with Seb being so childish or he's still horrified at the idea of Tillingford Hall looking like B&Q.

"Accessibility is the key." Guy rakes his hand through his floppy blond hair. "Make it happen."

"Which of us?" asks Seb. "Is it grounds or house?"

He looks between the two of us, his jaw twitching. "Oh, grounds – probably – just sort it out, will you?"

"Tell me what the budget is and consider it done," I say with bravado, while I'm utterly daunted inside.

"Thanks, Charlie. I'll email you later. It's getting late – you can all knock off now." Guy zips up his Barbour and walks away.

"Let me know if you need any help, Charlie," says Seb.

"Does she look like someone who needs help?" snaps Steve.

"C'mon, I was just trying to be nice. It's going to be a daunting task finding the right contractor to get all the paths laid in time for the Christmas concert."

He's not wrong there.

"You're not *daunted*, are you, Princess?" Steve says, putting his arm around me.

I say nothing, looking challengingly at Seb.

He looks levelly from me to Steve; then looks me steadily in the eye and slightly shakes his head. He shoves his hands in his pockets and walks off.

"What the …" I spit.

"Prick," adds Steve. "What's it to him whether we're together? Is there something you need to tell me, Princess?"

"No!" I say firmly.

By now, the evening's drawing in; so, as it's Friday, I invite Steve back to mine for a cuppa which turns into a beer, a takeaway from our local Indian, the Shimla, and then a night of non-stop bedroom athletics.

***

"Who are you speaking to?" Steve's muffled tones come down the stairs the next morning. He's chosen to have a bit of a lie-in rather than come with me to take Bertie for his walk. He's promised to have breakfast ready for me when I get back. I'll see how he rises to the challenge of keeping it vegan.

"Just my mum!" I call back.

"Who's that you're talking to?" Mum asks on the other end of the phone.

"Oh, just Alice," I lie. I'm not ready to tell her about Steve yet. Although I think he's lovely, and he's swept me off my feet, it's really early days.

And I can just hear the way she's going to say, "*A tradesman*?" when I tell her about him.

"Now, Darling. I still need to know if you're going to even out my table this Christmas. The canon theologian has accepted our invitation; so if you're not coming, I'll need to think of someone else to sit next to him."

"I guess I'll be there, then." I try but fail to sound enthusiastic as I attempt to squeeze into my wellies while simultaneously holding my phone and fending off Bertie, whose tail is wagging so fast it's actually become invisible.

"Is there something else you want to do this year?" she asks, sounding almost hopeful.

I put her on speaker phone so I can shrug on my jacket. "Are you trying to get rid of me?"

"Of course not, Tottie! We love having you with us for Christmas. I just wonder if you're getting a bit bored with it by now. Maybe the Tillingfords will invite you to stay?"

"Perhaps." They haven't said anything and I don't have any expectations that way. I grab Bertie's lead morosely. I do love Christmas at my parents'. Nothing could be more traditional: mulled wine and mince pies around the fire after the midnight choral service; a huge tree festooned with the decorations we all made as children, joined by my nephew and nieces' fresher attempts; a huge lunch, with turkey and all the trimmings.

But it will be my thirty-eighth Christmas round that table; and I wonder if, maybe, I should be making my own Christmas traditions.

And it sounds like she's starting to wonder about that too.

"I won't be able to come down until the last minute anyway. Guy's putting on a Christmas concert here, on the twenty-second of December, as a kind of opening event." I pick up my keys as Bertie nearly scratches down the door. "But he still hasn't found a suitable act."

"What about the Wells Cathedral Choir? The dean's always saying he thinks it would be good experience for the choristers, and good publicity for the cathedral, to do more choir tours."

I can feel my breath quicken at the thought of twenty-four rustling choir robes filing into the ballroom. Then I check myself, thinking how Steve would laugh at me for letting it get to me. "I have no idea if that's the kind of thing Guy had in mind. I can suggest it, though, if you can check the date."

Suddenly, I get a notification that Tristain is trying to get through to me just as Steve comes down the stairs, stark naked, and Bertie's howling to get outside.

"I've gotta go, Mum." I open the door so the beagle can rush ahead of me. "Someone else is trying to get through."

"Okay, Darling. Let me know about the choir!"

"I will!"

I swipe to answer Tris.

"Hey, Tris. What's happening?"

"Who's Tris?" growls Steve, frowning.

I open the door and turn my back on him so I can hear Tristain better: he keeps breaking up and Bertie's dashed a hundred yards ahead of me, chasing after a squirrel.

"Gotta go!" I mouth to Steve, battling the wind to get the door shut behind me.

"I thought you'd got rid of your phone, Tris."

"I've got a burner I use for emergencies."

"Is this an emergency?"

"Erm … well … we've been chucked out of the house in Batheaston. The owners are like trying to sell it now and they sent the bailiffs in, so we thought it was time to go. We didn't want no trouble. So we've got nowhere to go for Sarr-wayn now."

"What about Glasto?" I ask.

"We were going to do our own rituals in the garden, so we hadn't booked up and now it's full – if you can believe that! Apparently, it's become a big thing now, so they're having to control it with tickets and stuff."

"I thought the whole point was that it was just a kind of turn-up-and-shag kind of thing."

"Yeah. Sad, innit?" says Tristain wistfully. "Everyone's getting on the effin' alternative lifestyle bandwagon now, so you kinda have to do your own thing if you want to be different. So we thought we'd pop over to yours, seeing as there's the ley lines and Seb said we was welcome for Solstice. We reckoned we could maybe come a bit early."

"A *bit* early! It's nearly *two months* early! And I don't think Seb's even *mentioned* it to Guy yet." Guy's so going to freak out. "How many of you are there?"

"Just the house – maybe fifteen, sixteen, couple of dogs."

"I'll have to check with Guy. I mean, we weren't expecting you and it's not really for me to say it's okay, so just hang on in there for a moment. I'll call you back in ten."

"Okay. I hope he says 'yes', cos we're just in the lane outside."

I hang up. Shit! They're not giving me much room for manoeuvre.

I could phone Guy, but I'm literally fifty metres from the house. I whistle for Bertie, and he comes running to me. I feel bad invading Alice and Guy's family breakfast, but there's literally no point phoning when I'm this close. I go to the kitchen door and knock politely. Guy appears looking slightly bleary-eyed, his hair a little tousled.

"Hey, Charlie, come in. We're just having breakfast." Over his shoulder, I can see Alice and Hatty at the table. "Want some coffee?"

"No thanks, Guy."

I shove Bertie in the boot room. *No Dogs in the Kitchen* is a strict rule at Tillingford Hall these days.

"What's up?" asks Alice, obviously reading the stress in my face.

"Er … well … you remember Tris and Ama?"

She nods.

"They've joined a kind of, um, community," I try to explain.

"A commune?"

"Something like that." I look down at my boots to check I haven't trodden mud on the floor.

"And?"

"Well, they've been chucked out of their, er, accommodation. They were planning to go to Glastonbury for this big Samhain festival, but they can't get in. So they were wondering if they can come here and camp for a few days," I gabble.

"What on earth gave them that idea?" asks Guy, somewhat accusingly.

"Well, when Tris and Ama brought me down here, Ama realised that the Great Oak sits directly on the Spine of Albion ley line. She was practically licking it until we dragged her back into the van. But when Seb came to get me from Bath their …" I hesitate to use the word *priestess*, "group leader, Selena, said they wanted to come and visit for Solstice, on the strength of what Ama had said. *Seb* said they could. I told him he'd just heaped up a whole load of trouble for you, but he said it was a 'polite' invitation. I don't think they really know what that is."

"Oh, Seb!" Guy runs his hands through his hair, making it even more messy. "Sometimes, he's too nice for his own good!

Seb's definitely not in the "too nice" category as far as I'm concerned.

"You'll just have to tell them to find some other field," Alice says.

"They're literally at the gate. Shall I tell them to leave?"

Guy looks thoughtful for a moment.

"What's a ley line?" Hatty asks into the silence.

"They're kind of invisible tracks that some people think have a special kind of magnetism or energy. Lots of ancient monuments like Stonehenge are built on them. People think that the ancient folk knew better than us how to connect with the energy of the universe and these lines meant something to them. There are still people nowadays, like the friends I'm talking about, who really believe there's some kind of special energy in some places – like here."

"Let them come," says Guy.

"What?" says Alice, dropping her teacup loudly into her saucer.

"Yeah. I'm not going to uninvite them, especially not if they're right outside. If there really is a ley line running through here maybe that's something we could explore."

Alice stares at him incredulously. "Seriously?"

"Why not? It doesn't mean much to *me*. But if nature worshippers want to come here and have a big love-in with the Great Oak, they're guests like any other. I want to be open and inclusive here."

Alice rolls her eyes and looks away with a sigh.

I'm about to say, "I don't think it's a big love-in *with* the Great Oak, but a big love-in *under* the Great Oak you want to worry about," but Hatty's there and it's too late to warn him. I'll explain some other time what tends to go on with Selena's lot at Samhain.

"We'll obviously have to lay a few ground rules, though," says Guy. Then we talk briefly about what our reasonable expectations are. They can stay for one week and then they need to go. We'll get Portaloos but they won't arrive for a few days, so they'll have to dig a couple of pits; they'll have to get water from the outside pipe in the stable yard. No noise before seven AM or after ten PM. Dogs always on leads and that's about it – nothing too heavy.

I call Tris back and lay down the Ts and Cs. I also explain that we need to meet them by the Great Oak and show them the ropes. And I add that we're all just trying to finish breakfast, so they'll have to give us an hour. I call Bertie out from the boot room and stride back to the cottage, leaving Guy, Alice and Hatty to their breakfast.

Bertie's obviously disappointed to have such a short walk, but I promise him he can come out to meet my friends after breakfast.

Chapter Sixteen

"You said you was talking to your mother." Steve brandishes a spatula as I walk through the door. "Who the hell is Tris?"

I frown as I take off Bertie's lead and hang it over the banister. "Hello, Steve, nice to see you too!"

"Don't you 'hello Steve' me! Who were you talking to?" he slams down the frying pan, sending a couple of mushrooms flying across the worktop.

"Tris – he's an old friend from Bath." I'm about to go on, but Steve interrupts.

"An ex?" he says, beating the hell out of some innocent scrambled eggs in another pan.

"Erm … kind of." I take off my coat.

"Well, I hope you're effin' staying away from him, that's all I can say."

"That could be kind of difficult as he and his friends are going to be camping here for a week," I say mildly as I sit down to take off my wellies.

"What the heck?"

"Tris *and his partner Ama*," I add pointedly as I wrench off welly number one, "are part of a sort-of New Age community and they're going to be staying in the grounds – down by the Great Oak – for a few days to celebrate Samhain."

"What the hell is that?" says Steve, spatula in mid-air.

"It's the pagan autumn festival," I explain calmly as I start to wrestle with the second boot.

"Hmm. I don't like the idea of a bunch of New Age crusties camping here."

"This is *Guy's* home and he's happy to welcome them. In fact, they've already arrived and he's meeting me down by the Great Oak in half an hour to help them set up their camp."

As welly number two pops off my foot, Steve mutters something under his breath that sounds like "Effin' liberal snowflake." And then, more sweetly, as though none of that conversation just happened, he says, "I hope you've got time for my lovely breakfast, Princess. It's a Steve Special."

"Thanks, Steve. It looks amazing. Thank you for doing separate pans."

He looks momentarily puzzled. "I always use a different pan for the eggs." Then understanding dawns on his face. "Ah, yeah, cos of that vaygan thing."

"So I won't be having any eggs, obviously."

"All the more for me then!" He tips all the eggs on his plate, with a cheerful, pirate-like laugh.

The mushrooms and tomatoes are delicious. He's added some kind of sauce; I can't think what, as there's not much in my cupboards yet, but it's delicious, with a real depth of flavour.

Almost like he's added the bacon fat.

But he wouldn't do that, would he?

Steve can't stay as he's got his kids coming today. He offers to take me down the drive to meet our guests on his way out.

"Bloody hell!" he says as we approach the Great Oak. Some tents are up already, dotted around a large, painted teepee and someone's already managed to get a fire going.

There are three camper vans there: Tris's manky white Vee-Dub, an old silver Caravelle and a shiny Elddis: one they've clearly just hired from somewhere. Milling around the vehicles are an assortment of unusual-looking folk. I can see Tris and Ama sitting on the steps of their van, with the thin girl, whose hair is now in a tidy plait, and a couple of others from the Batheaston house. In the driving seat of the Caravelle is a wiry man; he has a big shock of dark hair in a quiff, with massive sideburns, like Wolverine from the X-Men. Leaning on the bonnet is a huge guy wearing antlers.

"I hope your boss knows what he's getting himself into letting these effin' hippies in. Good luck, Princess," says Steve with a lopsided grin. "See you tonight. I'll pick you up from the vicarage at seven PM sharp, okay?"

"Oh yeah – forgot about that."

I promised I'd go with Alice, Hatty and Guy to a children's Hallowe'en party hosted by the local queen bee, Elizabeth Pemberton, in the village. Lots of adults are invited, including me because I'm Hatty's godmother. Steve will pick me up from there because we're going on to a party at the Rugby Club in Alton.

They're both fancy-dress dos, so I'll have to think of something quickly.

Bertie and I get out of Steve's black crew cab, and he zooms off.

A moment later, Guy arrives with Hatty, Alice and Seb in the Rangie. My god-daughter's eyes widen as she takes in the sight of the rapidly forming camp.

"Why are they camping here?"

"They've come for Samhain: it's an ancient autumn festival to celebrate the coming of the darker half of the year." I explain.

"Like Hallowe'en?"

"A bit. I think Hallowe'en is one of those English festivals that has some pagan ideas mixed in with Christian ones. When Christians came to this country, we never bothered changing the name of some of the old pagan festivals, like Eostre, the spring festival."

"Christmas is full of pagan traditions," adds Seb. "Like yule logs, holly and mistletoe."

"But why are they camping *here* and not by the house, where the toilets are?" asks Hatty. For a small child, she does seem particularly interested in hygiene facilities.

"Firstly," says Alice firmly, "because we don't really want them all coming into the house – there are too many of them." I can hear her thinking, "*And they're pretty grubby and I don't trust them not to nick the Thomas Lawrences.*" But she adds, "Also, because this oak is special."

Tris catches sight of me, lopes up and attempts to kiss me but I sidestep him, and it becomes a fumbling air-kiss. Definitely no more Tris for me; not just because of Steve but, since that last day in Bath, I've gone right off that idea. Ama's not far behind and gives me a hug.

"Hey, Alice," says Tris.

Alice met Tris and Ama when she came to visit me in Bath last summer.

"Alice, my friend, congratulations!" says Ama.

Alice looks slightly panicked as she gives Ama a much deeper hug than I expected, given how she feels about my friends; it's almost like Alice is whispering something to her.

"Your auras are looking really settled today," Ama adds.

Alice nods. "This is Hatty." I can see Hatty's trying not to stare at Tristain's dreadlocks and Ama's flowing black dress, block-printed with skulls. And then the guy with antlers approaches and her eyes nearly pop out of her head.

"Meet Herne," says Tris.

"Hey, Friends." Herne's antlers rock about as he acknowledges each of us with a nod.

"What's so special about this tree?" Hatty asks me, returning to our earlier conversation.

"It's called the Great Oak. It's the biggest, oldest oak tree in the grounds of Tillingford Hall, maybe even in Hampshire."

I pick up a couple of acorns and start to fiddle with a pencil and a couple of nails I had in my pocket.

"Oak trees are really amazing," says Herne.

"This one is extra amazing because it's over five hundred years old," Guy explains. "That means it was already a sapling taller than a man when *Amber Lynn* died. It's so famous, it appears in books and lists of some of the most special trees in Britain."

"Woooow!" Hatty leans forward with an exaggerated drop of the jaw and raised eyebrows.

"And they say that Charles II hid in an oak tree while a whole army of Roundheads trooped past him. That's why we have lots of pubs called The Royal Oak," adds Guy.

"But, yeah, oaks can support like literally thousands of different kinds of bugs and creepy crawlies," says Herne, "and squirrels, birds, bats and …"

"Ew! Bats!" Hatty shudders.

"Aw, bats are great little creatures," says Ama, gently. But Hatty doesn't look convinced.

"Do you hear that high drumming sound?" asks Herne and we all prick our ears to listen. "It's a woodpecker!"

"What's a woodpecker?"

"Look – there he is!" Ama points to the black-and-white bird with a red top knot, clinging to the trunk, drumming away.

"Did you know a woodpecker's tongue is so long that it curls around inside its head like a cushion, so it doesn't smash its brains out when it's knocking on wood like that?" says Herne.

"And look at that jay," adds Guy, pointing to a cheeky one flying off with an acorn in his beak. "He's going to bury that somewhere for later. But most likely he'll forget it, and it'll grow into a new oak tree."

Hatty laughs. "Can *we* plant some acorns, Mummy?"

"Of course! I'm sure Charlie can show you how."

"Or we could make … acorn men!" I show her the little guy I've made: two acorns stuck together with a nail and more nails for hands and feet, and a face drawn on with the stub of pencil.

Hatty's enchanted and starts to gather pocketfuls of acorns.

"I'm going to make a whole family of acorn men. And they can have a little house, just in this hollow bit here."

"Leave some for the squirrels," says Herne, chuckling.

"I want to be a squirrel!" Hatty holds up her hands like little paws, sticking out her front teeth and hopping about, which makes everyone laugh.

"Come on, Hatty, we can make acorn men later – we've got Hallowe'en costumes to finish!" says Alice. Hatty runs back to the car and scrambles in.

Chapter Seventeen

I never in my life thought that, one day, I'd be heading to a kids' Hallowe'en party with a nearly-peer-of-the-realm, dressed as the Incredible Hulk, and Alice in full *Pride and Prejudice and Zombies* regalia. I can't believe she's watched that film. I would have thought that messing around with Dear Jane's beloved work like that would be enough to give her The Vapours!

With some last-minute creativity, involving hastily-gathered leaves, a bin bag (I've just had a big delivery of a hundred per cent recycled plastic ones) and a stapler I borrowed from Guy, I've made a kind of Green Man costume for myself.

The Green Man is this spirit from English folklore who appears every spring to make the land green again. But, in a nod to Samhain, this one's past his best, waiting for winter. I think the coronet of leaves around my head, done with the wire from an old coat hanger, is quite effective; but it's not nearly as good as Hatty's costume.

She's dressed in a full Elizabethan farthingale dress and has a papier mâché head, complete with curly wig, under her arm. If she wants to, she can pull the stiff cardboard ruff up over her actual head so that it looks like she's had her head cut off. It's crudely done, but funny on an eight-year-old and the dress itself is quite authentic-looking. Goodness knows where they got it. For all I know, there's a huge chest full of beautiful dresses up in the attic at Tillingford Hall or, more likely, Guy just bought it for her. He does seem to be on a one-man mission to spoil the kid.

Looking at Alice's little girl, so pretty and happy in her beautiful outfit, I think with a pang how, if I even had a daughter, she'd have to make do with a cat costume made out of a black leotard and tights and a sock for a tail. But she'd still be *my* little girl and I'm sure she'd be the naughtiest Hallowe'en cat. You can but dream. And at least *I* won't need a costume by then, because I'll be so haggard by the time I finally have a kid that I'll frighten everyone just as I am.

But I'm not going let myself get all morose. We're going to a party and there's going to be plenty of free booze: real champagne, by all accounts. Although this is a kid's party starting at five PM and being held in the Old Vicarage by Elizabeth and Mike Pemberton, who are very posh by all accounts, I've heard that, last year, the adults used it as an excuse to have a bit of a booze up. It doesn't seem to have put her off doing it again.

Alice insists she really doesn't want a drink at this time of the afternoon and is more than happy to drive, so we all pile into her zippy new Mini. Guy removes his Hulk head so he can fit in the front seat and I snuggle up in the back with Hatty, who keeps throwing *Amber Lynn*'s head at me, until Alice snaps at her.

"We should have gone in the Rangie," says Guy, slightly tetchily.

"I'm not insured to drive it," replies Alice reasonably.

"I'll add you on." Guy taps a note on his phone. "And we need to have a meeting about the concert."

Alice sighs.

"What?"

"I'm just a bit tired, Guy. I was hoping we could have tomorrow off, seeing as it's half term."

"Well, it might be for Hatty, but it's a normal working week for me. When else are we supposed to talk about these things?"

I tune out from this minor domestic as Hatty's now asking me which is my favourite of Henry VIII's wives.

I'm struggling to remember the names of any of them apart from *Amber Lynn* but luckily, when I mention her, Hatty seems pleased. "Why is she your favourite?"

"Erm … because she's got the prettiest name?"

"My name's Hatty, which is short for Harriet, which is a girl's version of Henry."

"Charlie's short for Charlotte."

"Like the spider in *Charlotte's Web*."

And so we carry on in this vein until we draw up on the village green.

"Look, *I'm* still working full time," I hear Alice say as she puts the car into park mode.

"You don't have to, you know," Guy mutters.

"Not the time or the place, Guy!" she squeaks and then turns round and mouths "sorry" at me, but I shrug and get out of the car. Seems there's trouble in paradise already.

Guy, without his Hulk head, is helping Hatty out of the car. "Pass me your head." Hatty giggles. He hands the papier mâché monstrosity to me so he can unclip her from her car seat and get her out. Surely an eight-year-old can undo a seat belt?

He's about to set her on the ground when she puts her arms up and says, "Carry me."

"Don't be silly, Hatty! You're eight years old, not a baby," says an exasperated Alice. "And Guy needs to put on his monster head." Then she mutters something that sounds like "Not that we'd notice the difference."

Guy lifts Hatty up anyway. "Can you bring it for me, Alice?"

She scowls as she goes round to the passenger side to pick the green rubber mask up.

So we process to the Old Vicarage, with the Incredible Hulk carrying *Amber Lynn* to her execution, her head handily pre-severed. I shuffle along in my shabby vegetational outfit, shedding leaves all the way, *Amber Lynn's* head in my hands, and a blood-spattered Alice follows behind with the Hulk's head in hers.

The path up to the front door of the detached Georgian vicarage is lit with a trail of tealights in jam jars wrapped in black crepe paper with spooky faces cut out of it. There are two massive jack-o'-lanterns – one laughing, one scowling – on the front steps. We stop on the path to sort out our costumes before we knock on the door. Alice hands Guy his monster head then adjusts Hatty's collar so that it covers her face and vaguely gives the impression that she's been decapitated – at least enough to convince a child her age or smaller. Alice takes the Amber Lynn head from me and puts it a little roughly under Hatty's arm, adjusting the little girl's hand on her hip to keep it in place.

If she's spent every evening this week helping Hatty make this fantastic costume as well as her own zombie one, no wonder she's tired (and, frankly, a bit grumpy).

When we ring the bell, a petite woman looking like a giant pink meringue in a fluffy blond wig – or possibly Glinda the Good Witch from the Wizard of Oz – answers the door.

"My goodness, who's this?" she asks.

I bet she says that to all the kids.

"Amber Lynn," comes a little voice from inside a collar, "and here's my head!"

Elizabeth, our hostess is laughing. "And the Hulk and … don't tell me … *Pride and Prejudice and Zombies*?"

Alice nods.

"And I don't think I've met this leafy person before. I'm guessing you're Charlie."

"I am the Green Man who dies at Samhain," I say in a lugubrious voice.

"How wonderfully pagan!" Elizabeth replies.

The leaves on my costume are gradually dropping off the bin bag and smell a bit musty, but I think it's not bad for a last-minute effort. And the decay kind of contributes to the overall effect.

"Well, do come and have some witch's brew and see if you can't stay alive for a few more minutes!" Elizabeth leads us into a large, candle-lit kitchen full of adults in costumes of varying degrees of inventiveness, and a few who are just in dark clothes and vaguely spooky masks.

Hatty runs off to find Elizabeth's twins, Lily and Poppy, while Elizabeth doles out bright green prosecco with raisins bobbing up and down in it.

"None for me, Elizabeth," says Alice. "I'm driving."

"Go on, Darling," says Guy, pulling off his Hulk head so he can knock some back. "We can leave the car here and get a cab back."

"No … it's okay. It's too early in the day for a drink."

Elizabeth thrusts a plastic cauldron towards us, filled to the brim with the little round chocolates. "Maltesers?"

"Wow! I haven't had these for years." I grab a few and munch. "Mmm, they're so good!"

"Aren't they just?" says Elizabeth excitedly, like I'd just praised her home-made cheese straws.

"Elizabeth eats Maltesers with everything!" Alice shovels about six into her mouth at once. "I have no idea how she manages to stay so slim."

"Constant stress! Darcy's got some snacks in the oven which will be ready soon, and there's pumpkin soup on the Aga – just help yourselves. Anyway, I must go and supervise the children's games now. Do come and help if you can be bothered, otherwise just stay and eat and drink!"

"I'll help," says Guy to Elizabeth. "Why don't you just relax, Alice, and forget about Hatty for a few minutes?" He kisses her tenderly on the forehead, with a look of concern.

He dons his Hulk head again and she softens a little. "Thank you, Guy. That would be nice – it's been a really full-on week. I'd still like to *watch* the games, though."

So we go through to the living room, where the kids have an amazing time with Guy the Hulk and one of the other dads in charge of the games. There's a lot of shrieking and shouting. Even Hatty, who's normally a quiet, calm child, is screaming like a banshee while a tiny pumpkin chases her round the room. She keeps hitting it with her severed head to try to fend it off. I hope the pumpkin-child's costume is protecting them from brain damage, although the little creature doesn't seem unduly fazed by the onslaught. I can't help chuckling to myself: the kids are so adorable and Guy's great with them.

All of a sudden, I'm feeling a bit emotional. I fancy a cigarette but when I ask Alice to nip outside with me, she looks at me like I've got the plague.

Chapter Eighteen

I walk out into the garden for "a breath of fresh air" and a chat with some of the more louche guests who are having a smoke outside: a zombie nurse and a Frank-N-Furter, who's lounging in the lap of a huge Frankenstein's monster.

As I light up, a tall, willowy woman, all in white, with long ash-blonde hair and pointy ears floats into the garden.

I think I know who this is, apart from Galadriel, the elven queen of Lothlorien from *The Lord of the Rings*, obviously.

"Hey, Sahara, come and join us," says Frank-N-Furter, waving a packet of fags, confirming the identity of the lady in white. She doesn't look quite how I expected. Apart from her height, she looks a bit wan and tired, and rather ordinary, not supermodel glamorous.

I hear a familiar voice behind me. "She's given up."

"No way!" says Frankenstein's monster, with a sound of muffled surprise through their rubber mask.

"Yes, way," says Galadriel.

Aware of the presence behind me, I turn round and come face to face with a giant-sized version of Legolas the Elf, complete with bow and arrow. I've never seen a chunkier Legolas in my life. He looks more like someone from *Gladiators* than a fey, elven warrior. That familiar, unwanted shot of desire hits me in guts.

Legolas-Seb gives me a quizzical but friendly look as he

takes in my pathetic bin-bag-and-dead-leaves costume. I notice a stowaway spider dangling off my arm and I feel each of its eight eyes is gazing at me balefully. The spider certainly gives my costume a more Hallowe'eny feel, but I wish I was dressed as a sexy vampire or a tarty zombie, clinging to Steve, so I could look Sebastian in the eye and show him I've moved on.

"What's triggered this clean-living frenzy?" the zombie nurse asks Galadriel-Sahara, oblivious to the unspoken drama between me and Sebastian.

"It's time. I've given up all stimulants and depressants: no tea, coffee, alcohol or nicotine; no legal highs; and definitely, definitely nothing illegal. I'm as clean living as a Mormon now." Sahara laughs a deep throaty laugh that sounds like the result of smoking too many fags.

The zombie nurse takes a drag on a vape. "Aren't you worried you'll get fat?"

"No, Sweetie, I'm not: I could do with adding a few pounds." Her brother puts his arm around her waist and kisses the top of her head. The monster looks at Frank-N-Furter agog – or as much agog as you can from behind a rubber mask. "I'm never going back to modelling. From now on, I'm going to live for myself and find my happy weight. I only came out to check what phase the moon is in: I've got some bulbs to plant."

"Biodynamics now, is it? You always were a crank," laughs Frank-N-Furter.

"Charming!" Sahara retorts playfully, then turns to me. "I don't think we've met before."

Seb gently touches my arm, sending an unwanted thrill all the way up to my ear, "This is Charlie."

"Oh!" she says, a little frostily. "The arsonist." I shuffle around and look at my feet, not wanting to catch Seb's eye. "Interesting costume. Are you a bonfire waiting to be lit?"

"She's the Green Man in autumn, Sassy," Sebastian corrects her, not taking his eyes off me.

My heart clenches as he's the only person this evening who's understood my costume.

I don't want him to understand me, though.

I don't want him to be here at all, looking all huge and muscly and gorgeous.

Sahara locks her elbow with mine. "Let's have a chat." She leads me back into the house. Though I'm slightly terrified of her and what she's going to say, I welcome the excuse to get out of Seb's aura. I can just about cope with him when he's in old holey sweatpants and a manky old T-shirt; but that costume – especially the elven sword – is doing things to me I really don't welcome.

I notice the skin of Sahara's arm feels rough against mine. I glance down at her thin arms poking out from her costume and notice a tracery of silvery scars on her wrists and nausea rises in my throat.

We find an empty room, a cosy snug, painted dark green, with a sofa and a telly. It's gently lit with a couple of side lamps resting in the alcoves either side of a small fireplace. There are no Hallowe'en decorations in here and it's calm and restful.

Sahara takes a proper look at my costume, then she sits down on the sofa and pats the seat next to her. I sit down. "That's very *you,* Charlie. Seb's told me everything about you – didn't miss out a thing. Despite you trying to set light to him, he's never stopped caring about you."

I feel the heat rising in my cheeks. "I'm with someone else now." I'm aware that sitting on the leaves is crushing them into the upholstery and shedding crumbs on the floor, so I stand up again.

"Charlie, there's something about Steve you should probably know."

"*Don't!* If you've got me here to tell me to get back together with your brother, you're wasting your time, particularly if you're going to slag my boyfriend off."

I just want her to shut up. I'm sick of all these upper-crust people judging Steve just because he's working class, so I deflect the conversation back to Seb.

"Your brother cheated on me, Sahara. Last year, I thought we were going steady, but it turned out it was just a casual thing."

"He was hurt when you went to that Samhain festival in Glastonbury."

"I can't believe he told you about that." I look away. Samhain was not my finest hour; I hadn't even realised he knew about it. "To be fair, I didn't know what was involved when I agreed to go."

"But you went along with it anyway."

"*He'd* been shagging Guy's mum for *years*," I retort. "He had no right to wonder who *I* was sleeping with!"

"What he had with Maxine was … weird … and really bad for him. He was desperately hurt when she ran off with the family silver and left him to burn – literally, it turns out, eh, Charlie? Maxine was a constant in his life. But when he tried to tell her it was over because he'd met you, she promised him she'd help him set up a surf school in Polzeath. She also said she'd go to the police and tell them what he'd been up to if he didn't collaborate with her. He was going to tell you he couldn't be with you the weekend everything kicked off, but he didn't know how to do it."

I flop down next to her, sick to my stomach, my mind reeling, oblivious to the mess I'm making on Elizabeth's sofa.

"Then suddenly she was gone. It was like when our mother died, all over again."

"What?"

"Our mother took her own life," says Sahara matter-of-factly. "He promised he'd look after me but what was he supposed to do? He was only nine and our father packed us off to separate boarding schools the next academic year. He's spent his whole life feeling guilty that he couldn't keep that promise."

For a moment, the room seems to tilt; a strange blackness fills my mind.

"I'm so sorry," I manage to whisper. Guy told me their mother had died. But I didn't know how.

"It's hard enough for a child to lose a parent but, with suicide, they'll always wonder why they weren't good enough to keep their mum or dad getting up for them every morning," admits Sahara. "And to be separated from their family, their home, their pets when they are grieving and so young – it doesn't help.

"What happened to Seb this summer – losing you, Maxine and Neville all in one weekend – triggered his PTSD. What on earth were you thinking, Charlie?" She doesn't sound angry, just bewildered and sad. "Setting fire to his home! He's homeless now – and he could've died."

I look at the ground.

"I was angry, I guess."

"At least that tells me you might have had *some* kind of feelings for him, then."

Some kind of feelings? I think.

Hell, yeah.

I thought I loved him, I finally admit to myself.

I've never, in all my life, felt the kind of passionate connection with someone I thought I had with Sebastian.

"He wasn't in a good way when he came back," explains Sahara, flicking a tear from her eye. "He hadn't been answering our calls and we were just about to start hunting for him, when I got a call from a hospital in Truro. He'd contracted pneumonia while sleeping rough and they were about to discharge him so they were asking me to put him up for a bit because he had nowhere else to go."

"He was sleeping rough?"

"He couldn't stay here. And he was skint and needed to lay low so what else was he going to do?"

"Shit …" I bite my lip.

"His PTSD got really bad. He's been having flashbacks and nightmares. But he's been having EMDR therapy since he came back and I think it's helping a bit."

"Alice said he'd been at the Priory last year, before I met him. She just assumed he was there for addictions."

"No, Sweetie. That time, it was because he was burnt out. I sent some of my designer pieces to auction so I could pay for him to spend a couple of weeks at the Priory – I'd do anything for him. But addictions, no! *I* was the one with the substance abuse issues, never Seb. He said one of us had to stay sane if we were going to stay alive at all, but the responsibility took its toll on him. I struggle to forgive myself for burdening him with that as well. But I don't think I'll *ever* forgive that bitch Maxine for what *she* did to him." She clutches at the elven pendant around her neck; I can clearly see the scars on her wrists now. "He was so desperate for someone to love him; she could make him do anything she wanted. Seb's only addiction is wanting to be loved, that's why he works so hard. It's like he believes he can win people's approval by doing things like restoring that bloody garden."

"The walled garden?"

"Yes! He was often there until it was completely dark, but then Guy threw him out before he could finish it. He tried to ask for some money, for some help, but understandably Guy and Giles didn't see why they should give him anything after everything he'd done. So he just went – didn't try to explain, didn't put up a fight – because he's like that."

Sahara gets up from the sofa and glances out at the people smoking in the garden as though she's itching to cadge a fag off them. I feel like a scruffy little hobbit next to her elven stateliness.

I'd believed Alice when she'd said Seb was a waster who smoked dope in his camper van. But now I'm thinking about how he single-handedly restored the walled garden in a matter of months (even if he did do it to impress Maxine); and all the things that Guy and Sahara have told me about him; and everything that I felt instinctively when I first got to know him.

It's unlike Alice to jump to conclusions, but it looks like she might have got this one completely wrong. And it's unlike me to take on someone else's views lock, stock and barrel. But I guess her assumptions suited my angry frame of mind last summer.

It sounds like the party's winding down now. The volume has increased but the games have finished, and the doorbell keeps going. We can hear mums and dads starting to collect their sugar-crazed offspring for challenging bedtimes throughout the village.

"If it hadn't been for Guy, we would probably be even more messed up than we are. But Seb … he's so desperate to sort himself out. He just wants to be … *normal*: to be a regular guy, set up a little carpentry business, have a couple of kids, give them a carefree upbringing in the countryside. But Maxine had such a stranglehold on him – she promised him so much. She ruined his life, the selfish cow. I can see how it must look, Charlie, but Seb's …"

Guy, no longer wearing his Hulk head, opens the door and Sahara jumps up to meet him. "I'm glad you two have found each other. What's the matter, Darling?"

"I'm worried about Seb." Sahara rests her head on his shoulder as he puts his arm around her. I bristle for Alice, but Alice has already explained to me how Guy, Seb and Sahara have this weirdly close relationship. They're meant to be "like siblings" but given that Guy and Sahara used to be engaged, and Seb was sleeping with Guy's mother, I'm really not sure what that means.

"Me too," Guy admits, "I don't think I'll ever stop worrying about you two." He kisses the top of her head. She looks up at him, her eyes moist and he looks down at her with a furrowed brow and wipes a tear from her cheek with his thumb.

"Oh!" says Alice, standing in the doorway with Hatty.

Guy disentangles himself from Sahara. "Shall we go?"

"Yes," says Alice weakly. "I think we'd better."

I give Hatty a quick hug, scattering crushed leaves over the carpet, and they're off. Sahara's wafted off somewhere so I go back into the garden for a much-needed cigarette.

A few minutes later, Elizabeth comes into the garden looking agitated, pointing her wand at me in a way that doesn't seem too friendly. "Ah, *there* you are! Your lift is here."

"Thank you, Elizabeth, I'll be along in a minute," I reply, taking another drag of my half-finished cigarette.

"I'd rather you came immediately!"

"Okay." I stub out the cigarette and rustle towards her.

When we reach the conservatory, out of earshot, she says "I don't mean to be awkward, Charlie, especially as we don't even know each other yet – and it's really none of my business – but I'm going to say, anyway, that I can't approve of your choice of company."

"What?" I turn to her incredulously.

"Steve Silver is *persona non grata* in this village. I'm surprised Guy didn't say anything to you!"

Maybe that's because he's polite and knows when to mind his own business, I think. But I say, "We're perfectly happy with his work up at the Hall."

"I'm not talking about him *professionally;* he's done good work for us too. I mean, *socially.*"

"This isn't some kind of class thing, is it?" Because that would seriously piss me off.

"Of course not! I'm just saying, Charlie, *be careful*."

Suddenly, a man in a gimp mask and a ripped, blood-spattered T-shirt, wielding a real chainsaw crashes into the living room with a roar. A couple of small children run shrieking behind the sofa; the others shrink away, apart from two tough-looking boys who say "Wow!" and "Cool!"

"Take him away!" shrieks Elizabeth, glaring at me. "This is a children's party, Mr Silver and this is *not appropriate*!"

Steve whips off his mask and my shock turns to a smile as I glimpse his mussed-up silver hair and his handsome face, alight with laughter.

"Sorry, Mrs Pemberton, just having a laugh," says Steve, unable to wipe the grin off his face.

"Well, please go and laugh outside! Charlie!"

"We're going! I'll see you outside, Steve."

Reluctantly, he heads for the door.

"I'm really, sorry, Elizabeth. He's just a bit of a tease."

"That's not all he is, Charlie – just ask around and you'll soon find out!"

"I hear you," I say, bewildered. "Thank you for inviting me. It's been lovely."

"Don't mention it. Hopefully, we can get to know each other better under calmer circumstances. I'll tell Alice when my next Champagne-and-Malteser evening is, and you can come too – alone: it's strictly ladies only. Please take care of yourself." She has a look of genuine concern on her face.

When I get outside, Steve's holding the door of his crew cab open for me, peering at me in the dim streetlight. "What the hell are you wearing?"

Chapter Nineteen

The next weekend, we're all sitting round the kitchen table – me, Guy, Milan, Mrs Powell, Sahara and Alice – staring at an empty flipchart. Bertie's sitting on my feet, keeping them toasty.

A big plate of Mrs Powell's buttery choc chip cookies is tempting me; but I take a slice of carrot cake, which she assures me is made with vegetable oil, not butter, and has plant-based frosting. Seb, wearing a baggy brown jumper full of holes, is making a pot of herbal tea, with lavender and verbena from the walled garden, which Alice, Sahara and I are glad to share with him while the others have coffee from a huge cafetière.

Elizabeth is standing in front of the flip chart, marker pen poised.

"Right, everyone. Sorry to do this on a Saturday but it's the only time when we're all available. We've got seven weeks to pull together a line-up for a Christmas concert. It's going to be high-end and exclusive. We're giving away fifty seats to friends, family, influencers and potential major donors, and charging a hundred and fifty pounds a ticket for the remaining hundred and fifty tickets, which includes drinks and canapés. We need an exciting programme that will draw in a hundred and fifty high-paying customers in seven weeks. Does anyone know any suitable performers?"

Alice refused point blank to have anything to do with the Christmas concert or the summer gala ball. She told Guy she's a curator, not a tour guide, and she'd be terrible at organising an event. She said that even the thought of it was massively stressing her out. I thought it was going to break them; but he just apologised, said he loved her and the last thing he wanted was for her to be stressed. The next thing we knew, Elizabeth was suddenly in charge.

She read engineering at Cambridge and managed a team of fifty – mostly men – in an aerospace company before she had The Twins. She's now a full-time mum and is using her enormous spare energy and brain power to run pretty much every committee in the village. Guy's chosen well, not least because it might give the good people of Tillingham a break.

Elizabeth is also – despite being formidable and having had that bizarre dig at Steve – actually really nice.

Guy's also got Sahara on board to do the PR. With over a hundred thousand followers on Instagram and a pretty hefty contacts book, she's well placed, even if her brain power and organisational skills are the size of a pea compared to Elizabeth's.

Alice dips a cookie in her tea. "Desmond is friends with Gayane Harutyunyan, the Armenian violinist who played at the Last Night of the Proms this year. Maybe he could ask her. Or she could suggest a few people if she can't do it herself."

"Sure!" Elizabeth writes down "Gayane" without attempting to spell Harutyunyan: a challenge too great even for Elizabeth's massive brain.

"I know a man who does a Tom Jones act at the Coach and Horses," says Mrs P and there's a moment of silence.

"I could ask Elton," says Sahara quietly.

I feel like flicking a piece of soggy cake at her with my teaspoon.

Of course Sahara knows Elton John.

Seb strokes her arm. “I don’t think he’d do it, Sassy. He’s like retired now, isn’t he?”

“Don’t you remember at that party, how he said he’d do anything for us?”

Seb looks down sadly. I wonder what he’s thinking. His saggy, lumpy brown jumper makes him look like an old teddy. I try to squash the thought that I just want to give him a big hug.

I’ve done a lot of pondering since that conversation with Sahara at the party. I realise that perhaps, in reality, things between me and Seb weren’t so clean-cut as I’d had them in my own mind. We were seeing each other regularly but hadn’t actually spoken about going exclusive. Then there was my Samhain last year. And in a way, he was cheating on Maxine with me, as much as the other way round. But that doesn’t make it better, just more complicated than I saw it at first.

And I had no idea he had so much childhood trauma to deal with. Seb didn’t tell me anything about himself. In fact, he lied about who he was. And when I discovered the truth – or some of it – I just took Alice’s judgement at face value.

“You know what, Sahara?” says Guy, “I think if Elton John was willing to do something here, given that he’s officially retired – and it would be the most massive thing in music since Oasis got back together – we should make it part of an open-air festival in the summer, probably the summer after next. I’m not sure we’re quite ready for someone as big as Elton just yet.”

Sahara looks a bit put out, but I’m quite sure Guy’s right.

“Hey, Bro, what about re-forming Johnny Incorrigible and

the Boiling Kettles?" asks Seb, grabbing a cookie, and Guy laughs.

"What's that?" I whisper to Alice, who's had a cookie collapse and is trying to get the goopy bits out of her mug.

"A band they had at school," she explains, sotto voce. "I think Seb was the drummer. Guy says he's a brilliant musician."

That's not helping, Alice.

I fall into a reminiscence about Saturday nights in Neville, Seb picking out his favourite riff with his clever fingers in moments of relaxation between our lovemaking. But I quickly put that inappropriate thought out of my mind. I look up and catch sight of his full lips as they meet his mug. I quickly flick my eyes towards the flip chart, carefully avoiding looking at Seb any more.

Meanwhile, a discussion has gone on about the Alton Brass Band and some friends of Milan's in London who run a Czech folk group: they do polkas and Czech Christmas carols in traditional costume, which sounds charming.

"What about some old English Christmas carols?" asks Seb, grabbing yet another cookie. "Not just the usual *Hark the Herald* and that, but the old folky ones like the *Wassail Song* and *King Herod and the Cock*. Our friends out there," he waves in the direction of the grounds, "do a set with Herne on the hurdy-gurdy, Wolf playing shawm and Gwendoline with her timbrel. They're really good – kind of like Florence and the Machine's second album. You know, the one with the harp but less rocky."

"Hmm," says Guy, dubiously. "I'm not sure about King Herod's cock, but they do kind of owe us for their keep, so it might be a good way for them to pay us back."

"Oh, I completely forgot!" I say, "I *do* have an idea. Actually, it was my mother's suggestion – the Wells Cathedral Choir. Obviously, they'll come if Dad asks them to and she's already checked they're free on that date. We'd have to cover the cost of the coach, the choirmaster's overtime and a slap-up tea for the boys. But other than that, they'll do it for the publicity and to help us out."

"That would be fabulous," says Guy. "Who doesn't love a chorister at Christmas?"

"I'd love to do a proper high tea for the little darlings," coos Mrs P. "It'll be just like the old days, when you used to bring all your friends back from school," she says, looking dotingly at Guy.

"Oh! Can you do your butterfly cakes?" says Seb, smacking his lips.

"Of course! But only for the choir – I'd have to do at least three dozen extra if you got your hands on them!"

Guy and Sahara laugh; Seb pretends to look put out while Sahara pushes some carrot cake towards him. It feels like a private joke between the three of them.

"So, how soon can we confirm the choir?" asks Elizabeth, looking at me.

"I can phone Mum straight after this. She'll tell the dean to ask the choirmaster to put it in the diary."

"Handy your father being a bishop!" says Guy, with a laugh.

"I guess it has some advantages," I agree, although I've never really seen it that way before.

"And let's do the English folk carols as well," adds Guy.

"I like the idea of involving our visitors. Although, it'll be the day after the solstice, so they might still be at some festival miles away from here. Can you talk to them, Seb? And Milan, could you speak to your Czech band and see if they might be available just to be on the safe side?"

Elizabeth makes sure everyone knows what they're doing, then winds up the meeting.

"Who's going to the cricket club fireworks?" asks Mrs P as we help her clear away the tea things.

Everyone, apparently – I'm meeting Steve there – so we agree to go down in a couple of cars.

Chapter Twenty

I go to check up on Bertie in the boot room and give him a doggy tranquiliser. I doubt he'll hear the fireworks in the village all the way over here at Tillingford Hall, but he's so highly strung, I don't want to take the risk of him totally stressing himself out, especially as no one's going to be here.

I put the pill into a treat and give it to him, making a big fuss of him while his tail thumps a hundred beats per second on the flagstone floor. I've also got a massive marrow bone for him to enjoy while we're out. The disgusting meaty smell makes me almost gag as I pull it out of its plastic wrapper, but Bertie's ecstatic.

Somehow, I end up in the back of the Range Rover. Guy is driving, Alice is in the front passenger seat and Seb is sitting next to me. Hatty's with her dad this weekend, otherwise she'd probably be creating a welcome barrier between me and Seb in the middle seat. As it is, I'm crackling with static, like a long-wave radio that can't quite find a station.

I have no intention of talking to Seb. But I'm itching to ask him more about that folk band and whether they do *The Ten Joys of Mary*, which is one of my favourites.

'The Chase', the pub where Seb and I met, was full of beardy, real-ale types and folky people, who would often start impromptu jamming sessions. I don't remember the particular combo he mentioned. Certainly, I've never seen Herne playing a hurdy-gurdy; I'd definitely remember *that* no matter how many pints of Crusty Bath Ale I'd drunk.

There *was* a band playing when Tris introduced me to Seb. I remember us talking about music for hours and me thinking how gorgeous Seb was. And I do remember going back with him to Neville "for a nightcap".

As I reminisce now about that first time we made love, I'm acutely aware of the bulk of him sitting next to me in the back of the Range Rover. We could reach out and take each other's hands here in the dark and no one would know.

"How's it going with Steve?" asks Seb out of the blue. I instantly snap out of my reverie.

"Great, thanks."

"Cool. Glad you've met someone."

"What's that supposed to mean?"

He sighs and turns towards me, saying with a tone of resignation, "I'm just wishing you well, Charlie. Literally, just that. But look, I know, I *just know* you're going to think this is sour grapes, but I'm going to say it anyway, because, despite everything I do care about you ..." He hesitates.

"Go on, spit it out then!"

"I'm actually a bit worried about you."

"You? Worried about me?"

"Yes, Charlie. And I just know you're going to take this the wrong way, but I couldn't live with myself if I didn't say something. I'm worried about *you and Steve.* He's got a bit of a reputation. I know you can hold your own but ..."

"It's not really any of your business is it, Seb?" I point out.

Seb turns to look out of the window and the remaining five

minutes of the journey pass in awkward silence.

Although I had put it out of my mind, I can't help remembering what Elizabeth said about Steve. And maybe Sahara was trying to tell me something about him at the Hallowe'en party but I shut her down, turned the conversation to Seb and learned all those shocking things about his past that have had me thinking all week.

What's wrong with these people? Steve's been nothing but charm personified – apart from the chainsaw massacre thing; but that was just a Hallowe'en prank.

When we park in the temporary car park on the outfield, I can't wait to get out of the car. Seb trudges towards the beer tent, his hunched shoulders silhouetted against the roaring bonfire, the fierce light burnishing his hair.

I try looking for Steve, but my eyes are bedazzled by the contrast between the crackling flames and the darkness of the night sky.

"Hello, Princess," says a gruff voice at my shoulder and then he's got me in his arms, sweeping me downwards before pulling me back up for a kiss. "Let's get hammered!"

And so we stroll towards the beer tent, hand in hand. There, we spot Seb, leaning on the bar, looking lost and disconsolate as he orders a Coke.

"What can I get you?" he asks when he sees me and Steve approach.

"A couple of pints of Old Cressy," says Steve.

"And what will you have, Charlie?" asks Seb.

Steve's eyes crinkle at the corners. "You're such a joker!"

"I was just asking Charlie what *she* wanted," replies Seb, deadpan.

"I'll have one of those two pints of Old Cressy," I say, pointedly. I'm well aware of the point Seb's just made and I don't appreciate him making it. "But don't worry, I'll get them."

"Your call." He takes his Coke and walks away.

"I can't let you buy me a drink, Princess. And I'm not sure why you didn't let that posh git pay for the drinks when he offered," Steve mutters.

"Posh" is a pretty vague and relative term. I've been called it myself, though I certainly don't think of myself that way. But I do wonder … just how posh *are* Seb and Sahara? I don't think Seb's *that* posh. True, he went to Winchester College and he's friends with Guy, but he's just this bloke: a chippy, not an investment banker or something. And he seems pretty skint, judging from his clothes and the fact he lives with his sister in a friend's cottage, and comes to work on a pushbike.

Now the weather's closing in, I feel pretty bad about his camper van. I've been wondering why he didn't claim on the insurance. I've been thinking about it quite a lot and I have various theories. It was either because it wasn't insured (most likely) or because he didn't want the police involved, in case they started asking awkward questions about all kinds of other things, including maybe me.

I guess I'll never know why; but I do know it's my fault the guy doesn't have wheels.

Still, he probably deserves it, I remind myself.

The display's started already, so we pour out on to the field with a few hundred others, trying not to spill beer from our wobbly plastic pint glasses. Most of the village school seems to be here, with their families. And I guess people come from the surrounding villages, maybe even Alton and Alresford as well, for this display.

And then I spot a pair of antlers towering above the sea of light-up deely boppers and woolly hats and realise that the entire traveller contingent has wandered over here too.

"Look! It's one of your effin' crusties. Aren't they meant to have left by now?"

"That was the plan, but they've literally got nowhere to go. Guy said they could stay a bit longer while they're looking around for somewhere."

"Blimey, he's a soft touch, isn't he? Next thing you know, their friends will be turning up and you'll have a real problem on your hands. Effin' druggy weirdos, with dogs on strings. They'll be nicking stuff from the house next."

I don't remind Steve that some of these "effin' weirdos" are my friends; or that he and I enjoy an occasional smoke of not-entirely-legal substances ourselves.

"Oi! Get away from that fire!" Steve yells.

He hands me his pint and rushes forward to grab a little tyke in a black Nike hoody who's getting too close to the massive bonfire. A bunch of kids have been leaning on the hazard tape and pushed over the stakes that were holding it up so there's nothing to mark the safe zone. Steve grabs the kid by the shoulders and yanks him back to where we are.

"Oi! Dad! You're hurting me."

"I'll hurt you more if you don't stop effin' mucking about! Now you behave – I've got someone I want you to meet."

"You must be Tyler," I say to the boy, who looks eleven or twelve.

"Yeah." He's looking at me.

"Be polite!" Steve growls.

"Hello." The boy holds out his hand.

I take it and give it a squeeze. "It's nice to meet you, Tyler."

"Can I go now, Dad?"

"All right. But don't go near that effin' fire again. And make sure you're back by nine!"

"Can I have a tenner for a burger?"

Steve swears under his breath, pulls out his fat wallet from his back pocket and gives the kid a note. "Tell your sister to come and find me if she wants one," he calls after the receding figure.

As I finally start paying attention to the display, I hear *Firework* by Katie Perry playing while the sky lights up like the fourth of July. And then we're on to *Rocket Man*, which reminds me of Sahara's suggestion of getting Elton John in for our concert. I wonder if she really could have pulled that off? I'm assuming she met him through her modelling career, but then I wonder how Seb seemed to know him too. Maybe their family is well connected.

But then, aware of Steve standing behind me, his arms around me, keeping me warm, I just settle back into enjoying the fireworks.

I particularly like one type of rocket that makes rosehip red and apple green shapes in the sky when they explode. They remind me of the onion and carrot seed heads in the walled garden. And there's the kind that bursts quietly before sending glittering, shimmering flakes, like autumn leaves shivering off the trees on to the ground; and catherine wheels, like giant sunflowers.

Then two enormous explosions, like the heralds of Ragnarök, make the whole village shake and the *1812 Overture* starts up.

Through the "oohs" and "aahs", the sound of children laughing and shouting and the general chatter, you can hear a hundred dogs howling in terror and rooks cawing in alarm as they circle the village.

Chapter Twenty-one

"Penny for 'em, Princess?" asks Steve, putting his strong, hairy arms around me in bed the morning after the fireworks. I can still smell the smoke in our hair. Although I enjoy being out and about with Steve – he's funny, good-looking and knows how to have fun – I like the moments when we're calm and cosy together in my cottage even more.

But I can't tell Steve what I'm really thinking about.

Why was Seb trying to tell me he was worried about me: about me *and Steve*? He knows *we're* never going to get back together again, so it can't have been just some kind of anti-Steve manoeuvre. And why would Elizabeth mention Steve's "reputation"?

As Steve tries to get my attention again, I decide I don't care. "Fancy a smoke?"

"Why not?"

I roll over while he reaches for his tobacco pouch, takes out the little plastic baggy tucked behind the normal tobacco and makes us a nice, fat spliff.

"So, how about the shrubbery?"

He takes a drag and then passes it to me.

Smoke curls round me as I exhale. "What about it?"

"Aren't you going to get us in to clear it?"

I prop myself up on my elbow to look at him "Not really. Milan can easily do that with the tools we've already got. I don't have a budget to get you guys in to do that as well as the tree work."

"Oh, come on, Princess. There's the bit round the lake too. Don't tell me you're going to try and clear that just with Milan?"

"Well, no. But it's a project for next year anyway. I don't think we'll be able to open that area up to the public for a while. Why are you asking?"

"I've got this lad, Ged, see? Son of a mate of mine. I owe this bloke a favour so I said I'd take this lad on. But I've got to make sure I've got enough work for him to do. Once we've taken down that cedar, that's the end of the list you gave me."

"I can't make up work just so you can keep your mate happy, Steve. Perhaps Ged can do some casual work when we need him."

"But Princess ..." He kisses my shoulder in that way he does, which means further conversation will be impossible.

There's a knock at the front door.

"I'd better go and see who that is!" I say, jumping up.

"Can't be important on a Sunday," he complains, trying to pull me back into bed.

"Must be important if they can be bothered to come all the way over here," I argue. I wrest myself from his grasp, pull on my robe and hurry downstairs, just as there's another, louder, knock on the door.

It's Alice and Sahara.

There's a hard frost outside and a wan orange sun offers no heat but sets the frosted seed heads outside my door sparkling.

"Can we come in?" Alice asks. She's shivering, even though she's wearing her inside-out squirrel coat.

"Of course. What's up?"

"We wanted to talk to you about the social media campaign before Alice has to go back to London," Sahara explains. "Alice is meant to be doing some reels about the history of the house; but I think it will help her relax and be more natural on screen if we could do them as a conversation between you two. You're the only one on the team who knows enough about art history to chat with her."

"Did we get you up?" Alice asks as I draw my dressing gown around me.

"Kinda. What time is it?" I ask, trying to tidy up my hair a bit.

"Eleven."

"I had no idea it was so late! But it *is* Sunday."

"Are you going to let us in?" Alice pointedly rubs herself with her gloved hands and stomps her feet.

"Of course, sorry. It's just …"

"Ew! Have you been smoking weed again?" Alice sniffs me suspiciously before I have a chance to finish my sentence.

"Erm …" I bite my lip.

"Oh, Charlie, *seriously*?" scolds Sahara.

"Like *you* can talk!" I also start to shiver as the cold starts to find its way up my robe.

"I've completely given up! You think it's harmless, don't you? Well, I'm telling you, it isn't! You should come to DRAGS with me," she adds.

"What's that?"

"Drug and Alcohol Group Support. You should try it."

"Thanks. I'll bear that in mind, Sahara."

"Let's come back later, Sahara. Send me a text when you're ready, Charlie," says Alice, turning away.

"No wait. I'll just open the windows. I'm really sorry."

"I can't go in there!" Alice insists.

"It'll only take a minute to clear the air, Sweetie," Sahara calls to her.

"I'm not risking it," says Alice over her shoulder. "I'll come back later."

"She was fine with it when she came to stay with me," I mutter to Sahara.

"Are you pregnant?" Sahara asks gently to Alice's receding back. She stops stock still, hugging herself defensively. Then she turns round and looks at us with a furrowed brow but a smile playing on her lips.

"She *is!*" says Sahara, rushing to hug her. "Alice! This is amazing! I can't believe I'm going to be an auntie!"

"And me!" I say.

Neither of us is related to the baby, but we'll definitely be its aunties.

"Guy must be over the moon," I say.

But Alice is looking tearful. "He doesn't know."

"Sweetie!" Sahara envelopes her in a bony hug while I stand shivering on the doorstep, my mouth working up and down like a stranded grouper's. "Why on earth haven't you told him?"

"Who is it?" Steve shouts down from upstairs.

"Alice and Sahara," I call back, leaving the door open to fumigate my disgusting, messy cottage.

"Come back to bed," he calls from upstairs. Alice wrinkles her nose.

"No, you get up," I yell back. "I'll make us some breakfast."

"Come back to bed, Princess," he insists.

"Sorry, girls, I'm going to have to talk to him. Why don't we talk up at the house in a few minutes?"

"I think we need a *private* conversation," says Sahara, looking pointedly at Alice.

"OK. Brunch here in an hour? I'll get rid of Steve. And I promise I'll have this place spotless and fumigated."

Alice and Sahara scurry away, shivering, as I shut the door then climb up the stairs.

"I kind of want to get up now, Steve," I say from the bedroom doorway. "Alice and Sahara really need to talk before Alice goes back to London, and I want to have a shower and some food."

"Time for a quickie, though."

"Not really, Steve. It's eleven already and this place is a tip. I've promised them brunch at twelve."

He looks cross. "Fine," he growls, throwing off the duvet, marching into the bathroom ahead of me and locking the door so I'm left on the landing crossing my legs. There's a big bang as he throws the toilet seat upwards and it hits the wall; a big bang as he throws it back down again and lots of stomping as he thumps around.

He refuses breakfast and leaves without so much as a goodbye kiss.

An hour later, Alice is sitting in my kitchen devouring some mushrooms on toast while Sahara has a detox tea, and we try to warm back up after I've had all the windows open.

"Look, Alice, it's none of our business, but you didn't answer Sahara's question. Why haven't you told Guy?"

Alice looks away tearfully. "I've been so stressed, I only realised a couple of weeks ago, so I went to the doctor. It turns out I'm already twelve weeks gone. I must have got pregnant the first time we slept together – I hadn't been on the pill since I broke up with Phil and I just wasn't thinking. I guess Guy wasn't either."

"*Please* tell him, Alice. He has a right to know," says Sahara. "He loves you so much. I've never seen him so happy, so sure of himself, so excited for the future. Knowing he was going to be a daddy would ..." She gasps, pushes back her chair and walks over to the sink, tears streaming down her face. She pulls half a dozen squares of kitchen towel off the roll and blows her nose noisily.

Alice and I look at each other awkwardly while Sahara pulls herself together.

"Why don't you want to tell him?" I ask gently.

"I don't want to be part of some Tillingford project: phase one, pack Dad off; phase two, open the house to the public; phase three, find a wife, have a baby, or two or three. I'm a mother already and I'm not sure I really want to go through all that again."

"You wouldn't get rid of it?" says Sahara, horrified.

"No! I'm just saying, having babies isn't a picnic."

"I wouldn't know," says Sahara, tears starting in her eyes again as she sits down. "Let *me* bring up the baby if you don't want it!"

"Of course, I *want* the baby! I'm just a bit tired and emotional, and this is a really big deal. It's all happened much quicker than I expected – we've only been together for three months. I don't want Guy to marry me just because he feels he has to."

"But he's already proposed to you – and you turned him down!" says Sahara.

"What?" I gasp. "You *turned him down*?"

"I can't believe he told you, Sahara! Are you going to be our Camilla Parker Bowles?"

Sahara recoils with hurt. "I keep telling you, Alice. I don't love him *like that*. Our engagement was very short-lived, a very stupid idea and entirely my fault. *I* asked *him* when I was distressed and vulnerable; and I guess he didn't know how to say "no". And it was a long time ago. Guy's completely crazy about you, Alice. Don't break the heart of the best man that ever lived; he's already had enough heartbreak in his life, and he really needs you."

"I don't want him to *need* me. I want him to *love* me. I don't want to be part of his programme."

Sahara looks thoughtful.

"I understand how it could look that way and what can I say? Guy's a passionate, ambitious man, who goes full tilt at everything he wants to achieve. Only you can decide if he loves you for yourself and you love him for himself too, not just the glamorous friends, the fancy car, the big house and the title, hey, Alice? Think about it from his point of view. I don't want to be mean – because I think you're lovely and I've never seen Guy so happy – but here you are, a not very well-off single mum, plucked from obscurity, with someone else's child in tow. You're not exactly on the *Sunday Times* Rich List or Miss UK, are you? If he had some kind of 'Tillingford Project' in mind, don't you think he might have aimed a bit higher?"

Alice looks like she's had a slap in the face, but I'm kind of with Sahara on this one, although I notice Sahara's shaking, like it's really cost her to be this confrontational.

Chapter Twenty-two

"Can I have your attention everyone?" says Elizabeth in a voice that was going to get everyone's attention anyway while two besuited consultants fiddle with a projector. Behind them, a flip chart, a banal grey triangle, is reflected a hundred times in the golden mirrors of the ballroom. "I'd like to introduce India and Oliver from ColoRING, who are going to lead our team-building session today."

The Edwardian curtains have been drawn so we can see the PowerPoint projection. Alice is on edge, looking up at them as though in fear that they'll drop into tatters at any moment.

Mrs Powell has a face like thunder. She's wearing a sticker saying, "Hello. My name is Christine". I think we all feel a bit exposed now. Finding out Mrs P's first name was a bit like seeing a picture of Margaret Thatcher in her bra.

"Haaaai," says the female consultant, flicking her immaculate balayage over her shoulder. "Thank you so much for the introduction, Liz."

No one calls Elizabeth "Liz": I can see her bridle while Alice stifles a laugh.

"I'm India Garton-Jones and this is my colleague, Oliver Bentley. We'll just give you a little intro to ourselves and then give you the chance to let us get to know you, with a little icebreaker."

"So, I'm India, like I said," says India, clicking her remote to bring up a slide that has a picture of her on it and "India Garton-Jones", printed in a clear sans-serif font, in case we still hadn't quite got it. "After uni, I spent five years as a brand manager at Proctor and Gamble, and then I decided to have a complete career change and go into HR. We did a ColoRING away day with our staff and I loved it so much I joined the team; and I've been here ever since. We always start by sharing our favourite coffees," she giggles self-consciously, "because what's a better way of warming things up and getting a conversation going than coffee? My favourite's a caramel macchiato. And I have a cat called Pudding," she adds with a soppy grin as she brings up a picture of her fluffball on the PowerPoint. A couple of people say "Aw" and "Ah"; and she simpers as she says, "And so I'll hand over to Oliver."

"Hey there. I'm Oliver. I graduated from the University of the West of England in Human Resources Management this summer, and I joined the ColoRING team in September. I love meeting new people, so we're going to have loads of fun. I like a latte and our family dog's called Turnip."

Alice lets out a snort. She grabs a tissue and pretends to be blowing her nose. It's all I can do to keep a straight face.

Guy's fiddling with his phone, looking slightly embarrassed. I don't know if this team building day was his idea or Elizabeth's, but I'd rather be at the wholesaler's choosing plants for the pots on the front steps.

"Charlie, what do you think?" asks India.

I have literally no idea what the question was.

"Yeah. Great. Definitely …" I stammer. I'm looking up at the PowerPoint hoping it'll give me a clue about what they're yammering on about but it's just a big picture of Oliver gurning while holding a scruffy Border Terrier that could definitely be called Turnip. And then I snigger. Everyone's looking at me. Elizabeth is glaring.

"I'm sorry … I just …" I was about to say, 'zoned out there' but that's way too rude so I offer "I just wasn't quite sure what you mean."

"Yeah, Charlie, I asked whether you'd like to do the icebreaker with teas and coffees or if we should crack on and have a break later," India explains patiently.

"Oh, sorry! Yes. Let's crack on – lots to do," I gabble.

"Okay, so we're going to get into pairs and tell each other our favourite coffee or a beverage of your choice, if you're not a coffee drinker. And, if we've got pets, what they're called and any of their funny little habits. If you've not got a pet at the moment, think about a pet you had in the past or one of your friends' pets." India uses an upward inflexion that makes the statement sound like a question. She goes round the room giving us each a coloured card at random. "Link up with the person with the same colour as you."

Alice and Guy have been paired up, so Guy swaps with Amy, our new fundraiser; and Alice gets Jerry, the handyman Seb hired last week. Elizabeth is with Milan. Mrs Powell, who's been appointed Catering Manager, is linked with Shelley our finance/admin person. Sahara, who is now officially in charge of PR and marketing, is with Jane, who is the new Housekeeper.

And guess what? I've been put with Sebastian.

We glare at each other. "So what's your favourite coffee?"

"You know I'm off all that, Charlie; no buzz, no nonsense."

"And how's that going?"

"Pretty sweet, actually. You should try it."

"Hmm. So, what about pets?"

"I had a dog called Ranger. He was a golden retriever, and I adored him. He used to sleep in my room, and I would tell him everything, especially once Mum died. But Dad shot him."

"What?" I gasp.

"Yeah. He was proper wound up cos I'd cut up Sassy's Barbie's dress, cos she stuck heart stickers on my Airfix Spitfire. He shot the dog to teach us both a lesson, he said."

"Oh my God!"

"Yeah. He was mental – psychotic you might even say." He looks at me significantly.

"So, now that's broken the ice," says India brightly, "let's try a game!"

Oliver is handing out more coloured cards while India explains the activity. "On these cards are values or qualities, like loyalty, hard graft, ambition, fairness, intuition, leadership. If you think you have these qualities or hold these values, or it's a quality you really want to work on gaining, keep the card. If not, give the card to someone that you think has those qualities. Now, some of them might sound negative to some people, but we need all these qualities to build a good team; so we're not judging, here: we're just trying to get to know each other. If someone gives you a card you don't agree with – that's fine, just find someone else to give it to."

And so we look at our cards. I've got "determination" (nope), "imagination" (maybe), "hard graft" (aspiring), "ambition" (probably not), "kindness" (maybe), "leadership" (definitely not: I'll give that one to Guy or maybe Elizabeth), "stability" (not really sure what that one means; but if it means that I've stayed in the same dead-end job for ten years, then I guess it applies to me) and "maturity" (I know I don't deserve that one, but I want it and so I decide I'm going to keep it). There are also "spontaneous" and "intuitive": I think I'll keep those too.

"This one's for you." Sebastian's drawn a hedgehog on the back of one of the cards.

"Oh *thanks*. Are you saying I'm prickly?" Or are you just a massive prick yourself? I think.

"You should change your name to Holly."

I'm about to write "loser" on a card for him but it would only prove his point; and I want to keep that "maturity" card.

So I hand him the "hard graft" card. He stares at it for a moment but says nothing. Then I go around the room and hand "leadership" to Elizabeth, and "determination" and "ambition" to Guy. Then I give "kindness" to Amy, who I don't really know yet, but she seems nice enough and I want to give her a boost as she's just joined the team. And that leaves me with "stability" and "maturity", which don't feel right at all. I think Mrs Powell might take it amiss if I give her "maturity" and I really want that one for myself, although it would have felt better if someone had given it to me. I'm not sure if "stability" is a positive or a negative but, as India said, it's not really about that.

Someone hands me "laid back" and I also get "uncompromising", which I'm not quite sure what to make of.

India and Oliver make us get in a circle and hold up our cards with the words facing us. We realise that the colours on the backs are significant. Guy has lots of red and yellow cards.

Alice has lots of blue and a couple of green ones. The "relaxed", "spontaneous", "fun" and "intuitive" cards I've been handed are all yellow, and "stability" and "maturity" are green. Mrs Powell and Milan have entirely green cards, and Amy is green and with a few yellows. Elizabeth is mostly reds with a few blues.

But what does it all mean? I'm actually intrigued now.

India and Oliver explain that to build a good team you need all the different colours. And it's helpful to know who has which ones, but not to judge them: it's to allow you to understand how they tick so you can work better together.

When we go for a break, I can't help thinking how Seb got lots of the same colours as me. I pick up the cards he's left on his chair; he's got some of the same ones as me, as well as "kindness", "creativity" and "generosity", which I don't have. "Maturity" isn't in his pile and – let's face it – it shouldn't really be in mine either.

"Now if you could all please take your seats," India says.

"We're going to do another activity," Oliver announces.

"You don't say," I think.

"On these sheets, you'll see some situations and ways you might react to them. For example, we've got 'I've been given a hundred-page document to read by tomorrow'. The options for your reactions are 'I panic' or 'I put my other work on hold and focus on it' or 'I finish what I have to do today and then take the document home to work on overnight'. It's like a multiple choice," says Oliver.

"It *is* a multiple choice," says India, with a fake grin and a look of frustration in her eyes.

Luckily, Alice has been paired with Sebastian this time;

so I get Amy, the fundraising girl and I'm enjoying getting to know her. She's sparky and bright and really sweet. We work through the scenarios and have a giggle about essay crises at uni, doing presentations with bra straps showing or dates with spinach between your teeth. It turns out Amy's parents have an allotment, so we end up chatting about that for a bit when we've finished. She says her dad can't wait to retire; he's already got Tetley Tea man slippers and a flat cap in preparation. He sounds lovely, and her childhood growing up in Gloucestershire sounds idyllic. She just seems like a really happy, well-adjusted person.

I look across at the others and see that Guy looks bored with Mrs Powell; Sahara and Milan look like they're having a very passionate conversation, presumably about philosophy or politics as that's all he seems to be interested in discussing; and Alice is holding Seb's hand. "What's *that* all about?" I think, with a strange flutter of irritation in my stomach. Is he wheeling out the sympathy vote again?

But, God, that thing about his dog.

I wonder if it was really true.

Guy told me they had a difficult childhood but, surely, only a monster would do something like that.

I can only begin to imagine how much damage that kind of experience could do to a sensitive child.

Chapter Twenty-three

It's not long before lunchtime comes around and I find myself in a huddle with Elizabeth, Sahara and Alice. So much for mixing and team building. We agree to step outside the ballroom and sit in the salon for the break. Alice lets us bring our drinks in, so long as we promise on our lives not to spill.

"Did you see how Guy swapped partners for the icebreaker?" Alice moans, putting her mug on a coaster to protect the ornate Victorian coffee table. "He thinks he knows me so well, but we've only been together for a few months."

Elizabeth puts a hand on Alice's arm. "Of course he knows you!"

Alice rearranges the pile of art books on the table. "Sometimes I wonder. Like him thinking I'd be able to manage the events."

"He's just enthusiastic," says Sahara. "He's like a big puppy, jumping up at everything exciting he comes across."

"That's the point of today," says Elizabeth. "If *you* can understand that he's an enthusiast – and he's full of new ideas and doesn't always think things through – and *he* can understand that you're more of a thinker, who needs time to analyse and process things and go through them in a detailed way, then you could work brilliantly together. You complement each other. He's a great CEO and you're going to be a fabulous curator. Project management is my thing.

Sahara's a brilliant communicator, and she's got the charisma to pull everyone in."

Alice is peering disconsolately into her mug. "I've just found out who my new boss is going to be at the London Portrait Gallery."

"Oh?" Elizabeth invites her to say more.

"Rollo Bumpstead."

"What? The guy on the *Arty Farty Show*?" I ask.

"Yes. He's very ambitious – I'm sure I'll be doing all the work, and he'll be taking all the credit."

"So why don't you just leave?" asks Sahara, picking a piece of lint off the sofa.

"Because I feel I should see things through, at least to keep the department going until Rollo settles in."

"Why?" I ask. "You've been there fifteen years. You don't owe them anything. And it's not like anyone's going to die if the department shuts for a couple of months."

"Guy's finishing at Hogghedge next week," adds Sahara. "He'll be down here full time then. Why don't you just hand in your resignation and come down too?"

"Hatty would have to change schools."

"You can't keep looking for the fly in the ointment, Alice." says Elizabeth. "I'm a governor at the school and I know we have a space for Hatty in year three. She'd be in the same class as Lily and Poppy, so she'd already have friends to help her settle in."

"I'm not sure I'm ready to give up work."

"But you'd be working here," points out Sahara.

"And you could finish your PhD," I add.

"I'm just not sure I should be putting all my eggs in one basket."

"Do you love Guy?" asks Elizabeth.

"Of course!" Alice protests.

"Do you trust him?" Elizabeth goes on.

"I think so."

"Alice," says Sahara, "Guy is the most honourable, trustworthy man on the planet."

"You are actually nuts, Alice!" says Elizabeth standing up in frustration. "You need to hand in your resignation and get your bony arse down here right now."

"And you've got to tell him," says Sahara, putting her hand gently on Alice's knee.

"Tell him what?" says Elizabeth.

"Yes. Tell him what?" says Guy from the doorway.

Sahara and I jump up from the squashy sofas and signal to Elizabeth to exit hastily with us, leaving Alice with Guy.

***

"So, we're going to have a bit of silliness now – the ColoRING way," says India, with the kind of enthusiasm Liz Truss demonstrated for the Chinese pork markets.

We look at one another in dismay.

"I think we're missing a couple," Oliver comments to her.

"Guy and Alice have been called away," Elizabeth explains. "I don't think we should wait for them."

Next thing we know, we're playing a game of Twister involving our colours. So I've got my right hand on a yellow, my left foot on a green; Elizabeth's tiny bottom is in my face;

and Sebastian is arched over me, trying his best not to touch me, which is pretty much impossible under the circumstances. Very inappropriate feelings run down my spine and into other places I can't even mention.

I pull myself out from the awkward tangle of bodies. "Sorry. I need the loo."

I excuse myself from the room, thinking, "Whoa! That was *soooo* inappropriate!" I bump into a very cross-looking Mrs Powell, who's fanning herself in the corridor, grumbling about having menus to plan.

We commiserate about the stupidity of it all.

"I can't help wondering if Guy's a bit out of his depth with this kind of thing."

Mrs P pulls an odd face, and I realise Guy and Alice are coming out of the library. He's got his arm around her and she's beaming. She glances across at me, raises her eyebrows and smiles as they walk back into the ballroom.

Guy carefully closes the door behind me and Mrs P as we come in.

"I have an announcement to make!"

He has the stupidest grin on his face; but he looks like a man in his prime who is absolutely not out of his depth.

He politely asks India and Oliver to leave.

We all look at each other. This is serious.

"I am delighted to announce that my darling Alice has just made me the happiest man in the world."

We all start to whoop and cheer and beam at Alice, who's looking mortally embarrassed but very happy.

When the noise subsides, Guy goes on. "Not only,"

he chokes back the emotion that's constricting his throat, "has she *finally* agreed to be my wife," we all clap and whoop again, "but she also has some amazing, fantastic news … which apparently some people in the room sussed out before I did!" he says with mock peevishness, glancing at me and Sahara.

"She's expecting!" gasps Mrs P.

"Yes!" Guy does a fist pump. "As well as making me stepfather to lovely Hatty, Alice – my beautiful, clever, wonderful Alice – is also giving me a baby of my own! Come here, Darling!"

Alice, red as a beetroot, comes up to the front of the room. Guy pulls her to him and kisses her on the top of the head while she leans into his chest.

"I couldn't be happier!"

He seems six inches taller, glowing with pride.

I'm pleased for them, I really am. But somewhere gnawing inside me is that hollow emptiness. The pain of it almost makes me gasp. Guy will be an amazing father for Alice's baby. As well as being solvent(ish), attractive, decent, he's welcomed Hatty like she's his own and he clearly adores children.

I can't say I've seen the same level of enthusiasm for parenting from Steve. In fact, I'm quite sure Steve wouldn't want any more kids. And, even if he did, I definitely don't want to have kids with him, I suddenly realise.

But I do want to have children; more than anything.

Sahara, tears streaming down her face, is giving Alice and then Guy a hug and everyone is following her. The new staff, like Amy and Jerry, are a bit hesitant, but Guy pulls each of them in for a big hug anyway. They can be left in no doubt that everyone who works at Tillingford Hall is part of the family.

"So, team, if you'd all like to sit back down again," he says. He laughs and wipes a tear from his eye as we all settle down. "That's not the end of it. Alice is freaking out because the summer gala ball is two days before her due date."

We all start talking at once.

"Shhh! And also, she thought I was expecting her to give up work and organise everything. But I'm not. I've explained to Alice that if she wants to be head curator here, there's a job with her name on it. If she wants to stay at the London Portrait Gallery, I will employ someone else. And if she took that role on, she would only be in charge of the collections – nothing else. Everything else will be dealt with by all of you. So, I need a Head of Visitor Experience who will manage all our outward facing work. This person will oversee events, catering, visitor services, comms and fundraising. And I'm delighted to say that Elizabeth has already agreed to take this role on."

Huh. She kept that one quiet, I think, glancing across at Elizabeth as everyone claps.

She stands up and walks to the front of the room, looking nothing other than totally professional. "Thank you. I'm really excited to be part of the team here. And, just to reassure you, I will be resigning from some of my voluntary roles to focus on this, which is going to be a full-time paid position – something I've been needing for a long time! I'm so grateful to Guy for giving me this opportunity."

"I'm sure we're all looking forward to working with you." Guy continues. "Meanwhile, there's all the background work: maintaining the building and grounds; health and safety; and accounts, HR and so on. I will be managing this for now, but I will be looking – advertising if I need to – for a chief operating officer, to take over all or some of this. If anyone has any ideas about anyone we could approach, please do come and talk to me because, ultimately, I'd like to focus on strategy and managing the wider estate and … being a dad." Here, he stops and grins at Alice again. "Not just to Bump but also to Hatty. There are going to be some big changes for her and Alice in the next few months. I want to be able to support them both through that, not worrying about fixing the loos or the leaking roof."

Everyone cheers again. I've never seen Guy look so happy.

He holds up his hand for silence. "Lastly, though this is, of course, absolutely brilliant news and I want to shout it from the rooftops, I beg that everyone here keeps this to themselves until Alice, Sahara and I have decided how to handle the PR. As you know, I am – I was – according to *Tatler*, Britain's twenty-ninth most eligible bachelor," he says with a wry smile. "And someone somewhere is, for reasons unfathomable to me, going to be vaguely interested in all this. We can't keep it to ourselves for ever; but we just want to get the messaging right, not least to protect Alice and Hatty, who aren't used to the public eye at all." He smiles knowingly at Sahara. "So please, please just keep it under your hats for now. We'll give you an update as soon as we can."

"Sahara, can you lead us in a moment of mindfulness just to get us back into the ColoRING zone?"

"Sure," says Sahara. She invites us all to take a few deep breaths, close our eyes and visualise a sunny tropical beach: the private beach of an exclusive boutique hotel. We can hear the waves on the sand, feel the sand beneath our feet and see beautiful shells washed up on the tide line. As the sun goes down, we walk back into the hotel and into the conference suite, where there's a meeting, a PowerPoint presentation on a screen and flip charts; and we're all suited and booted and ready to work.

It's weird. It works. So when Oliver and India come back in, we take their next activity vaguely seriously.

It starts with a questionnaire that we have to do on an app which feeds the results back on to the screen. Oliver shows Mrs P how to do it on his smartphone, as she only uses a brick.

Surprisingly, I feel like I've actually learned something from it.

I don't like what I've learned, though.

Apparently, translating the neutral management speak we're all having to use today, people find me cantankerous. Also, although I'm passionate about my subject, I'm not very good at getting that across, so I'm seen as quite unenthusiastic; churlish, even.

This doesn't enhance my mood but definitely gives me food for thought.

Thankfully, it's not long before the training day is over. Then there's plenty of champagne and elderflower pressé and several kinds of cake for everyone, and it goes out of my head.

Chapter Twenty-four

"Ugh. Let's get up," I groan on a Saturday morning a couple of weeks later. "I need a shower."

I'm at Steve's nursing another hangover after our usual heavy night at the pub.

"I need a shit! Go and use the family bathroom."

I throw on a robe and stomp across the landing. I'm just about to turn on the water when I hear the doorbell. He doesn't answer. It rings again. The Amazon man doesn't ring twice, I reckon, so it must be something important. I go down and find Tyler, a girl I assume is Rogue and a middle-aged woman I guess must be Nicola standing on the doorstep.

The kids wordlessly push past me into the living room. I hear the TV go on and the kids start arguing about who's got control of the remote.

"Hello," Nicola says, neutrally. "Are you his latest or just another one-nighter?"

"Erm … probably his latest?" I pull the robe tighter round me. "My *name's* Charlie."

"Look, Charlie," she says very quietly as she leans in. "I know you'll just think this is the ex-wife being a bitter old bat but watch out for him – seriously." She bites her lip. "He seems like a charmer, but he can be a bit …"

Steve appears at the top of the stairs.

"Is she talking to you?" he yells up at me.

"Not really."

"Don't believe anything she says." I can't quite tell if this is banter or he's deadly serious.

"Why the hell didn't you answer the door?" she shrieks at him. "You forgot again, didn't you?"

"No – I was just having a hard dump."

I excuse myself and go up for my shower while Steve and Nicola carry on their barney in the kitchen. Just as I come out of the shower wrapped in a towel, there's Nicola on the stairs.

"Sorry, just gotta use the toilet. Won't be a sec."

Seeing me on the landing, Steve dashes up the stairs, with a hungry look on his face.

He puts his arms round me so my towel's in a precarious position. I try to grab it to keep my modesty as Nicola comes out of the bathroom. He has his back to her; she stares at me, then does a throat-slitting action while looking significantly at him.

What does *that* mean?

"Bye!" she calls as she runs down the stairs and lets herself out.

Steve grunts before he whips off my towel and leads me back into the bedroom. "Now, where were we?"

"The kids are here, Steve."

"So what? They're watching TV."

"It's late, I'm hungover and I want some breakfast!"

I always seem to be hungover in the mornings with Steve.

"But you're naked! You can't expect me to ignore that luscious body of yours, can you?" He playfully pushes me on to the bed. I give in, but it's only him who's enjoying it. As soon as he's done, I get up, light a cigarette, light one for him and start getting dressed while he watches me. I feel like one of those slappers in a B-movie. And when I glance in the mirror I look like one, my half-dried hair all over the place and bags under my eyes.

"Come on! Fry up!" He throws yesterday's jeans and T-shirt back on and we head for the kitchen.

"Only beans, tomatoes and mushrooms for me, if you have them."

"When are you going to stop this vaygan rubbish? What's wrong with you?"

"I've been vegetarian since I was twelve and a vegan for the past three years. I don't see why I should change."

I grab the box of mushrooms.

"It's not healthy."

"Do I look unhealthy to you?"

"Yeah, pretty shit."

"Oh, thanks," I say, laying into the mushrooms with one of his expensive Japanese knives.

"You should wear makeup more often. And you could do with a few more pounds on you. I don't like a skinny woman."

"Well, you seem to have liked me so far."

"Yeah, well, that was sex that was. But we've been together for a few weeks now. If we're going steady, you'll need to shape up a bit."

He throws a whole pack of sausages in a pan.

"'Scuse me? What century are we living in?"

"Huh?"

"I mean, that's a bit sexist."

"What are you talking about? I just said I like a bit of meat on my women."

"Exactly. What about my wit and sparkling personality?"

He laughs.

I hurriedly grab a pan for the mushrooms off the shelf and put it on the hob, hiding my face behind my loose hair.

Since we got together, Steve's been looking out for me: coming up to the Hall after his contract work is done to do some extra work for me before it gets dark; getting in some groceries for me because I hadn't had a chance to go shopping; lifting heavy things for me, not to mention the gifts, the fancy nights out.

I thought he was the perfect gentleman, but now I'm gobsmacked.

"Go and tell the kids we're eating in a few minutes," he commands.

I leave the kitchen and go into the living room.

"Hello kids."

They totally ignore me.

"*Hello*, Rogue. *Hello*, Tyler. Good morning! Dad's making a fry-up."

Rogue flicks her eyes away from her phone for less than a millisecond and Tyler looks away from the TV momentarily.

I grab the remote and turn off the TV.

"Oi! I was watching that!" roars Tyler.

"Hello, Tyler. So nice to see you. How are you? Would you like to join us for brunch?" I sound exactly like my mother. Even though I swore I'd never be like her, I'm now starting to understand why she spoke to kids like that. "Now please would you get off the sofa and come and wash your hands in the kitchen."

"What about *her*?" says the little tyke.

"Rogue is obviously going to put her phone away, go and wash her hands upstairs and set you the good example I know she can."

God, I really do sound like a headmistress, but I have no idea how else to do it.

Incredibly, Rogue does exactly what I ask, albeit a bit resentfully.

It's not long before we're all sitting round the kitchen table eating fried food.

"Pass the tomato sauce," Rogue tells her little brother. "Oi! Don't take all of it, you prick! Can't you see it's almost finished?"

"Piss off, Rogue," replies her silver-tongued brother. "I'll have all the ketchup if I want it."

"No, you bloody won't!" Their dad takes the whole bottle and pours all that's left down the sink.

"Daaad! Oh my God, that's sooo unfair!" says Rogue, giving Tyler the skunk eye.

"Now you lot. What shall we do today?"

"Watch TV," says Tyler, displaying a mouth full of half-chewed sausage.

"Go to Gunwharf Quays," says Rogue, mashing up her leftover beans into a disgusting mess.

"I'm not driving all the way to bloody Portsmouth and getting stuck in the queue for the Quays car park for half an hour. Are *you* coming with us this time?" Steve asks hopefully, turning to me.

"Sure"

"Great. So, what would *you* like to do?"

"I think Portsmouth sounds fun." I try not to laugh at the face Steve pulls. "We can go to the Historic Dockyard and then go shopping at Gunwharf Quays."

Rogue gives me a momentary flicker, which looks surprisingly like gratitude, while Tyler slumps in his seat.

"I've heard they're firing the canons on HMS *Warrior* at noon today." I have no idea if this is true, but it sounds like the kind of thing they might do.

Tyler sits up. "What, like real canons?"

"Yep. Massive, great big ones."

"So, it looks like that's what we're doing today, then." Steve starts clearing the plates. He doesn't look too happy. "Bloody expensive getting all of us in there."

"Don't worry, I've got an Art Pass, which gets us in half price. We can take a picnic if you're worried about the cost of a meal." But I know full well that Steve's not going to want a picnic in the middle of November; he might be an outdoor man but he loves his creature comforts, and he likes to enjoy the money he earns. Grumbling about the cost of things is the habit of a lifetime and has nothing to do with his actual income. Like I said, I've never met a poor tree surgeon. "Come on kids – plates in the dishwasher, sauces in the cupboard."

And they do.

They actually do what I ask.

And I hear them talking to each other with something approaching interest about the day out we're going to have. Rogue's got her eye on a Juicy Couture top she thinks she can just afford with her birthday money; and she wants to start getting some ideas for Christmas presents. Tyler's practising his exploding noises. I think I might actually enjoy this.

But as we get in the black crew cab, I'm still wondering what Nicola meant with her throat-slitting gesture. Was it that she was going to slit my throat for being with Steve? Or was she was trying to warn me about something?

I can't say Steve was overly charming this morning.

Chapter Twenty-five

"You'll have to do something else today, then," says Steve, arms crossed as he confronts Sebastian under the massive, dead cedar tree, while Bertie cowers at my feet.

The autumn storms have created loads of work for him the past few weeks, but Steve is finally at Tillingford Hall to do this one last job.

Sebastian rubs the back of his neck. "Mending the fence is urgent if we don't want sheep wandering into the ballroom."

"I don't give a shit if there's lions in the library or cows in the kitchen: that's not my effin' problem. I've got the cherry picker coming in half an hour."

"There must be a hundred other trees you could do today that need a cherry picker," argues Seb, waving his arm across the expanse of the estate. The bare skin of his bicep shows through a hole in his jumper. I can't take my eyes off it.

"We're only hiring a flippin' cherry picker for a grand a day because this cedar's completely dead and it's too dangerous to climb. Bloody health and safety, innit?" Steve pings his harness. "It's gotta be done today. I'm not sending the effin' cherry picker back."

"This is bloody ridiculous," says Seb.

"Too right it is!" The red mist starts to cross my eyes.

"This is the problem with each of us doing our own thing!" Seb throws down his drill and scratches at his beard in frustration.

"We need to be more coordinated, but *she* won't talk to me!" He gestures sharply in my direction. "How am I supposed to work with someone so … abrasive and cruel?"

My chest tightens with a surge of anger. "*Cruel? Me?* What about *you*? You lied to me. You strung me along, for months and months, while you and Maxine got on with your conniving little schemes."

Seb clenches his jaw, gritting his teeth as he stares back at me, silent and seething. I know he knows I'm right, but he refuses to admit it. I take a step closer, feeling the tension thicken between us.

"You disgust me!" I say in a low voice.

Seb recoils like he's been struck by a serpent. I turn away, crossing my arms across my chest, trying to control my shaky breath. I feel like the backlash of its tail has stung me across the face too. I don't want to look at him.

I don't know why I said that.

He doesn't disgust me. He *frustrates* me. But I can't unsay it now.

He draws himself up to his full height, which is considerable, and takes a deep breath.

"I know what I did was wrong and stupid, Charlie. Maxine bewitched me. I'd have done anything for her, but not for *love*; she was a manipulative bitch, and she preyed on me. She was blackmailing me – I had nowhere to hide."

"Last year you pretended to be someone you weren't just to get into my knickers!"

"I *got into your knickers* because you fancied me."

"What the hell?" Steve spits, pulling me round to face him.

"This public-school turd's your ex?"

"Not so much an ex as a big mistake!" I retort, my heart burning as I see the fury in Steve's face. But I can't try to pretend I don't still have feelings for Sebastian.

"Yes, it *was* a mistake," Seb says. Another shard of glass embeds itself in my heart, adding to the many he's already stuck there. "But I lied to you about who I was to *protect* you, Charlie. You know what I was involved with! I should never have put you in danger by seeking out a relationship with you at all. And then you tried to kill me!"

"That's nothing to what I'm going to do to *you* in a minute!" barks Steve, starting his chainsaw. "She's *my* woman now. And if I ever see you less than two metres from her, you'll effin' know about it!" He slices a line in the turf with the saw – him and me on one side, Seb on the other – spraying us all with mud and grass.

"You're both nutters!" Seb rubs his neck as he takes a few steps back from the whining chainsaw. "You deserve each other!"

He stalks off towards the broken fence and starts to poke it. Bertie runs after him. I want to call my dog back, but I think he's safer with Seb right now and I dare not even look in their direction.

"Why didn't you tell me he was your ex?" Steve growls.

"It didn't seem relevant."

"Not *relevant*? I've a right to know who you've been sleeping with!"

Whoa! I don't think so!

But he hasn't cut the motor on the chainsaw, so I give in

before I crap myself. “Sorry … I just didn’t think.”

“Look at me!”

“I’m a bit scared to be honest, Steve.” I don’t take my eyes off the ground.

He cuts the motor.

“Sorry, Princess. I just didn’t like the idea of you hanging around your ex,” he says gruffly.

“He’s not really my *ex*, Steve. We slept together a few times. Then I discovered he was lying to me, sleeping with Lady Tillingford and nicking the Tillingfords’ art, so I set fire to his camper van.”

Steve laughs out loud.

“What, like actually set it alight? With him inside?”

“Yes. It was a write-off.”

“Attagirl!” he says with a big grin and puts his arm around me.

“There’s not a snowball’s chance in hell of us ever getting back together,” I say with confidence.

Suddenly, I spot Guy stalking across the lawn in his Barbour and Hunter wellies; Bertie careering along behind him. “What’s going on?” He ignores the dog and confronts me.

“A work schedule clash. Seb’s got to fix the fence but Steve’s here to do the cedar, right over where the fence has broken.”

“For goodness’ sake!” Guy runs his hand through his hair in exasperation, “What other work can the tree surgeons do today? Or why can’t you all just fix the fence together before the cherry picker gets here? Why am I even getting involved in this?”

“We didn’t ask you to, Guy. We can sort it out ourselves! Steve, how long is the cedar likely to take?”

"Probably all day. It's massive."

"Bugger!" says Guy. "Seb," he says, calling him over, "is there anything temporary we can do, just to secure the fence, if all of us work together?"

"S'pose. But if we'd just talked about it, or had a proper schedule, we wouldn't be in this mess, Bro," says Seb, his hands in his pockets.

"I know, but that's not helping right now, is it?" Guy answers, exasperated. "Come on, Team. Let's get this done."

Steve mumbles something about it not being his job; but he glances at Guy with the look of a kid when the headmaster's about.

"We could ask Tris, Herne and Wolf to help," I suggest. Despite the weather, our friends down by the Great Oak still don't seem to have found another place to go.

"I'm not working with effin' crusties! There's enough stolen equipment at car boot sales without adding my stuff."

To give him credit, despite his misgivings, Steve does then lend us a hand. Between us, we manage to cobble together something that should hold for the next week or so until Seb can get on to it properly.

Just as we're finishing, Steve gets a call from Cherry Aid, the cherry-picker guys, saying they're at the gate. He scoots over to his crew cab to drive down and let them in. I could tell, from the way Steve was eyeing me up, that he wanted me to come with him so he could get me away from Seb. But I didn't offer, and he couldn't make a fuss about it in front of Guy.

"It's a shame about this cedar," says Guy, kicking the trunk once Steve's gone. "What are we doing with the timber?"

"We can try to save as much of it as we can," I suggest. "How long's it been dead do you think?"

"Four or five years at least," Guy replies.

"Shouldn't need too much seasoning then," says Seb, patting the trunk "It must've been awesome when it was alive," he says staring up into the skeletal branches.

"There's nothing like a cedar," I agree, thrusting my hands deep into my pockets and gazing up, but Seb ignores me.

"What do you think we could make out of it?" asks Guy.

"I can do rough-hewn benches with a …" he hesitates, "a chainsaw. Or we could take it to a sawmill and have them make planks out of it – if you've got the budget, that is."

Guy looks dubious.

"How does he know all this stuff?" I ask Guy, since there's clearly no point addressing Seb directly anymore.

"It's what I do. I'm a cabinet maker by training," Seb mumbles, without looking at me, rubbing his beard.

"So, you weren't totally lying when you said you were a chippy?"

"No," he says, kneeling down to ruffle Bertie's ears.

"Although the Twerton bit?"

"I wasn't lying about that either. I kind of I grew up in that part of Bath."

"You *kind of* grew up?"

He rolls his eyes at me. "Har har. I mean, my parents' house was technically in Twerton, but it's probably not what you'd expect. Look, is it okay if I borrow Milan to help with the hoarding outside the stables today? It's not really a one-man job. The builders are starting tomorrow. I said I'd have everything ready for them, and I've wasted enough time on this fence."

"I can't spare him!" I insist. "He's draining the ornamental pond behind the shrubbery today because the stonemasons are coming tomorrow."

"Damn. I should've spoken to you about it before."

"Yeah, really, that would have helped." I zip up my jacket as a gust of cold wind finds its way down my neck.

"Can *you* help?" We both turn to Guy.

"No. I've got an urgent meeting with the estate manager. We're too late to get the winter wheat into two fields and we're going to have to make another plan. You'll *have* to work together."

"No way!" I say at the same time Seb says, "We can't do that."

"You two will just have to iron out your differences and learn to cooperate." Guy takes off his glasses and runs a hand across his face, his frustration plain.

I look at Seb and I can tell he's thinking the same as me. We can't tell Guy what just happened before he got here: he'll send Steve packing instantly if he hears about it; and we do need to get the cedar done.

"We don't have enough staff!" I moan.

"I am aware there's a lot to do but frankly this isn't about staffing: it's about structure and communication. I'm advertising for a COO but I need a Facilities Manager to oversee and coordinate all maintenance operations. I'm going to advertise this week. You're both welcome to apply for the Facilities Manager job; although, of course, only one of you can get it, if I don't find someone better."

He stalks off, dragging his hands through his hair.

"This is all your fault!" I shout at Sebastian.

"Huh?" He takes several steps away from me as Steve's black crew cab comes back into view, followed closely by the bright red cherry picker.

"You should've shut up about us not being coordinated. Now one of us is going to end up being the other's boss!"

Chapter Twenty-six

"I'm sorry, Charlie – you just have to face up to it." Alice lolls on my sofa. She's just issued an edict from Guy that the entire estate is a zero-tolerance zone for drugs and annoyingly points out that this isn't news: it's actually in my contract.

As if I'd bothered to read it.

"After what happened in the summer, when Hatty and her friends nearly ate some of Maxine's eddies, Guy declared Tillingford Hall a drug-free zone. He should have made that clearer to you when you started. He's pretty cross now he's found out about you smoking dope in the cottage."

"Well, who told him? You? Sahara?" I wrap my arms tighter around my knees.

"He kind of worked it out for himself. Sahara and I actually tried to cover up for you, Charlie. Herbert was allowed to because he was a Rastafarian. Giles's father knew that when he took him on in the seventies; and Herbert always confined his smoking to the potting shed or the cottage."

"So that's why they call it a potting shed," I quip.

But she doesn't laugh.

Alice used to be sweet and funny. I don't know what's got into her recently. "I hardly ever smoke weed in here. You just happened to catch me that one time."

"And when I was with you in Bath. And, apparently, you've been doing it outside the pub."

"That's not part of the estate! How do you know about that anyway?"

"Things don't go unnoticed in Tillingham." Alice rubs her back and rearranges the cushions.

"What is this? Some kind of witch-hunt?"

"No, Charlie. But why do you think people aren't mad keen on you smoking weed?"

"Stop patronising me!" I clench my fists as I walk up and down.

"I'm trying to do the opposite. That's why I'm asking *you* to explain it to *me*."

I roll my eyes. "It's illegal-ish. It makes you paranoid and can lead to psychosis. It makes Guy look bad if the employees are found lurking round the pub doing weed. You're worried about your baby. Everyone thinks Sahara's going to start heroin again if she catches so much as a whiff of dope. I get it. But I'm not harming anyone. I sometimes think you're all out to get me!"

"Hmm. What was that about paranoia?"

"You're so … bourgeois, Alice! And frankly, you've become pretty snooty and patronising since you became Lady of the Manor!"

"I'm sorry you think I've become snooty. But if being bourgeois means trying to be healthy, responsible and follow the law, then, yes, I am bourgeois – and proud of it. I'm just wondering if you're planning on growing up any time soon?"

"Piss off, Alice!"

I turn my back on her.

There's a long silence.

"Charlie." Her tone is softer than I know I deserve. "I'm *trying* to help you. I stuck my neck out to get you the job here. I could see how unhappy you were in Bath. I thought this would be a really good opportunity for you to get a fresh start and a step up the career ladder; and look how you're repaying me. Maybe it wasn't the Physick Garden that was the problem."

Before I can express my outrage, there's a knock on the door.

I walk across and open it.

I'm confronted with six foot four of man-mountain in my doorway, wearing a baggy old fleece and a bobble hat.

"Oh. It's you."

I'm not surprised he hasn't taken Steve's threat too seriously: he's dealt with far more dangerous people in the past; and stuff like that just doesn't seem to bother him.

"Guy wants you both up at the house."

Is it my imagination or is Seb looking smug?

He's so damn gorgeous when he smiles. I hate him.

I sigh and grab my warm Silver Tree Surgeons jacket while Alice unwinds herself and stretches like a cat. Seb helps her up, gets her silly pink coat and she smiles gratefully up at him. When he helps her on with it, I notice his hand brushes her neck and I shudder as the hairs stand up on the back of mine.

Suddenly, my stomach twists with longing for him and I can almost feel the way our bodies used to intertwine when we were lovers, the heat of him. I'm so angry with myself for not being able to forget that, so angry with him for being … for being *Sebastian*.

He's brought a torch, but he gently reminds me to take mine for the way back. Why does he care whether I break my stupid neck stumbling over a tree root? I wordlessly snatch mine off the hook by the door and call Bertie to join us.

"So, what's this all about?" I grumble as we head towards the house, trudging through the piles of soggy leaves Milan should have cleared from the stable yard.

"Work," Seb answers,

"Does the man never let up?" I ask with a curse.

I can sense Alice tense. I must remember my boss is her future husband and be more careful what I say about Guy in front of her. I'm not sure this whole "family enterprise" was such a good idea. It feels like living with my parents again. People always on my case, people … *caring* … but I push *that* thought down. If I wasn't grumpy before, I definitely am now. Luckily for Bertie, he's a couple of feet away from me or he might find my boot in contact with his stupid, doggy butt.

"Please take a seat," says Guy imperiously as we enter his office. Between the ornate, fitted dark-wood bookcases, a huge portrait of some Tillingford ancestor stares down at us.

Bertie snuffles around, looking puzzled, as though he's expecting to find Bailey in the room; then flops down on the old dog bed that's still by the marble fireplace.

"Phew, Bertie!" Guy wafts his hand in front of his nose as Bertie gets comfortable with a little toot.

I can't help laughing, but Alice doesn't look too pleased as she sits down on the sofa and puts her feet up. I take one of the carver chairs with sagging velvet cushions opposite Guy, who's sitting behind his enormous banker's desk; Seb takes the other. We simultaneously push back our chairs to draw Alice into the circle.

"I'll cut to the chase," says Guy. "The Christmas concert is four weeks today and the gala ball is now in just over six months' time, and we don't have time to pussyfoot around. I have heard what you've had to say about staffing, Charlie. I know we need more manpower, so I've arranged for a loan to cover salaries for the next few months, hoping Amy can make up the budget shortfall somehow. Tris, Herne and Wolf have agreed to keep helping us, while they're still here, to pay for their keep. And I've found two new guys who can start on a trial basis next week. Pawel is a friend of Milan's from the Czech Republic, who's currently doing casual work on a building site in London and is happy to join us. Jayden is one of my mentees from the scheme I'm involved with to help lads in Southwark who are at risk of getting into gangs. He finished a carpentry course at sixth-form college last summer. He's keen to start over somewhere new, a long way from the drugs scene." He looks pointedly at me.

"So, we're now a bit tighter for accommodation. Pawel can move in with Milan in the keeper's cottage and either Jayden can move in with you, Charlie, or he can have the cottage and you can have the room next to Hatty's on the top floor here. Either way, obviously, no overnight guests."

What? They're even trying to stop me sleeping with my boyfriend now. Maybe I should just move into Steve's, where I can be treated like an adult. But then I remember how Steve was with me the weekend we took the kids to Portsmouth, and the incident with Seb and the chainsaw yesterday, and decide that wouldn't be a good idea.

"As I said at our training day, I need to hire a Facilities

Manager to oversee the practical work with the buildings and grounds. But I don't have three months to advertise, interview, select and wait for someone to hand in their notice to come here. So I've decided to recruit internally. As of tomorrow, Sebastian will be taking the role."

So the guy that stole precious art from Tillingford Hall is now going to be its Facilities Manager? Great. That makes a whole bunch of sense … not.

"So, Charlie, how does that sound?"

How does that sound? Absolutely terrible!

I know that a grown-up would congratulate Seb and say they were looking forward to working with him. But as Alice pointed out so nicely just now, I'm not a grown-up, so I'm going to say exactly what I think.

"I'll admit I'm gobsmacked, Guy." I take a deep breath because I'm starting to feel a bit wobbly. "I'm actually astonished that you would put the person responsible for stealing half your collections in charge of them! Are you out of your mind?"

Guy recoils. "Sebastian has all the necessary skills and expertise for this role. And, if trusting my best friend is being 'out of my mind' then, yes, that's what I am. What I'm more concerned about is having dangerous people on site." I shrink into my chair, knowing what's coming. "I'm told Steve Silver threatened Seb with a chainsaw."

"He was just being protective," I reply, pulling at a loose thread on the cushion.

"Possessive more like," says Sebastian. "His exact words were 'She's *my* woman now. And if I ever see you less than two metres from her, you'll know about it.' And then he drew a line in the ground with his chainsaw – with the motor running."

Alice gasps and turns to me. "Charlie, are you really sure you want to be with someone like that?"

"Well, what if I do? Maybe I like it that he's strong and passionate."

"Unhinged, more like," says Sebastian, rubbing his neck.

"I feel like you're all ganging up on me!"

I'm close to tears.

"See? Paranoia," mutters Seb.

Guy stands up and crosses over to the fireplace, propping himself up against it like they do in those period dramas. It certainly makes him look imposing. "We're not ganging up, Charlie. We're rallying round you. You've only been here for a few weeks, but I've lived in this community my whole life. I can honestly tell you that Steve, while he's a great tree surgeon, is not good news in the domestic department. Ask Nicola. Funny how often she *bumped into cupboards*."

I recall that throat-slitting gesture.

And then it hits me. Steve was only being charming to draw me in.

I've literally got into bed with a nutjob.

And I've acted like a spoiled teenager and alienated anyone who's tried to help me.

I've really messed things up again, haven't I?

Bertie's sitting on my feet and I bend over to rub his silky ears so the others can't see that I've started to cry.

"I know it's a lot to take in, Charlie," says Guy, more kindly than I deserve. "I know we've been working Saturdays to get things done, but I think you should take tomorrow off to mull things over. Just turn off your phone and have a complete rest."

"Okay," I mutter into Bertie's ear, trying to stop the tears coming.

"Shall I walk you back to the cottage?" he asks.

Why are they being so nice to me?

"I'm fine." I feel humiliated. I know I've massively overreacted; but instead of giving me the sack, he's treating me like a favourite child who's exhausted herself with a tantrum. "I've got Bertie and a torch."

I flick the tiniest glance of gratitude at Seb for reminding me to bring one; but he's leaning forward, elbow on one knee, propping up his head in one hand while he rubs the back of his neck with the other.

Alice grabs a Post-it note off Guy's desk, scribbles something on it and says, "Let me at least come to the door with you."

I get up from the carver chair and call Bertie to follow me.

"Take care, Charlie," says Guy as I leave.

Seb's stance hasn't changed and he doesn't look up.

When Alice and I reach the back door she says, "You need to spend tomorrow lying on the sofa, under your duvet, binge-watching Jane Austen movies. Here's our Amazon Prime and Disney+ logins. I hope you can work this out, Charlie – we really want you to stay." She gives me a hug and hands me the Post-it note.

I really want to stay too.

Apart from the fact that this is the most interesting job I've ever had and could be a real game-changer for my career, I have nowhere else to go. And despite the way I'm behaving, I do really like these people.

Chapter Twenty-seven

When I get back to the cottage, I feed Bertie, turn up the heating and send Steve a carefully worded text to put him off bothering me. I notice a missed call from my mother. I'm not sure whether it's a good idea to get back to her now, when I'm feeling so overwrought. If I don't, though, she'll only pester me to tomorrow; so I decide to get it over and done with. I curl up on the sofa, with a blanket round me, practising my snuggling techniques for my unexpected day off tomorrow, and get out my phone.

"Jane's phone."

"Oh, hello, Dad. How come Mum's not there?" I put him on speakerphone so I can rearrange the blanket.

"She's making a crumble, and her hands are covered in flour," he explains. "Don't you want to talk to your old dad?"

"Of course I do, Dad! It's just that I usually speak to Mum. I guess you've always got better things to do."

"Not *better*, Poppet. What could be better than speaking to my only daughter?"

I feel a tear prick my eye and suddenly I'm sniffing.

"What's the matter, Tottie? Things not okay up in Hampshire?"

"No!" I wail and suddenly I'm full-on snivelling, reaching across for the box of tissues on the coffee table.

"Tell Daddy."

"I've totally messed things up, Dad!"

"Have they sacked you?"

"No – not quite. It's … really complicated." I just don't know where to start. Or how much to reveal. As little as possible probably, but I have to say *something* now.

"There's this guy I liked, but we broke up quite spectacularly in the summer. Now it turns out he's working here, and we just can't get along because of what happened before. But he's just been made my boss, which is really annoying. And then I started seeing this *other* guy recently but he's … Dad, I'm scared! It turns out he's a dangerous nutjob. Used to hurt his wife and stuff. People tried to warn me about him, but I didn't want to hear – he was so charming, I thought he might be good for me. But now he's threatened the first guy."

"Oh dear, what a pickle you've got yourself into," he says, laughing.

"Dad! It's not funny – Guy Two threatened Guy One with a chainsaw!"

"The dangerous nutjob bit isn't funny at all," he agrees gravely. "Do you need to involve the police?"

"I hope not." I gather the blanket more tightly round me.

"Well then, let the nutjob down gently and hopefully he'll just go away. But this other man, Guy One, the one you work with – you said you really liked him. Do you mean you were in love with him?"

I take a deep breath.

"I might have been. But I'm so angry with him I hate him now. He did something really awful."

"Are you sure you really hate *him*? Maybe you hate *what*

he did. Maybe you're just angry and struggling to forgive him. But remember, Poppet, not forgiving someone is like drinking poison and expecting *them* to die."

"What the hell does that mean, Dad?"

I feel so confused.

"When someone hurts you, the hurt is yours – it's *inside you.* The only person who can control that, can *feel* it, is you. The person who hurt you could be literally oblivious to what they've done, and you'd be still eating yourself up. People think that by not forgiving someone, they are punishing that person for what they did; but the only person it hurts is them."

"But I can't forgive him I feel so angry."

"Is your anger like a rock you're clinging to – something certain and safe you understand?"

"Yes!"

"If you're clinging to that rock, you're never going to move on, are you? You're just hanging on feeling angry and stuck; being smashed up by the waves crashing over you, while you could be swimming free, letting the water carry you instead."

"I guess. But how? How do you forgive someone?"

"Just let it be. Accept that something happened and just let it go."

"Just like that?"

"Just like that: every day, again and again. Do you remember Matthew eighteen, verse twenty-two, Tottie? The one when Peter asks Jesus how many times he should forgive someone who wronged him, and Jesus says, 'Seventy times seven'? Some hurts never really go away; but so long as you hold on to them, they have the power to keep hurting you, like holding a knife to your chest. But let them go and they can't do you any harm."

"Wow. I guess I could think about that."

"Sermon over! Shall I get your mother?"

"No, Dad, don't worry. I'm sure she'll let me know what she wanted, but can you ask her to text me rather than calling? I'm having a duvet day tomorrow."

"Sounds like a good idea, Poppet."

"Thanks, Dad."

I turn my phone off and go up to run a bath. I lie brooding until my tears mingle with the bath water, and I'm spent, and the water goes cold. I start to drift off, too lazy to get out; I wonder if I could get hypothermia that way. When I start shivering, I realise I should just get into bed and let Bertie come under the covers with me.

I fall into a fitful sleep, punctuated by strange dreams. I'm teaching at a school, when a maniac bursts in and starts shooting the kids. The children's bodies are lined up in the school playground. Black birds fly down and start to peck out their eyes, until a lumberjack starts up a chainsaw and they all fly off.

I wake up, startled and horrified; but the chainsaw noise doesn't stop.

Bertie starts to nuzzle me and whine for his breakfast.

Steve must be here, I think, suddenly alert, my heart pounding. Now he's done the cedar, his work at Tillingford Hall is finished; so why is he working here?

I throw on some clothes, my heart pounding, and go downstairs.

I almost scream as I hear a strange thump outside the front door. But I'm too scared. Nothing comes out of my mouth as

I whip round to look through the frosted glass. Bertie starts barking but I can't see anyone there.

I grab the biggest knife from the rack, my heart in my mouth, and open the door.

There's no one there.

But when I look around, I spot, carefully placed to one side of the door, a three-foot high sculpture of a raven, wings outstretched. Even though it's been crudely done with a chainsaw, not a chisel, it somehow manages to convey the feeling of flight and the sleek elegance of the bird.

I take a deep breath and relax my grip. Only Sebastian could make something like this, I think, remembering the carved benches and the little gonks in the walled garden.

Steve would use his chainsaw only for cutting down trees – and threatening people. I'm sure if he had wanted to bring me a present, he'd have knocked and made a big fuss about giving it to me. It would have been something expensive and flashy, like a designer watch. And he'd definitely have expected sex afterwards.

I put away the knife and feed Bertie before he starts gnawing my ankle. Then I go out to look at the sculpture again. How did Seb know which bits to cut away to make that complex shape? How did he manage to do something so intricate with a chainsaw?

I'm crying now.

Why did he make this for me when I'm trying my best to hate him, when I'm being so obnoxious towards him? I cringe as I remember I even told him he *disgusted* me.

And why a raven?

Chapter Twenty-eight

I'm shivering in my dressing gown, staring at the thing, when Sahara appears on the garden path, startling me.

She stops for a moment and admires the sculpture too.

"He thinks it's your spirit animal."

"Why? I think a fat old toad would be more appropriate. Or a prickly hedgehog," I say with a sniff as I remember the picture he drew when we had the ColoRING day.

"No, a raven is good for you, Charlie. Ravens are intelligent and resourceful."

"They live off carrion and peck each other's eyes out. The collective noun is an unkindness of ravens," I reply sadly.

"Yes, some people use that term for a flock of them. But, in folklore, they're also associated with magic and the spirit of the universe. They can be spirits of transformation and protectors on unknown paths," she adds.

"Now you're really starting to sound like Ama!"

She laughs gently. "They're loyal and playful too."

"Playful?"

Sahara puts her skinny arms round me and takes me back into the cottage. "Come on, Charlie. You'll catch your death. I came to see you were okay."

"I will be."

She makes me sit on the sofa, with a blanket around me, lights the wood burner and starts to make some breakfast.

"But why did he make it?" I ask once we're sitting at the kitchen table with our vegan porridge, made with oat milk, sprinkled with raisins and munchy seeds.

"It's a peace offering. He really cares about you, Charlie – more than you want to realise. But you're doing your utmost to push him away. I know you're finding it hard to forgive him. And, honestly, I can totally see why you think what he did was beyond forgivable. But can't you at least just try to be a bit less antagonistic? He's more than aware of his own faults; he doesn't need everyone else to point them out to him."

I add some more oat milk to my porridge. "Isn't that true of all of us?"

"Perhaps. But some people are more self-aware than others. And he's definitely one of those."

"Why are you being so nice to me, Sahara?"

She hands me some agave syrup. I drizzle it slowly on the porridge.

"Because … despite everything you're doing to keep us all at arm's length, I like you. We're all worried about you and … it's the right thing to do," she answers, clearly bewildered at my question. "Seb told me about his promotion."

"It was quite a humdinger. I suppose you're really pleased for him."

I put the syrup bottle down really carefully, resisting the urge to slam it on the table.

"No. I don't think either of you should have that job. Guy's trying to do too much too quickly, like he always does. I think that level of responsibility will break Seb if he has to do it for too long, especially if he faces a lot of conflict." She rubs the back of her neck. "*You're* more capable of doing that job, but not until you've sorted your head out and learned to be more of a team player. And even then, I don't think your heart would be in it – the gardens are your passion, not planning and paperwork," she adds. She takes a mouthful of porridge.

"To be honest, Sahara, I'm ready to quit. I just feel like it's all getting a bit much."

"I can understand that."

"But it's not really Seb being my boss which upsets me. I mean, I'll still be in charge of the grounds, I suppose. Seb's just got to try and coordinate the workers a bit better, so that'll be good for everyone. No, what really upset me was this nannying that's going on – no drugs, no sex and Alice basically telling me to grow up."

"That must've been hard to hear." Sahara adds some syrup to her porridge.

"Too right it was!" I dig my spoon in again.

"How did it make you feel?"

I pause as I reach into myself for the true answer. "Hurt and inadequate."

"Why?"

Again, there's something there, deep inside of me. Some truth that I'm not admitting to myself. "Because I agree with her and that feels really uncomfortable. I *do* need to grow up. I *want* to be a grown-up, but I just don't know how."

"Sometimes, when we haven't seen an example of maturity that we want to model ourselves on, it's hard to find a path to follow."

Sahara gazes at her spoon while I ponder this for a moment.

"Yeah, maybe that makes sense. I don't want to be a headmistress or a bishop like my mum and dad, or like Alice or Guy – all kind of workaholic and ambitious and organised. But I do want to have a home of my own, a dog." I ruffle Bertie's ears. "A partner, maybe? Kids?"

"Just maybe?"

"I might not be able to get pregnant: I drink and smoke tobacco and dope, and I'm nearly forty. And I still have to meet the right person. I thought Steve might have been – he's well off, foxy, practical – until I realised that there's no way he's ever going to want to have more kids. He told me about Rogue and Tyler straight away; but I hadn't realised that waitress who works in the pub, Darcy, is also his, until she called him 'Dad' the other day. And then there's his scary streak. He was such a gentleman when I first met him, but he is becoming a bit … controlling. And then, this thing with Seb yesterday was totally OTT. I *think* he was just joshing, like when he turned up at the Hallowe'en party with the chainsaw."

"But Nicola wasn't joshing when she got the restraining order on him."

"What?" I gasp, staring at her, my spoon frozen in mid-air.

"We should have told you earlier," Sahara admits. "But … no, there are no buts. We should have warned you immediately."

"People *have* been *trying* to warn me about him. But no one said anything directly, and I heard what I wanted to hear. I thought you were all just being snobs."

"No! Everyone in the village knows he's violent. Nicola would turn up to work at the vet's surgery with a black eye, a bruised arm and say she'd fallen, but eventually she took her courage in her hands and told him where to go. And to be fair, he did back off and promise to reform and she had no further trouble. That's why he was allowed to have the kids to stay again. And I guess everyone wanted to believe he could reform; that he deserved another chance. But – as you put it – there's this scary streak."

"Oh shit! What am I going to do?" I ask, fiddling with the label on the syrup bottle.

"Do you love Steve?"

"I thought he would be good husband material."

"Do you love him?"

"He's very good in bed."

"Charlie. Answer the question."

"No."

"Then you should tell him."

She looks hard at me with those amber eyes, flecked with green, that are so like her brother's.

"I'm scared to," I admit.

"Then let him down gradually … play hard to get, be distant, tell him you've got a headache. See if you can make it fizzle out."

"I can try. But I don't think Steve's the fizzling out kind." I draw my knees up on to the chair, hugging them to my chest. Suddenly, I get three texts in a row, my phone buzzing madly on the wooden table; and I can see they're all from him.

"Whatever happens, Charlie, you're family now. And we will look after you – if you'll let us."

I bite my lip to stop myself crying and nod.

She gets up and goes over to her bag, which she dumped

by the door when she came in, and pulls out a plastic box. "Mrs Powell's sent you these." The box is full of home-made choc-chip cookies. "They're vegan – she looked up a recipe specially for you!"

"Aw, that's so nice."

I start to sniff.

Even Mrs P wants to look after me.

"Now, Sweetie, why don't you wrap yourself up again, have a cookie and get *Pride and Prejudice* up on the TV?"

"I don't know if I want to watch something romantic."

"Yes, you do – the moody version with Keira Knightley! You need some catharsis and some true love and some lovely Regency costumes to inspire you for the gala ball next summer. Now, do you want tea or oat milk with your cookies?"

"You don't have to do that."

"But I am. And I'm going to wash up too, while you snuggle down!" She stops me protesting with a wave of her hand. "I insist!"

"Tea please, then, Sahara."

"I'll leave the bag in, shall I?" She flips the kettle back on.

"Thanks. I like it strong."

"I guessed as much." She laughs as she pulls the tea bags back out of the cupboard.

"One of us will come down at lunchtime, just to see how you're doing. Today is a complete day off for you. There's a box of tissues there for the bit when she turns Mr Darcy down. I'll take Bertie for his walk if you like."

"Thank you." I smile up at Sahara.

"Don't mention it, Charlie. I really hope you can get some rest today."

She lets me help her clear the table but insists on doing the washing-up while I go and use the bathroom. By the time I get down, she's already taken Bertie out and put the cookies on a plate on the coffee table.

When I first heard Sahara Seaton-Smyth was Sebastian's sister, I was sure I wouldn't like her; but now I've got to know her, I think she's lovely.

And, apart from being as thin as a rake, she looks so much like her brother: her smile, the colour of her eyes, the way she touches her neck when she's stressed …

I feel so sad for her. She's so beautiful, but what good has it done her? With her anorexia, addictions and ravaged wrists, waiting helplessly for a player like James Irving-McAuley to come back to her, she's almost like a character in a Greek tragedy. And yet she still finds space in her heart for idiots like me.

I can think of worse people to have as a sister.

Chapter Twenty-nine

I spend most of the film crying my eyes out. Not for Elizabeth and Mr Darcy or Jane and Mr Bingley but just crying: crying about everything. Crying about how I've cocked things up. Crying that Sebastian is so messed up, and so annoying, but so gorgeous. Crying that Steve isn't what I was looking for and turns out to be a nutjob. Crying that I didn't get a promotion that I didn't even know was there and didn't even want. Crying because I'm so tired and my body feels like a bloated sausage.

And then I must have fallen asleep because I wake up to hear someone knocking on the door. I jump up and grab all the snotty tissues off the floor so I can put them in the bin before I stumble over to answer.

When I eventually get to the door, there's Sahara again.

"Hey Charlie. Were you asleep? Sorry to wake you. I just thought I'd come and make you some lunch."

She's brandishing a bag from A Little Treat that looks like it's crammed with yummy things. She pulls out a box of Christmas chocolates and hands it to me. It's a vegan one, with lots of happy cows and calves wearing Santa hats and, on the back, it says, "Thank you for choosing vegan, signed Mama Cow."

"I found the suppliers myself," she says, proudly.

"Thank you, that's so sweet of you. I was going to make pumpkin soup."

I point to a small knobbly fellow on the countertop who

missed being made into a Hallowe'en lantern and has been sitting there ever since.

"Wonderful. I like mine spicy. Do you?"

"Yes, a bit of ginger and chilli would pep me up!" I shuffle over to my well-stocked spice rack and pull out a few jars.

"Listen, you can say no, but I wondered if we could invite Seb to eat with us?"

Although he's the last person or, maybe, the second-to-last person I want to see right now. I don't want to appear petulant by saying "no", especially as he's now my boss. "Okay. He grew the pumpkin, after all. He may as well eat it."

She opens the window. "You can come in!" she calls.

"I didn't know he was literally just out there! Don't let him in – I look shit!"

"Never to me, Charlie," he says through the window, and my insides turn to mush. Oh my God, *why*? Why does he have to do this to me? And is that an entirely appropriate comment from my boss? I can't believe this pain in the arse is actually my manager now.

Sahara lets him in anyway.

I rush up to the bathroom to wash my face and brush my hair; and put on a jumper and some jeans. Seb's seen me in a lot less but there's a difference between looking alluring in the altogether when you're somebody's lover and looking scuzzy in PJs when you're someone's direct report.

When I come down, Sahara's frying onions and spices and is just adding the pumpkin. It smells mouthwatering.

"Come and sit down, Charlie. "We've just made a pot of verbena tea, if you'd like some."

"Yes, please, that would be nice. Are you sure I can't cook?"

"Nope. I'm cooking. You two have some talking to do."

Seb and I look at each other awkwardly for a moment.

"Seb," I say, just as he clears his throat to speak.

He pulls at his beard. "You go first."

"No, you."

"Charlie, I'm sorry about the way Guy's decided to do things. I didn't ask to be your boss. I know you don't want me to tell you what to do. But it's not going to be like that. He just wants someone to coordinate our projects so we can make sure whatever we're working on each day doesn't clash. If we need to hire equipment, we can book it on the same day to save costs and that kind of thing; so I want us to sit down and work it out together. But to do that, I need you to be okay with talking to me."

I take a deep breath.

"I'm sorry I've been a pain. I'm okay with talking to you. More than okay … I …"

He gently touches my hand for a second and the hairs on my neck stand up. I dare not look in his eyes: there's no denying the spark between us, however unwanted, is still there.

"I really liked the sculpture, the raven. It's beautiful."

The fact that it's true doesn't stop it being hard to say.

"I'm not very good at expressing myself sometimes," he says awkwardly. "It's a peace offering, Charlie."

"I know. And I accept it."

He looks relieved and he pours some verbena tea into our mugs. "This has been the worst … well, probably, the second worst year of my life and I've completely messed everything up

– I mean *everything*. I know that. And I totally understand why you tried to kill me." He looks down at the table while rubbing the back of his neck.

"I didn't *try* to kill you! When I set fire to Neville, I was just cross! Well, livid, actually." I plonk my mug down. "It was more like a prank than attempted murder."

"I *could've* died, though, Charlie." He stares into the mug he's cradling.

"But you didn't," I insist.

Seb looks steadily at me and there's a pointed cough from over by the cooker, where Sahara's beavering away.

"But, yes, I admit, you *could* have died and I'm sorry. I know it's my fault you lost everything. You could've had me charged with arson but you didn't; so thank you for that too."

"I know I deserved your anger, Charlie, but that van was … Well, it was precious to me. Neville wasn't just a van, he was my home and, after what you did, he was a complete write-off. And he wasn't insured, which I know is my fault. But still … he was my only asset. And I'm really skint, so I haven't been able to replace most of my stuff. Why do you think I've been wearing clothes from the charity shop? Luckily, you took that Thomas Lawrence portrait with you when you went, otherwise that would've been lost too."

"Like all the other ones you stole," I point out. I take a swig of tea.

"I didn't steal them. Maxine removed them from her husband's collection."

Sahara coughs again.

"Look, Charlie. I've done some pretty terrible things, and I know I shouldn't keep making excuses for my poor behaviour. I'm trying to own up to my own responsibilities in all of this. It's going to take a lifetime to make it up to Guy, so the least I can do is make *this* work – to help him get Tillingford Hall open; and to prove to him that I am a competent human being and that he's right to trust me."

"So, this is all about you redeeming yourself in Guy's eyes?" I say, twisting the mug round in my hands.

"No! I'm trying to apologise to everyone and trying to pull myself together – for me, for Sahara … for you," he adds shyly. "I'm trying to ask you to please try and work with me. Why do you have to be so … so *prickly* all the time?"

"Because that's just how I am!"

But in my head, I'm wondering if I'm defensive because I feel like whatever I do in life never seems to be quite good enough: being a disappointing girl to a mother who only liked boys; not being able to actually sing in the choir or have a chance of winning at any school sport; missing out on the changing-room camaraderie. All of it has definitely coloured the way I see myself. It's hard to fit in when you're used to being an outsider.

"Can't you just chill and accept that, despite *everything* you've done to put me off, maybe I really like you?" he says.

I scowl at him: this is too much information right now.

"The grumpier you get, the more I can't take my eyes off you, Ravengirl."

"That's so inappropriate," I mutter as I look at some lint on my jumper.

I can't let on that my heart rate has doubled and my stomach is in knots. He can't take his eyes off me. Even when I'm grumpy, which is a lot. And … *Ravengirl*?

"Sorry to break the mood, here," says Sahara, feebly attempting not to smile. "But do you have a blender, Charlie?"

"In the middle drawer."

I still can't look at Seb. I can't believe he'd say something like that – admit he's still attracted to me and give me a nickname – in front of his sister, especially not now he's my manager.

But I just can't help the corner of my mouth turning up.

Ravengirl?

It just won't go away, will it? This thing we have.

And then Sahara's making too much noise with the blender for us to carry on the conversation, so I go and get glasses, bowls, spoons and side plates for the garlic bread she's got baking in the oven; and we lay them on the table. Seb's hand brushes mine as he puts down a spoon just where I'm laying a plate: the static prickles right up my arm.

Sahara doles out the soup in silence. It's too hot to eat, so we're stirring it and blowing on it.

"You grew this pumpkin," I say eventually, to fill the void.

He looks up at me.

"I was very impressed with what you did in the walled garden, Seb. Bowled over, actually. I can't believe you did that all by yourself, but I guess love gives you wings," I can't help adding, unable to put down the knife yet.

"Yes, it does," he stares at me, a confused look on his face.

"Was she impressed?" I ask.

"She?" he replies, puzzled, rubbing the back of his neck.

"Maxine."

He puts his spoon down. "I didn't do it for Maxine."

"Why then?" I gasp, gripping the table.

"For myself. For therapy. And for Guy and Giles and Tillingford Hall."

"Oh."

Suddenly, my north-facing wall's the one with the sun on it.

"Guy is the only person on the planet, apart from Sahara, who's always taken my side; who's always believed in me. He's my best friend, my brother … sometimes, even my dad," he looks sheepish. Sahara nods, knowingly.

Now I get it.

Now I understand why Sahara could never have married Guy and why Alice has to believe her.

"I wanted to do something to thank Guy for the home he's made for me and Sahara; the care and love he's given us for twenty years. I just didn't know I'd run out of time."

"Couldn't you see the contradiction in what you were doing? Trying to restore Guy's garden while you were selling off the family silver and sleeping with Maxine?" I feel nauseous.

"Of course I could! And it was tearing me apart. I told you… she took advantage of me cos I was all messed up and vulnerable. When I was in Cornwall, I realised… her heading off to America? Best thing that's happened to me for a long time. Out of sight, out of mind. I won't lie to you, Charlie – I've got my issues. But I'm taking responsibility for them and working on them. I want to be a grown-up, you know? I want to believe I can hold down an honest job, manage people, be a good mate. Maybe even be a husband and a dad … in the not-too-distant future."

I feel like he's just held a mirror up to me; that we're like two people on the same journey.

"At DRAGS, they talk about steps," he says, "it's all about taking small steps every day, yeah? But you also need a big goal – the reason you want to get better – that's the key. That's my big goal, just being a good dad someday. Giving some kid the life I didn't have."

"I hope so, Dearest Brother. Then I can be an auntie. It's the nearest I'll ever get to being a mum."

Sahara looks sadly into her soup; and we eat in silence for a few moments.

Seb clears his throat. "So, all I'm asking, Charlie, is that we can move on and try and work together."

"Yes, that's fine. I'll try to be more professional and cooperative."

Seb manages a weak smile. Sahara bites her lip and looks away.

And inside I'm kicking myself.

He's obviously talking about more than just our professional relationship.

Prickly.

He's right.

Why am I being so damn prickly?

Chapter Thirty

"See, I told you." Steve surveys the travellers' camp from a distance as we sit on a log, sharing coffee from a Thermos. Bertie is snuffling round in the drifts of leaves at our feet.

I've been trying to put Steve off as much as I can, but I'm not ready to tell him things were over between us just yet. "Let him down gently," Dad and Sahara had both said; and I think they're right.

The coffee is really milky but I dare not mention it, so I just take little sips.

"I said they'd bring in their friends and you'd have trouble shifting them, didn't I?" Steve reminds me.

Annoyingly, he's spot on. Guy said it was fine for a *few* extra people to join for the solstice, so long as they definitely leave by Christmas. But I can see that they're all going to say they've got nowhere else to go. Guy's not hard-hearted enough to turn away homeless people at Christmas, so they're probably going to be here well into the new year. And somehow, every day, another vanload of travellers seems to appear.

Alice is starting to get really worried about security in the house. She didn't mind a handful of our friends camping out in the grounds; but now, all kinds of people we don't even know have joined them. And they could start bringing *their* friends too.

While he doesn't want to evict them so close to Solstice,

Guy's worried enough about it to have installed security cameras at the gate. He'd have loved to have had a gatekeeper living at the lodge once again; but he obviously can't afford that, so CCTV will have to do.

We're also having to build proper composting toilets in the field. Guy's intending to use the area for a glamping site in the summer anyway so he sees the construction as an investment. But it would've been good if we could've done it after the Christmas concert, which is now just four days away.

Guy has decided we're going to build them along the model of the Icelandic ones he and Seb remember from their Gold Duke of Edinburgh's Award expedition. Icelanders call them *snyrtings*. Of course, Seb and Guy went to *Iceland.* They couldn't have just gone to the Lake District, like the kids from my school did, could they? Guy says the *snyrtings* are more pleasant to use – and much cheaper and more environmentally friendly – than a chemical Portaloo.

If only Seb hadn't made that "polite invitation". But I don't really want to discuss any of this with Steve because he'll only keep saying he was right all along, so I change the subject.

"Alice is hating work now her old boss has left. She's met the guy who's going to be her new boss at conferences and stuff before, so she knows she won't get on with him. Guy's been trying to persuade her to leave London, come to live here permanently and put Hatty in the village school. But she's dragging her heels, even though Hatty really isn't happy at her old school any more."

"Must be crazy! Some aristo proposes – you grab him by the bollocks and move in as soon as you can, I say."

"Well, quite. But Alice has principles! And one of those is her hard-earned independence."

Steve's holding the open Thermos over my cup for a top up. I cover it with my hand to show I don't want any more, but he reacts too slowly and a scalding drop falls on to my skin before he tips the Thermos back up.

"What's the point, when The Honourable wants to look after her?" Woman like her, with a kid, can't afford to be too choosy.

"That's why we're good together: I've had more than enough kids, you're not up for it and we can just have fun – my feisty woman and me." He puts his arm round my shoulder and gives me a squeeze.

"Who says I don't want kids?"

"You're joshing me, right? You're too old!"

"I'm only thirty-seven!"

"I thought you was early forties."

Oh my God! Not another one. I understood how I looked "old" to Cobain. But Steve, who I reckon is around fifty, should have a better idea of what a woman of forty looks like, and also know how touchy women can be about turning forty.

"Plenty of women in their forties have babies," I point out.

"Well, not with me you're not! I'm about to be a grandad!"

"What? *Rogue's pregnant*?"

"Don't be stupid. She's only fourteen," he splutters.

"Well, it's not unheard of," I point out.

"Not *my* effin' daughter!" Steve looks like he's about to explode.

"Oh, of course not," I say hastily, trying to appease him. "Darcy, then."

We've never talked about Darcy. Steve's never introduced me to her, which I find a little hurtful, but I'm not going to pretend I don't know he's her father.

"No, not Darcy. My *eldest*!"

"What?"

Who is his eldest?

"Yeah, Paula's kid."

"Who's *Paula*?"

"My ex-wife." He shakes the dregs out of his cup.

"You've got *another* one?" I ask as he screws the cup on to the Thermos.

"Yeah, I told you about her!" He slings the flask into his backpack.

"No, you didn't. You never mentioned her!"

"Course I did. Paula had Katie when we were, like, eighteen or something. And then it went tits up and she moved to Oz. Katie's having a baby boy next week, so I've booked our tickets to go out and see her. We're spending Christmas out there."

I stand up. "Who's 'we'?"

"You're actually kidding me, Charlie! You, me – we're going to Australia for Christmas."

"But I don't want to go to Australia for Christmas!"

"But I've booked it and everything," he growls.

"You should at least have discussed it with me."

"It was meant to be a surprise – sweeping you off your feet and all that. I've spent a bloody grand on your effin' ticket! There's no way you're not coming with me."

"You'll have to cancel it!"

He grabs my wrist.

"You go and pack your effin' suitcase right now."

Bertie starts growling.

"I don't even own a suitcase, Steve. And I don't want to go to Australia. It was very *kind* of you to buy me a ticket …"

His fingers press into my flesh.

"But I have plans, and there's too much to do here. I can't afford to take time off."

"What?" He looks at me unbelievingly.

Bertie's barking frantically. Steve aims a kick at him but doesn't let go of my wrist and misses.

"There's the Christmas concert on Friday. And I always spend Christmas with my family," I insist, my voice raised. My wrist is really starting to hurt now. Nut roast and sprouts with the canon theologian suddenly seem very appealing. "I *wanted* to introduce you to them."

An ugly look is coming over Steve's face and he's not letting go.

"And *you* didn't discuss that with *me*!"

I catch sight of Guy striding across the lawn in our direction.

"I'm trying to *now*!" I scream so Guy will hear.

Steve spots Guy and lets go of my wrist. There's a deep red mark. Bertie's going nuts, teeth bared, growling at Steve but keeping just out of kicking distance.

"What's going on?" Guy demands.

"What's it to *you*?" retorts Steve.

I try to pull my sleeve over my wrist, but it's too late: Guy's seen the mark.

"I heard raised voices. Bertie was upset. I came to check everything's all right, and I can see that it isn't," replies Guy.

"Steve's just leaving."

Steve gives me a filthy look, turns his shoulder to us and stomps off across the rough grass towards his crew cab. Bertie follows him, barking and snapping at him, until I call him off.

"What happened?" asks Guy with a furrowed brow.

"Don't worry about it." I look down and put Bertie's lead on.

Guy takes a deep breath.

"Okay. It *is* none of my business; but I saw the mark on your arm. He hurt you, didn't he?"

I look away. I don't want Guy's sympathy. This is *my* fault and *my* battle. Suddenly, my lip wobbles and a tear rolls down my nose. I take a deep gasping breath in and sniff back the tears. "Bertie, come on!" I yank on his lead.

"I tried to warn you!"

"I *know*! That doesn't make me feel any better, Guy. I'm going home to take some time out."

"Are you going to be okay?"

"I expect so," I retort over my shoulder as I stomp off with Bertie towards my cottage.

As I round the corner of the shrubbery, I hear heavy footsteps running towards me and my heart pounds in my chest as I spin round.

"Oh! Seb! It's you! Thank God. It thought it was …"

"Charlie, sorry. I didn't mean to startle you!" He gently cups my elbows and looks into my eyes. "Tell me to go away if you don't want me here, Charlie, but I heard what happened and I just had to check you were okay." Breathless with concern, his forehead wrinkling, he looks at me as if he could read a report of what's just happened on my face.

"Thanks, Seb. I'm just going home for a bit. I feel a bit shaky, to be honest," I admit as he lets go of my arms.

"Want some company?"

I nod.

Seb is a big guy; he's definitely the man I'd want on my side if there was ever a bit of trouble kicking off. I feel safer knowing that someone will be there to stand up for me if Steve comes back.

Someone I can … *trust.*

We arrive at the cottage. I reach behind my scruffy, oversized Christmas wreath to turn the door handle.

"Don't you lock it?" Seb asks as Bertie pushes past me and noses in his breakfast bowl.

"I don't have anything to steal!"

I unclip my dog's lead and hang it up.

"It's not your *stuff* I'm worried about!" He locks the door behind him and checks the window locks. "You should definitely lock it from now on, especially when you're at home alone."

I take a deep, rasping breath.

"Seb. I'm scared!" I admit, turning to face him.

Chapter Thirty-one

Sebastian looks at me with concern. He hesitates, perhaps deciding whether to give me the hug I so badly need. Instead, he takes my hand and turns it over, his cypress scent teasing me with memories of last summer, before it all went wrong between us.

He oh-so-gently pushes up my sleeve and looks at the red weal on the skin. There's a clear imprint of Steve's fingers on my arm. The mark is starting to turn dark, a deep bruise. Then his eyes meet mine, blazing, but he doesn't say anything.

I go over to the sink to run my arm under cold water. "I should get some arnica," I mutter as I turn on the tap.

"Arnica won't cut it, Charlie: this one's for the police." Seb gets out his phone to take a picture, but I brush it away and turn my wrist over to hide the mark. There's a big dark patch on that side too, where Steve's thumb pressed into the flesh.

"I don't want to get involved with the police," I explain as the water runs over my arm.

Seb bites his lip. I know he understands.

I'm shaking now and Sebastian pulls at his beard, concern creasing his forehead. "I'll make some verbena tea."

"Thank you." I attempt to smile. Verbena tea seems to be Seb's answer to everything. "There's a bunch of verbena drying over the sink," I point out.

He puts the kettle on and pulls out the teapot. I move to one side so he can fill the kettle.

"I rescued it from the walled garden before it died down for the winter," I say as he grabs a few sprigs and crumbles them into the pot. "You're a really talented gardener, you know, Seb. I'll still bowled over by what you did – on your own – in the walled garden."

He lowers his head, then smiles down at me shyly. "It's nice of you to say so, Charlie."

"I mean it," I say gently as I watch him work.

"Thanks."

He pours boiling water on the herbs.

"I really appreciate this, Seb."

"It's nothing."

"It's not 'nothing', Seb. You're being *so kind.* Guy intervened when he saw Steve hurting me; but then he just said he'd tried to warn me, like it was all my fault."

"Trouble is, Guy's clueless – he just sees the good in people. He doesn't understand that manipulative people can be seriously persuasive – and very good at hiding their true colours."

And I suddenly start to understand how what happened between him and Maxine was even possible.

"I won't even ask how you ended up with him," he says.

The cold water's made my arm so numb now, I can't feel my fingers, so I turn off the tap, dry myself and go to sit down.

"It just kind of happened … you know, like us. There you were, in the pub, we got chatting. You invited me back – just one Saturday night leading to another."

I'm aware of Seb's eyes fixed on my lips as I speak.

"It wasn't like that for *me*, Charlie." His voice catches as he looks me in the eyes. "I saw you in The Chase, with Tris and that lot, and you took my breath away. But it took me a couple of weeks before I worked up the nerve to ask him to introduce us. I don't reckon you'd even noticed me until then. But once we'd started talking… wow. Don't you remember how we talked for hours and hours about all the stuff we love to talk about – music and gardens and art and nature and folklore. And when they chucked us out, ages after closing time, and you agreed to come back with me, I couldn't believe my luck! We were so good together, Ravengirl. After that, I lived for my Saturdays."

I can hardly breathe as he tells me this: I thought *he* was the one who saw "us" as just a casual thing. I believed *I* was the one who could hardly get from one end of the week to the other if I didn't know whether I'd see him that Saturday.

And now it turns out he felt the same way. And I had no idea.

"I thought you were the one who could break her spell."

My heart clenches and I take a ragged breath. "Seb, you don't have to talk about this. You don't need to explain anything to *me*."

"But I *do* – I want you to *understand*. I know you don't want us to be anything other than colleagues, and I get that. But it really sucks that you still seem to think so badly of me. I've messed things up … that's on me … but I'd do anything to earn back even a bit of your respect. It means so much to me. I wish you could see me as I really am. So please just let me tell you my side of the story, yeah?"

"Okay."

I settle into my chair. This could take some time.

"When I realised how I felt about you, I told her I was done with her little scheme. But she blackmailed me. She said she couldn't live without me, that I was the only thing keeping her going in her loveless marriage and how could I think of leaving her so alone? She promised me that if I kept helping her, sleeping with her," he shudders, "she'd help me set up my dream surf school in Polzeath. Working for Guy was only ever meant to be a temporary thing, so it was … you know … tempting."

He pours the verbena tea into two mugs. I take my mug silently, sure there's more he has to say.

"I told her I *couldn't*, that I wanted to be with *you*. But she said if I didn't cooperate with her, she'd rat on me to the police… to Guy, and Giles and tell everyone that it was just me who had been stealing the pictures. I couldn't see a way of proving I was only her accomplice, so she had me there.

"When Giles told Maxine he was planning to bring someone in to catalogue the collection, she tried to get the pictures out of the door quicker; and it got harder to get rid of them."

He takes a sip of his tisane.

"She had me swap the pictures for coke and sometimes heroin, though it killed me to be doing it, especially the heroin,"

"Because of Sahara?"

"Yes. After Sassy was in the Priory, I promised I'd never have anything to do with heroin – as a user, a dealer, anything." He closes his eyes for a moment and takes a deep breath before continuing. "Maxine would give or sell the drugs to her rich friends in London, but *that* night she wanted cash. That proper pissed Scorpio off. If you and Tris hadn't stepped in, I don't even want to think how it might've gone down.

"And then, you remember how you came back to Neville to spend the night with me, and you took the Thomas Lawrence portrait?"

"*Rescued it*, I like to think."

"You must already have known what I was doing to have realised it was there."

"Yes. Alice had worked out that someone was taking pictures from Tillingford Hall. When she saw you with Debbie in the pub, she worked out what you were up to. She was staying with me for the weekend. I'd introduced her to Debbie at the market because I thought she'd think Debbie's tacky Jane Austen pictures were funny. Alice recognised her style of painting straightaway. She realised that she was the one who was making copies of the pictures from Tillingford Hall so you could spirit away the originals without anyone noticing. I was shocked that you were stealing the art from Tillingford Hall, but I didn't care that much about that. No, what got me totally worked up was discovering you were sleeping with Maxine!"

Seb puts his head in his hands, then rubs his neck. "Oh God. I hate that it's true; I'd do anything for it not to be."

"I was just livid that you'd cheated on me. That's why I set fire to your stupid camper van!"

"Well, obviously, it drew the police's attention."

I look down into my mug. "I was so angry with you, I wasn't thinking. I literally didn't care what happened to you."

"I hadn't realised you were so *passionate*, Charlie!"

"Well, I am! Most of the time we were together, I was a bit drunk or half stoned. It probably didn't give you the impression of what I'm really like."

He looks away. "Would you have slept with me if you hadn't been?"

"God, yeah!"

I clap my hands over my mouth.

I'm not supposed to be admitting I still fancy the pants off him, not even to myself. But the cat is out of the bag now.

Sebastian looks at me and the light in his eyes burns me up. For a moment, the space between us is so laden with charge that my thoughts actually stop.

Eventually, he looks away and pushes his chair back, with a loud scrape on the tiled floor; he takes a shuddering inhalation and walks over to the window.

"It got quite sketchy with the drug dealers after that. Their Russian Mafia overlord wasn't exactly thrilled to lose that Thomas Lawrence portrait. And then the shit hit the fan here too."

"Yeah, Alice told me a bit about what happened when Lord Tillingford and Guy realised Maxine had done a runner."

"Guy told me to keep out of his way. That hurt worse than Maxine's betrayal. To be honest, once I'd got over the shock, I realised that things being over with her was a relief. But the way it happened was shit – the way I was so disempowered, had no say in it; that none of it was under my control and the way it made me look so stupid. The way I was painted as the bad guy.

"Guy asked me to leave, but the people I was really hiding from were Scorpio and his gang. I actually threw away my phone and hid. Not in Polzeath – that would have been too obvious. It was brutal: I had nowhere to stay, no money, no transport, no job, no friends, no family.

"And I'm not very good on my own. When I'm not busy, it's harder to forget, harder to fight my demons. I did a lot of thinking – I mean, a lot – way too much, probably. I realised that if I'm ever going to be a regular guy, I need to take more responsibility for my own actions. But also, I couldn't stop ruminating about how every woman I've given my heart to has broken it: first my mother; then Sassy, with her crazy escapades and her suicide attempts; Max … you …"

My mouth drops open. *Me* break *his* heart? I'm about to say something, but he goes on.

"Charlie, I know you don't feel the same way about me as I do about you. And yeah, maybe I shouldn't have dumped all this on you – not now, after everything with Steve. But I'm just asking … begging … can we please at least try to get along as colleagues, maybe even friends? It kills me when we fight, when you slap me down. One day, I hope you'll be with a good guy who truly sees you, loves and cherishes you, like you deserve. Not a prize arsehole like Steve. Until then please let me tell you that I never want to see anything bad happen to you. I'll have your back, if you'll let me, as long as you need."

His eyes are burning so intensely, boring into mine in a way that makes it completely clear he's deeply in love with me, that I have to look away.

I sit in stunned silence, pick up my mug and stare at the gritty bits at the bottom. I have to say something, anything. I think about joking about how I still officially can't stand him but, after this speech, I can't. I just can't say that, even in jest, because it wouldn't be kind.

And it wouldn't be true.

But I still don't know whether I can forgive him for not telling me he was already in a relationship – no matter how crap it was – when we got together. And I'm not sure I can trust someone who stole from his best friend and dealt drugs, even under coercion.

Sebastian stands up and goes over to the window. He stares out for quite some time before saying, "Well, these *snyrtings* aren't going to dig themselves." He grabs his waterproof from the hook. "I get it if you need more time, Charlie, but do you think you could get back to work? I'm desperate to finish them before dark, and we're two men down because Jerry's got an emergency dental appointment and Guy's run into town to grab CCTV equipment for down here."

"He's installing CCTV for my cottage?"

"Just as a precaution," replies Seb, levelly.

Now I'm properly scared. And my brain is reeling from everything he's just told me.

"But look, I totally understand if you need a bit more time to process everything."

I do need time to process everything – everything he told me about himself – as well as deciding whether to tell the police about what just happened with Steve. I'm also chewing over how I'm going to "let the nutjob down gently", as both Sahara and my father suggested.

But right now, I'm too scared to stay here on my own. "I'd rather get back to work."

Chapter Thirty-two

"Jayden has to knock off early to catch the train back to London."

"Wow. He's going already?"

I'd been so caught up in my own worries, I'd totally forgotten that the holidays are nearly here and Jayden had a two-week trip to spend Christmas with his granny in Barbados booked before he started working with us.

"Let me just get a few layers on."

"Bring a waterproof. It's starting to drizzle."

My Silver Tree Surgeons jacket is the only properly waterproof jacket I've got, so it will have to do, even though I feel kind of weird and dirty wearing it after what Steve just did.

I wrap up, throw Bertie a treat to keep him busy in the kitchen, lock up and get on the quad bike behind Seb, coiling my arms around his waist. We career over the bumpy ground towards the travellers' camp. I can feel the warmth of Sebastian's bulk even through his waterproof. It feels so good to be holding him again; I want to rest my head on his strong, solid back.

A thick drizzle has started to fall; and twilight is already closing in, even though it's just past two o'clock.

"We should've just got Portaloos for now," grumbles Seb with a grimace as we arrive at the scene where Milan, Pawel and Jayden are digging out deep pits; Herne, Wolf and Tristain – his dreadlocks bundled into a massive tam – are barrowing the mud away.

I can see why we need all hands on deck to try to get this finished. We still have to erect the huts over the pits to make proper *snyrtings*.

"It certainly would've been easier," I admit as I watch Wolf struggling over the mud with another teetering wheelbarrow of soil. His hair, which is normally sprayed into a Wolverine-like quiff is flopping damply over his forehead. "Or we should have used the mini diggers when the car park contractors had them in."

"At least the ground isn't frozen," Seb points out.

"And at least we got the car park and paths done last week."

Milan's now six feet down in a pit, digging out squidgy earth and sending it up in a bucket. Herne adds it to the barrow, which he'll take away as soon as its full, to deposit the mud on the growing pile in the corner of the field.

"I wonder if we've bitten off more than we can chew."

"We might just have to finish tomorrow or get more of the travellers to help us."

Then it starts to rain properly.

"Looks like you haven't put the supports in yet, Seb!" I point out. "Let's get them in quick! With this rain, the sides might collapse."

I'm horrified to think what could happen to Jayden, Milan or Pawel if one of the pits caves in with them inside it.

"God! Yeah, sorry. I was so distracted."

"It's understandable."

He picks up some planks and gives instructions to the gang, who start to lower them into the holes.

"How many more of you are coming?" I ask Wolf.

He shrugs.

I laugh, realising I should've known better than to ask someone like Wolf a question like that. I know some more guests might arrive today at some point, maybe tomorrow. The solstice is in two days' time, so I'm sure they won't be late for that.

"It's kind of cool that they think this is a good place to celebrate Solstice," I say, passing Seb another plank and noticing he's now got mud on his face.

Only Sebastian Seaton-Smyth could look foxy with mud smeared across his cheek. I'm willing him to wipe it off because that earthy look is doing funny things to my insides. I'm coming to accept the idea that I might be able to get along with my new boss, but I definitely don't want to be feeling *that* way about him; not until we've resolved a lot more of our crap anyway.

"I wonder if the ley lines really are as strong as Ama and Selena say?"

Seb smiles indulgently. I don't think he really believes all that stuff. I'm not really sure I do either; but I like the idea that humans and nature are all part of the same spiritual world. There are so many things in this life that we can't see and can't explain, like the way I just feel safer when Seb's around.

But now, even with all the lads around me, I can't help looking over my shoulder, my ears straining for the sound of a chainsaw.

The diggers are doing well, so Seb and I start to do as much as we can to assemble the huts without having them in place, to save time later. He's got all the parts ready and labelled but there's a lot of nailing and screwing, and a couple of tricky roofing joints to make. Even though I'm just passing him nails and tools, he assures me I'm making it much easier and saving him heaps of time.

It reminds me of the time I watched a couple of ravens building a nest together: one flew in with bits of twig and straw – even a section of hazard tape and a manky blue paper face mask – while the other tucked them all in neatly. I was mesmerised. After an hour they stopped; one put its beak inside the other's, like they were kissing, and they preened each other.

Suddenly, our radios crackle into life, rousing me from my reverie. "Come in Seb."

"This is Seb. Go ahead."

"Where are you, Seb?" We hear Guy's crackly voice over the radio.

"At the *snyrtings*."

"Good. There's something kicking off at the gate. Take a someone strong with you and go and see what's up. I'll be down as soon as I can."

"I'll bring Jayden. Over."

Seb and Herne help Jayden out of the pit. Jayden's a good choice: he's not as tall as Seb or Guy, but he's a prize-winning boxer; well built for a nineteen-year-old. Jayden jumps on the back of the quad bike, and he and Seb zoom down to the gate while I climb into the pit to get shovelling.

I'm dying to know what's going on at the gate; but Milan and Pawel, in their classic hard-working way, are more interested in getting the job done before it's dark so they can get back to the keeper's cottage and crack open a Staropramen. As the weather worsens, I can hear they're picking up the pace – they're not the quitting kind – but I'm already exhausted from shovelling the soil, which is getting heavier and rockier as we get further down.

Seb has only been gone a few minutes when I hear the muffled roar of the quad bike returning. Herne calls down to help me back out of the pit. I'm already aching and soaked with the sweat, which is building up inside my jacket, and rain that has found its way down my neck, so I'm not sorry to leave my station.

"What's up?" I ask, trying to wipe mud off my jacket and just smearing it everywhere.

"Steve!" shouts Seb over the sound of the engine.

"What do you mean?" I shout back.

Seb cuts the engine and climbs off, closing the distance between us so we can talk normally.

"He's down at the gate, and he won't go till he can talk to you."

Cripes! I should've known Steve wouldn't back down that easily.

"Couldn't you just send him away?"

"He won't go! The latest group of campers turned up, but they didn't have a phone between them. There was one … Weasel, I think he's called. Do you remember him from The Chase?"

"What? The tiny Irish one, with ginger hair and tattooed knuckles, who's always starting fights?"

"That's him. Well, he decided to climb over the gate and walk up to the house to ask for help. But just as he got up on to the bars, Steve turned up."

"Oh no!" I gasp.

"Yeah. And Steve started swearing at them for blocking the drive. He obviously didn't realise that Guy had locked the gate because of *him*. He was somehow expecting just to drive in. He started calling them 'crusties' and 'pikeys' and said they were trespassing. They told him they'd been invited but, of course, he didn't believe them, so he marched through the middle of them and tried the gate. Weasel was still trying to climb over the bars and – get this – Steve grabbed him and tried to pull him off."

"Steve *grabbed Weasel*? Crazy-as-hell Irish Weasel?"

"Yep. Steve started to thump him, so things got a bit lively. When Jayden and I got down there, there was a full-scale scrum, with Steve at the bottom of it. By the time Guy had arrived, he'd climbed out from under the pile of fur, feathers and tie-dyed boho pants, looking a bit worse for wear."

Seb's grinning. But I'm biting my lip because, although it sounds kind of funny and I'm not sorry Steve got what he deserved, I'm now more scared than ever.

"Why's he here?"

Seb's smile fades instantly. "He said he was coming to fetch you to the airport."

"Shit. I'm not going – obvs."

"Guy told him that he wasn't welcome here any more and he should get on his way. But Steve said he wasn't going anywhere until you came out and told him yourself. We decided it was best for you to explain, rather than us getting feisty with him."

"I'm so embarrassed. All this trouble I've caused Guy – and you, and everyone – cos of my own stupid lack of judgement."

"Take it from me, Charlie, it can be really hard to see what's going on when you're *inside* a relationship, even when it's obvious to everyone else." He looks at me, his eyes filled with pain, understanding and pleading. I take a moment to process what he's saying, what he's offering me, my eyes not leaving his.

"Quits?" The word slips out of my mouth as a question, but I think we both know it's more than that. It's the start of a process, a journey we're about to begin together.

"I think so, Ravengirl."

I manage a tiny, brave smile; I've got so much to digest, but this isn't the time or the place.

He takes my muddy hand in his, pulling me back to the present.

Right now, I've got to face up to Steve.

"You've got this, Charlie. You've got to tell him yourself where to get off."

Chapter Thirty-three

Seb gets back on the quad bike and I climb on, put my muddy arms around his thick waist and lean my head into his broad back as he starts the engine. We tear down the drive, each second bringing me fearfully closer to my now-nemesis; each second another moment I can cling to Sebastian for strength and comfort.

The journey is all too short and it's only moments before we reach the gate and the crowd parts to let us through.

Guy's frowning deeply, juggling his radio and his phone from one hand to the other. His floppy blonde hair, darkened by the rain, is plastered to his head. "Here they are!"

"What the hell's going on, Princess?" says Steve. His hair is mussed up, his nose is bleeding, and he's sporting a black eye and a disgusting cauliflower ear. His eyes flash angry fire as he watches me unwrapping myself from Sebastian and climbing off the quad bike.

There are five strong steel bars between Steve and me, and I'm glad of them.

I can feel Seb standing right behind me and I'm aware of Guy and Jayden either side of me. Tristain is next to him and Ama and their friends are nearby. Even Milan and Pawel have arrived. Drawing courage from this show of support, I take a step nearer the gate.

I hold my head erect and speak loudly and clearly so

everyone can hear. "I don't want to go to Australia with you, Steve. In fact, I don't want to go anywhere with you. I don't feel safe, loved or respected by you, and you can't offer me what I want from a relationship."

There are some low whistles of admiration and a few claps.

"Is *he* making you say that?" says Steve pointing at Seb accusingly, while he wipes some blood and snot away from his nose with the back of his other hand.

"You see, Steve, that's exactly what I'm talking about! I am a person! I have a mind, a will and a heart of my own. I don't need to take my cues from other people, especially not you."

"But we're so good together, Princess."

"Hmm."

His black eye is starting to puff right up and is making me want to puke.

Tris titters and Steve glares at him, his face like thunder.

Some of the others – Selena, Ama and Gwendoline – are whispering together and sniggering, which does nothing to wipe the ugly fury off Steve's face.

I stretch my arm out behind me and Seb's huge, gentle, calloused hand clasps mine, strengthening my resolve. Tris takes my other hand, and Guy puts his hand on my shoulder.

"I'd like you to leave now, Steve," I say loudly.

"Not until you come with me!"

Everyone gasps.

"Long distance flights are killing the planet, my friend," says Tris. "Best off staycationing."

Everyone starts to laugh, except Steve who's looking enraged, his lips curling back in a snarl. If there's anything a man like that can't stand, it's being made fun of.

"I'm not your friend, you effin' hippy! How are you going to stop me taking my woman to Australia if I want to?"

"I'm not *your* woman!" I shout at Steve. "You have no respect for me!"

And then Seb steps forward and says mildly, "If you're after Charlie, you'll have to go through me first." And then Tris, Guy and Jayden all step forward, shoulder to shoulder and say exactly the same thing. Herne, with his antlers, and Wolf too – cracking his knuckles. Even Ama, Gwendoline and Selena step towards the gate. Weasel starts grinning and cackling, smacking his fist into his hand.

Selena's trying to look all imposing and ice queeny and not laugh, her white eyelashes flickering with the effort. But then she bursts out with a sound like a walrus snorting. I've never heard a noise like it! And then Gwendoline and Herne and all the other campers start laughing too and Steve's … Well, you can imagine how a man like Steve would react to twenty people – and *crusty hippies* at that – laughing at him.

But it's not funny.

Not to me.

Steve is backing off, a psychotic look in his eye.

He's absolutely apoplectic, about to blow a gasket as he opens the door of his crew cab and gets in, without for a second taking his eye off me. Then he guns the engine, reversing into the road at top speed, almost ramming into a horse box coming the other way. The woman driving it gets out to have words with him. But he's already miles away, which is probably just as well for her, or she and her horses would be mincemeat.

Everyone's cheering, but I'm shaking.

My personal bodyguards gather round me, asking if I'm okay.

"Am I the only one that didn't find that funny?" I ask quietly.

"Definitely not," says Seb, gravely.

"I was laughing at Selena, not him, Fam," says Jayden.

"He's a psycho, Charlie," drawls Tris.

"I'm sorry, Guy. Sorry everyone. I'm sorry to have caused all this trouble," I whimper.

"No, Charlie, *he's* the one who's caused the trouble," says Guy gently. Then he stands on a tree stump to get everyone's attention. He's an imposing figure at the best of times, but the added height and his general air of authority leave us in no doubt as to who's in charge here. "It's going to be dark soon and we've got eight new guests to settle in and three *snyrtings* to finish. Seb and Jayden, help me get the floodlights and generator set up so everyone else can keep working; then I'll take you to the station, Jayden, if you're all packed."

"Safe," says Jayden, with a nod; and everyone starts to disperse to their various tasks.

"Selena, Ama," Guy says, taking them aside. "I'm going to need you to step up to the plate and see our new guests in – I'm just too tied up – and Selena, when I'm back from the station, I'll need to have a word about your departure. We need to get everyone out by midday on the twenty-second. The concert guests will be arriving from four, and we can't have you lot going down the drive when the great and the good are coming up it."

In the half-light, I see a determined look flash across Selena's face. I wonder if they're really intending to leave at all.

"Herne, Tris and Wolf, please go with Milan and get the *snyrtings* finished. Charlie, go into the house and ask Mrs P for *a formula* – she'll know what I mean."

"Thanks, Guy, but I'm not going to rest until we're done here."

And he flashes me a look of gratitude, which I barely deserve.

It's completely dark and we're all soaked by the time Guy declares we've finished, and we can turn off the floodlights and the generator. Milan and Pawel have disappeared off to the keeper's cottage for some Staropramen and a nice plate of pork and dumpling stew. Pawel's sister makes it in industrial quantities, and they keep it in bags in their freezer for nights like tonight.

I do not envy the campers, who now have to try to get clean and dry in an assortment of crowded tents and camper vans, with no hot water worth speaking of.

"If you guys want, you can come over to the cottage for a shower," I say to Herne, Wolf and Tristain, who are now all looking like creatures from the black lagoon.

Tris leans in for a kiss, which lands on my cheek as I turn my head. "No need to fret, M'lover – we'll be fine."

If I'm honest, I'm quite relieved I'm not having to open my doors to them, because who knows who else might decide they want a hot shower too and where it might all end? But I'm also nervous about going back there alone.

"Are you going to be okay, Charlie?" asks Seb, streams of water running from his hair. "Guy's worried about you being in the cottage all by yourself tonight. He thinks you and Bertie should sleep up at the house."

I feel my shoulders slump. "I don't feel right up there. It's so fancy schmancy, and I love my cosy little cottage. I mean, Steve's not likely to come back, is he? He's got to get his flight in the morning."

"Maybe if you're not going with him, he's not going to go at all. He could still be rampaging around here," reasons Seb, the rain trailing from his jacket.

"But he really wants to be there for his first grandchild," I reply, wiping my wet face.

"Even if he does go, it won't be until the morning. I don't want to scare you, but there's nothing to stop him coming back in the night."

"Can't *you* stay?" I plead, my stomach in knots.

I can't look at him. I can't admit how much I want him to stay with me; and I'm scared of how I might just break down if he says "no". The danger that Steve poses is really hitting me now, and my emotional and physical exhaustion is just making it all seem even worse.

Seb looks down at me steadily. "Do you want me to?"

"*Would* you?"

I try to keep my voice even. I don't want to sound so desperate, but I'm flooding with relief at the thought that he might stay.

"If you're sure? I feel like, sometimes, you still can't stand me."

I take a deep breath and almost smile, the weight of terror lifting from my shoulders.

"Well, officially, *yes*." I twist my mouth into a sheepish grin. "But could we suspend hostilities tonight? I mean, would you stay in Jayden's room? I'd be in mine, obviously. And no funny business or anything?"

He laughs.

"Don't flatter yourself, Charlie. I'm not going to spend what's left of my energy this evening trying to seduce someone who 'officially can't stand me' – I'm not *that* desperate!" He grins. "But I do have some conditions, Ravengirl."

"Oh, it's like that is it?" I huff sarcastically, folding my arms across my chest. I can't stop a smile from playing on my lips, enjoying the warmth of this gentle banter between us.

"Yep! If you want my official bodyguard services then it's no drink, no drugs and no smoking."

"Fine," I retort. "I might have to step outside for a quick fag, though. And definitely separate rooms. Strictly professional."

"Strictly professional," he agrees.

"Although in recognition of your services, I might be able to downgrade your threat status from 'officially can't stand' to 'risk of severe annoyance'. How's that?"

He replies with an eye-roll and a grin.

And so he phones Guy and Sahara to tell them the plan (and I'm sure I hear a little whoop from Sahara, but maybe it was just a crackle of static on the phone).

Chapter Thirty-four

"Are you sure you don't want a shower while I make the tea?" I ask Seb when we get in, to Bertie's ecstatic welcome.

Seb rubs the back of his neck awkwardly. "I'll be fine, if I can just borrow a towel. I'm sure I'll dry off by the fire."

I feed Bertie, put the kettle on and go up to get clean and dry, leaving Seb attempting to clean himself up and dry his long, curly hair with a towel.

When I come down, there's a pot of tea on the table; Seb's stoked up the wood burner and is toasting crumpets. I bring him a towelling bathrobe I found in the linen cupboard. He's soaked through: he looks longingly at it for a second, then says, "Sod it!" and agrees to go up for a quick shower.

Five minutes later, he comes down in the robe and hangs his wet stuff on the clothes horse in front of the wood burner; it starts to steam. He admits he was actually dripping wet, not to mention filthy and sweaty. But he did mention it and now I'm trying not to think about what lies under the robe. Except my heart and my body won't let me forget, even if my head is trying to.

I smear jam on the crumpets and put the plate on the coffee table in front of him. Bertie jumps up and nicks one and we laugh as he drags it under the kitchen table to eat it.

Seb grabs one and eats it almost in one bite. "Mmm. That's my kind of crumpet!" He looks across at me with a raised eyebrow.

"Oh, give over! I wouldn't have you down as the *Carry On* type."

"And you'd be right, but you gotta laugh sometimes … otherwise you'd cry!" He snatches another one.

"I'm sorry about what happened at the gate today."

I put my crumpet on a plate and cut it in half.

"It's not your fault, Charlie. Man's a tosser. You really told him where to go. I wish I'd had your courage with Maxine. Instead, I was a coward and let it go on for years and years. You were a lioness. There was a lot of love for you out there this afternoon, Ravengirl – all those dudes standing shoulder to shoulder at the gate."

"I'm sure I didn't deserve it. It was all my fault and I'm still pretty scared," I admit, drawing my feet up on to the chair and hugging my knees to my chest. "I'm glad *you're* here now."

"*Are* you?"

"Yes," I say meekly. "I feel safer with you here and I'm glad I've got Bertie with me too. I feel like Steve could be back at any time. My phone's been pinging like mad. I was ignoring it because I was desperate to get the *snyrtings* finished, but I think it was probably him. I'm not sure he's the kind of man who knows when to give up."

I stare into the fire for a moment, aware of Seb's silent gaze on me but unable to turn and face him and find out what it means.

"I'll get on with the supper," I say, jumping up.

"I'll help you."

We both move to the kitchen table where we chop potatoes, swede, parsnips, carrots, chillies and herbs. We have *The Archers* on and we chat about Christmas. He likes what I've done to decorate the cottage in the traditional way, with holly and ivy.

While we're waiting for my signature veggie stew to cook, I light a couple of scented candles and we just flake out on the sofa, snuggling under throws at either end. We watch soaps, with a cuppa each, and Bertie snoozes between us. If I wasn't so hungry – and so acutely aware of Seb right next to me in nothing but a bathrobe – I'd probably doze off myself.

"This is nice," Seb says when Emmerdale ends. "I haven't done this … well, ever really."

"What? You've never just sat on a sofa and watched TV?"

"No, I mean *this* – tea, the soaps, dinner in the oven, clothes drying by the fire, dog. It's very … normal … and grown up."

"Yeah, just like an old married couple," I drawl dreamily and then quickly sit up straight. "Not that we'd ever be like that – either of us. I mean, we're both just too boho and we'd never just settle down – and certainly not with each other!" I gabble, my nerve endings jangling as I notice how his eyes are trained on my lips while I speak.

"Would it be so heavy? Snuggling up on the sofa after a hard day at work, kids in bed, cup of Horlicks, rubbish on the telly and bedtime beckoning?" He sounds wistful.

My stomach does a flip as I catch sight of a bit more thigh under his robe than I think he intended me to.

"Yes, I mean – no." I'm just flapping around now. "Look, I don't know. Of course I want to settle down – some day – with someone sensible and hard-working, and kind and *solvent* and … sexy," but the last word fades into a whisper and catches in my throat. He leans towards me, and I think he's about to kiss me.

The oven timer goes off and I jump up like a scalded cat. "Must check on the dinner," I squeak. I poke and prod the hearty chunks of vegetables which have gently softened in the pot. "Yes, it's definitely ready."

I dollop out two big platefuls, while Seb pours us each a glass of apple juice.

"This looks so good." He cuts thick wedges of bread from a granary cob from A Little Treat. After a few mouthfuls of my casserole he says, "Mmmm. This is really tasty. Sassy's into some kind of raw paleo stuff at the moment, which is proper dismal at this time of year. I keep offering to cook, but she won't have it – that pumpkin soup was a welcome exception. I feel like I haven't had a square meal for days."

"Just as well I made lots, then!"

I dole out second helpings. The hard work today has really taken it out of me and I'm as hungry as a horse; but eventually, we're stuffed – even Seb, who must need twice the calories I do to keep his enormous frame going.

"No pudding, but you can have a couple of Sahara's vegan Christmas chocolates, and some Hobnobs if you like."

"Yeah, sure."

We egg each other on to get the washing-up done while the kettle's boiling; and then flop on the sofa, each with a cup of camomile. The TV's on; but we're both so tired, we're nodding off before we've even really finished our tea.

"Do you think it's too early to go to bed?" I ask, yawning.

Seb turns to me with what I think is a hopeful look but then he yawns too.

"We should make up the bed," I say, something catching in

my throat which makes me sound more husky than I intended.

Seb's suddenly alert. "What?"

I'm puzzled by his reaction.

"Jayden will have left his own sheets on there. But you don't have to change them if you can't be bothered, I guess."

"I thought you said something else!"

The air crackles with tension as I wonder what bit of "we should make up the bed" he might have misheard. *What did he hear?* "Make up in bed" maybe? The thought makes me smirk; I'm almost tempted to lean across and tell him that's exactly what I did say.

"Where are the clean sheets?" he asks, interrupting my lascivious thoughts.

"There's a linen cupboard on the landing. I'll just lock up here and follow you up in a sec."

I lock the door and put the key on the windowsill. Then I shut Bertie in the kitchen, with a couple of dog biscuits and a bowl of water. I make sure the wood burner is properly shut, and I blow out the candles we had on the table.

By the time I get up the stairs, Seb has almost finished making his bed so all I can do to help is put a pillow in its case. My stomach is double-back flipping as I watch him bend over to smooth out the nice clean duvet, the line of his glutes showing under the robe. I catch another flash of thigh as he straightens up.

"Thanks for staying, Seb."

"That's okay, Charlie. You know I really care about you, even if I'm still on your 'annoying' list. I want you to feel safe."

Safe from the outside world, but locked in my own cosy

home with hunky Sebastian Seaton-Smyth, who I fancy the pants off – not that he's wearing any right now – and feeling that, if I wanted, I could just give him the right signal and neither of us would get any sleep tonight.

That doesn't feel safe at all.

And I'm sure it's a mistake we'd both regret.

Chapter Thirty-five

As I rub my chilly feet on the cold under sheet to try to warm up my bed, I wonder how I managed to make such a mistake trusting Steve. I should have seen that being wooed like that – the fancy restaurant, shopping together that first weekend – I was letting him buy me.

But I was in a bad place, like Hansel and Gretel lost and starving in the wood, and he offered me a gingerbread house.

It makes me cringe now I see it clearly.

I can also see that it's easy to be manipulated by someone who can spot your weakness when you're sad and desperate.

Like Maxine did with Seb, I guess.

I don't want to go down this dark path; but in the coldness of my lonely room, I start to wonder what it must have been like: their first time. He was just nineteen and Sahara had somehow got him into modelling for Calvin Klein. Social media hadn't quite taken off back then, but I remember that poster being everywhere: the billboards, the bus stops, the back of magazines.

When I met Seb last year, he was a scruffy, bearded man in his prime, with long, curly hair, tied back with a piece of twine. I never would have recognised him as that oiled-up boy with a buzzcut, in the Calvin Klein ad, my friends fancied when we were at uni. *That* guy wasn't my type at all. I smile to myself remembering how that was a period of my life when Alice and

I used to debate the relative merits of Colin Firth and Matthew Macfadyen as Mr Darcy; the oiled-up buzzcut boy definitely wouldn't have featured on our list of potential beaux.

I never really noticed that Calvin Klein poster but, obviously, most of the country did.

What would that kind of attention do to a vulnerable young person?

Did Maxine deliberately set about seducing him? Maybe she'd already had her scheme in mind for a while and was biding her time. Or maybe she was just frustrated and lonely. Being married to a gay man can't have been easy. Maybe the criminal collaboration wasn't part of her original plan. I guess I'll never know. And I don't really want to.

But nineteen! I could technically have a child that age myself, the age Jayden is now; and Jayden, for all his muscle, is definitely just a kid. Milan's twenty-five and getting married next year, and even he barely seems grown up to me.

Maybe Seb was just a lost boy, pining for his mother's love, longing for his dad to show him some kindness. Despite the therapy and the years passing, maybe that's still all he's looking for.

My heart clenches as I think how prickly I've been towards this gentle soul who only wants to be loved.

Or maybe Seb was more flirtatious with Maxine than he likes to admit. Perhaps there was a bit of laddish bravado to sleeping with his friend's mother. He told to me last summer, that he'd fancied her from the first time he'd come to Tillingford Hall, when he was fourteen. Then I remember that sickening moment he told me he felt "like a god" when he'd first slept with her.

I turn over, unable to get comfortable anywhere.

Why did he have to tell me that? If he really cared about me as he says he did, why would he have stuck the knife in like that? Was he trying to protect the memory of the boy he once was, making out it was what he really wanted back then? I still don't understand whether he was really in love with Maxine when he was nineteen; whether she really broke his heart. Maybe she did, a long time ago, but is the adult Seb just angry that he's been used, blackmailed into committing crimes?

Maybe he feels like I do now: scared, confused, dirty, used.

I really liked Steve at first. He was sexy, and he was fun. When he swept me off my feet and promised to treat me like a princess, I was flattered and kind of relieved. After being skint for years, it only took a bit of luxury to turn my head. Maybe that was *my* weakness: that underneath it all, I was sick of my scuzzy lifestyle and just wanted to have wearable clothes, a decent home, a nice kitchen.

And be a mum.

And it turned out, with three batches of kids already, that definitely wasn't on Steve's agenda. I don't know why he didn't tell me about Darcy or Katie. Maybe he just doesn't think about them that much. Maybe I should have asked a few more questions before I signed on the dotted line; but you don't tend to ask people how many sets of children they have on a first date. And you don't generally ask people if they're psychos or have ever had restraining orders placed on them. It's a pity my friends didn't think I should know that before I even went on that first date. To be fair, though, I only told Alice where I was going, and she wouldn't have known that about him.

That first weekend with Steve, I thought we could have something special; but it wasn't long before something about him made me feel deeply uncomfortable. And now I understand that pretty much everything that we did was his idea, his choice. To him our relationship was just a bit of fun, but I was – I am – looking for something more.

I'm now sure I want a meaningful, dependable and life-long loving relationship with a decent man. I want to have a household and children with someone I can respect and trust.

But can I trust Sebastian?

I don't know.

But I do know I feel safer with him sleeping in the next room.

And with that thought, I finally start to drift off, my physical exhaustion winning over my anxiety. Before long, I'm dreaming about a huge beach party; everyone's there: Tris and Ama, Selena and all the others, even Guy and Alice. Milan and Mrs P are cooking on a giant barbeque. Hatty and The Twins are playing; dogs are barking. The dream is so vivid, I can smell the smoke from the barbeque, and the dogs are barking louder and louder. I'm looking at the scene from the water but there are sharks everywhere and everyone's screaming at me to get out, but I can't move! The sharks are coming, but I can't move.

And then I'm awake and Seb's shouting at me, towering over me, grabbing the duvet and trying to rip it off me.

"What the f*** are you doing?" I scream in terror.

"Charlie! There's a fire! The stairwell's full of smoke. The only way out is the windows!" He throws open the sash window, grabs my pillows and duvet and throws them down to the ground ten feet below to make a softer landing. He rips the sheet off the bed and makes me grab the other end so I can climb out and only have to fall a couple of feet. Then he climbs out of the window and jumps down on to the duvet, with a parachute roll and a grunt. He gets up unsteadily, rubbing his ankle. Then he puts his hands on my shoulders and looks at me.

"You okay?"

"I think so," I gasp, shaking uncontrollably as I look up at him. "You?"

"Yep, but I left my phone in there! You?"

"Yes. Me too."

"We'll have to phone from the Hall!"

And then my mind clears and I realise I can't hear barking any more.

"Bertie!" I scream.

Seb picks up the raven sculpture and smashes it through the glass door.

"Seb! No!" I cry as acrid smoke pours out of the kitchen, making me cough.

But he dives straight into the house, taking no notice of the broken glass strewing the floor.

He's back out in a second, carrying the dog.

My heart, which must have stopped for a moment, seems to start again. And for just a second, I'm flooded with relief to see them both: until I realise Bertie is limp.

"Bertie!" I shriek as Seb hands him to me.

"Onto the bike!" Seb orders hoarsely, blood pouring from his bare feet.

I follow him unquestioningly and we scoot away from the cottage on the quad bike towards the Hall, the warm, limp dog in my arms.

Bertie's not breathing!

The quad bike careers right up to the kitchen door and Seb slams on the brakes so that we almost fly through the kitchen window. He smashes the keycode into the door and runs to the landline phone in the kitchen to call the fire brigade.

I'm cradling Bertie to me, rubbing him, but I can't feel any breath, any heartbeat, but I can't believe he's gone: he's still so warm!

I have no idea whether you can do CPR on a dog, but it's got to be worth a go. I love this mutt; I don't want him to die!

I rush into the boot room and lay Bertie on the floor, open his mouth on autopilot to check for obstructions, thanking God that I had to do compulsory first aid training for work each year. Then I begin to pump his chest with what I hope is about a sixth of the pressure I'd use on a human, crying "*Stayin' alive, stayin' alive ...*" And I keep going.

"What are you doing?" asks Seb.

"CPR!" I wail, tears streaming down my face. "His barking saved us and I'm not going to give up on him! *Stayin' alive, stayin' alive.*"

I hear a weird gasp and look down as Bertie's eyelids flutter and his tongue lolls in his mouth.

I'm aware that Guy's now appeared in the kitchen and he and Seb are talking frantically, but my focus is all on Bertie.

"*Stayin' alive, stayin' alive.*"

Bertie gasps again, then gives me a weak doggy grin. I pick

him up and hug him and rub him and make a fuss of him. I can't believe it worked! He gives me a big lick and tears spring to my eyes.

I start to pay attention to what's going on around me and become aware of the acrid stench in the air, as the fumes from the burning cottage start to drift across the whole estate and percolate into the kitchen. I lay Bertie on his bed, make sure there's water for him and rush out of the boot room. I look up to see smoke and flames raging behind the stable block: flecks of amber rush up into the night sky in a column twenty, thirty feet high or more. The cottage has become a raging furnace; and the way it's going, there's a risk it's going to set other things alight.

Seb rushes back on to the quad bike. "Bertie okay?"

I give him the thumbs up, and he grins for a millisecond.

"What about your feet?" I gasp. The kitchen floor is smeared with blood.

But he's already started the engine and can't hear me. "I've gotta go to the gate to let the fire engines in," he shouts, zooming off.

My heart clenches as I look after him. I knew Seb was brave, but this complete oblivion to his own safety in the service of others is something else. I close my eyes and pray for his safety, pray that the blood loss from his feet is sustainable.

Thinking how he careered off in nothing but his robe, I realise I'm just in my knickers and a vest and the cold out here is starting to hit me. I run back into the boot room and grab an old coat, which looks like it's been used to line the dog's bed, a random woolly hat from the pegs, and a pair of wellies two sizes too big.

Then I hear a massive groan and a crash outside, like the roof of the cottage has caved in or something huge has collapsed. I run out of the house and can hear distant shouting, barking and caterwauling. It sounds like the whole travellers' camp is in turmoil.

I don't want to leave my dog; but I'm desperate to know what's going on out there, and I keep being startled by the noises. Bertie licks my hand as I crouch down to stroke him, then pushes it away with his nose and raises his head and grins. He totters to his feet and nudges me away.

"Do you want me to go?" I ask.

Bertie nudges me again and grins weakly. I move towards the door, and he settles down on the bed.

As I rush out on to the drive, I can see the flashing blue lights round the corner lighting up the sky and the trees. But they're not moving up towards the house.

What's keeping them?

Chapter Thirty-six

I must look really silly, running down the drive in wellies, with next to nothing on underneath my flapping waterproof; but I don't care. I'm desperate to know what's happening, why the fire engine is stuck and why there's such a commotion at the camp.

No wonder Seb and Guy use quad bikes to get about, I think, puffing: it's actually a really long way down the drive. Before I make it as far as the Great Oak, Guy is careering back up the drive towards me, followed closely by two fire engines. I lose my balance, fearful of being run over, and fall sideways on to the verge, which is still soaking from the afternoon's rain.

Guy yells something at me as he rushes past – was it "Don't go down there"? – but I can't hear him properly over the roar of the fire engines and I don't care what he thinks. I want to see what's happening.

A police car zooms past in the fire engines' wake.

I round the corner of the drive by the camp to find a tree lying halfway across the road. Several massive branches have been cut and dragged back on to the verge to make a kind of path around it; and the verge has been churned up by the fire engines' wheels, as they've veered past. The drive is the only way up to Tillingford Hall, unless you go cross-country on a quad bike, so I guess the fire brigade had no option but to clear the tree branches from the road while the cottage burned.

My little house must be razed to the ground by now, along with my five laundry bags of rags and ten boxes of crap. And our phones … and the clothes Seb was wearing last night. Now all I own in the world are the knickers and vest I'm wearing.

I stop in the blue, strobing lights and pull the old coat around me, coughing and retching. Trying to run when my lungs were still full of smoke wasn't the best idea.

I can hear that there's a huge commotion in the camp and, as I approach, I see that it's the Great Oak that's fallen.

After the initial shock of realisation – a terrible kick in the guts of grief and bewilderment – I start to question how it could have happened. It was a totally healthy tree. Sometimes, a wind funnel can do that, even to a healthy tree; but it's been a completely still, if wet, night and an oak as huge and deep-rooted as this one should be able to withstand the mightiest storm.

There are two police cars parked up nearby, lights flashing, and a police van full of coppers is coming up the drive to join them. Then I see two officers dragging a wiry, middle-aged man, handcuffed, into a patrol car. Another is gingerly carrying a massive chainsaw.

The man isn't going easily and he's effing and blinding at them.

It's Steve!

He must have brought the Great Oak down single-handedly. Only a tree surgeon would have the skill to do that. But how did he manage it right under the noses of the campers?

When I'm sure Steve is in the car, I start to howl.

This is *all my fault*.

That beautiful, famous, ancient oak tree has been felled

because of some crazy guy's vendetta against me. Everyone's going to be devastated. Guy's going to be furious about the cottage, and the stress and time-wasting four days before the concert. Bertie may not survive the night. And I've got nothing left in the world but my vest and knickers.

I sink into the achingly cold, muddy grass on the verge and sob uncontrollably.

Ama appears by my side and silently puts her arms around me.

She always seems to know when someone's in trouble.

For a few minutes, she just rubs my back.

"Hey, Charlie. This isn't your fault. No one blames you."

"But the Great Oak!" I wail. "It will take five hundred years to grow another one like it. It's utterly irreplaceable."

"It's heartbreaking!" She's got tears in her eyes too and we both start crying. After a couple of minutes of sobbing, she takes my hand and gets me on to my feet. "Come with me."

"I'm not sure I should show my face, Ama. This is going to ruin everyone's Solstice celebrations! Selena will be livid; everyone's going to be so angry with me."

"I think everyone's too shocked to be angry, Charlie. And, anyway, I came to find you because the police want to talk to you."

"Oh shit!"

"As a witness," she explains.

"Oh, right," I say, sniffing and trying to pull myself together. We walk towards the police cars. I glance at Ama, her face alternately livid blue, then in deep shadow.

"Here she is," says Ama to a female police officer, then she vanishes into the crowd like a wraith.

A second police van comes up the drive from the road and yet more officers jump out and start milling around the camp. This is obviously the most exciting thing to happen in mid-Hampshire for years and they all want a piece of the action.

"Charlotte Patcham?" asks the officer.

"Yes."

"I'm Inspector Tanya Burton. I'll need to ask you a few questions."

"Okay."

Suddenly, Seb's at my side. "Charlie's had a bit of a shock tonight – we all have, to be honest. Do you think you might be able to come up to the Hall to take our statements? We could sit at the table, in the warm, and have a cup of tea?"

I want to hug him but instead I start to shiver uncontrollably.

"I think that would be a good idea," agrees the Inspector as she takes in the way Seb and I are dressed. She barks some orders at some of the other police officers. A young PC gets into the driver's seat of the nearest police car and Inspector Burton hands me one of those foil 'blankets' and jumps into the passenger seat, indicating that I should get in the back, next to another officer. Seb says he'll follow us on the quad bike.

We progress steadily up the drive, with the roar of Seb's quad bike behind us, and arrive at the house a minute later. I let everyone in through the kitchen door and go into the boot room to check on Bertie who jumps up and greets me joyously. He seems none the worse for wear. I fall to my knees and give him the biggest hug and kiss, while he licks my face.

"He's pleased to see you," says Inspector Burton.

"And I'm so, so pleased to see him! Bertie got caught in

the fire! I thought I'd lost him – but Seb went into the kitchen to rescue him; and I did CPR, and he survived!" Among all this devastation, there is at least a ray of joy.

"CPR on Seb?"

"No – the dog!" I explain with a croaky laugh.

"And that worked?"

"I must have managed to get enough movement in his chest to get things going again."

"Well, I never!" she says. "Now how about this tea?"

"Sit down, Charlie. I'll make the drinks," says Sebastian.

"No one's getting any tea until I've looked at your feet!" I insist, my voice still hoarse.

"What?" he looks down, bewildered.

"You're bleeding everywhere!"

He looks down at the blood oozing from the soles of his feet. "Shit! I hadn't even noticed."

Inspector Burton picks up her radio and has a brief exchange. "The paramedics are right behind us."

"I can do it!" I insist.

"No, Charlotte. The paramedics need to check you both over for shock and smoke inhalation. And anyway, I need to talk to you. Let's wait for the professionals."

Her tone brooks no argument, so Seb sits down with his feet up while the other officer, PC Nick Jones, helps me make the drinks. Inspector Burton also sits down and asks us to call her Tanya.

Someone's added a few Christmas mugs to the cupboard; I get one with a laughing Santa on it, while Tanya gets "Santa's little helper", which has a picture of a gurning elf. I find some of

Mrs P's mince pies in the magic, never-empty Tillingford Hall cake tin. I literally don't care they're not even vegetarian, let alone vegan: I just need some sugar.

"We've charged Mr Silver with trespass, arson, attempted murder and criminal damage, although I expect there will be some other things we can add to the list." Tanya reaches across towards the plate of pies, her face grim. "We've been wanting to catch up with him about a couple of other things for a while. He'll be spending Christmas in custody."

Despite my exhaustion, I feel some kind of hysterical joke about trifles coming on, but I can't quite make it gel. I realise it wouldn't go down all that well with a police officer who is conducting an investigation into arson and attempted murder at God knows what time on a wet December night.

Once the paramedics arrive, Seb submits to having shards of glass tweezered out of his feet. Sitting in his bathrobe, munching countless mince pies while giving a statement to Nick, he looks as relaxed as if he were having a salon pedicure. Tanya takes a witness statement from me in the snug, which is quieter, warmer and more private than the kitchen, and where I can wrap myself in cosy throws. About half an hour later, by which time I've almost lost my voice, Guy appears looking haggard and we move back to the kitchen.

Guy slumps down at the table and puts his head in his hands. "They've managed to get the fire under control, so it won't spread. But there's nothing left of the cottage. I'm sorry, Charlie. All your stuff is gone."

"Don't worry about my stuff! Apart from a few sentimental things, it was all worthless shit! But I'm sorry, Guy! I'm sorry about your lovely cottage and the Great Oak. This is all my fault." I burst into tears.

He puts his hand over mine. "No, Charlie, it really isn't – just put that thought right out of your head." He grabs a mince pie, eat it in two bites, then gets up to make himself some coffee from the fancy Nespresso machine on the countertop. "God, I'm tired." He rakes his hands through his hair.

The police officers each take a mince pie and accept another cup of tea before we see them off at about four AM.

I'm feeling too wired to sleep right now. "I'm not sure it's even worth going to bed!"

Guy yawns. "Well, I'm going. You two can do what you want. I've disengaged all the intruder alarms, so you can go where you want. The guest bedrooms on the top floor are already made up for the visitors we've got coming for the concert. But they won't be here for a few days, so you can go up there if you want or just – whatever."

He looks from me to Seb as though he's just processing that we were both in the cottage and Seb is wearing nothing but a bathrobe. But he's clearly too tired to know what to make of it.

"What do you want to do, Charlie?" says Seb, once Guy's left. He gets up and winces slightly as he puts weight on his bandaged feet.

The first thing I want to do is light up – but I can't. There probably isn't a single fag or half ounce of tobacco within two miles, so I chew my nails instead. Then I take a deep breath.

"I want to apologise."

"What for?" he asks gently as he grabs a glass from the cupboard.

"For setting fire to Neville."

"Guess we're a fair way past that now?" He has his broad back to me as he fills the glass with water.

"I've never apologised for it; it was a reckless thing to do – you could've died. I never meant you any real harm, but I guess I hadn't thought it through." I burst into tears yet again.

"Hey, hey. Come here, Ravengirl."

He gently pulls me up from my chair so he can put his arms around me.

I rest my head on his broad chest.

"What if you'd been roasted alive or just died from the smoke inhalation?" I mumble.

"It was a possibility."

His voice sounds different from here: even more resonant.

"I hadn't thought how frightening it would be for you, and how difficult it might be for you to lose Neville … and all your stuff. I wasn't thinking at all. I was just so angry."

"Maybe you were jealous?" he says quietly into my hair.

"Maybe." I can hear the strong, steady thud of his heart. "And upset that you'd lied to me."

"Because you cared?" he asks, gently unwrapping me from him so he can look at me; but I can't meet his gaze.

"Yeah. A lot, Seb. I cared *a lot*!"

"And now?"

I look at him and his expression is patient, his eyes unfathomable, as though he wants the answer to be mine, and mine alone.

"I still care now, Seb." And then, in a whisper, I add, "*A lot.*"

He takes me in his arms again and rests his chin on the top

of my head, his heart thudding louder now.

"Thank you for staying with me last night, for saving my life, for going back to get Bertie – even if that was completely mad and you've made a disgusting mess of the kitchen floor!" I say with an awkward giggle, thinking about the bloody footprints we still haven't mopped up. "If something had happened to you tonight, I'm not sure I'd ever have forgiven myself."

"But it didn't, did it?"

"No."

"And now we're here," he whispers. "And we're okay."

He takes a deep, shuddering sigh, then gently unpeels my arms from around his body, leaving me feeling cold and alone. He goes back over to the sink, drinks the glass of water, rinses the glass, puts it on the sideboard, all with his back to me so I can't see the expression on his face. Then turns to me, suddenly looking exhausted.

"We should get some rest."

"There are two sofas in the snug," I point out.

"Charlie, in a few minutes this'll all hit me. Then I'll start reliving some of the roughest times in my life. At best, I won't sleep at all, and I'll try to battle my demons with my eyes open. At least then, I can doomscroll reels of wood-turning or those people who make tables out of epoxy resin with stuff embedded in it, to keep me distracted. At worst, I'll drift off and have nightmares. I tend to be quite noisy when that happens. Either way, I'd keep you awake. So I'll go up to the salon and you can sleep down here – Bertie will keep you company." He turns to leave. "I hope you can sleep okay, Charlie."

"I hope you can get *some* rest," I whisper, feeling terrible that tonight's adventures will have put back his recovery from PTSD by God knows how long. Weirdly, the way he's opened up to me, shown me his most vulnerable self, sets my heart racing. If he hadn't just given that speech, I'd have run after him and begged him not to leave. Even though I've just downgraded his threat status from "risk of severe annoyance" to "friend zone", I can't expect him to sleep in the same room as me after everything we've said and done recently, no matter how much I want him to stay close to me – nightmare or not. We're both probably still in a state of shock. And who knows what crazy, reckless thing I might be driven to by the sight of him lying horizontal in nothing but a skimpy bathrobe.

When I'm settled on the sofa in the snug, with a couple of throws over me, Bertie joins me. He licks my face for several minutes until he eventually gives a stinky yawn and we both fall asleep, my arm around him like he's a big hot water bottle.

I sleep fitfully between nightmares about a raging inferno at a Bee Gees concert.

Chapter Thirty-seven

Each picture, mantelpiece and windowsill in Holly Cottage, Sahara's home on Tillingford Manor Farm, is festooned with ivy and yew. There are swathes of greenery wound round the banisters, interwoven with fairy lights and dripping with painted wooden decorations. It's Christmassy in a beautiful, understated, cottage-core way. No tacky tinsel here. A scented candle, with the most heavenly frankincense fragrance, is burning in the grate, which adds to the festive atmosphere.

I've been staying with Seb and Sahara since the fire a couple of days ago. Although Guy and Alice said they could make room for me, the Hall is full of Guy's guests and actually living inside a vast country house isn't really my scene.

Luckily, there's a sofa bed in the living room at Holly Cottage and a downstairs cloakroom I can use for my basic needs; but obviously I have to go upstairs to use the bathroom when I need a shower. The two-up, two-down cottage is pretty cosy for all three of us: Seb has to bend his head wherever he goes, as the ceilings are so low; and we three are continually bumping into and brushing past one another. We've agreed we can cope with it for the few days up until Christmas, and we'll worry about "what next" in the new year.

When Sebastian came back to work at Tillingford Hall in October, he moved into James's cottage, with Sahara, since living in Neville was no longer an option. The alternative was sharing the keeper's cottage with Milan; but Seb's so close to his sister, he obviously prefers to live with her and cycle up to the Hall each day. And she welcomed his company. He clearly enjoys living with her and I can see, as they interact with each other, why Guy said their spirit animals are doves: they're both so gentle and so devoted to each other.

It's nothing like the relationship I had with my brothers, which was a real dog-eat-dog existence that usually left me as mincemeat.

Since Seb saved my life and I downgraded his threat status from "risk of severe annoyance" to "friend zone", we've been getting along, steering well clear of talking about What Happened Last Summer and focusing on getting ready for the Christmas concert. If I take WHLS out of the equation, I just can't stop myself getting all hot under the collar whenever I think about him.

Brushing past Seb in his bathrobe on the landing this morning, without ripping it off him, was one of the hardest things I've had to do all week and I'm wondering if we're approaching "good friends (with a strong undercurrent of lust)" status. The look he gave me and the awkward way he walked as he hurried into his bedroom made me wonder if he wasn't thinking the same thing.

And, although right now I have no idea where it's going, I have to admit I prefer feeling warm, light-hearted and … *excited?* rather than the seething ball of rage I have been for the past few months.

I have my moments when that feeling of anger and distrust comes back. But I'm practising accepting it and then letting it go, just like my father said, and it's working … mostly.

Sahara hands me a red tablecloth printed with tiny gold stars so I can lay it out on the table. She's putting the finishing touches to a delicious-smelling curry, which is bubbling away in a beaten-up casserole dish on the Aga. Now the weather's turned freezing cold and the cottage itself is none too warm, she's finally surrendered her raw food diet; so it's all go in the kitchen, especially with Bertie sticking his nose in every cupboard.

"It's so sad about the Great Oak," says Sahara as I spread out the cloth.

Seb adds a jug of water and a bottle of Tillingford Manor Farm apple juice to the table. "It's more than sad, Sassy. It's a bloody tragedy."

The story's gone viral and Guy's had to hire a crisis management company to hush up what triggered Steve to cut down the oak. I'm immeasurably grateful to him for that. He and Sahara both know how painful it is to have your love life dragged across the media. He understands I don't have the resilience to cope with anything like that right now, especially after the shock of losing everything I ever owned. Even if I did bravely say it was worthless shit.

Guy's buildings insurance should cover the rebuilding of the cottage. But the claim will be delayed for months while there's a full investigation into how it burnt down. I was meant to be responsible for insuring the contents but imagine if I'd got around to doing that. So basically, I'm stuffed. And skinter than ever.

I didn't really own anything of worth or of great importance; but literally everything I did own – from my phone to stories I wrote at primary school and all my clothes, including Alice's little black dress (which I hadn't got around to returning) and the new clothes Steve bought me – are now all soggy ashes. My laptop's melted but luckily my workplan was saved in the Cloud, so at least I haven't lost all the work I did; but lots of my messages and photos have disappeared.

Seb gets three pasta bowls out of the warming drawer (James's cottage may be tiny, but it's got all the mod cons) and puts them on the counter for Sahara to fill. "With Steve in custody, hopefully we can have a peaceful Christmas."

"I've heard he's appearing at the magistrate's court tomorrow. If there's any justice, he'll be sent down for a long time," says Sahara, scooping rice into the bowls.

I breathe a deep sigh of relief as I lay out the knives and forks: I've been so scared the past few days, thinking he might break out and come back for me. I did wonder whether to reach out to Nicola, his ex, but decided I'd rather not dwell on what happened. I feel safe here, with Bertie, Seb and Sahara, and Allegra and her family in the manor house on the other side of the farmyard, and that's enough.

Sahara puts down a pretty, painted bowl filled with home-made raita. I look at it suspiciously; but when she confirms it's made with soya yoghurt, I spoon some on to my plate. "The travellers disappeared quickly once the Great Oak was down – Selena said there was too much negative energy there now."

"With only two days to Solstice, they needed to find somewhere else to go, pronto." Seb agrees, taking the raita from me.

"Tris says Selena found a place near Stonehenge where they

can go for the solstice; and then they'll try and get somewhere permanent in the new year," I say, fork halfway to my mouth. Did you know Selena's thinking of actually setting up a retreat centre?"

Sahara and Seb look at each other with raised eyebrows.

"I think we'll miss Tris, Herne and Wolf's muscle power, though," says Seb.

"They actually made themselves quite useful in the end, didn't they?" says Sahara.

"Totally. As well as helping build the *snyrtings*, they cleared quite a lot of rhododendrons and the area around Pan's Pavilion too. So we're a week ahead of schedule now and I can relax and enjoy Christmas a bit. I was thinking I was going to have to work right through the holidays," I admit. "But overall, I'm still glad they've gone."

"I'm really relieved," says Seb.

"I couldn't believe it when you invited them."

"Not *this* again!" he rolls his eyes and tuts exaggeratedly. "It wasn't quite like that now, was it, Ravengirl?" He looks directly at me with one eyebrow raised, quizzically.

"Hmm." I really don't want to fight about this. Now it's all over, it just seems quite funny. But I was genuinely worried we were going to have a full-scale settlement by the Great Oak by the spring; it would have been Guy's headache but our fault – like quite a lot of what's happened recently at Tillingford Hall.

Sahara digs a fork into her curry. "I wasn't at all convinced they were going to leave before the Christmas Concert. I'm just glad that Guy didn't have to evict them. I think that would have been really awkward, especially at this time of year."

"True. It's also handy that we've got time to clear the site before the concert and won't have to worry about all our hoity-toity concertgoers driving past a huge traveller camp," I say, waiting for my curry and rice to cool.

"I can't imagine they'd be that chill about it," agrees Seb. "Guy wanted to be open and inclusive, but I think he's quite relieved he doesn't have to be *that* open and inclusive!"

"He's a darling," says Sahara wistfully. "But yes, I don't think he's quite ready for open house at Tillingford Hall – any old waifs and strays welcome!"

"What do you still need to do to get ready?" Seb asks me.

"I've just got to fine-tune the topiary and plant up the containers on the front steps with cyclamen, skimmia and ivy. But the wholesalers are doing a big drop tomorrow and it will only take me and Milan the morning to do. Nothing else is really relevant for the concert – the drive's done, the toilet block, the stable-yard planters and the car park – so I think Milan and I will probably be getting greenery to decorate the house and that kind of thing. So if you need him to help you with muscle stuff, just ask."

"Thanks," he beams at me, and I can't help thinking how much nicer this is than fighting all the time. "So, what's your thinking about the walled garden?"

"Second of January!" I reply enthusiastically.

"Great way to start the new year," says Sahara.

"The walled garden's going to be my absolute favourite project!" I beam "Of course, you've done most of it already, beautifully." My heart melts when I think how he completely restored the whole thing by himself, and so carefully, with all those lovely little details. “But maybe we can go and have a look at it tomorrow so I can start thinking through what I need to do and maybe order some stuff, so it’s ready for us to start after the holidays.”

“I’d really rather leave it until after Christmas if you’re chill with that. I’ve got so much to do before the concert, and then there’ll be a lot to clear up afterwards.”

“Talking of which, Dearest Brother, we must practise!”

Chapter Thirty-eight

While Sahara and Seb clear the table and I stack the slimline dishwasher, I feel a nicotine craving building up. I tell them I'm just taking Bertie out. As I grab his lead, Seb tunes his guitar: an old one Guy lent him after I burnt his treasured Gibson to a crisp in the camper-van fire.

Once outside, I grab the disposable vape I keep hidden in the planter outside the front door. I'm not wearing my coat and I'm freezing, feeling super self-conscious in the glare of the security light, while Bertie looks enquiringly at me, so I only take a few drags.

When I come back in, Sahara has made us each a festive mug of hot chocolate, with stacks of whipped plant cream, cinnamon sticks, cute little dairy-free chocolate stars and a sprinkle of edible glitter on top.

Hatty would adore something like this; it's certainly very Instagrammable.

Seb's playing *Come As You Are* and doing his best Kurt Cobain impression.

"That's not really going to get me in the mood to sing *Santa Baby*, is it?" grumbles Sahara, taking a sip of her chocolate from a pretty mug with a holly-leaf pattern.

So he starts picking out a few chords, plucking awkwardly at the guitar.

Fifties swing isn't really his style.

"*Santa Baby*?" I ask, grabbing the dusty bongo drums that scull around the living room so I can do the cheeky base rhythm. "Why?"

"Guy said I had to."

"He's not forcing you, Sassy."

"I know, but I owe him so much and this is such a tiny thing, really." She stands up and shakes herself a little. "Okay, okay … I can do this!" Then a look of deep concentration comes on her face, she tosses her head and does a kind of sexy starlet pose, with a hip thrust to one side, one knee crossing the other. She sticks out her bottom, pouts, then dips her finger in the cream still piled on the top of her mug and sucks it with a sexy sigh.

"*Babababum*," sings Seb, starting to pluck out the tune on his guitar. "*Ba bum, ba bum, ba bum*."

It sounds so daft after he's just been yelling Nirvana songs, I just want to burst out laughing; but I don't want to put Sahara off, so I concentrate on my bongos.

Then Sahara starts to warble about how she wants Santa to put a sable under the tree for her. She can hold a tune, but she's no singer.

She suddenly stops.

"God, this is so cringe!" she says crossly. "I can't even sing. And this is an awful song! It glamourises fur and it's full of kinky double entendres! I don't know why I agreed to do this."

"Because, Darling Sister, you're a superstar. And telling everyone you're performing has helped Elizabeth sell loads more tickets. She's added twenty standing-room-only ones for a hundred quid each! That's another two grand."

"I know all *that*, Dearest Brother, but what I mean is *why singing*? And why *Santa Baby*? The lyrics are awful, and it's got a really tricky rhythm. It's so hard to get the words in the right place! And anyway, I was a model, not a *singer*! I'm a complete amateur."

"Nobody cares! They just want to see *you*, Sassy. They probably think we're going to turn up in nothing but our pants. Seriously … you could stand there and smile and they wouldn't give a toss *what* you did."

"You could camp it up and make it funny," I suggest. "You could channel Eartha Kitt or Kylie or Madonna and dress up like one of them. Well, not Eartha, maybe …"

We listen to a few versions and agree Eartha's original is the best, but Kylie's got a kind of girl-next-door sweetness about her that feels the most appealing.

"But I can't do any of those," wails Sahara. "I don't know what Guy was thinking!"

"Nor me! I mean, there's millions of songs he could have asked you to do," I agree.

"I guess he just didn't have time to think it through, Sassy."

"At least he didn't ask you to do *Fairytale of New York*," I point out.

"God, yeah! I love the tune but *those words*!" gasps Sahara. "That would've been a million times worse."

"Or *Baby, it's Cold Outside*," says Seb.

"Definitely a bit rapey," I say, and we all shudder.

"*Santa Baby* is all kind of saucy and sexy and people don't see me as that kind of girl. My model persona was all skinny and moody, not some kind of curvy bombshell wearing fur and Tiffany diamonds."

"Why don't you do some other song?" I suggest.

"Like what?" Seb takes a deep swig of his hot chocolate. When he lifts his face from the mug, there's cream all over his upper lip and I just want to lick it all off, but I manage to resist as I grab the guitar before he can pick it up again.

My ragged gardener's fingernails reach for the strings and, like a lonesome stranger returning home after years abroad, I pick out some chords and sing:

Silent night, holy night!
All is calm, all is bright.

Seb is gazing at me with more than surprise in his eyes.

"I didn't know you played!"

"You've got such a lovely voice," says Sahara.

"I trained as a chorister and learned classical guitar and piano," I explain. "But I haven't played or sung for years."

"Why did you stop?" asks Sahara.

"I guess I'd just had enough and I needed a break. I got sick and tired of being told I wasn't as good as my brothers. And music was just another way for my parents to squeeze me into their mould, so I just stopped as soon as I could. I didn't do any music once I'd left school."

"That's a shame," says Seb. "If I was as talented as you, I'd definitely have kept it up."

"Oh well." I turn away to hide the hurt that's deep inside me. I did love music, but I kind of gave it up as an act of defiance. Now I realise that didn't really hurt anyone but me. But I don't want to dwell on that now; I want to help these good, kind people who've welcomed me into their home, and make sure Guy gets a concert to remember.

Maybe the thousands of hours of practice and that talent buried somewhere down there could come in useful at last.

So, I carry on picking out the chords. Seb and Sahara join in with the second verse:

Silent night! Holy night!
Shepherds quake at the sight:
Glories stream from heaven afar,
Heav'nly hosts sing Alleluia!
Christ the Saviour is born!
Christ the Saviour is born!

And I add a descant harmony, soaring above Seb and Sahara's melody.

I see them exchange a *What the ...?* kind-of look, raising their eyebrows in admiration. It makes me feel alternately smug, remembering how good I am, and sad that I never did anything with my skill and have hidden my light under a bushel for so long.

"What's your favourite carol, Seb?" I ask to avoid an awkward silence when we reach the end of *Silent night*.

"*It came upon the midnight clear*."

"Interesting – a connoisseur's choice!"

I pick out the chords, the strings starting to sting my flabby fingertips.

He can only remember the verse he had to sing solo as a child – the one about universal peace:

Yet with the woes of sin and strife
The world has suffered long;
Beneath the angel-strain have rolled
Two thousand years of wrong;
And man, at war with man, hears not
The love-song which they bring:
O hush the noise, ye men of strife,
And hear the angels sing.

I'm transported back to the first carol concert I ever attended, when one of my many brothers – I think it was Tom, but it could honestly have been any of them – had taken the treble solo. I shudder, overcome with nostalgia mixed with mild panic.

"Seb had such a pure voice as a treble," Sahara reminisces. "Just as well they didn't make you a castrato!"

Seb crosses his legs and glares at me.

His lovely bass-baritone voice is definitely a greater gift to the human race than a fine treble. Not to mention his other assets, I think, letting my loose hair hide my face as I bend over the guitar.

Sahara gets up and tugs Seb's hand. "Come on, time for our meeting!"

"Where are you going?" I ask.

"DRAGS."

"Will you be okay here on your own?" asks Seb.

"Come with us!" says Sahara. "It's the last one before Christmas, so it's an open meeting tonight. Anyone's welcome."

I don't like the sound of it, but neither do I fancy sitting here on my own. I guess I could go to the Tillingford Arms; I'd surely find someone to chat to there. But I'd end up being squeezed for gossip about Steve; and it feels a bit desperate to go to the pub on my own while my friends go to a drug and alcohol support group.

"Yeah, sure," I find myself saying and just catch Seb and Sahara exchanging a glance. What is it? A glint of relief? Triumph? Surprise? I'm not quite sure. I've no idea why I said "yes".

"I just don't fancy sitting here on my own," I say, as much to myself as to them.

But maybe there's something for me to hear at DRAGS tonight.

Chapter Thirty-nine

The new floodlights highlight the huge Christmas trees that stand proudly either side of Tillingford Hall's imposing front door. The light reflects off the oversized shiny baubles, making sparkles dance all over the gravel drive, the stone walls, and the concertgoers in their finery, who are snaking their way from the car park to the main entrance of the house.

I wonder if Guy's regretting asking Jonathan Nutter, a family friend and retired Royal Navy commander, to run the security for the event. Jon decided to name his new company after the most famous vessel he served on. I'm not sure he thought through the acronym for Ark Royal Security Enterprises, which is now emblazoned on the back of the fluorescent tabards that only came back from the printers this afternoon.

Despite the uniforms, the security people are doing a great job of directing the traffic in the new car park, showing guests across to the house and directing those who need it to the new toilet block in the old stable yard. We're certainly not expecting *these* guests to use the *snyrtings*, half a mile from the house, however proud we are of them.

Most of the guests are people the Tillingfords already know; but some of the tickets have sold to the general public, who seem very keen to have a brush with the nobility and get a good look inside the house, which hasn't been open to the public since the 1920s. The Ark Royal security team will see that the guests stick to the ballroom for the concert and the dining room for the refreshments afterwards.

Elizabeth looks like a tiny knight in shining armour in her mermaid-line dress covered in silver sequins. She seems tense but calm as she presides over the whole affair from the bottom of the stone stairway leading up to the front door, grasping her clipboard and pen like a sword and shield.

Guy and Alice are standing in the entrance hall with Guy's father, Giles, Lord Tillingford, who's come down for the occasion with his partner, Alice's former boss, Desmond Kingston-Campbell. They are greeting all our visitors personally, and a little queue is starting to build up.

Guy looks fantastically handsome in his dinner jacket, while Alice is looking amazing in strappy diamante heels and a beautiful empire-line dress in ice-blue chiffon, which hides her faint bump. She's had her mousy, frizzy hair highlighted and smoothed; it hangs on her shoulders in beautiful golden waves. She's sporting massive diamond earrings and a monster diamond necklace – which I assume are the famous Tillingford Diamonds – and looks every inch the aristocrat that she will soon become.

It's amazing what the right hairstyle, diamonds and the love of a good man can do, I think wistfully.

Sahara, in a holly green wrap-over dress (which almost makes it look like she's got some curves), is supervising Hatty and the Pemberton twins, who are usherettes with me. Each little girl is wearing a red velvet dress, with a white sash, white tights, black patent shoes and a big white satin bow in her hair.

"My mummy's wearing a dress like Elsa's," says Hatty in

a quiet moment, referring to the ice queen in Disney's *Frozen*. "She looks really pretty!"

"She does," agree The Twins.

"I love her sparkly shoes," says Poppy.

"Our mummy looks like a fish," adds Lily.

And I laugh because, although Elizabeth's dress sits nicely on her petite, well-toned frame, they're not entirely wrong.

"You look lovely, Charlie – all floaty and shimmery," says Poppy.

I glance down and wonder if the plunging neckline on my black satin dress is a bit vampy for a Christmas concert. "Aw, thank you, Poppy. I had to buy it specially."

"Because all your stuff got burnt." Lily looks down at her red velvet number grimly. "I wish all our stuff would get burnt so we could get some clothes we *actually like*."

My family have rallied round to help me out but, by the time I'd bought a new phone and work clothes, I couldn't really ask for party clothes too; so I was pleased to find this dress reduced in a Winchester boutique because there was a ruck in the seam, which I managed to tease out. I added a string of sequins around the neckline and hem to make me look a bit more Christmassy. Despite being a dress, it does feel very *me*, maybe because there's something of the raven about it. With some fake tan on my neck and shoulders to even out the real tan on my face and forearms (the inevitable consequence of my outdoor job), smoky eyes, dark lipstick and my hair up in a tight chignon, I think it kind of works. It certainly makes me feel more alluring and feminine.

I receive a lecherous glance from an old buffer with a stick, who attempts to kiss my hand. His wife, sporting the Harrods helmet hairstyle she's probably been wearing since 1982, gives him a dig in the ribs and says they can perfectly well find their seats without help, thank you very much.

Seb is "backstage" in the kitchen, supervising the afternoon tea with Mrs P and helping the choirmaster keep the choirboys under control. I'm relieved we're not working near each other this evening. Just remembering how he looks every inch the former Calvin Klein model in his hired but perfectly fitting dinner suit is seriously raising my blood pressure, and I could do without that distraction.

Earlier this afternoon, we walked past the back lawn just as an impromptu *decani* versus *cantoris* football match was starting up. I was about to get stressed out about those slide tackles on the lawn I've so carefully renovated, but Seb turned to me and said, his eyes sparkling, "Takes you back, doesn't it?" At that moment, I felt only sweet nostalgia and realised that being at a choir school wasn't all bad. And it also hit me that it was all a very long time ago and all the kids performing tonight – even the tenors and basses, who are mostly sixth formers – are so young they're literally the next generation from us.

And some of the tiny ones were so cute: I just wanted to take them home and feed them dinosaur pasta and Penguin bars. There was one little boy, stocky with curly blond hair and ruddy cheeks, who was pretty much how I imagine Seb must have looked when he was nine. Before everything went wrong for him.

There's a lull in the stream of visitors for a moment, so I tear myself away from that recollection and glance into the ballroom just to take it all in. It's lit by candles (with a couple of standard lamps at each end of the room to ensure adequate lighting, as required by health and safety procedures). At one end is a dais that has a huge Christmas tree on either side and a Steinway concert grand piano hired for the occasion (as the piano in the salon needs a bit of work to bring it up to concert standard). At the other end, the enormous ornamental fireplace is filled with huge logs crackling gleefully. Pawel and Milan are on standby with fire extinguishers and fluorescent fire marshal tabards, as requested by the Hall's insurance company.

Nestling on the marble mantelpiece is one of the garlands of yew and holly, wrapped round with red satin ribbon, and bedecked with dried orange slices, cinnamon sticks and pine cones, which the girls and I made yesterday. The other ones are hanging over each of the six enormous windows and an extra huge one hangs over the French windows. It's so beautiful! And so amazing to see the ballroom as it should be: full of people.

I become aware of a presence at my elbow and a scent of driftwood and cypress. I turn to find Sebastian in his dinner jacket, his hair neatly tied back in a black satin ribbon that, I only just realise, perfectly matches my dress. He's gazing at me and, for a second, I feel like it's just me and him.

"You look stunning, Ravengirl," he says sotto voce and my heart bursts into flames.

I open my mouth to reply, not sure anything's actually going to come out.

If last night Seb was in the "friend zone (with a strong undercurrent of lust)", tonight he's …

There's a cough and I turn with a smile to a severe-looking, grey-haired couple who are holding out their tickets. Seb melts away while I show them to their seats.

Then I hear familiar tones in the entrance hall. "Sorry we're late! The taxi that was meant to bring us from the Tillingford Arms just didn't turn up. The landlady, lovely lady – Gaynor, isn't it? – brought us over!"

"You're most welcome, My Lord," says Giles.

Guy, shaking his hand warmly, adds, "Lovely to have you here, My Lord."

"Thank you, My Lord, Mr Tillingford," says the Bishop of Bath and Wells with a tiny bow. "I think we can use first names now we've got that over with, don't you?" He laughs. "Just call me Rod. Where is she, then?" He cranes his neck to look for me. My father is looking very Anglican and festive in his fuchsia bishop's cassock.

"My, my, it's the prodigal daughter!" He gives me a very affectionate hug as I come up to greet him. "And don't you look beautiful?" He seems surprised.

My mother hugs me too. "Yes, Darling. You do look lovely!"

It's the first compliment I think I've had from her in about ten years, and I'm knocked speechless.

"Mum, Dad, meet my god-daughter, Hatty!" I say, as she comes running up.

She does a little curtsey and shakes their hands in a very becoming and appropriate manner, which can't fail to please them.

"May I show you to your seats, My Lord, Mrs Patcham?" she says. I'm so glad I did that little rehearsal with her: she looks as pleased as punch that she got it right and they seem pretty impressed with her as she leads them away.

Suddenly, I hear a commotion at the door as a woman calls out at the top of her voice, "Daaarling!"

I swivel round to see who's just uttered this exclamation. There on the doorstep is a very glamorous blonde woman, whose frozen brow makes her seem twenty years younger than the tall, extremely handsome man in his mid-sixties beside her. He looks uncannily like Guy. The woman is carrying a tiny white Bichon Frisé dog that looks like a pompom with eyes.

There's a look of panic in Alice's eyes as she glances at me.

Then I turn round to see Seb approaching me, as if he's about to ask me something.

He clearly hasn't spotted her.

"Char…" he begins, then stops dead in his tracks and freezes as he sees who is on the doorstep.

I don't need a further confirmation that this is Maxine, the former Lady Tillingford, Guy's mother.

I had no idea she was coming.

Seb starts to turn away, but she's caught sight of him.

"Sebaaastiaan," she drawls in her faint American accent, one arm outstretched as she paces towards him, the ridiculous white pompom of a dog held firmly under the other arm.

Seb's eyes light up with a strange kind of fire. He steps behind me and puts his arms round my waist. For a second, I think he's being affectionate, claiming me for his own in front of her; and then I realise what he's doing: he's pinning my arms to my side so I can't move!

I feel his beard on my neck as he whispers. "Play nicely, Charlie – this is Guy and Alice's night."

My heart is doing at least two hundred beats per minute as my feelings escalate into a tornado of outrage.

How dare he! How dare he second-guess how I'd react? How dare he tell me how to behave? How dare he take my power, use his strength against me?

I swore I'd never let a man do that to me ever again.

And how dare *she* come here and speak to him like that? Like they're long-lost friends! My arms are tensing and I'm trying to pull them free so I can deck her; but Sebastian does some clever little thing where he grabs both my hands and spins me round so that I can't escape, and he can introduce me politely to her.

So that's how it is!

All this work I've done; everything I've struggled with to become friends with him again; and it turns out he's just back where he was last summer!

He must have known she was coming and here he is, flirting with her all over again. Just when I thought we finally had something.

Well, I'm not going to be taken in again!

Alice's eyes are boring into me, pleading: "Let's not have a scene here!"

Sahara intervenes, sweeping Maxine and her chevalier into the ballroom, not a moment too soon.

Seb hands me to Alice, and she grabs my hands. "Not here, Charlie. Not now!" She hisses, leading me to the cloakroom under the stairs, the rasping of my hyperventilation echoing up the grand staircase. She jabs the code into the security pad. "1710, the year the house was built," she reminds me in an urgent whisper – and pulls me inside.

The awful moment of being introduced to Maxine (God, I hate that name: it's the kind of name you want to spit if you have to say it at all) has passed and my breathing is normalising. But I'm still enraged.

How can he be so calm?

How did I let him control me like that?

"I know you want to kill her, Charlie, but please can it wait until afterwards? She's staying here all Christmas, so you'll have plenty of opportunity: carving knives, poison in the mince pies, electrocution by fairy lights!"

She starts to laugh slightly hysterically.

"Cyanide in the marzipan?" I suggest, but I'm not laughing.

"Whatever!" she exclaims and laughs. "But *please, please* just wait until after the concert! I know I should have warned you she was coming; I just totally forgot to tell you: we've all been so busy. This is my first public appearance with Guy and the biggest event that's happened here for years. Please don't ruin it for us!"

"Okay." I calm down slightly, aware I've already caused Guy more than enough trouble since I arrived here. "I just can't believe what that woman *did!* To Seb, to Guy, to *Giles* for God's sake."

"She's not a perfect human being, Charlie, and I know she hurt everyone. But, remember, she sacrificed her happiness for Guy. If it wasn't for her courage and love, he would have been mashed into some hospital bin before he'd even seen the light of day. And, despite all the other awful things she did, she was a good mother to him. And wicked witch or not, she's Bump's granny!" Alice holding her arms protectively around her tummy;

my heart softens. "I need you either to sit this out in the kitchen or *behave!*" she says with steel in her voice.

She opens the panelled door and slides out into the hall.

Guy looks quizzically at the two of us. "Ah, there you are, Darling! Are you ready?"

Alice straightens her dress and takes a deep breath.

"Yes."

She is glowing and radiant, looking every part the aristocrat's fiancée. He kisses her on the cheek, puts his hand on the small of her back and guides her gently towards the ballroom. I lock myself back inside the cloakroom and try not to let my mascara run.

The last thing I need tonight is panda eyes.

Thank God I don't have to perform, like Seb and Sahara.

Chapter Forty

I can do this. I can just go quietly down to the kitchen and come back up when the drinks are being served. And I can be politely indifferent if I happen to spot *her* again.

I reach for the lock. But there's a shuffling, swooshing sound as twenty-four choristers start to gather in the hall, right outside my hiding place.

I can hear the audience in the ballroom quietening to a hush. Then Guy gives a short welcome address. There's a bit of laughter, and some clapping.

The shoving and shushing just outside my little room suddenly stops. There's a spine-tingling silence for several seconds before the purest sound, like a crystal blade cutting the ether, breaks out right in front of me.

A single treble is singing:

Once in royal David's city stood a lowly cattle shed.

And then the shuffling starts up again as the choir processes into the ballroom. I actually can't breathe as the treble's voice fades into the distance, until I can barely hear him ending the verse:

Mary was that mother mild,
Jesus Christ her little Child.

Then, after a beat, the whole choir – bass, tenor, alto and descant – burst into full harmony for the second verse of the carol.

As I lean back against the oak panelling, I take a deep, shuddering breath. I finally begin to notice the smell of cinnamon, orange and clove wafting from the Christmassy reed diffuser propped on the cistern.

How did I end up sitting in the downstairs loo of an English Country House, hoping I'd never have to come out and face the music?

It's Seb.

It's all because of him, damn him.

It's all because of how we met in The Chase; how we loved each other but neither of us was honest about what else was going on in our lives. He said he did it to protect me, and I want to believe him. But seeing Maxine at last – seeing how radiant and charismatic she is – I finally understand how a horny nineteen-year-old could have seen her when she was the age I currently am. Having seen the look on his face when he saw her just now, I tell myself there's nothing, nothing at all I can do to come between them: she has such a powerful magnetism, so much control over him; and they have such a long history.

Why did I have to fall in love with someone so weak, someone I just can't trust?

And why did she have to turn up right here, right now, and ruin everything?

I thought we'd started to bind ourselves back together, with tiny gossamer threads, until she came crashing in, like a hornet smashing through a spider's web. Just when I was so happy to have reached the “friend zone (with a strong undercurrent of lust)”, she had to push him back into “officially can’t stand” status in my heart.

And I remember how Seb grabbed me. How dare he!

I look at my wrists and arms, but there is no sign of trauma: no marks, no bruising.

I realise Seb caught me, held me, but he didn’t hurt me. He was trying to stop me embarrassing everyone, especially myself.

And I start to sob, clutching my stomach, feeling so empty, like there’s a choirboy-shaped hole in my life. The music becomes more muffled, as though the ballroom door has just been closed. Seconds later, someone’s knocking very gently but insistently on the door of the loo. I open it a crack.

“Are you okay?” Elizabeth whispers.

“Not really,” I say through a hiccough.

“Well, can you go and be ‘not okay’ downstairs?” she hisses. “When the music stops, they’re going to be able to hear you!”

I creep out and Elizabeth wordlessly squeezes my arm with a sympathetic smile and points me in the direction of the servants’ stairs. “And while you’re down there, can you see if you can find Sahara? I haven’t seen her for a bit. I just want to check she’s all set for later.”

I start to make my way down the stairs and find Sebastian coming up them; he’s frowning deeply.

“Charlie!” he whispers, his breath catching. “What’s the matter?”

“What do you think?” I growl at him.

“You have to put that aside just for now. We’ve come so far, Charlie. We’ve been so good together this week. I’m sorry about what happened just now. I promise I'll explain and make it up to you. This isn't the time and place for a row. I really need you to be okay *right now*," he whispers urgently, rubbing his neck. "I can't have *two* of you falling apart on me!"

"What?"

"Shhh." He puts his finger to his lips, takes my hand and leads me downstairs. When we're definitely out of earshot of the concert, he says, "Sassy's having a panic attack."

"Shit!"

"She says she can't sing in front of *that lot*!" He points upwards, towards the ballroom.

"But she's *got* to! She's the reason half of them are here."

"I *know*! But saying that's only making it worse. Please will you talk to her? I need you to help her. I know how strong you can be when you have to, Charlie!" He looks desperate.

I take a deep, ragged breath and he squeezes my hand. His face is so close to mine I can feel his breath on my cheek, and I can I smell cypress and driftwood.

I feel like my heart's going to tear in two.

I so want things to be okay, for us to be back in that "friend zone (with a strong undercurrent of lust)" that felt so amazing; but right now, I want to scream and shout and relegate him to the "never a snowball's chance in hell of me ever speaking to you again" level.

But I can't do that.

I can't do it because the people I'd be letting down would be Guy and Alice.

And I can't do that, not after everything they've done for me. I have to put all that aside and focus on Sahara and the concert.

I may be a deluded fool, but I make a resolution that I'll stay in the "friend zone" just for now.

It's where everyone needs me to be.

I'll question it and rationalise it some other time.

A few sprays of Rescue Remedy, fifteen minutes of deep-breathing exercises, some yoga stretches and a mug each of verbena tea eventually calm Sahara and me down.

She helps me clean up my panda face and tells me, in no uncertain terms, that if I don't trust Seb and hold on to where we made it to this week, she'll never speak to me again. And I realise that would make me desperately sad, because I've become very fond of her.

By the time Herne and Gwendoline's folk band have done their little medley and Elizabeth comes to get us, all is calm, all is bright. And we three have made a plan of how we're going to wow the audience.

Elizabeth hurries us all up the servants' stairs and into the entrance hall; and then she marches ahead of us to give Guy a signal from the ballroom door. He clocks me standing there *with* Seb and Sahara; he does the faintest double take before announcing us.

"And now, in a slight change to the advertised programme, my oldest friends, Sahara and Sebastian Seaton-Smyth, *and* our new head gardener, Charlotte Patcham, will perform together for the first time a song that needs no announcement."

I breathe a sigh of relief that he hasn't named the piece: we forgot to tell him we weren't doing *Santa Baby.*

The room is hushed, the only noise the crackling of the flames in the great fireplace and the slight rustling of a few of the more restless choirboys' surplices.

I sit at the piano and play an E so Seb can tune his guitar; then I run my fingers over the keys, producing a couple of arpeggios to get the feel of the thing, while a couple of older audience members cough awkwardly. My heartbeat must be almost at the top end of the metronome. I make a point of not looking at anyone; the last thing I need right now is to catch Guy or Alice's eye, or, worse still, my parents.

I focus on the feel of my fingers on the keyboard, the sound of the notes in my ears and the resonance of the instrument through my entire body, and the muscle memory begins to kick in.

Of course I can still play!

You don't forget how to do something when you've practised as much as I did.

I begin to reproduce on the piano the chords I was playing on the guitar yesterday: C major, G7, C major, F major. Seb begins to join in, picking the strings to break the chords into cascading arpeggios, and then I nod to Sahara. We all three start to sing the simple melody:

Silent night! Holy night!

There's a sigh of approval from the audience.

All is calm, all is bright.

A couple of older ladies start to hum along.

Round yon virgin mother and child.

And then a gentleman in the front row starts to join in with the words:

Holy infant, so tender and mild.

By then, a few dozen people are singing quietly along.

Sleep in heavenly pe-eace,
Sleep in heavenly peace.

When we start the second verse, I begin with the descant, my voice flying high and alone above all the other harmonies filling the room. And then a couple of the trebles from the Wells Cathedral Choir add their voices; the choirmaster nods approvingly, so the others come in too. I'm feeling more courageous and really giving it some welly, while focusing on those arpeggios on the piano. And the adrenaline and the feedback from the audience is giving my hands wings: I'm starting to add some trills and some more sophisticated finger work, filling out the melody with harmonies enhanced by Seb's beautiful guitar playing. And then we come to the end of the third verse, and everyone falls quiet. I look at Seb and we take the final line around once more, just the two of us:

Jesus, Lord, at thy birth.

And the effect is electric: there's a telling two-second silence before everyone in the audience jumps to their feet and erupts into rapturous clapping.

"Encore, encore!" they cry.

I bend over to Sebastian and whisper, "*We wish you a merry Christmas?*"

"Hell, yeah," he replies with a wink.

I smash out the old favourite on the piano as he somehow works out the chords from my hashed-up rendition full of wrong notes. But no one really cares because we're all yelling for more figgy pudding, and everyone's clapping and stomping along.

Then we really have finished; and everybody's applauding, laughing, talking and starting to move away from their seats. And Seb's leaning over me, whispering in my ear, "We're so good together, Ravengirl." His beard lightly brushes my neck, sending thrills down my spine.

But before I can respond, we're surrounded by well-wishers; and Sahara is hugging me, thanking me so much for being a complete genius and an absolute lifesaver. I'll take that!

And some champagne appears in my hand and I'm not going to turn it down, DRAGS or not. And there are all these interesting people who want to talk to me, including a TV producer who's going to be filming a fly-on-the-wall documentary about Tillingford Hall in the new year – Guy kept that one quiet! She says she'd particularly like to feature the gardens and thinks I'll be great on camera.

My mother battles towards me through the scrum. "Darling, that was amazing! I'm so glad you've kept up your music!"

I don't tell her I literally haven't touched the piano since I went to university nearly twenty years ago.

"And where's the marvellous young man who was singing with you?" says Dad.

"I'm not quite sure." I look around and see no sight of Seb. "I'll go and look for him."

He's not in the dining room, where Mrs P and the caterers are serving mulled wine and mince pies (or champagne for an extra tenner a glass: Amy's good at this fundraising business); nor is he in the entrance hall, where people are starting to collect their coats from the improvised cloakroom. Hatty and the Twins careen past me, chased by two little boys in lederhosen. "Who the hell are they?" I wonder. "I don't remember seeing Captain von Trapp walking in."

As Hatty twirls around me, I ask, "Have you seen Seb?"

"He went that way!" she sings as she pirouettes past, pointing in the direction of the salon. She starts to scamper up the stairs, where thankfully one of the Ark Royal team stops her before the other children go rampaging all over the house.

I can hear voices in the salon, so maybe there's a group of family and friends gathered in there. Before he lets me through, the Ark Royal guy cops a good look at my cleavage as he checks the brass staff badge pinned to the merest bit of fabric where a lapel would be.

I push open the salon door.

"Oh!" I gasp.

Sebastian and Maxine are sitting close to each other on the sofa, deep in confidential conversation, that damn ridiculous Bichon Frisé on his lap. Sebastian's arm is resting along the back of the sofa, not quite touching her shoulders but as near as dammit.

Chapter Forty-one

"What the hell is going on in here?" I demand, storming towards the sofa.

Sebastian jumps up, Maxine's little dog sliding off his legs letting out a startled "yip" as it bumps into the coffee table on its way down.

Maxine doesn't get up but replies, "Sebastian and I are having a little *private* tête-à-tête, Honey."

"Right, well. I can see where I'm not wanted!" I say fiercely as I back towards the door.

Seb gets up and comes towards me with what I suppose is meant to be an appeasing look on his face. "Charlie! Wait! It's not what it looks like. I'm having things out with Maxine. We haven't been in touch since … since last summer and there's a few things I needed to get off my chest."

"Huh. And what might those be?"

He draws himself up to his full height, towering above me.

"Firstly, which I think she knows already, that I don't love her. And I never have. I had a crush on her once, a long, long time ago, when I was very young and stupid, and then … well, and then it was just sex."

"And I feel exactly the same!" Maxine stands up and looks me in the eye. "It was just a kind of game for me. You know, half the women in the country were hot for him and there he was, right on the doorstep, ripe for the picking. It was so easy – and just so obvious. It gave me a kind of kick knowing a million women envied me. And he was a good pupil. Maybe you should thank me for teaching him everything he knows."

I want to vomit.

"How could you *do* that to him?" I ask, outraged on behalf of the vulnerable nineteen-year-old that Seb was.

"Oh come on, Honey. Don't tell me you've never had sex just for the sake of it!"

I open my mouth, but nothing comes out.

"Are you telling me you had a deep emotional connection with any of the people you slept with at Samhain last year?" asks Seb.

I shut my mouth tight.

"You see, Charlotte," says Maxine, "sometimes it is just about sex."

Seb turns to her angrily. "But back then I thought we *had* something, Max. When we first … *started,* I really did think I was in love with you. When you dropped me like a hot coal for that photographer bloke, you broke my heart. I didn't know then what it felt like to be *really* in love. I didn't know what we had wasn't the real deal."

"Aw. Poor ickle motherless boy." She chucks him under the chin.

I can see he's instinctively about to grab her wrist to stop her taunting him; but he grits his teeth and simply steps out of range of her pointy fingernails. I'm in utter admiration of his self-control because my fists are balling up and I want to clock her.

"If you were so heartbroken, why did you keep coming back?" she asks.

"Because, as you say, it was easy. You were always up for it, always wondering where your next shag was coming from. And then, when you got me involved in your little scheme, well, you had me by the bollocks, didn't you? Silly, naïve little me: it hadn't occurred to me that you'd blackmail me too, that you'd tell them it was me and *only* me stealing their stuff. And then, when I wanted out, you promised me Polzeath – and you promised you'd give it all up and come with me. I should've known you were lying."

"Yes, you should've; we're two of a kind, Sebastian," purrs Maxine.

"No we're bloody not, Max. I'm *nothing* like you! And I'm going to spend as long as it takes – my whole life if I have to – *proving* I'm not. I just want to be a regular guy. I feel like you stole that from me."

"Don't be ridiculous! You and your silly sister can't blame your issues on me. I did my best to help you have a stable, happy childhood, even though you were none of my concern. I only took you under our roof for Guy's sake – he was so desperate to have a brother and a sister. As far as I was concerned, you two were just like any other waifs or strays he might have dragged in, like those flea-bitten hedgehogs he used to rescue from the cattle grid."

Sebastian straightens himself up but, behind his mask, I can see him crumpling and I want to go to him and hold him up. Instead, I just burst out with anger: "You bitch! How can you be so cold and cruel?"

"Would you rather hear that I have feelings for him? That I want him and me to get back together and live in a cottage by the sea after all?"

"No! But you don't have to kick him in the balls either!"

"Do you think it's been easy for me to be married for thirty-five years to a man who couldn't give me any physical affection or give me more children? Having secret affairs? Always having to hide, to pretend? Not being able to be with the only man I've ever loved, the *father of my son*, until now, *thirty-five years* after I had his child? The adored child I now have to leave behind in another country just as he's about to make us grandparents?"

A silence hangs between the three of us.

"So, Seb, what was the second thing?" I ask.

He looks momentarily lost.

"Ah yes … *that*." He takes my hand. "I told her that I love you."

Suddenly, the whole room seems to spin and yet come into focus: the swirly Persian carpet, the carved marble fireplace, the polished walnut-wood Bösendorfer piano, with its silver-framed photos of the Tillingford family meeting the great and the good.

I must be overwrought.

I don't think *that*'s what he just said.

"Sorry … what?"

"Charlie, I love you," he repeats clearly and he catches me, strong but so gentle, his hands under my elbows as my knees weaken. "Any chance you can downgrade my threat status another level? Maybe to *potential date material*?" he looks at me with a wry smile but pleading eyes.

I can't help but laugh. I start to close the slight gap between us and cup my hand around his cheek.

Before I can answer, Maxine makes a fake retching noise

and scoops up her stupid, pretend dog, making as if to leave.

"I think I can go one better than that," I tell Seb in a husky voice. "How about changing it to *definitely shaggable*?"

"Ah, here you are, Darling," says my mother from the doorway and my cheeks burst into flame. I dare not turn to face her; but I pray the chandelier will fall down right now and cause a major distraction, ideally crushing me in the process.

"I hope we're not interrupting anything," says my father, his fuchsia cassock only one shade brighter than my cheeks.

"Oh no, we were just chatting about old times!" Maxine assures them. Her smile doesn't reach her eyes.

"Aren't you going to introduce us, Tottie?" my mother asks me.

So I introduce Maxine as "Guy's mother". She bristles.

"It's been delightful meeting you. I must go and find my son to congratulate him on such a splendid evening," says Maxine. She scoops up her silly little excuse for a dog and, tottering out on her Christian Louboutins, leaves the four of us alone in the salon.

And then I introduce Sebastian Seaton-Smyth. My parents are clearly satisfied, maybe even impressed, at the company I'm keeping these days. Dressed in his dinner jacket, with his beard trimmed and golden curls neatly tied back, Sebastian looks tonight like just the kind of sophisticated gentleman they'd approve of, not the scruffy, homeless carpenter who's so much more my type.

"Is this Man One?" My father asks me.

"Yes," I croak, almost dying with shame that my father would bring up that conversation.

"Are you any relation of Jack Seaton-Smyth the cricketer?" he asks Seb.

"He's my uncle."

"How very splendid! We were in the first eleven at Monmouth together and we still play for the Old Monmothians every year. A very solid chap indeed. I'm godfather to your cousins Lucretia and Iona. I suppose that makes Nigel your father?"

"Yes," says Sebastian guardedly.

"Bad luck. I heard he didn't handle things all that well after Madeleine died."

"You could say that," admits Sebastian.

Since the chandelier seems unlikely to fall on me, I'm now wishing a great big hole would open up in the floor and suck me down into the depths, where not a soul will find me.

"You do look so very like her," my father continues.

"So I'm told," Sebastian replies, his jaw tight.

"Well, you seem to have turned out all right," Dad goes on, oblivious. For a clergyman, he can be incredibly indelicate sometimes. "And at least you got that humungous trust fund she left you. And Twerton Manor must come to you eventually?"

"What?" I gasp, turning to Seb. "I thought you didn't have two pennies to rub together!"

He starts to pace the room, rubbing the back of his neck. "It's complicated, Charlie! Sassy and me are utterly skint because my father's the only trustee and refuses to release the funds. We've spent a decade trying to sue him, and the solicitors' fees have been killing us."

I flop down on the sofa.

Just how posh are Seb and Sahara? I wondered a few weeks ago.

Now I'm starting to get a picture.

But I decide I won't think about that now: my head's so messed up already.

"You sing so beautifully," my mother tells Seb, thankfully changing the subject. "And your voice blends so perfectly with Charlotte's. What a lovely pairing." *Please make it stop!* Even at my age, my parents are still really good at embarrassing me. "But anyway, we can't stand here chatting all evening, we need to get going! You're all packed aren't you, Tottie? Do you have something to change into?"

"The coach is leaving in ten minutes, Poppet," says my father, "so you'd better hurry up."

"Packed?" says Seb, his face falling.

"I'm spending Christmas at Mum and Dad's."

"I-I just assumed you'd be spending it here."

"No one actually invited me. But in any case, Christmas is about family, and I always spend it with my parents – and my brothers and their families. Midnight Mass at Wells Cathedral is really something! You'd love it – it's *sooo* Anglican!"

"I know I would, but I have other plans," he says. And I think his eyes are trying to tell me that those other plans might involve me. "Charlie, please don't go. Not yet!"

"But Mr Simpson's already counting the boys on to the coach!" insists my mother, clearly torn between seeing me paired up with this handsome, pre-approved young man and getting the choristers home by midnight.

"Charlotte," says Sebastian in his most polite voice. "I wonder if you'd consider staying with us until Christmas Eve? I could drive you over to Wells in the afternoon so you wouldn't miss your family's Christmas celebrations."

"Well, that sounds fair," says my mother, clearly coming down on the side of the pairing.

"Okay," I say, "if you're sure."

"Of course. Let us know when you think you'll get there, Tottie. See you on Christmas Eve!"

And with that, my parents each kiss me on the cheek and rush out of the room.

I flop on the sofa and exhale a very deep breath. "Seb …"

But before I can even begin to frame my thoughts into full sentences, his arms are around me, his lips on mine, soft and warm, sending crazy tendrils of electricity over my whole body. Our kiss deepens and goes on and on: far, far longer than is strictly decent in someone else's house.

Chapter Forty-two

A wan, grey light filters into Sebastian's tiny bedroom under the eaves of Holly Cottage. I roll over to spoon him and sit up suddenly, my heart pounding.

His side of the bed is cold and empty!

"*Nonononono!* Don't do this to me, Seb! Not after all we've been through," I plead with him in my head. Snapping on the bedside lamp, I notice a folded piece of paper on his pillow.

I carefully unfold it.

Inside, there's a beautifully drawn picture of a raven, with a limp dove in its claws; the dove has hearts for eyes. He's written in florid, forward-sloping handwriting:

Can't wait to see you later, Ravengirl.

I lie back on the pillows, holding the paper to my chest.

His nickname for me is so cute and seeing it actually written down tickles me. I wonder if I should have one for him, but nothing in particular comes to mind; Seb is just Seb, for now. This is the first note I've ever had from him – apart from that hedgehog drawing, I remember, laughing to myself – so the first *love note*, then. And the first time we've slept in a proper bed in an actual house.

My whole body tingles when I remember what we did on the sofa in the salon at Tillingford Hall last night, when Seb discovered how very floaty my skirt was.

And then I roll myself up in the duvet, wishing he was here, just holding me.

We made love so passionately last night, making up … and making up for lost time.

But it felt different from how it used to. It wasn't just unbridled pleasure, like we shared on those nights in Neville. A deep all-encompassing feeling of love and belonging pervaded every cell in my body, as if, somehow, I'd come home. And yet it was no less exciting for that.

If only he was here right now.

I need to know where he's got to – and I'm starving – so I throw on some clothes, hastily use the bathroom and fly down the stairs to the kitchen. Bertie leaps up to greet me.

"Hi Sahara. Where's Seb?"

"He's out!" she says with a mischievous smile.

"Huh." I scratch my dog behind his ears and earning a big face lick.

"Sleep well?" Sahara smirks as she puts the kettle on.

I bite my lip. "I hope we didn't keep you awake?"

She doesn't answer, which makes me think the creaking of the floorboards at various points in the night probably made it hard for her to get much shuteye, but she doesn't seem put out. In fact, she comes over and gives me a huge hug. "I'm so, so glad you two have made it up." She kisses me on the cheek. "I've never seen him happier."

"Did you know he had it out with Maxine last night?"

"Yes. He told me he finally plucked up the courage to tell her what he really thought of her. He said he was inspired by you standing up to Steve."

"Oh my God! No way! I thought I handled *that* really badly. I mean, look what happened!" I slump down at the table, shaking as I relive the shock of what I went through a few nights ago.

Sahara puts a steaming mug of lemon balm tea in front of me.

"Maxine wasn't likely to come after him with a chainsaw though, was she?"

"So, what's Seb up to, then? Why did he rush out?"

"I'm not allowed to say." Sahara puts her finger to her lips. "You won't see him all day."

My face falls. I'm intrigued about what he could be up to; but then I suddenly remember Maxine's up at the Hall. "It's not a workday, though. What's he doing?"

"He said he had some urgent stuff that he wanted to get out of the way before Christmas – maybe tidying up after the concert?" suggests Sahara, slicing through a sourdough loaf from A Little Treat.

"But Elizabeth and the events team are doing all that," I protest. What if he's changed his mind about *us*?

"I'm quite sure he's genuinely gone to work – there's still a lot to do."

A little smile is playing round her lips; I can tell there's something she's not telling me.

What if there's something she doesn't know, and he *has* gone to make up with Maxine?

I don't like the tight feeling in my guts that thought gives me, so I make myself replay the conversation we three had in the salon last night. He said *in front of her* that he loves me! And *she* seems to have little more than contempt for *him*.

This time, I *have to* trust him. I *want* to believe that everything they both said last night is true.

It certainly feels better than harbouring rage and suspicion all the time.

I watch Sahara put the sliced sourdough into the toaster. "I should go and help, then. I hadn't planned to work today because I was meant to be going to Wells with my parents last night. But as I'm around, I might as well go to work." Especially if I can use it as an excuse to check up on what's going on up at the Hall. I just can't quite let the thought go.

"I think you should take the day off. You've had quite a stressful time recently and I'm sure you could do with some down time."

"But I feel bright-eyed and bushy tailed!"

Sahara laughs, raising an eyebrow as though she knows what brought *that* on.

"I only had maybe half a glass of champagne last night, so I'm not hungover. It feels weird."

"It's a good feeling, though, isn't it?"

I have to agree: I hadn't realised it was possible to wake up feeling clear-headed after a party and it's actually quite nice.

"If you're at a loose end, you can help me with the next batch of mince pies, if you like. I've had this huge order from a deli in Winchester. And for some reason, Guy wants a couple of dozen for the Christmas feast at the Hall. I don't think Mrs P was very pleased," she says, giggling.

"Sounds fun, but I should go and lend a hand up there." I'm trying to see if I can get her to spill the beans.

"Actually, if you wouldn't mind, I could really do with some help." We're surrounded by about a hundred and twenty pies, which must surely be enough! Her eyelids are flickering, which I think might be her tell.

Just as my toast pops up, her phone rings. She glances at the number, looks startled, puts her hand on her chest and takes a deep breath. She runs upstairs to take the call in private.

While I spread hedgerow jelly on the toast, I can hear Sahara speaking on her phone for just a few seconds; I then hear the creak of the floorboards above my head, as she paces up and down for some time afterwards. I finish my tea and toast and start washing up.

Eventually, she comes down; her face is blotchy, as though she's been crying.

She comes over and enfolds me in a tight hug.

Then she looks at me and her face breaks into a huge smile, even though her eyes are sparkling with tears. "We're going shopping!" she squeals.

"Okay!" I say, puzzled. Looks like the call was good news.

Shopping is not a pastime I often indulge in; but my wages went into my account yesterday, so I'm not quite as skint as usual. A girly shopping trip with Sahara Seaton-Smyth's got to be something worth experiencing, even if only to see the reaction of the passers-by as I stroll down the street with the *Face of the Noughties*.

In any case, the gifts I've got for my parents so far are a bit lacklustre. And my brother Henry says my niece Daisy isn't into *Frozen* any more, so would I mind getting some Bratz stuff? (I do mind, but I'll find something else I think she'll like.) And

I guess I should get the canon theologian something. There's a Christian bookshop in Winchester I could visit, although maybe giving a canon theologian a theology book would be like taking coals to Newcastle.

And then I realise with horror that I haven't got Sahara and Seb anything at all!

Yes, shopping is a must! I can easily get Sahara some scented candles or a lovely scarf or a pretty cushion: I can see the kind of thing she likes from the way she keeps her home. But I have literally no idea what to get Seb on my limited budget. He could certainly do with a new jumper, but I want to give him something more thoughtful.

Sahara, Bertie and I pile into a really old Land Rover. Sahara tells me it's James's pride and joy; but he left the keys behind when he ran off to Zanzibar and didn't tell her *not* to drive it, so she doesn't see why she shouldn't, especially as she doesn't have a car of her own at the moment.

Once we're in Winchester, we leave Bertie in the Land Rover for a few minutes while we drop the pies off at the deli.

"Thank goodness!" says the lady behind the counter. "We've already had five people asking for these this morning. I've taken their numbers, so I can call them and let them know they're in now. Everyone loves them. I actually think yours are nicer than the ones with beef suet in."

Sahara beams.

"These are for you." The deli lady hands over a box of marzipan fruits. "They're vegan – no egg."

"Aw, thank you, Sue. You didn't need to," says Sahara joyfully.

"Well, of course not, but it's Christmas! I love giving people little things they're not expecting, don't you?"

"Yes!" agrees Sahara.

And then Sahara insists on treating me to lunch, so we find a little vegetarian cafe that's happy to have Bertie, so long as he's well behaved. They even give him a little Santa-shaped dog biscuit that he quietly munches under the table.

After that, we go shopping in a couple of boutiques and vintage clothing shops. I insist on trying Oxfam too and I find a beautiful deep purple velvet dress, which I can't believe hasn't already flown off the hanger because it's perfect for Christmas. Sahara's thrilled to find a genuine vintage crochet-and-suede hippy dress.

She agrees to a selfie with the volunteers in the shop. It's funny to see how excited they are about it.

Then we go to a shop that specialises in cashmere, and she tries on a powder-blue roll neck. She's thrilled when the size eight doesn't fit her and she needs a ten. I've never known a woman to be happy about putting on weight, but I'm so pleased for Sahara. She says it's the first time her BMI has been anything other than dangerously low.

"Good job you ditched that raw food diet!"

"God, yeah," she says with her throaty ex-fag-smoker's chuckle. "Why do you think I made an extra batch of pies today?"

So in a quaint little teashop, we celebrate by having full fat oat milk hot chocolate and vegan gingerbread men decorated with little Christmas outfits. Each table has its own mini tree and they're playing traditional English Christmas carols. It makes me so nostalgic and so excited for the service at Wells tomorrow evening.

We look outside and realise it's starting to get dark.

"There's snow on the way," says the waitress, looking out into the dark.

"No way! It never snows in Hampshire at Christmas these days," Sahara replies.

But the first few flakes start to come down just as a solo, canned chorister sings *In the bleak midwinter*, and I shiver with the magical loveliness of it all.

Sahara looks at her watch. "We'd better get back."

"Yeah. Bertie's not going to survive much longer on a few pieces of biscuit. Oh no! What about Seb's present? I haven't got him anything yet!"

We have a moment of panic, until Sahara looks out of the window. "Mr Stanley might have something."

So we race across the road to Stanley's Treasures, just as the proprietor, who looks older than most of his wares, is about to turn round the "Open/Closed" sign. Sahara explains our predicament and persuades him to let us come in for a few moments.

I explain what I'm looking for, and he says he has some old carpentry tools at the back. He helps me select an old Edwardian rabbet plane, which is apparently nothing to do with bunnies but used for creating notches in wood. I have no idea if Seb already owns one or whether he'll even like it; but it's exquisitely made, as these old Edwardian tools often seem to be. And it reminds me of the kind of gizmos and grundlygrunches they had in *The Victorian Kitchen Garden*.

We thank Mr Stanley for staying open for us and he wishes us a merry Christmas.

Then I see that the kitchen shop next door is still open, and I have an idea.

I hurry inside and come out with a small, heavy bag.

When we get back, Seb's still not home. It's been dark for three hours, so I wonder what on earth he's been doing and those doubts about what could be going on at Tillingford Hall start creeping back into my mind. Maybe Sahara's in on it too? But then I remember she detests Maxine, and I can't imagine she'd ever cover up for her.

When he does eventually appear at Holly Cottage, it's nearly seven o'clock and he seems completely wiped out. I feel bad for not having been there, helping, but he reassures me it's fine.

Despite his exhaustion, Seb insists that we're going to watch *The Box of Delights* – a must for the Seaton-Smyth children every Christmas, apparently. But by the time we've eaten, he's fallen asleep on the sofa; so I just snuggle up to him under a throw while Sahara and I watch the first two episodes. Later on, when the fire's died down and Sahara says, "Good night," and takes herself upstairs, I gently wake Sebastian up and we stumble up to bed, where we just sleep in heavenly peace together.

Chapter Forty-three

Seb wolfs down the cranberry pancakes Sahara's made in two seconds flat, insisting he's got work to do.

"On Christmas Eve?" I complain. "You promised to drive me to Wells today. What was the point of making me *abandon my family* and stay here when I'm not even *seeing* you? When are we going?"

"Hey, Ravengirl, just chill! I'll take you after lunch!" He drains the dregs of Christmas tea from a Santa mug.

"But we'll arrive after the start of the 'Nine Lessons and Carols' from Kings!" I squeak. "Mum will have a fit! We can't start peeling the sprouts until the head chorister sings 'Once in royal David's'."

Sahara and Seb burst out laughing.

"*You've* got *The Box of Delights*," I point out.

"Yeah, but it's not like end-of-the-world stuff if we don't watch it – there's gotta be like loads of times when we haven't. Like when *she* was in Tokyo." He nods towards his sister as he rummages in the bowl by the door for the quad bike keys.

"Or when *you* were shagging that anarchist girl. The one who insisted on getting hammered on absinthe in the ninth *arrondissement*, instead of celebrating Christmas, because she was a hard-line atheist," Sahara points out.

"God, that was the worst time of my life – never again." Seb shakes his head sadly. "Christmas is too precious to waste being wasted. But seriously. I've just got to do another couple of hours."

I catch him looking at Sahara as though there's some big secret I'm not in on.

"What?" I look at them both. "*What's the big secret*?"

"There's no secret!" A smile plays around Sahara's lips. "But I do need to make those mince pies for the Hall, and I promised the vicar some for the midnight service refreshments as well."

"I think you're making up mince pies to keep me out of mischief!"

"Well, someone has to," she says, laughing and slipping another pancake on to my plate.

Bertie looks up at me expectantly and whines a little. Sahara's put a little Christmas-pudding print bandana round his neck. He looks so sweet that I can't resist giving him a tiny piece.

Seb kisses his sister on the top of her head, then he comes round to my side of the table. He pulls me up on to my feet and kisses me so deeply and passionately that I'm left in no doubt that whatever he's up to at the Hall is most certainly nothing to do with Maxine.

"Be good, girls!" he calls to us both from the doorway, with a wink.

"More Christmas tea?" Sahara pours me another mugful. I chide her for waiting on me, but she says it's lovely to have me around.

I can honestly say I'm really enjoying spending time with her too; but I'm on edge all day, alternately feeling puzzled, excited, nervous and slightly peeved. I can't really settle into present-wrapping, mince pie-making, Bertie-walking or

Box-of-Delights-watching. Sahara's already told me twice I'm worse than a five-year-old waiting for her stocking.

And can you blame me? Lunchtime passes and Seb *still* isn't back. The choristers of King's College, Cambridge, are just finishing up with *Hark the herald* and it's already dark by the time we hear him coming in. Whatever he's cooking up had better be good: my brothers won't forgive me for not doing my fair share of sprout-peeling and will impose some fine on me, like putting out the bins!

Seb looks shattered, but it doesn't stop him giving me the sweetest kiss. He buries his face in my hair. "Mmm. You're so good to come home to. I'm going up for a shower!"

"But when are we *actually leaving*, Seb?" I ask as he nonchalantly puts one foot on the bottom stair.

"When I'm *ready* – in half an hour or so?"

"What?! I'll be late for supper!" I wail. "And then *you* won't get home until God knows when!"

"Look, Charlie. After all these years, you're still doing Christmas with your mum. Maybe, just maybe, she could be pleased that you're turning up at all. And maybe you and I could make some new traditions?"

"Hear, hear," says Sahara.

I'm practically hopping from foot to foot, we're so late now and Bertie is as restive as me, picking up on my mood. Sahara looks like she wants to slap me and insists I have a spray of Rescue Remedy.

By the time Seb comes down, his face pink and his hair wet and tousled, I've got my bag packed, my boots on and my coat in my hands.

"You're keen," he says with a grin.

I pull a face.

"Or are you just scared of Mum?" he laughs, shrugging his jacket back on.

Maybe that's nearer the truth.

"Come on, hurry up, Ravengirl. We gotta go! What are you waiting for?" he gabbles.

"Okay, okay!"

Sahara hands him a hamper "for the journey". At least she's not suggesting it's so late now we might as well eat here before we go, so we do actually, finally walk out of the door.

I assumed Seb would borrow Lord Tillingford's Range Rover but when I get outside there's no sign of it. But there is a brand-new electric Volvo EX30 SUV sitting in the farmyard.

"Who's car's this?" I ask.

"Mine!" Seb winks as he tosses the keys in the air with one hand and catches them behind his back in the other.

"What?"

"Yep. I thought it was about time to buy a proper car. And before you say it," he says, putting his finger on my lips, "its carbon footprint across seven years, even allowing for manufacturing, assuming recharging on renewables, is four times lower than my old VW camper van. And I downgraded it from the leather seat option, so it's totally vegan too."

He opens the boot and inside is a crate for Bertie, with a cosy blanket and some Christmas chews. He pops Bertie in the crate and puts my bag next to it.

"How on earth did he afford it?" I wonder as I get into the passenger seat.

Shit! He's not been drug dealing again, has he? Trading stolen art?

But I don't want to spoil Christmas by thinking about that. Right now, I just want to get to Wells in time for the midnight service, so I keep quiet as I sink into the ridiculously luxurious heated seats. He switches the stereo from Nirvana to Classic FM.

But then, instead of turning right into the village, which would take us towards Winchester and the A31, he turns left out of the farm on to the country lane that leads to Tillingford Hall.

"Where are we going?" I ask tetchily.

"I just need to pick up something from the Hall," he says softly, putting his hand on my arm.

I sigh and roll my eyes. I'm really grateful to him for driving me home so we could have some time together; but I'm now *so late* I'm kind of wishing I'd just gone on the train or gone with my parents the other day. Although, I admit to myself, we wouldn't have had that first amazing night together. And I have really enjoyed my time off with Sahara.

The Hall looks beautiful in the snow. Big flakes have settled on the Christmas trees by the front door, in all the details of the mouldings around the windows and outlines the whole building, giving it the look of a gingerbread castle. Seb parks in the stable yard, helps me out of the car and opens up Bertie's crate.

"What are we doing here, Seb?" I ask. The snow's starting to fall again; and right now, I just want to keep warm and dry in the car and get on our way.

"I just need to show you something."

"What?" I sigh.

"You'll see!" He takes my cold hand in his big, warm calloused one and leads me towards the walled garden, Bertie following with interest.

Chapter Forty-four

Seb parts the ivy that still hangs down over the door to the walled garden, dislodging some clumps of snow, which plop on the ground. He unlocks the door and pushes it open; Bertie shoots through, eager to explore this new territory.

This had better be good, I think grumpily, visualising my entire family gathering in Wells Cathedral for my father's star moment of the year.

Right in the middle of the garden, where once stood a large, nearly dead apple tree in a dilapidated brick planter, is a beautiful little garden house: a sort of a gazebo, made from rough-hewn oak. It still displays the nobbles, bumps and contours of the massive branches from which it's clearly been made.

The path to the gazebo is lit with candles in storm lanterns. "Wherever did he get so many of them?" I wonder. Over-sized glass baubles hang from the eaves, and the building is lit from inside by more lanterns.

For a moment, I'm speechless.

"Do you like it?" he asks after a minute, searching out my thoughts.

"I love it!" I gasp and turn towards him. His eyes are dancing, meeting mine with joy. "It's the loveliest thing I've ever seen!"

My eyes mist over as he bends to kiss me gently on the lips. I pull his head closer to mine, entwining my hands in his golden curls, so that we're pressed together, seeking each other out, kissing deeply and passionately while the snowflakes pirouette around us.

Eventually, he draws apart from me.

"Come inside!"

Suddenly aware of the cold and damp, I willingly follow him.

Inside, it's cosy, with throws and a woven rug in front of a proper wood burner. There's a sofa, a pull-down table, mini fridge and a tiny, compact cooker. Gently warming on the hob is a small Le Creuset pan containing some red liquid, with cinnamon sticks and star anise floating in it.

On a small coffee table, there's a two-foot Christmas tree adorned with natural decorations, like the ones I used for the ballroom but with the addition of some little birds cut out of balsa wood: some of them painted black, like keen-eyed ravens; some of them white with pink beaks, like doves. The most heavenly smell is wafting from the tree, which is a real Norway Spruce – all spiky needles and a proper Christmas tree scent.

"Did you make *all this*?" I gasp.

He nods, his eyes sparkling.

"Does Guy know?"

"Yes. But he understood why I wanted to keep it secret from you. He said it was just the kind of thing I was going to do anyway, and he couldn't stop me if he tried. And if we told you, you'd say it wasn't in keeping with the way Victorian kitchen gardens looked, and we should be doing something more useful and authentic."

"That's true! But I don't care – it's the loveliest thing I've ever seen."

He beams. "I've been doing it for ages but, obviously, I suddenly needed to get it finished in time … for this. Come and sit down." He pats the space next to him on the sofa. "Guy says we'll Airbnb it in the summer; but for now, it's just for you and me."

"Airbnb? But isn't it just a garden room? Where will people sleep?"

He gets up to open the door to what I assumed was a cupboard. Inside is the world's tiniest shower room. I'm stunned: how did he manage the plumbing?

"And this is a sofa bed," he explains, sitting back down and patting the cushions.

He gets two mugs out of the cupboard above the cooker, then he pours the red, steaming liquid out of the Le Creuset pan.

"What's this?" I ask, blowing on it to cool it down. It smells like mulled wine.

"It's crab apple toddy, my own recipe."

I take a sip. It's rich and sweet and punchy and really doesn't need any alcohol.

Seb puts his mug down on the tiny coffee table, takes my mug and puts it next to his, then he takes my right hand.

"Charlotte." He looks deep into my eyes. "Thank you."

"For what?" I ask, thinking that I'm the one who's been doing all the receiving here.

"For forgiving me." He turns over my right hand and slowly kisses my palm. Then he takes my left hand. "For trusting me," he adds, kissing that palm. "And for giving me another chance." He kisses me on the lips, then his hands find my waist as he gently pulls me down on top of him and we sink on to the sofa.

"And thank *you*, Sebastian," I whisper when I come up for air.

He sits up and looks at me. "What for?"

"For forgiving *me*, for saving my life and for helping me to start a new one."

"Then are we definitely quits?" A broad grin spreads across his face.

"Yes. Definitely."

He picks up his mug and hands me mine. "To new beginnings!"

"To new beginnings," I agree, clinking my mug against his.

He smiles and goes over to the compact oven. Inside are two individual Le Creuset casserole dishes. He points at them and silently raises his eyebrows, and I burst out laughing.

"It's not *all* about Le Creuset, Seb!"

"Oh." His face crumples in mock-disappointment. "I thought you were just after some new cookware!"

Then he grins, comes over to where I'm sitting and gives me a friendly hug, a gesture which totally melts me. I am passionately in love with this man; but it's lovely also to be friends, and to laugh together, to be affectionate and to appreciate each other as souls, not just bodies.

How we were before – weekend lovers – sex was all we ever had time for. I missed out on so much by not getting to know the real Sebastian and not learning new things about myself by seeing my soul mirrored in his eyes.

But now I think we might be learning what true love is.

And, as if to prove the point, dinner's appearing on the pull-down table! What could be a more loving gesture than making a delicious meal for the special people in your life?

I realise I'm starving. I hardly ate today, on edge as I was, and now I've got a huge appetite. And he's been working so hard: he must be really hungry too. We guzzle the casserole (however did he have time to make that as well as everything else, I wonder?) with some chunky bread, dipped in good olive oil from Sahara's hamper.

We talk about Christmases past, our favourite Christmas films and where we'd dream of spending Christmas if money were no object. I say I can't think of anywhere nicer than this. And then there are baked apples with vegan custard, all washed down with more of Seb's delicious crab apple toddy.

"That was amazing, Seb. I feel bad that I've done absolutely nothing towards this."

"Charlotte, you've done everything! You inspire me."

My lip trembles and my eyes start to swim. "I can't believe you're being so lovely to me when I've been pretty horrible to you all autumn."

"Hey, hey, Ravengirl. Come and sit with me." He moves over to the sofa. "I understand why you were angry with me – I deserved it. And I will spend as long as I need to, to completely win back your trust."

"You have it already, Seb."

"Are you sure?" he asks, looking into my eyes from under a frown.

"Yes!"

And then he kisses me deeply.

"And you know what?"

"What?" I ask, still a little teary.

"You can spend the rest of the Christmas holidays making it up to me!" His face breaks out into a grin, and I shove his arm playfully with my hand; but it's only a moment before I'm pulling off his jumper and he's got hold of mine. Then we're shedding more layers. We laugh as he struggles to open the sofa bed and gets his hair caught in the mechanism. And I'm wondering where to put Bertie, who seems more than curious about what's going on.

It seems like only a moment later that I wake up, groggily, grab my phone and see that it's nearly ten o'clock. "Oh shit!" I gasp, sitting bolt upright. "If we go now, we might just make it in time."

"Charlie!" Seb puts his hand sleepily on my arm. "I'm not rushing anywhere. And we *won't* make it in time."

"But it will be the first time ever I haven't been at the midnight service with my family."

"Good," he says bluntly.

"What?" I furrow my brow. "Just because …" I'm about to go into a rant about him not understanding because he doesn't have a family, but he puts his finger gently on my lips again.

"Charlie, you just thanked me for helping you to start a new life. And this is it."

He picks up my phone and hands it to me. "Please call your mother and tell her you'll be there in time for lunch tomorrow."

"I can't do that!" I cry.

"I dare you!" His face breaks into a broad grin.

Trembling, I speed dial Mum while I pace around the tiny space.

"Oh, Darling! Thank God. The canon theologian's got

Covid and I'm uneven for tomorrow! I don't suppose that lovely Seaton-Smyth boy could join us to make up the numbers?"

I almost drop the phone, and Seb looks at me with the warmest smile.

"Yes, Mum, I'm sure he'd like that!" I wink at Seb, who blows me a kiss back.

"And are you here yet? The cathedral's so packed I can't see where you are!"

"I'm still at Tillingford Hall, Mum. I, uh, I got a bit caught up with things. D-do you mind if we skip the service and just come up for lunch t-tomorrow?" I stammer.

"You don't need to ask my permission, Darling. You're an adult. You just do what you need to! I can't wait to see you, tomorrow, though. Must dash – the archdeacon's waving at me."

And with that she hangs up.

Again, I almost drop the phone. Did an alien just abduct my mother? Or have I just not been listening for the past twenty years?

I suddenly realise that – despite her advice, her concern (often about the daftest little things), and occasional badgering – my mother has never once, in my adult life, made a decision on my behalf or actually told me what to do.

Maybe it's been me that's been passing judgement on myself all this time.

I look down and see Seb lying on the sofa bed, leaning on his elbow, smiling at me.

"See? That wasn't so gnarly, was it?" He takes my phone from me and puts it on the table.

Over his bare shoulder, through the little mullioned

windows, I can see the snow falling once more over our very own Victorian kitchen garden. The tracery of the espaliered apple trees, the cordoned pears and the cavolo nero outlined in snow.

I sit down and he takes a lock of my hair and moves it away from my face so he can kiss me again.

"I've got something for you," he says.

I'm worried my Christmas gifts are going to be rubbish compared to whatever amazingly thoughtful thing he's come up with.

He sits up, reaches behind the sofa and hands me a big, handmade wooden box, about eight inches square and nearly three feet tall. He must have made it specially. I can't imagine what goes in a box like this.

"Go on," he says gently as I hesitate.

I sit up and pull the blanket around me. And then I carefully open the box.

Inside is a little oak sapling in a pot.

Seb's eyes crinkle. "He's just over a year old."

"Oh my God!" I lift the little tree out of the box as tears spring into my eyes. "Is this … is this the Great Oak's *baby*?"

He nods. "I planted this acorn the weekend I met you two summers ago."

I hold the little plant in my hand, staring at it, stunned.

"And there are others." He strokes my hair.

"Others? What? Other babies?" I look at him and then back to the baby tree I'm holding.

"Yuh-huh, hundreds. I planted my first one when I was, like fourteen."

"So, the Great Oak *has a twenty-year-old child?*" I squeak.

"Yeah, loads! I'll take you to see them and all the others tomorrow – if I can remember where they all are!"

"Sebastian, that's beautiful."

"And so are you, Charlotte."

He takes the tree from my hand to place it safely back in the box, leaving the lid off so it can get some light.

He reaches across to kiss me again and I cling to him so hard.

I can't bear for my soulmate to let me go ever again.

"And there's just one last thing." He gently eases himself away from me.

"Really?"

Can there be any more? My heart's so full.

He hands me a large manilla envelope. Inside are details of a three-bed cottage in Tillingham.

"The court settlement came through yesterday, so I put in an offer on it – and it's been accepted!"

"Oh my God, Seb. That's amazing!"

"It's end-of-chain so we could be in by February."

"*We*?"

"Of course, 'we', Charlie. Please, please, my darling Ravengirl, will you come and live with me?"

I'm so stunned, I don't know what to say.

Seb gets down on one knee and looks up at me, taking my hands in his. "Charlie?"

Bertie barks.

"I've got the Volvo and the Le Creuset set now," he says in a pleading voice, with a silly grin, squeezing my hands.

"This Le Creuset set," I purse my lips to stop myself laughing, "which one is it?"

"The thirteen-piece orange one, with the shallow casserole dish and salt-and-pepper mills!"

"Hmm," I say slowly, teasingly, well aware he's spent well over a grand on designer pans just because I rather like them. I take one of his curls in my hand and wind it round my finger, as though I'm pondering this difficult question; I can see he's in agony.

"Of course I'll live with you, you daft boy!"

I jump on him so he can't get away, but he tips me over. We roll over and over on the rug, while Bertie barks and wags his tail until I think either his head or his tail might fall off.

And, although I've missed taking part in my family's traditional Christmas for the first time in my life, as Seb and I lie on the sofa bed in our cosy little hideaway, watching the snow falling thick and fast in the walled garden at Tillingford Hall, I can honestly say this is the best Christmas ever.

Epilogue: Christmas Day

Christmas Day at the Bishop's Palace is always nuts. Once we've got rid of the forty invited guests, who come for a champagne reception after the morning service, there are still twenty-four of us, mostly immediate family, for lunch. And then there's the compulsory walk in Bishop's Park, which we have all to ourselves, as it's closed to the public on Christmas Day. And then there's evensong to get through after that.

Luckily, my three married brothers are all hands-on dads; and their wives form a great crack catering team. So everyone's pitching in, and no one feels overwhelmed.

As well as hitting it off with all four of my brothers, Sebastian's popular with my nephews and nieces. He's called on for umpiring, dinosaur rides and fixing the inevitable Christmas morning toy breakages and malfunctions. I've never seen him look so much in his element. I can see why he wanted to teach kids to surf: he's a total natural with them.

I don't get him to myself until late in the evening, when the family has finally given up drinking eggnog round the embers of the fire and my brother Edward – the only one, apart from me, who doesn't have kids – eventually slopes off to bed in a drunken stupor. I feel quite smug that I'm still bright eyed and bushy tailed, if a little sleepy.

"I haven't had a chance to give you *my* presents yet," I remind Sebastian, when we finally get up to our room and

I hand him two parcels. "Open this one first."

He unwraps the knobbly-bobbly one, cushioned in bubble wrap.

"Bubble wrap, Charlie?" He raises his eyebrow.

"I know, I know. It's *plastic*. But that's how the shop man wrapped it."

He gives a theatrical stage "tut" as he unpicks the sticky tape.

"A rabbet plane. Sick! This must be, like, really old!"

"It's Edwardian."

He runs his hands lovingly over the wooden parts. "I've got a modern one, of course, but this is … *beautiful*. They don't make 'em like they used to. Thank you."

He gives me a little kiss, then looks expectantly at the next box: a cube.

I hope he likes it.

I hope my last-minute idea doesn't fall flat.

"Le Creuset?" He looks first at the mini casserole, then at me, his brows knotted. "So now we have six. Perfect for a dinner party."

"Open it!" I say, impatiently.

"Okay, okay!"

He pulls the tiny casserole dish out of the box and takes off the lid. "Acorns?"

"Look closer."

"Acorn men!" he laughs and looks at me, though I can see he's still not quite getting it. Then he takes each one out and lays them on the duvet. There's a big fat one, a medium sized one, two tiny little ones and a horizontal four-legged one.

I breathe a sigh of relief as Seb's face breaks into a huge smile. "A family of them!"

He looks at me and his eyes begin to smoulder.

"Better get started then, Ravengirl."

THE END

Invitation

Seb and Charlie
Invite you to their housewarming
Raven Cottage
23 Honey Street, Tillingham, Hampshire
1st March from 7 PM.
Bring a musical instrument!

Acknowledgements

Praise be to God for the example of his loving forgiveness by which we are invited to live in peace with one another; and whose Holy Spirit has strengthened and encouraged me to bring light and joy to your days with my happy love stories.

I've had so much support from so many people to get this book together. I will do my best to thank everyone who has helped. I apologise if there's anyone I've forgotten.

Firstly my family: Martin and the boys who each contribute in their own way; my parents for their everlasting support; my brother for his editorial comments; and my sister for always being there. I'd also like to thank all my cousins of various generations, especially Michael, for their kind and loyal support for my writing career.

I'd also like to thank Imogen Papworth, my Commissioning Editor at Audible for taking me on, and the whole team at Audible Studios for their work on my books. I'm thrilled to have entered into this collaboration. Nathalie Buscombe's narrations are brilliant and it's really exciting for a new author to be able to hear her work acted out by a professional.

Then there is my writing tribe: the Romantic Novelists' Association, especially the London Chapter and our little local Romance Round the Park group. The manuscript of this book went through the RNA New Writers' Scheme – twice – and is a better book for it; so thank you to the anonymous volunteers who read those first two iterations. I also have an amazing ally in Monica Galante, the world's best beta reader. She's so full of encouragement, but not afraid to offer plenty of suggestions and positive criticism (you can find her on Fiverr @monicag98). I also had some helpful comments from Alicia Hastings (also on Fiverr @writing_away) and keen ARC reader Chris Brady.

Once again, my thanks go to my fellow authors, Ruth Kramer, Angela Pearse, Katharine Light and Helen Hawkins, for reading and commenting on the final version.

Louise Clairmonte has done a fantastic job with the copy-editing. If you find any mistakes, they're certainly my fault, not hers!

I'm sure you'll agree that the illustrators, Sajeela Kiran (find her on Instagram @sajee_artandpatterns) and Dijana Peter (@burntredhen on Fiverr), and the cover designer, Berni Stevens (www.bernistevenscoverdesign.com), have done a beautiful job on the cover.

I'd like to thank the real Bishop of Bath and Wells, the Rt Revd Michael Beasley, who gave me his permission to assign his ancient office to the fictional Rod Patcham. I should also acknowledge that the fictional Tatchester Cathedral is the invention of John Masefield, the author of *The Box of Delights* and my use of it is an affectionate acknowledgement that for me, like the Seaton-Smyth children, Christmas wouldn't be Christmas without the delightful BBC adaptation of that book.

If there were a way to thank the producers of *The Victorian Kitchen Garden* and its late presenters, Peter Thoday and Harry Dodson, for the lifelong joy and inspiration this wonderful BBC documentary has afforded me, I would certainly do so. Let this acknowledgement be that way for now.

And lastly, I'd like to thank you, my readers, without whose lovely reviews, kind comments and general encouragement I would not be able to keep writing.

God bless you all.

Flora

Lumina Publications Charity Partner Scheme

Lumina Publications supports charities.
You can find out more about this scheme
at www.floradunn.com/partners.

Flora Dunn: about me

I wrote my first book when I was five. It was about a cow and a bed because those were words I knew how to spell. Then I wrote a three-page graphic novel, *The Crazy Book*, about some skateboarding kids who went back in time, a kind of unholy marriage between *Graham's Gang* and *A Traveller in Time*, and seventy-two issues of a magazine about Bunnyland called, rather obviously, *The Bunny*.

I fell in love with romance when I read MM Kaye's *The Ordinary Princess*, a touching children's book about a sassy runaway princess called Amy, which was one of the first books to turn traditional fairy stories on their head. Later I got into Jane Austen, the Brontës and all the classics, until I finally picked up a Mills and Boon and my fate was sealed.

When I'm not being a mother, wife and professional charity fundraiser, I'm writing feel-good, funny romances and now I want to share them with you.

Whether they are about romance, friendship or camaraderie, love stories – how we feel about other people, how we treat them, how we make mistakes and are forgiven and learn to forgive in our turn – are what makes the world go round. You can tell those stories in a light-hearted way but that doesn't change the depth of the message, that true love is what sustains our very existence. Even The Bible is a love story between God and his people (and that ending when you think it's all over, but it isn't, is just the best plot twist ever).

My stories are set in and around the modern-day fictional village of Tillingham in leafy mid-Hampshire (known to some as Jane Austen Country).

Christmas at Tillingford Hall is my third published book. It follows on from *Summer at Tillingford Hall* which tells the story of how Alice and Guy got together. It was a finalist in the Romantic Novelists' Association Debut Book of the Year Award 2025. *Christmas at Tillingford Hall* will be followed by Sahara's story, *A Gala Ball at Tillingford Hall*.

I have also published *A Little Treat on Honey Street* which is about how Laura helped the villagers of Tillingham to save the village shop, and found love along the way.

All these books are (or soon will be) available as audio books from Audible.

I write from a posh shed set in a beautiful garden in Southwest London. I live with one boring fat cat, one mad skinny cat, between one and three nearly-grown-up boys (depending on the time of year) and my husband, a hunky gardener with a growing collection of tractors. When I'm not working or writing, I can be found in my kitchen baking cakes (which I try not to eat) or cooking my home-grown veg (which I do).

Keep in Touch!

If you would like to learn more about the village of Tillingham, the romance of the English countryside and hear about my forthcoming books, exclusive offers, events and giveaways, then please sign up for my newsletter at www.floradunn.com or follow me on Instagram @floradunnbooks.

More from Flora Dunn

Summer at Tillingford Hall

Finalist

Romantic Novelists' Association

Debut Novel of the Year 2025

According to Tatler's *Little Black Book*, The Honourable Guy Tillingford is Britain's twenty-ninth most eligible bachelor, after the Marquess of Granby and grime artist Tornado.

With a seven-year-old daughter, Hatty, to care for, studious divorcee Alice Merrow doesn't have time for celebrity gossip. She's on secondment to Hampshire's famous Tillingford Hall for one job – to catalogue Lord Tillingford's unrivalled collection of miniature portraits. She knows Guy is way out of her league and couldn't be interested in a tired single mum like her… could he?

When Alice and her flamboyant boss, Desmond Kingston-Campbell, realise that everything – and everyone – at Tillingford Hall are not as they seem, their discoveries could tear the Tillingford family apart.

And can Guy get over supermodel Sahara Seaton-Smyth to find true love with a woman who could help him put Tillingford Hall on the map and drag his family into the twenty-first century?

Praise for Summer at Tillingford Hall

"I adored the setting – I could easily picture the house and its inhabitants – and Alice and Hatty were so likeable and authentic that I was rooting for them the whole way. *Summer at Tillingford Hall* kept me guessing till the end."
Hannah Langdon, author of *Christmas with the Lords*

"A delightful romantic read that combines heart, humour, and a touch of nostalgia. A perfect choice for fans of romance and those looking for a feel-good book. Whether you're a long-time romance reader or new to the genre, there is something for everyone."
Reader, Cheam

"I was drawn into the world of Tillingford Hall from the very first chapter and I enjoyed it so much!"
Angela Pearse, author of *Amusing Miss Austen*

"A gorgeous 5* read!"
Helen Hawkins, author of *A Concert for Christmas*

"*Une romance douce et enveloppante, comme un bon thé pris au bord d'un jardin anglais.*"
A sweet, involving romance,
like tea taken in an English garden
@whywomenread on Instagram

"Charming and a cut above. Narrator was excellent."
Anon on Audible

A Little Treat on Honey Street

Laura's worked hard for her legal career and dreams of the future lifestyle her workaholic boyfriend, Rob, can give her. Her bubbly flatmate, Nadia, can't imagine why she'd want anything else.

While Granny's in Sorrento, Laura returns to the charming Hampshire village of Tillingham where she grew up, to care for her grandmother's pets, Tibbles the cat and the Coronation Chickens. She's dismayed to find that A Little Treat, the village stores and teashop she loved as a girl, is about to close down. Unless the villagers can club together to buy it and turn it into a community shop, it will become another holiday cottage and the heart will go out of Tillingham.

Can the committee chair, the cricket-playing curate, the Reverend Matthew Causton, and Laura's friends, new and old, pull things together in time to save the shop?

And does Laura's ex, gentleman farmer James Irving-McAuley, mean it when he says after all these years that she's The One and he'll stop at nothing to get her back?

Available now on Amazon as both eBook and paperback and on Audible as an audiobook early in 2026. For signed gift editions visit www.floradunn.com

Praise for
A Little Treat on Honey Street

"A Little Treat is full of funny antics, great characters, a swoony romance and men you just want to kick up the backside 😂 I highly recommend this book for all romcom lovers, it's the perfect summer read!"
Angela Pearse - author of *Amusing Miss Austen*

"What a cute summer read! The cozy village feel, all of the baking, and a handsome farmer make for the ultimate feel-good romance read. If you love a romance with a good mix of humor and heartfelt moments definitely give this one a read."
@Bookish_Aly_Cat on Instagram

"This is a charming story, well-plotted and with heartfelt characters. Highly recommended and would also make a lovely gift purchase for someone who enjoys romantic fiction."
JLTR on Amazon

"A warm-hearted and engaging romantic novel, set in a country village, this book is a delight – a real treat!"
Lynne Shelby, author of *Rome for the Summer*

"A Little Treat is another wonderful Flora Dunn novel set in Tillingford, which is fast becoming my favourite fictional village. Vibrant characters, an evocative setting and a perfectly paced plot make this an English country romance to remember."
Ruth Kramer, author of Things we Do for Love and Science

Questions for book clubs

1. Do you like Charlie? Why / why not?

2. Were Charlie's parents right to offer her a 'better education' at a boys' school rather than send her to a mixed school or an all-girls school?

3. Why wasn't Guy very sympathetic to Charlie when Steve attacked her?

4. Do you think Charlie and Alice's friendship be changed by Alice's new circumstances?

5. Charlie and Steve disagree on whether they should have told each other about their past relationships. Should everyone have a 'kicking the tyres' conversation before they get into a serious relationship or is it better to let bygones be bygones?

6. Is the bishop right about forgiveness? Is it just a choice you make every day to let something go?

7. Was Sebastian brave, or just stupid, to try to rescue Bertie?

8. Should Charlie and Sebastian try for a family so soon when they've been through so much?

Send me your book club questions
via my website www.floradunn.com